HE SWUNG THE BOOK INTO THE SEA AND VANISHED
INTO HIS STATEROOM.

THE
MAN WITHOUT
A COUNTRY

BY

EDWARD EVERETT HALE

AND

OTHER GREAT STORIES

THE SPENCER PRESS

INTRODUCTION

The Man Without A Country ranks as one of the most inspiring tales of patriotism ever written. In this day and age, when no one thinks of these United States as anything but a firmly knit nation, it is difficult to realize that at one time it was necessary to inspire patriotic fervor by speeches, pamphlets and books. It was with an eye to showing what one's country means to its citizens that Edward Everett Hale wrote "The Man Without A Country." The story was first published in 1863 during the years when the nation was being torn by bitter strife, and though it had no foundation in fact, there were several historical incidents which gave the author ideas for his story.

When Scott wrote "Napoleon" he told of a pathetic incident which occurred after the overthrow of the great Emperor. Napoleon had surrendered himself to Captain Maitland of the "Bellerophon" and owing to some fantastic delusion, he regarded himself as a guest on board the ship. The English considered this attitude to be rather much of a joke, and it was not long before Napoleon was made a prisoner on St. Helena, despite his complaints that he was the victim of a breach of trust. Upon reading this story, Hale had the feeling that the English government would have been much wiser if it had allowed Napoleon to remain on the "Bellerophon." Thus he would have been carried from port to port, and never would have had the opportunity to communicate directly with anyone. This idea became the basic plan for Philip Nolan's punishment in "A Man Without A Country." There were several other half historical and half fictional facts which entered into this story. Hale used names of actual naval men and ships, though he was careful to place them in different localities and different times from those in which they actually existed. So the story of Philip Nolan—The Man Without A Country—inspired by truth, and colored by imagination, stands as a literary triumph in patriotic writing and is destined to incite a feeling of national loyalty wherever it is read

LEONARD S. DAVIDOW

Reading, Pa. 1937

CONTENTS

THE
MAN WITHOUT
A COUNTRY

THE MAN WITHOUT A COUNTRY

By Edward Everett Hale

I suppose that very few casual readers of the "New York Herald" of August 13, 1863, noticed, in an obscure corner, among the "Deaths," the announcement,—

"Nolan. Died, on board U. S. Corvette Levant, Lat. 2° 11' S., Long. 131° W., on the 11th of May, Philip Nolan."

I happened to observe it, because I was stranded at the old Mission-House in Mackinaw, waiting for a Lake Superior steamer which did not choose to come, and I was devouring to the very stubble all the current literature I could get hold of, even down to the deaths and marriages in the "Herald." My memory for names and people is good, and the reader will see, as he goes on, that I had reason enough to remember Philip Nolan. There are hundreds of readers who would have paused at that announcement, if the officer of the "Levant" who reported it had chosen to make it thus:— "Died, May 11, The Man without a Country." For it was as "The Man without a Country" that poor Philip Nolan had generally been known by the officers who had him in charge during some fifty years, as, indeed, by all the men who sailed under them. I dare say there is many a man who has taken wine with him once a fortnight, in a three years' cruise, who never knew that his name was "Nolan," or whether the poor wretch had any name at all.

There can now be no possible harm in telling this poor

1

creature's story. Reason enough there has been till now, ever since Madison's administration went out in 1817, for very strict secrecy, the secrecy of honor itself, among the gentlemen of the navy who have had Nolan in successive charge. And certainly it speaks well for the *esprit de corps* of the profession, and the personal honor of its members, that to the press this man's story has been wholly unknown, —and, I think, to the country at large also. I have reason to think, from some investigations I made in the Naval Archives when I was attached to the Bureau of Construction, that every official report relating to him was burned when Ross burned the public buildings at Washington. One of the Tuckers, or possibly one of the Watsons, had Nolan in charge at the end of the war; and when, on returning from his cruise, he reported at Washington to one of the Crown-inshields,—who was in the Navy Department when he came home,—he found that the Department ignored the whole business. Whether they really knew nothing about it, or whether it was a *"Non mi ricordo"* determined on as a piece of policy, I do not know. But this I do know, that since 1817, and possibly before, no naval officer has mentioned Nolan in his report of a cruise.

But, as I say, there is no need for secrecy any longer. And now the poor creature is dead, it seems to me worth while to tell a little of his story, by way of showing young Americans of to-day what it is to be A MAN WITHOUT A COUNTRY.

PHILIP NOLAN was as fine a young officer as there was in the "Legion of the West," as the Western division of our army was then called. When Aaron Burr made his first dashing expedition down to New Orleans in 1805, at Fort Massac, or somewhere above on the river, he met, as the Devil would have it, this gay, dashing, bright young fellow, at some dinner-party, I think. Burr marked him, talked to him, walked with him, took him a day or two's voyage in his flat-boat, and, in short, fascinated him. For the next year, barrack-life was very tame to poor Nolan. He occasionally availed himself of the permission the great man had given him to write to him. Long, high-worded, stilted letters the poor boy wrote and rewrote and copied. But never a line did he have in reply from the gay deceiver. The other boys in the garrison sneered at him, because he sacrificed in this unrequited affection for a politician the time which they devoted to Monongahela, hazard, and high-low-Jack. Bourbon, euchre, and poker were still unknown. But one day Nolan had his revenge. This time Burr came down the river, not as an attorney seeking a place for his office, but as a disguised conqueror. He had defeated I know not how many district-attorneys; he had dined at I know not how many public dinners; he had been heralded in I know not how many Weekly Arguses, and it was rumored that he had an army behind him and an empire before him. It was a great day—his arrival—to poor Nolan. Burr had not been at the fort an hour before he sent for him. That evening he asked Nolan to take him out in his skiff, to show him a cane-brake or a cotton-wood tree, as he said,—really to seduce him; and by the time the sail was over, Nolan was enlisted body and soul. From that time, though he did not yet know it, he lived as A MAN WITHOUT A COUNTRY.

What Burr meant to do I know no more than you, dear reader. It is none of our business just now. Only, when the grand catastrophe came, and Jefferson and the House of Virginia of that day undertook to break on the wheel all the possible Clarences of the then House of York, by the great treason-trial at Richmond, some of the lesser fry in that distant Mississippi Valley, which was farther from us than Puget's Sound is to-day, introduced the like novelty on their provincial stage, and to while away the monotony of the summer at Fort Adams, got up, for *spectacles,* a string of court-martials on the officers there. One and another of the colonels and majors were tried, and to fill out the list, little Nolan, against whom, Heaven knows, there was evidence enough,—that he was sick of the service, had been willing to be false to it, and would have obeyed any order to march anywhither with any one who would follow him had the order been signed, "By command of His Exc. A. Burr." The courts dragged on. The big flies escaped,—rightly for all I know. Nolan was proved guilty enough, as I say; yet you and I would never have heard of him, reader, but that, when the president of the court asked him at the close whether he wished to say anything to show that he had always been faithful to the United States, he cried out in a fit of frenzy,—

"Damn the United States! I wish I may never hear of the United States again!"

I suppose he did not know how the words shocked old Colonel Morgan, who was holding the court. Half the officers who sat in it had served through the Revolution; and their lives, not to say their necks, had been risked for the very idea which he so cavalierly cursed in his madness. He, on his part, had grown up in the West of those days in the midst of "Spanish plot," "Orleans plot," and all the rest. He had been educated on a plantation where the finest company was a Spanish officer or a French merchant from Orleans. His education, such as it was, had been perfected in commercial expeditions to Vera Cruz; and I think he told me his father once hired an Englishman to be a private tutor for a winter on the plantation. He had spent half his youth with an older brother, hunting horses in Texas; and, in a word, to him "United States" was scarcely a reality. Yet he had been fed by "United States" for all the years since he had been in the army. He had sworn on his faith as a Christian to be true to "United States." It was "United States" which gave him the uniform he wore and the sword by his side. Nay, my poor Nolan, it was only because "United States" had picked you out first as one of her own confidential men of honor that "A. Burr" cared for you a straw more than for the flat-boat men who sailed his ark for him. I do not excuse Nolan; I only explain to the reader why he damned his country, and wished he might never hear her name again.

He never did hear her name but once again. From that moment, Sept. 23, 1807, till the day he died, May 11, 1863, he never heard her name again. For that half-century and more he was a man without a country.

Old Morgan, as I said, was terribly shocked. If Nolan had compared George Washington to Benedict Arnold, or had cried, "God save King George!" Morgan would not have felt worse. He called the court into his private room, and returned in fifteen minutes, with a face like a sheet, to say,—

"Prisoner, hear the sentence of the court! The court decides, subject to the approval of the President, that you never hear the name of the United States again."

Nolan laughed. But nobody else laughed. Old Morgan was too solemn, and the whole room was hushed dead as night for a minute. Even Nolan lost his swagger in a moment. Then Morgan added,—

"Mr. Marshal, take the prisoner to Orleans in an armed boat, and deliver him to the naval commander there."

The Marshal gave his orders, and the prisoner was taken out of court.

"Mr. Marshal," continued old Morgan, "see that no one mentions the United States to the prisoner. Mr. Marshal, make my respects to Lieutenant Mitchell at Orleans, and request him to order that no one shall mention the United States to the prisoner while he is on board ship. You will receive your written orders from the officer on duty here this evening. The court is adjourned without day."

I HAVE always supposed that Colonel Morgan himself took the proceedings of the court to Washington City, and explained them to Mr. Jefferson. Certain it is that the President approved them,—certain, that is, if I may believe the men who say they have seen his signature. Before the "Nautilus" got round from New Orleans to the Northern

Atlantic coast with the prisoner on board, the sentence had been approved, and he was a man without a country.

The plan then adopted was substantially the same which was necessarily followed ever after. Perhaps it was suggested by the necessity of sending him by water from Fort Adams and Orleans. The Secretary of the Navy—it must have been the first Crowninshield, though he is a man I do not remember—was requested to put Nolan on board a government vessel bound on a long cruise, and to direct that he should be only so far confined there as to make it certain that he never saw or heard of the country. We had few long cruises then, and the navy was very much out of favor; and as almost all of this story is traditional, as I have explained, I do not know certainly what his first cruise was. But the commander to whom he was intrusted,—perhaps it was Tingey or Shaw, though I think it was one of the younger men,—we are all old enough now,—regulated the etiquette and the precautions of the affair, and according to his scheme they were caried out, I suppose, till Nolan died.

When I was second officer of the "Intrepid," some thirty years after, I saw the original paper of instructions. I have been sorry ever since that I did not copy the whole of it. It ran, however, much in this way:—

WASHINGTON [with a date which must have been late in 1807].

SIR,—You will receive from Lieutenant Neale the person of Philip Nolan, late a lieutenant in the United States Army.

This person on his trial by court-martial expressed with an oath the wish that he might "never hear of the United States again."

The court sentenced him to have his wish fulfilled.

For the present, the execution of the order is intrusted by the President to this department.

You will take the prisoner on board your ship, and keep him there with such precautions as shall prevent his escape.

You will provide him with such quarters, rations, and clothing as would be proper for an officer of his late rank, if he were a passenger on your vessel on the business of his Government.

The gentlemen on board will make any arrangements agreeable to themselves regarding his society. He is to be exposed to no indignity of any kind, nor is he ever unnecessarily to be reminded that he is a prisoner.

But under no circumstances is he ever to hear of his country, or to see any information regarding it; and you will specially caution all the officers under your command to take care that, in the various indulgences which may be granted, this rule, in which his punishment is involved, shall not be broken.

It is the intention of the Government that he shall never again see the country which he has disowned. Before the end of your cruise you will receive orders which will give effect to this intention.

Respectfully yours,

W. SOUTHARD, for the

Secretary of the Navy.

If I had only preserved the whole of this paper, there would be no break in the beginning of my sketch of this story,—for Captain Shaw, if it were he, handed it to his successor in the charge, and he to his; and I suppose the commander of the "Levant" has it to-day as his authority for keeping this man in this mild custody.

The rule adopted on board the ships on which I have met "the man without a country" was, I think, transmitted from the beginning. No mess liked to have him permanently, because his presence cut off all talk of home or of the prospect of return, of politics or letters, of peace or of war,—cut off more than half the talk men liked to have at sea. But it was always thought too hard that he should never meet the rest of us, except to touch hats, and we finally sank into one system. He was not permitted to talk with the men unless an officer was by. With officers he had unrestrained intercourse, as far as they and he chose. But he grew shy, though he had favorites; I was one. Then the captain always asked him to dinner on Monday. Every mess in succession took up the invitation in its turn. According to the size of the ship, you had him at your mess more or less often at dinner. His breakfast he ate in his own state-room,—he always had a state-room,—which was where a sentinel or somebody on the watch could see the door. And whatever else he ate or drank, he ate or drank alone. Sometimes, when the marines or sailors had any special jollification, they were permitted to invite "Plain-Buttons," as they called him. Then Nolan was sent with some officer, and the men were forbidden to speak of home while he was there. I believe the theory was that the sight of his punishment did them good. They called him "Plain-Buttons" because, while he always chose to wear a regulation army-uniform, he was not permitted to wear the army-button, for the reason that it bore either the initials or the insignia of the country he had disowned.

I remember soon after I joined the navy I was on shore with some of the older officers from our ship and from the "Brandywine," which we had met at Alexandria. We had leave to make a party and go up to Cairo and the pyramids. As we jogged along (you went on donkeys then), some of the gentlemen (we boys called them "Dons," but the phrase was long since changed) fell to talking about Nolan, and some one told the system which was adopted from the first about his books and other reading. As he was almost never permitted to go on shore, even though the vessel lay in port for months, his time at the best hung heavy; and everybody was permitted to lend him books, if they were not published in America, and made no allusion to it. These were common enough in the old days, when people in the other hemisphere talked of the United States as little as we do of Paraguay. He had almost all the foreign papers that came into the ship, sooner or later; only somebody must go over them first, and cut out any advertisement or stray paragraph that alluded to America. This was a little cruel sometimes, when the back of what was cut out might be as innocent as Hesiod. Right in the midst of one of Napoleon's battles, or one of Canning's speeches, poor Nolan would find a great hole, because on the back of the page of that paper there had been an advertisement of a packet for New York, or a scrap from the President's message. I say this was the first time I ever heard of this plan, which afterward I had enough and more than enough to do with. I remember it because poor Phillips, who was of the party, as soon as the allusion to reading was made told a story of something which happened at the Cape of Good Hope on Nolan's first voyage; and it is the only thing I ever knew of that voyage. They had touched at the cape, and had done the civil thing with the English admiral and the fleet; and then, leaving for a long cruise up the Indian Ocean, Phillips had borrowed a lot of English books from an officer, which in those days, as indeed in these, was quite a windfall. Among them, as the Devil would order, was the "Lay of the Last Minstrel," which they had all of them heard of, but which most of them had never seen. I think it could not have been published long. Well, nobody thought there could be any risk of anything national in that, though Phillips swore old Shaw had cut out the "Tempest" from Shakespeare before he let Nolan have it, because he said "the Bermudas ought to be ours, and, by Jove, should be one day." So Nolan was permitted to join the circle one afternoon when a lot of them sat on deck smoking and reading aloud. People do not do such things so often now; but when I was young we got rid of a great deal of time so. Well, so it happened that in his turn Nolan took the book and read to the others; and he read very well, as I know. Nobody in the circle knew a line of the poem, only it was all magic and Border chivalry, and was ten thousand years ago. Poor Nolan read steadily through the fifth canto, stopped a minute and drank something, and then began, without a thought of what was coming,—

"Breathes there the man, with soul so dead,
Who never to himself hath said—"

It seems impossible to us that anybody ever heard this for the first time; but all these fellows did then, and poor Nolan himself went on, still unconsciously or mechanically,—

"This is my own, my native land!"

Then they all saw something was to pay; but he expected to get through, I suppose, turned a little pale, but plunged on,—

"Whose heart hath ne'er within him burned,
As home his footsteps he hath turned
From wandering on a foreign strand?
If such there breathe, go, mark him well—"

By this time the men were all beside themselves, wishing there was any way to make him turn over two pages; but he had not quite presence of mind for that. He gagged a little, colored crimson, and staggered on,—

"For him no minstrel raptures swell;
High though his titles, proud his name,
Boundless his wealth as wish can claim,
Despite these titles, power, and pelf,
The wretch, concentred all in self—"

and here the poor fellow choked, could not go on, but started up, swung the book into the sea, vanished into his stateroom, "And by Jove," said Phillips, "we did not see him for two months again; and I had to make up some beggarly story to that English surgeon why I did not return his Walter Scott to him."

That story shows about the time when Nolan's braggadocio must have broken down. At first, they said, he took a very high tone, considered his imprisonment a mere farce, affected to enjoy the voyage, and all that; but Phillips said that after he came out of his state-room he never was the same man again. He never read aloud again, unless it was the Bible or Shakespeare, or something else he was sure of. But it was not that merely. He never entered in with the other young men exactly as a companion again. He was always shy afterward, when I knew him,—very seldom spoke, unless he was spoken to, except to a very few friends. He lighted up occasionally,—I remember late in his life hearing him fairly eloquent on something which had been suggested to him by one of Fléchier's sermons,—but generally he had the nervous, tired look of a heart-wounded man.

When Captain Shaw was coming home,—if, as I say, it was Shaw,—rather to the surprise of everybody they made one of the Windward Islands, and lay off and on for nearly a week. The boys said the officers were sick of salt-junk, and meant to have turtle-soup before they came home. But after several days the "Warren" came to the same rendezvous. They exchanged signals; she sent to Phillips and these homeward-bound men letters and papers, and told them she was outward-bound, perhaps to the Mediterranean, and took poor Nolan and his traps on the boat back to try his second cruise. He looked very blank when he was told to get ready to join her. He had known enough of the signs of the sky to know that till that moment he was going "home," but this was a distinct evidence of something he had not thought of, perhaps,—that there was no going home for him, even to a prison. And this was the first of some twenty such transfers, which brought him sooner or later into half our best vessels, but which kept him all his life at least some hundred miles from the country he had hoped he might never hear of again.

It may have been on that second cruise—it was once when he was up the Mediterranean—that Mrs. Graff, the celebrated Southern beauty of those days, danced with him.

They had been lying a long time in the Bay of Naples, and the officers were very intimate in the English fleet, and there had been great festivities, and our men thought they must give a great ball on board the ship. How they ever did it on board the "Warren" I am sure I do not know. Perhaps it was not the "Warren," or perhaps ladies did not take up so much room as they do now. They wanted to use Nolan's stateroom for something, and they hated to do it without asking him to the ball; so the captain said they might ask him if they would be responsible that he did not talk with the wrong people, "who would give him intelligence." So the dance went on, the finest party that had ever been known, I dare say; for I never heard of a man-of-war ball that was not. For ladies they had the family of the American consul, one or two travellers who had adventured so far, and a nice bevy of English girls and matrons, perhaps Lady Hamilton herself.

Well, different officers relieved each other in standing and talking with Nolan in a friendly way, so as to be sure that nobody else spoke to him. The dancing went on with spirit; and after a while even the fellows who took this honorary guard of Nolan ceased to fear any *contretemps*. Only when some English lady—Lady Hamilton, as I said, perhaps—called for a set of "American dances," an odd thing happened. Everybody then danced contra-dances. The black band, nothing loath, conferred as to what "American dances" were, and started off with "Virginia Reel" which they followed with "Money-Musk," which, in its turn, in those days should have been followed by "The Old Thirteen." But just as Dick, the leader, tapped for his fiddles to begin, and bent forward, about to say in true negro state, " 'The Old Thirteen,' gentlemen and ladies!" as he had said, " 'Virginny Reel,' if you please!" and " 'Money-Musk,' if you please!" the captain's boy tapped him on the shoulder, whispered to him, and he did not announce the name of the dance; he merely bowed, began on the air, and they all fell

to,— the officers teaching the English girls the figure, but
not telling them why it had no name.

But that is not the story I started to tell. As the dancing
went on, Nolan and our fellows all got at ease, as I said,—
so much so that it seemed quite natural for him to bow to
that splendid Mrs. Graff, and say,—

"I hope you have not forgotten me, Miss Rutledge. Shall
I have the honor of dancing?"

He did it so quickly that Fellows, who was by him, could
not hinder him. She laughed, and said,—

"I am not Miss Rutledge any longer, Mr. Nolan; but I
will dance all the same," just nodded to Fellows, as if to say
he must leave Mr. Nolan to her, and led him off to the place
where the dance was forming.

Nolan thought he had found his chance. He had known
her at Philadelphia, and at other places had met her; and
this was a godsend. You could not talk in contra-dances,
as you do in cotillons, or even in the pauses of waltzing;
but there were chances for tongues and sounds, as well
as for eyes and blushes. He began with her travels and
Europe and Vesuvius and the French; and then, when they
had worked down. and had that long talking-time at the
bottom of the set, he said boldly,—a little pale, she said, as
she told me the story, years after,—

"And what do you hear from home, Mrs. Graff?"

And that splendid creature looked through him. Jove!
how she must have looked through him!

"Home! Mr. Nolan! I thought you were the man who
never wanted to hear of home again!" And she walked
directly up the deck to her husband, and left poor Nolan
alone, as he always was. He did not dance again.

I cannot give any history of him in order; nobody can
now, and indeed I am not trying to. These are the tradi-
tions, which I sort out, as I believe them, from the myths
which have been told about this man for forty years. The
lies that have been told about him are legion. The fellows
used to say he was the "Iron Mask;" and poor George Pons

went to his grave in the belief that this was the author of "Junius," who was being punished for his celebrated libel on Thomas Jefferson. Pons was not very strong in the historical line. A happier story than either of these I have told is of the war. That came along soon after. I have heard this affair told in three or four ways,—and indeed it may have happened more than once. But which ship it was on I cannot tell. However, in one, at least, of the great frigate-duels with the English in which the navy was really baptized, it happened that a round-shot from the enemy entered one of our ports square, and took right down the officer of the gun himself, and almost every man of the gun's crew. Now you may say what you choose about courage, but that is not a nice thing to see. But as the men who were not killed picked themselves up, and as they and the surgeon's people were carrying off the bodies, there appeared Nolan, in his shirt-sleeves, with the rammer in his hand, and just as if he had been the officer, told them off with authority,—who should go to the cockpit with the wounded men, who should stay with him,—perfectly cheery, and with that way which makes men feel sure all is right, and is going to be right. And he finished loading the gun with his own hands, aimed it, and bade the men fire. And there he stayed, captain of that gun, keeping those fellows in spirits till the enemy struck,—sitting on the carriage while the gun was cooling, though he was exposed all the time, showing them easier ways to handle heavy shot, making the raw hands laugh at their own blunders, and when the gun cooled again, getting it loaded and fired twice as often as any other gun on the ship. The captain walked forward by way of encouraging the men, and Nolan touched his hat, and said,—

"I am showing them how we do this in the artillery, sir."

And this is the part of the story where all the legends agree; and the commodore said,—

"I see you do, and I thank you, sir; and I shall never forget this day, sir, and you never shall, sir."

And after the whole thing was over, and he had the Englishman's sword, in the midst of the state and ceremony of the quarter-deck, he said:

"Where is Mr. Nolan? Ask Mr. Nolan to come here."

And when Nolan came, the captain said,—

"Mr. Nolan, we are all very grateful to you to-day. You are one of us to-day; you will be named in the despatches."

And then the old man took off his own sword of ceremony, and gave it to Nolan, and made him put it on. The man told me this who saw it. Nolan cried like a baby, and well he might. He had not worn a sword since that infernal day at Fort Adams. But always afterward on occasions of ceremony, he wore that quaint old French sword of the commodore's.

The captain did mention him in the despatches. It was always said he asked that he might be pardoned. He wrote a special letter to the Secretary of War; but nothing ever came of it. As I said, that was about the time when they began to ignore the whole transaction at Washington, and when Nolan's imprisonment began to carry itself on because there was nobody to stop it without any new orders from home.

I HAVE heard it said that he was with Porter when he took possession of the Nukahiva Islands. Not this Porter, you know, but old Porter, his father, Essex Porter; that is, the old Essex Porter, not this Essex. As an artillery officer who had seen service in the West, Nolan knew more about fortifications, embrasures, ravelins, stockades, and all that, than any of them did; and he worked with a right goodwill in fixing that battery all right. I have always thought it was a pity Porter did not leave him in command there with Gamble. That would have settled all the question about his punishment. We should have kept the islands, and at this moment we should have one station in the Pacific Ocean. Our French friends, too, when they wanted this little watering-place, would have found it was pre-occupied. But Madison and the Virginians, of course, flung all that away.

All that was near fifty years ago. If Nolan was thirty then, he must have been near eighty when he died. He looked sixty when he was forty; but he never seemed to me to change a hair afterward. As I imagine his life from what I have seen and heard of it, he must have been in every sea, and yet almost never on land. He must have known in a formal way more officers in our service than any man living knows. He told me once with a grave smile that no man in the world lived so methodical a life as he. "You know the boys say I am the Iron Mask, and you know how busy he was." He said it did not do for any one to try to read all the time, more than to do anything else all the time; but that he read just five hours a day. "Then," he said, "I keep up my note-books, writing in them at such and such hours from what I have been reading; and I include in these my scrap-books." These were very curious indeed. He had six or eight, of different subjects. There was one of History, one of Natural Science, one which he called "Odds and Ends." But they were not merely books of extracts from newspapers. They had bits of plants and ribbons, shells tied on, and carved scraps of bone and wood, which he had taught the men to cut for him; and they were beautifully illustrated. He drew admirably. He had some of the funniest drawings there, and some of the most pathetic, that I have ever seen in my life. I wonder who will have Nolan's scrap-books.

Well, he said his reading and his notes were his profession, and that they took five hours and two hours respectively of each day. "Then," said he, "every man should have a diversion as well as a profession. My Natural History is my diversion." That took two hours a day more. The men used to bring him birds and fish, but on a long cruise he had to satisfy himself with centipedes and cockroaches and such small game. He was the only naturalist I ever met who knew anything about the habits of the house-fly and the mosquito. All those people can tell you whether they are *Lepidoptera* or *Streptoptera;* but as for telling how you can get

rid of them, or how they get away from you when you strike
them, why Linnæus knew as little of that as John Foy the
idiot did. These nine hours made Nolan's regular daily
"occupation." The rest of the time he talked or walked.
Till he grew very old, he went aloft a great deal. He always
kept up his exercise; and I never heard that he was ill. If
any other man was ill, he was the kindest nurse in the world;
and he knew more than half the surgeons do. Then if anybody was sick or died, or if the captain wanted him to on
any other occasion, he was always ready to read prayers.
I have said that he read beautifully.

My own acquaintance with Philip Nolan began six or
eight years after the war, on my first voyage after I was appointed a midshipman. It was in the first days after our
Slave-Treaty, while the reigning House, which was still the
House of Virginia, had still a sort of sentimentalism about
the suppression of the horrors of the Middle Passage, and
something was sometimes done that way. We were in the
South Atlantic on that business. From the time I joined, I
believe I thought Nolan was a sort of lay chaplain,—a chaplain with a blue coat. I never asked about him. Everything
in the ship was strange to me. I knew it was green to ask
questions, and I suppose I thought there was a "Plain-
buttons" on every ship. We had him to dine in our mess
once a week, and the caution was given that on that day
nothing was to be said about home. But if they had told us
not to say anything about the planet Mars or the Book of
Deuteronomy, I should not have asked why; there were a
great many things which seemed to me to have as little reason. I first came to understand anything about "the man
without a country" one day when we overhauled a dirty
little schooner which had slaves on board. An officer was
sent to take charge of her, and after a few minutes he sent
back his boat to ask that some one might be sent him who
could speak Portuguese. We were all looking over the rail
when the message came, and we all wished we could inter-

pret when the captain asked who spoke Portuguese. But none of the officers did; and just as the captain was sending forward to ask if any of the people could, Nolan stepped out and said he should be glad to interpret if the captain wished, as he understood the language. The captain thanked him, fitted out another boat with him, and in this boat it was my luck to go.

When we got there, it was such a scene as you seldom see, and never want to. Nastiness beyond account, and chaos run loose in the midst of the nastiness. There were not a great many of the negroes; but by way of making what there were understand that they were free, Vaughan had had their hand-cuffs and ankle-cuffs knocked off, and, for convenience' sake, was putting them upon the rascals of the schooner's crew. The negroes were most of them out of the hold, and swarming all round the dirty deck, with a central throng surrounding Vaughan, and addressing him in every dialect and *patois* of a dialect, from the Zulu click up to the Parisian of Beledeljereed.

As we came on deck, Vaughan looked down from a hogshead, on which he had mounted in desperation, and said,—

"For God's love, is there anybody who can make these wretches understand something? The men gave them rum, and that did not quiet them. I knocked that big fellow down twice, and that did not soothe him. And then I talked Choctaw to all of them together; and I'll be hanged if they understood that as well as they understood the English."

Nolan said he could speak Portuguese; and one or two fine-looking Kroomen were dragged out, who, as it had been found already, had worked for the Portuguese on the coast at Fernando Po.

"Tell them they are free," said Vaughan; "and tell them that these rascals are to be hanged as soon as we can get rope enough."

Nolan "put that into Spanish;" that is, he explained it in such Portuguese as the Kroomen could understand, and they in turn to such of the negroes as could understand

them. Then there was such a yell of delight, clinching of
fists, leaping and dancing, kissing of Nolan's feet, and a
general rush made to the hogshead by way of spontaneous
worship of Vaughan, as the *deus ex machina* of the occasion.

"Tell them," said Vaughan, well pleased, "that I will take
them all to Cape Palmas."

This did not answer so well. Cape Palmas was practically
as far from the homes of most of them as New Orleans or
Rio Janeiro was; that is, they would be eternally separated
from home there. And their interpreters, as we could understand, instantly said, *"Ah, non Palmas,"* and began to
propose infinite other expedients in most voluble language.
Vaughan was rather disappointed at this result of his lib-
erality, and asked Nolan eagerly what they said. The
drops stood on poor Nolan's white forehead, as he hushed
the men down, and said,—

"He says, 'Not Palmas.' He says, 'Take us home; take
us to our own country; take us to our own house; take us to
our own pickaninnies and our own women.' He says he
has an old father and mother who will die if they do not
see him. And this one says he left his people all sick, and
paddled down to Fernando to beg the white doctor to come
and help them, and that these devils caught him in the bay
just in sight of home, and that he has never seen anybody
from home since then. And this one says," choked out
Nolan, "that he has not heard a word from his home in six
months, while he has been locked up in an infernal barra-
coon."

Vaughan always said he grew gray himself while Nolan
struggled through this interpretation. I, who did not understand anything of the passion involved in it, saw that the
very elements were melting with fervent heat, and that
something was to pay somewhere. Even the negroes themselves stopped howling, as they saw Nolan's agony, and
Vaughan's almost equal agony of sympathy. As quick as he
could get words, he said,—

"Tell them yes, yes, yes; tell them they shall go to the Mountains of the Moon, if they will. If I sail the schooner through the Great White Desert, they shall go home!"

And after some fashion Nolan said so. And then they all fell to kissing him again, and wanted to rub his nose with theirs.

But he could not stand it long; and getting Vaughan to say he might go back, he beckoned me down into our boat. As we lay back in the stern-sheets, and the men gave way, he said to me: "Youngster, let that show you what it is to be without a family, without a home, and without a country; and if you are ever tempted to say a word or to do a thing that shall put a bar between you and your family, your home, and your country, pray God in his mercy to take you that instant home to his own heaven. Stick by your family, boy; forget you have a self, while you do everything for them. Think of your home, boy; write and send, and talk about it. Let it be nearer and nearer to your thought the farther you have to travel from it; and rush back to it when you are free, as that poor black slave is doing now. And for your country, boy," and the words rattled in his throat, "and for that flag," and he pointed to the ship, "never dream a dream but of serving her as she bids you, though the service carry you through a thousand hells. No matter what happens to you, no matter who flatters you or who abuses you, never look at another flag, never let a night pass but you pray God to bless that flag. Remember, boy, that behind all these men you have to do with, behind officers and Government and people even, there is the Country Herself, your Country, and that you belong to Her as you belong to your own mother. Stand by Her, boy, as you would stand by your mother, if those devils there had got hold of her to-day!"

I was frightened to death by his calm, hard passion; but I blundered out that I would, by all that was holy, and that I had never thought of doing anything else. He hardly

seemed to hear me; but he did almost in a whisper say: "Oh,
if anybody had said so to me when I was of your age!"

I think it was this half-confidence of his, which I never
abused,—for I never told this story till now,—which afterward made us great friends. He was very kind to me. Often
he sat up, or even got up, at night, to walk the deck with me,
when it was my watch. He explained to me a great deal of
my mathematics, and I owe to him my taste for mathematics. He lent me books, and helped me about my reading.
He never alluded so directly to his story again; but from one
and another officer I have learned, in thirty years, what I
am telling. When we parted from him in St. Thomas Harbor, at the end of our cruise, I was more sorry than I can
tell. I was very glad to meet him again in 1830; and later in
life, when I thought I had some influence in Washington,
I moved heaven and earth to have him discharged. But it
was like getting a ghost out of prison. They pretended
there was no such man, and never was such a man. They
will say so at the Department now! Perhaps they do not
know. It will not be the first thing in the service of which
the Department appears to know nothing!

THERE is a story that Nolan met Burr once on one of our
vessels, when a party of Americans came on board in the
Mediterranean. But this I believe to be a lie; or rather it is
a myth, *ben trovato,* involving a tremendous blowing-up
with which he sunk Burr, asking him how he liked to be
"without a country." But it is clear from Burr's life that
nothing of the sort could have happened; and I mention
this only as an illustration of the stories which get a-going
where there is the least mystery at bottom.

So poor Philip Nolan had his wish fulfilled. I know but
one fate more dreadful; it is the fate reserved for those men
who shall have one day to exile themselves from their country because they have attempted her ruin, and shall have at
the same time to see the prosperity and honor to which she

rises when she has rid herself of them and their iniquities. The wish of poor Nolan, as we all learned to call him, not because his punishment was too great, but because his repentance was so clear, was precisely the wish of every Bragg and Beauregard who broke a soldier's oath two years ago, and of every Maury and Barron who broke a sailor's. I do not know how often they have repented. I do know that they have done all that in them lay that they might have no country,—that all the honors, associations, memories, and hopes which belong to "country" might be broken up into little shreds and distributed to the winds. I know, too, that their punishment, as they vegetate through what is left of life to them in wretched Boulognes and Leicester Squares, where they are destined to upbraid each other till they die, will have all the agony of Nolan's, with the added pang that every one who sees them will see them to despise and to execrate them. They will have their wish, like him.

For him, poor fellow, he repented of his folly, and then, like a man, submitted to the fate he had asked for. He never intentionally added to the difficulty or delicacy of the charge of those who had him in hold. Accidents would happen; but they never happened from his fault. Lieutenant Truxton told me that when Texas was annexed there was a careful discussion among the officers, whether they should get hold of Nolan's handsome set of maps, and cut Texas out of it,— from the map of the world and the map of Mexico. The United States had been cut out when the atlas was bought for him. But it was voted, rightly enough, that to do this would be virtually to reveal to him what had happened, or, as Harry Cole said, to make him think Old Burr had succeeded. So it was from no fault of Nolan's that a great botch happened at my own table, when, for a short time, I was in command of the "George Washington" corvette, on the South American station. We were lying in the La Plata, and some of the officers who had been on shore, and had just joined again, were entertaining us with accounts of their misadventures in riding the half wild horses of Buenos

Ayres. Nolan was at table, and was in an unusually bright and talkative mood. Some story of a tumble reminded him of an adventure of his own, when he was catching wild horses in Texas with his adventurous cousin, at a time when he must have been quite a boy. He told the story with a good deal of spirit,—so much so, that the silence which often follows a good story hung over the table for an instant, to be broken by Nolan himself. For he asked perfectly unconsciously:

"Pray, what has become of Texas? After the Mexicans got their independence, I thought that province of Texas would come forward very fast. It is really one of the finest regions on earth; it is the Italy of this continent. But I have not seen or heard a word of Texas for near twenty years."

There were two Texan officers at the table. The reason he had never heard of Texas was that Texas and her affairs had been painfully cut out of his newspapers since Austin began his settlements; so that while he read of Honduras and Tamaulipas, and till quite lately of California, this virgin province, in which his cousin had travelled so far, and, I believe, had died, had ceased to be to him. Waters and Williams, the two Texas men, looked grimly at each other, and tried not to laugh. Edward Morris had his attention attracted by the third link in the chain of the captain's chandelier. Watrous was seized with a convulsion of sneezing. Nolan himself saw that something was to pay, he did not know what. And I, as master of the feast, had to say,—

"Texas is out of the map, Mr. Nolan. Have you seen Captain Back's curious account of Sir Thomas Roe's 'Welcome?'"

After that cruise I never saw Nolan again. I wrote to him at least twice a year, for in that voyage we became even confidentially intimate; but he never wrote to me. The other men tell me that in those fifteen years he *aged* very fast, as well he might indeed, but that he was still the same gentle, uncomplaining, silent sufferer that he ever was, bearing as best he could his self-appointed punishment,—

rather less social, perhaps, with new men whom he did not know, but more anxious apparently than ever to serve and befriend and teach the boys, some of whom fairly seemed to worship him. And now it seems the dear old fellow is dead. He has found a home at last, and a country.

Since writing this, and while considering whether or not I would print it as a warning to the young Nolans and Vallandighams and Tatnalls of to-day of what it is to throw away a country, I have received from Danforth, who is on board the "Levant," a letter which gives an account of Nolan's last hours. It removes all my doubts about telling this story.

To understand the first words of the letter, the non-professional reader should remember that after 1817 the position of every officer who had Nolan in charge was one of the greatest delicacy. The Government had failed to renew the order of 1807 regarding him. What was a man to do? Should he let him go? What, then, if he were called to account by the Department for violating the order of 1807? Should he keep him? What, then, if Nolan should be liberated some day, and should bring an action for false imprisonment or kidnapping against every man who had had him in charge? I urged and pressed this upon Southard, and I have reason to think that other officers did the same thing. But the Secretary always said, as they so often do at Washington, that there were no special orders to give, and that we must act on our own judgment. That means, "If you succeed, you will be sustained; if you fail, you will be disavowed." Well, as Danforth says, all that is over now, though I do not know but I expose myself to a criminal prosecution on the evidence of the very revelation I am making.

Here is the letter:—

"Levant," 2° 2′ S. @ 131° W.

DEAR FRED,—I try to find heart and life to tell you that it is all over with dear old Nolan. I have been with

him on this voyage more than I ever was; and I can understand wholly now the way in which you used to speak of
the dear old fellow. I could see that he was not strong, but
I had no idea the end was so near. The doctor has been
watching him very carefully, and yesterday morning came
to me and told me that Nolan was not so well, and had not
left his state-room,—a thing I never remember before. He
had let the doctor come and see him as he lay there,—the
first time the doctor had been in the state-room,—and he
said he should like to see me. Oh, dear! do you remember
the mysteries we boys used to invent about his room in the
old "Intrepid" days? Well, I went in, and there, to be sure,
the poor fellow lay in his berth, smiling pleasantly as he
gave me his hand, but looking very frail. I could not help
a glance round, which showed me what a little shrine he
had made of the box he was lying in. The stars and stripes
were triced up above and around a picture of Washington,
and he had painted a majestic eagle, with lightnings blazing from his beak, and his foot just clasping the whole
globe, which his wings overshadowed. The dear old boy
saw my glance, and said with a sad smile, "Here, you see,
I have a country!" And then he pointed to the foot of his
bed, where I had not seen before a great map of the United
States, as he had drawn it from memory, and which he had
there to look upon as he lay. Quaint, queer old names were
on it in large letters: "Indiana Territory," "Mississippi
Territory," and "Louisiana Territory," as I suppose our
fathers learned such things; but the old fellow had patched
in Texas, too; he had carried his Western boundary all the
way to the Pacific, but on that shore he had defined nothing.
    "Oh, Danforth," he said, "I know I am dying. I cannot
get home. Surely you will tell me something now? Stop!
stop! Do not speak till I say what I am sure you know,
that there is not in this ship, that there is not in America—
God bless her!—a more loyal man than I. There cannot be
a man who loves the old flag as I do, or prays for it as I
do, or hopes for it as I do. There are thirty-four stars in

it now, Danforth. I thank God for that, though I do not know what their names are. There has never been one taken away; I thank God for that. I know by that that there has never been any successful Burr. Oh, Danforth, Danforth," he sighed out, "how like a wretched night's dream a boy's idea of personal fame or of separate sovereignty seems, when one looks back on it after such a life as mine! But tell me,—tell me something,—tell me everything, Danforth, before I die!"

Ingham, I swear to you that I felt like a monster that I had not told him everything before. Danger or no danger, delicacy or no delicacy, who was I, that I should have been acting the tyrant all this time over this dear, sainted old man, who had years ago expiated, in his whole manhood's life, the madness of a boy's treason? "Mr. Nolan," said I, "I will tell you everything you ask about. Only, where shall I begin?"

Oh, the blessed smile that crept over his white face! and he pressed my hand, and said, "God bless you! Tell me their names," he said, and he pointed to the stars on the flag. "The last I know is Ohio. My father lived in Kentucky. But I have guessed Michigan and Indiana and Mississippi,—that was where Fort Adams is; they make twenty. But where are your other fourteen? You have not cut up any of the old ones, I hope."

Well, that was not a bad text; and I told him the names in as good order as I could, and he bade me take down his beautiful map, and draw them in as I best could with my pencil. He was wild with delight about Texas, told me how his cousin died there; he had marked a gold cross near where he supposed his grave was, and he had guessed at Texas. Then he was delighted as he saw California and Oregon; that he said he had suspected partly, because he had never been permitted to land on that shore, though the ships were there so much. "And the men," said he, laughing, "brought off a good deal besides furs." Then he went back—heavens, how far!—to ask about the "Chesapeake,"

and what was done to Barron for surrendering her to the
"Leopard," and whether Burr ever tried again,—and he
ground his teeth with the only passion he showed. But in
a moment that was over, and he said, "God forgive me, for
I am sure I forgive him." Then he asked about the old
war, told me the true story of his serving the gun the day
we took the "Java," asked about dear old David Porter, as
he called him. Then he settled down more quietly and very
happily, to hear me tell in an hour the history of fifty
years.

How I wished it had been somebody who knew something! But I did as well as I could. I told him of the
English war. I told him about Fulton and the steamboat
beginning. I told him about old Scott and Jackson; told
him all I could think of about the Mississippi and New Orleans and Texas and his own old Kentucky. And do you
think, he asked who was in command of the "Legion of the
West." I told him it was a very gallant officer named
Grant, and that by our last news he was about to establish
his headquarters at Vicksburg. Then, "Where was Vicksburg?" I worked that out on the map; it was about a hundred miles, more or less, above his old Fort Adams; and I
thought Fort Adams must be a ruin now. "It must be at
Old Vick's plantation, at Walnut Hills," said he; "well, that
is a change!"

I tell you Ingham, it was a hard thing to condense the
history of half a century into that talk with a sick man.
And I do not now know what I told him,—of emigration,
and the means of it; of steamboats and railroads and tele-
graphs; of inventions and books and literature; of the col-
leges and West Point and the Naval School,—but with the
queerest interruptions that ever you heard. You see it was
Robinson Crusoe asking all the accumulated questions of
fifty-six years!

I remember he asked, all of a sudden, who was President
now; and when I told him, he asked if Old Abe was General
Benjamin Lincoln's son. He said he met old General Lin-

coln when he was quite a boy himself, at some Indian treaty.
I said No, that Old Abe was a Kentuckian like himself, but
I could not tell him of what family; he had worked up from
the ranks. "Good for him!" cried Nolan; "I am glad of
that. As I have brooded and wondered, I have thought our
danger was in keeping up those regular successions in the
first families." Then I got talking about my visit to Washington. I told him of meeting the Oregon Congressman,
Harding; I told him about the Smithsonian and the Explor-
ing Expedition; I told him about the Capitol and the statues
for the pediment and Crawford's Liberty and Greenough's
Washington. Ingham, I told him everything I could think
of that would show the grandeur of his country and its
prosperity; but I could not make up my mouth to tell him
a word about this infernal Rebellion!

And he drank it in, and enjoyed it as I cannot tell you.
He grew more and more silent, yet I never thought he was
tired or faint. I gave him a glass of water, but he just wet
his lips, and told me not to go away. Then he asked me
to bring the Presbyterian "Book of Public Prayer," which
lay there, and said with a smile that it would open at the
right place,—and so it did. There was his double red mark
down the page; and I knelt down and read, and he repeated
with me: "For ourselves and our country, O gracious God,
we thank Thee that notwithstanding our manifold trans-
gressions of Thy holy laws, Thou hast continued to us Thy
marvellous kindness,"—and so to the end of that Thanks-
giving. Then he turned to the end of the same book, and
I read the words more familiar to me: "Most heartily we
beseech Thee with Thy favor to behold and bless Thy servant, the President of the United States, and all others in
authority,"—and the rest of the Episcopal Collect. "Danforth," said he, "I have repeated those prayers night and
morning, it is now fifty-five years." And then he said he
would go to sleep. He bent me down over him, and kissed
me; and he said, "Look in my Bible, Danforth, when I am
gone." And I went away.

But I had no thought it was the end. I thought he was tired and would sleep. I knew he was happy, and I wanted him to be alone.

But in an hour, when the doctor went in gently, he found Nolan had breathed his life away with a smile. He had something pressed close to his lips. It was his father's badge of the Order of the Cincinnati.

We looked in his Bible, and there was a slip of paper at the place where he had marked the text:—

"They desire a country, even a heavenly: wherefore God is not ashamed to be called their God: for he hath prepared for them a city."

On this slip of paper he had written,—

"Bury me in the sea; it has been my home, and I love it. But will not some one set up a stone for my memory at Fort Adams or at Orleans, that my disgrace may not be more than I ought to bear? Say on it,—

In Memory of

PHILIP NOLAN,

Lieutenant in the Army of the United States.

He loved his country as no other man has loved her; but no man deserved less at her hands."

MY DOUBLE, AND HOW HE
UNDID ME

By Edward Everett Hale

It is not often that I trouble the readers of the *Atlantic Monthly*. I should not trouble them now, but for the importunities of my wife, who "feels to insist" that a duty to society is unfulfilled till I have told why I had to have a double, and how he undid me. She is sure, she says, that intelligent persons cannot understand that pressure upon public servants which alone drives any man into the employment of a double. And while I fear she thinks, at the bottom of her heart, that my fortunes will never be remade, she has a faint hope that, as another Rasselas, I may teach a lesson to future publics, from which they may profit, though we die. Owing to the behavior of my double, or, if you please, to that public pressure which compelled me to employ him, I have plenty of leisure to write this communication.

I am, or rather was, a minister of the Sandemanian connection. I was settled in the active, wide-awake town of Nagaudavick, on one of the finest water-powers in Maine. We used to call it a western town in the heart of the civilization of New England. A charming place it was and is. A spirited, brave young parish had I; and it seemed as if we might have all "the joy of eventful living" to our heart's content.

Alas! how little we knew on the day of my ordination, and in those halcyon moments of our first housekeeping!

To be the confidential friend in a hundred families in the town,—cutting the social trifle, as my friend Haliburton says, "from the top of the whipped-syllabub to the bottom of the sponge-cake, which is the foundation,"—to keep abreast of the thought of the age in one's study, and to do one's best on Sunday to interweave that thought with the active life of an active town, and to inspirit both and make both infinite by glimpses of the Eternal Glory, seemed such an exquisite forelook into one's life! Enough to do, and all so real and so grand! If this vision could only have lasted!

The truth is, that this vision was not in itself a delusion, nor, indeed, half bright enough. If one could only have been left to do his own business, the vision would have accomplished itself and brought out new paraheliacal visions, each as bright as the original. The misery was and is, as we found out, I and Polly, before long, that, besides the vision, and besides the usual human and finite failures in life (such as breaking the old pitcher that came over in the *Mayflower*, and putting into the fire the alpenstock with which her father climbed Mont Blanc),—besides these, I say (imitating the style of Robinson Crusoe), there were pitchforked in on us a great rowen-heap of humbugs, handed down from some unknown seedtime, in which we were expected, and I chiefly, to fulfil certain public functions before the community, of the character of those fulfilled by the third row of supernumeraries who stand behind the Sepoys in the spectacle of the *Cataract of the Ganges*. They were the duties, in a word, which one performs as member of one or another social class or subdivision, wholly distinct from what one does as A. by himself A. What invisible power put these functions on me, it would be very hard to tell. But such power there was and is. And I had not been at work a year before I found I was living two lives, one real and one merely functional,—for two sets of people, one my parish, whom I loved, and the other a vague public, for whom I did not care two straws. All this was in a vague notion, which everybody had and has, that this second life would eventually bring out some great results, unknown at present, to somebody somewhere.

Crazed by this duality of life, I first read Dr. Wigan on the *Duality of the Brain,* hoping that I could train one side of my head to do these outside jobs, and the other to do my intimate and real duties. For Richard Greenough once told me, that, in studying for the statue of Franklin, he found that the left side of the great man's face was philosophic and reflective, and the right side funny and smiling. If you will go and look at the bronze statue you will find he has repeated this observation there for posterity. The eastern profile is the portrait of the statesman Franklin, the western of poor Richard. But Dr. Wigan does not go into these niceties of this subject, and I failed. It was then, that, on my wife's suggestion, I resolved to look out for a double.

I was, at first, singularly successful. We happened to be recreating at Stafford Springs that summer. We rode out one day, for one of the relaxations of that watering-place, to the great Monson Almshouse. We were passing through one of the large halls, when my destiny was fulfilled! I saw my man.

He was not shaven. He had on no spectacles. He was dressed in a green baize roundabout and faded blue overalls, worn sadly at the knee. But I saw at once that he was my height, five feet four and a half. He had black hair, worn off by his hat. So have and have not I. He stooped in walking. So do I. His hands were large, and mine. And—choicest gift of Fate in all—he had, not "a strawberry mark on his left arm," but a cut from a juvenile brickbat over his right eye, slightly affecting the play of that eyebrow. Reader, so have I!—My fate was sealed!

A word with Mr. Holley, one of the inspectors, settled the whole thing. It proved that this Dennis Shea was a harmless, amiable fellow, of the class known as shiftless, who had sealed his fate by marrying a dumb wife, who was at that moment ironing in the laundry. Before I left Stafford I had hired both for five years. We had applied to Judge Pynchon, then the probate judge at Springfield, to change the name of Dennis Shea to Frederic Ingham. We had explained to the Judge, what was the precise truth, that an eccentric gentleman wished to adopt Dennis, under this new name, into his family. It never occurred to him that Dennis might be more than fourteen years old. And thus, to shorten this preface, when we returned at night to my parsonage at Naguadavick, there entered Mrs. Ingham, her new dumb laundress, myself, who am Mr. Frederic Ingham, and my double, who was Mr. Frederic Ingham by as good right as I.

Oh, the fun we had the next morning in shaving his beard to my pattern, cutting his hair to match mine, and teaching him how to wear and how to take off gold-bowed spectacles! Really, they were electro-plate, and the glass was plain (for the poor fellow's eyes were excellent). Then in four successive afternoons I taught him four speeches. I had found these would be quite enough for the supernumerary-Sepoy line of life, and it was well for me they were. For though he was good-natured, he was very shiftless, and it was, as our national proverb says, "like pulling teeth" to teach him. But at the end of the next week he could say, with quite my easy and frisky air,—

1. "Very well, thank you. And you?" This for an answer to casual salutations.

2. "I am very glad you liked it."

3. "There has been so much said, and, on the whole, so well said, that I will not occupy the time."

4. "I agree, in general, with my friend the other side of the room."

At first I had a feeling that I was going to be at great cost for clothing him. But it proved, of course, at once, that, whenever he was out, I should be at home. And I went, during the bright period of his success, to so few of those awful pageants which require a black dress-coat and what the ungodly call, after Mr. Dickens, a white choker, that in the happy retreat of my own dressing-gowns and jackets my days went by as happily and cheaply as those of another Thalaba. And Polly declares there was never a year when the tailoring cost so little. He lived (Dennis, not Thalaba) in his wife's room over the kitchen. He had orders never to show himself at that window. When he appeared in the front of the house, I retired to my sanctissimum and my dressing-gown. In short, the Dutchman and his wife in the old weather-box, had not less to do with each other than he and I. He made the furnace-fire and split the wood before daylight; then he went to sleep again, and slept late; then came for orders, with a red silk bandanna tied round his head with his overalls on, and his dress-coat and spectacles off. If we happened to be interrupted, no one guessed that he was Frederic Ingham as well as I; and, in the neighborhood, there grew up an impression that the minister's Irishman worked daytimes in the factory village at New Coventry. After I had given him his orders, I never saw him till the next day.

I launched him by sending him to a meeting of the Enlightenment Board. The Enlightenment Board consists of seventy-four members, of whom sixty-seven are necessary to form a quorum. One becomes a member under the regulations laid down in old Judge Dudley's will. I became one by being ordained pastor of a church in Naguadavick. You see you cannot help yourself, if you would. At this particular time we had had four successive meetings, averaging four hours each,—wholly occupied in whipping in a quorum. At the first only eleven men were present; at the next, by force of three circulars, twenty-seven; at the third, thanks to two days' canvassing by Auchmuty and myself, begging men to come, we had sixty. Half the others were in Europe. But without a quorum we could do nothing. All the rest of us waited grimly for our four hours, and adjourned without any action. At the fourth meeting we had flagged, and only got fifty-nine together. But on the first appearance of my double,—whom I sent on this fatal Monday to the fifth meeting,—he was the *sixty-seventh* man who entered the room. He was greeted with a storm of applause! The poor fellow had missed his way,—read the street signs ill through his spectacles (very ill, in fact, without them),—and had not dared to inquire. He entered the room, finding the president and secretary holding to their chairs two judges of the Supreme Court, who were also members *ex officio,* and were begging leave to go away. On his entrance all was changed. *Presto,* the by-laws were amended, and the Western property was given away. Nobody stopped to converse with him. He voted, as I had charged him to do, in every instance, with the minority. I won new laurels as a man of sense, though a little unpunctual,—and Dennis, *alias* Ingham, returned to the parsonage, astonished to see with how little wisdom the world is governed. He cut a few of my parishioners in the street; but he had his glasses off, and I am known to be near-sighted. Eventually he recognized them more readily than I.

I "set him again" at the exhibition of the New Coventry Academy; and here he undertook a "speaking part,"—as, in my boyish, worldly days, I remember the bills used to say of Mlle. Céleste. We are all trustees of the New Coventry Academy; and there has lately been "a good deal of feeling" because the Sandemanian trustees did not regularly attend the exhibitions. It has been intimated, indeed, that the Sandemanians are leaning towards Free-Will, and that we have, therefore, neglected these semi-annual exhibitions, while there is no doubt that Auchmuty last year went to Commencement at Waterville. Now the head master at New Coventry is a real good fellow, who knows a Sanskrit root when he sees it, and often cracks etymologies with me,—so that, in strictness, I ought to go to their exhibitions. But think, reader, of sitting through three long

July days in that Academy chapel, following the programme from

TUESDAY MORNING. *English Composition*. "SUNSHINE." Miss Jones.

round to

Trio on Three Pianos. Duel from the Opera of "Midshipman Easy." *Marryat*.

coming in at nine, Thursday evening! Think of this, reader, for men who know the world is trying to go backward, and who would give their lives if they could help it on! Well! The double had succeeded so well at the Board, that I sent him to the Academy. (Shade of Plato, pardon!) He arrived early on Tuesday, when, indeed, few but mothers and clergymen are generally expected, and returned in the evening to us, covered with honors. He had dined at the right hand of the chairman, and he spoke in high terms of the repast. The chairman had expressed his interest in the French conversation. "I am very glad you liked it," said Dennis; and the poor chairman, abashed, supposed the accent had been wrong. At the end of the day, the gentlemen present had been called upon for speeches,—the Rev. Frederic Ingham first, as it happened; upon which Dennis had risen, and had said, "There has been so much said, and, on the whole, so well said, that I will not occupy the time." The girls were delighted, because Dr. Dabney, the year before, had given them at this occasion a scolding on impropriety of behavior at lyceum lectures. They all declared Mr. Ingham was a love,—and *so* handsome! (Dennis is good-looking.) Three of them, with arms behind the others' waists, followed him up to the wagon he rode home in; and a little girl with a blue sash had been sent to give him a rosebud. After this *début* in speaking, he went to the exhibition for two days more, to the mutual satisfaction of all concerned. Indeed, Polly reported that he had pro-

nounced the trustees' dinners of a higher grade than those
of the parsonage. When the next term began I found six
of the Academy girls had obtained permission to come
across the river and attend our church. But this arrangement did not long continue.

After this he went to several Commencements for me,
and ate the dinners provided; he sat through three of our
Quarterly Conventions for me, always voting judiciously,
by the simple rule mentioned above, of siding with the
minority. And I, meanwhile, who had before been losing
caste among my friends, as holding myself aloof from the
associations of the body, began to rise in everybody's favor.
"Ingham's a good fellow, always on hand;" "never talks
much,—but does the right thing at the right time;" "is not
as unpunctual as he used to be,—he comes early, and sits
through to the end." "He has got over his old talkative
habit, too. I spoke to a friend of his about it once; and I
think Ingham took it kindly," etc., etc.

This voting power of Dennis was particularly valuable
at the quarterly meetings of the proprietors of the Naguadavick Ferry. My wife inherited from her father some
shares in that enterprise, which is not yet fully developed,
though it doubtless will become a very valuable property.
The law of Maine then forbade stockholders to appear
by proxy at such meetings. Polly disliked to go, not being,
in fact, a "hens'-rights hen," and transferred her stock to
me. I, after going once, disliked it more than she. But
Dennis went to the next meeting, and liked it very much.
He said the armchairs were good, the collation good, and
the free rides to stockholders pleasant. He was a little
frightened when they first took him upon one of the ferry-
boats, but after two or three quarterly meetings he became
quite brave.

Thus far I never had any difficulty with him. Indeed,
being of that type which is called shiftless, he was only
too happy to be told daily what to do, and to be charged

not to be forthputting or in any way original in his discharge of that duty. He learned, however, to discriminate between the lines of his life, and very much preferred these stockholders' meetings and trustees' dinners and Commencement collations to another set of occasions, from which he used to beg off most piteously. Our excellent brother, Dr. Fillmore, had taken a notion at this time that our Sandemanian churches needed more expression of mutual sympathy. He insisted upon it that we were remiss. He said that if the bishop came to preach at Naguadavick, all the Episcopal clergy of the neighborhood were present; if Dr. Pond came, all the Congregational clergymen turned out to hear him; if Dr. Nichols, all the Unitarians; and he thought we owed it to each other, that, whenever there was an occasional service at a Sandemanian church, the other brethren should all, if possible, attend. "It looked well," if nothing more. Now this really meant that I had not been to hear one of Dr. Fillmore's lectures on the Ethnology of Religion. He forgot that he did not hear one of my course on the "Sandemanianism of Anselm." But I felt badly when he said it; and afterwards I always made Dennis go to hear all the brethren preach, when I was not preaching myself. This was what he took exceptions to,—the only thing, as I said, which he ever did except to. Now came the advantage of his long morning nap, and of the green tea with which Polly supplied the kitchen. But he would plead, so humbly, to be let off, only from one or two! I never excepted him, however. I knew the lectures were of value, and I thought it best he should be able to keep the connection.

Polly is more rash than I am, as the reader has observed in the outset of this memoir. She risked Dennis one night under the eyes of her own sex. Governor Gorges had always been very kind to us, and, when he gave his great annual party to the town, asked us. I confess I hated to go. I was deep in the new volume of Pfeiffer's "Mystics," which Haliburton had just sent me from Boston. "But how rude," said Polly, "not to return the Governor's civility and Mrs. Gorges', when they will be sure to ask why you are away!" Still I demurred, and at last she, with the wit of Eve and of Semiramis conjoined, let me off by saying, that, if I would go in with her, and sustain the initial conversations with the Governor and the ladies staying there, she would risk Dennis for the rest of the evening. And that was just what we did. She took Dennis in training all that afternoon, instructed him in fashionable conversation, cautioned him against the temptations of the supper-table,—and at nine in the evening he drove us all down in the carryall. I made the grand star-*entrée* with Polly and the pretty Walton girls, who were staying with us. We had put Dennis into a great rough top-coat, without his glasses, —and the girls never dreamed, in the darkness, of looking at him. He sat in the carriage, at the door, while we entered. I did the agreeable to Mrs. Gorges, was introduced to her niece, Miss Fernanda,—I complimented Judge Jeffries on his decision in the great case of D'Aulnay *vs.* Laconia Mining Company,—I stepped into the dressing-room for a moment—stepped out for another,—walked home, after a nod with Dennis, and tying the horse to a pump;—and while I walked home, Mr. Frederic Ingham, my double, stepped in through the library into the Gorges' grand saloon.

Oh! Polly died of laughing as she told me of it at midnight! And even here, where I have to teach my hands to hew the beech for stakes to fence our cave, she dies of laughing as she recalls it,—and says that single occasion was worth all we have paid for it. Gallant Eve that she is! She joined Dennis at the library door, and in an instant presented him to Dr. Ochterlony from Baltimore, who was on a visit in town, and was talking with her, as Dennis came in. "Mr. Ingham would like to hear what you were telling us about your success among the German population." And Dennis bowed and said, in spite of a scowl from Polly, "I'm very glad you liked it." But Dr. Ochterlony did not observe, and plunged into the tide of explanation,—Dennis listening like a prime-minister, and bowing like a mandarin,—which is, I suppose, the same thing. Polly declared it was just like Haliburton's Latin conversation with the Hungarian minister, of which he is very fond of telling. *"Quaene sit historia Reformationis in Ungariâ?"* quoth Haliburton, after some thought. And his *confrère* replied gallantly, *"In seculo decimo tertio,"* etc., etc., etc.; and from *decimo tertio* to the nineteenth century and a half lasted till the oysters came. So was it that before Dr. Ochterlony came to the "success," or near it, Governor Gorges came to Dennis and asked him to hand Mrs. Jeffries down to supper, a request which he heard with great joy.

Polly was skipping round the room, I guess, gay as a lark. Auchmuty came to her "in pity for poor Ingham," who was so bored by the stupid pundit,—and Auchmuty could not understand why I stood it so long. But when Dennis took Mrs. Jeffries down, Polly could not resist standing near them. He was a little flustered, till the sight of the eatables and drinkables gave him the same Mercian courage which it gave Diggory. A little excited then, he attempted one or two of his speeches to the Judge's lady. But little he knew how hard it was to get in even a *promptu* there edgewise. "Very well, I thank you," said he, after the eating elements were adjusted; "and you?" And then did not he have to hear about the mumps, and the measles, and arnica, and belladonna, and camomile-flower, and dode-catheon, till she changed oysters for salad,—and then about the old practice and the new, and what her sister said, and what her sister's friend said, and what the physician to her sister's friend said, and then what was said by the brother of the sister of the physician of the friend of her sister, exactly as if it had been in Ollendorff? There was a moment's pause, as she declined champagne. "I am very glad you liked it," said Dennis again, which he never should have said, but to one who complimented a sermon. "Oh! you are so sharp, Mr. Ingham! No! I never drink any wine

at all,—except sometimes in summer a little currant shrub,
—from our own currants, you know. My own mother,—
that is, I call her my own mother, because, you know, I do
not remember," etc., etc., etc.; till they came to the candied
orange at the end of the feast,—when Dennis, rather confused, thought he must say something, and tried No. 4,—
"I agree, in general with my friend the other side of the
room,"—which he never should have said but at a public
meeting. But Mrs. Jeffries, who never listens expecting
to understand, caught him up instantly with, "Well, I'm
sure my husband returns the compliment; he always agrees
with you,—though we do worship with the Methodists;—
but you know, Mr. Ingham," etc., etc., etc., till the move was
made upstairs;— and as Dennis led her through the hall,
he was scarcely understood by any but Polly, as he said,
"There has been so much said, and, on the whole, so well
said, that I will not occupy the time."

His great resource the rest of the evening was, standing
in the library, carrying on animated conversations with one
and another in much the same way. Polly had initiated
him in the mysteries of a discovery of mine, that it is not
necessary to finish your sentences in a crowd, but by a sort
of mumble, omitting sibilants and dentals. This, indeed,
if your words fail you, answers even in public extempore
speech,—but better where other talking is going on. Thus,
—"We missed you at the Natural History Society, Ingham." Ingham replies, "I am very gligloglum, that is, that
you were mmmmm." By gradually dropping the voice, the
interlocutor is compelled to supply the answer. "Mrs.
Ingham, I hope your friend Augusta is better." Augusta
has not been ill. Polly cannot think of explaining, however,
and answers,—"Thank you, ma'am; she is very rearason
wewahwewoh," in lower and lower tones. And Mrs.
Throckmorton, who forgot the subject of which she spoke,
as soon as she asked the question, is quite satisfied. Dennis
could see into the card-room, and came to Polly to ask if
he might not go and play all-fours. But, of course, she

sternly refused. At midnight they came home delighted,—
Polly, as I said, wild to tell me the story of the victory; only
both the pretty Walton girls said,—"Cousin Frederic, you
did not come near me all the evening."

We always called him Dennis at home, for convenience,
though his real name was Frederic Ingham, as I have explained. When the election day came round, however, I
found that by some accident there was only one Frederic
Ingham's name on the voting-list; and, as I was quite busy
that day in writing some foreign letters to Halle, I thought
I would forego my privilege of suffrage, and stay quietly
at home, telling Dennis that he might use the record on the
voting-list, and vote. I gave him a ticket, which I told him
he might use, if he liked to. That was that very sharp
election in Maine which the readers of the *Atlantic* so well
remember, and it had been intimated in public that the ministers would do well not to appear at the polls. Of course,
after that, we had to appear by self or proxy. Still, Naguadavick was not then a city, and this standing in a double
queue at town-meeting several hours to vote was a bore of
the first water; and so when I found that there was but one
Frederic Ingham on the list, and that one of us must give
up, I stayed at home and finished the letters (which, indeed,
procured for Fothergill his coveted appointment of Professor of Astronomy at Leavenworth), and I gave Dennis,
as we called him, the chance. Something in the matter gave
a good deal of popularity to the Frederic Ingham name;
and at the adjourned election, next week, Frederic Ingham
was chosen to the legislature. Whether this was I or Dennis, I never really knew. My friends seemed to think it
was I; but I felt that as Dennis had done the popular thing,
he was entitled to the honor; so I sent him to Augusta when
the time came, and he took the oaths. And a very valuable
member he made. They appointed him on the Committee
on Parishes; but I wrote a letter for him, resigning, on the
ground that he took an interest in our claim to the stumpage
in the minister's sixteenths of Gore A, next No. 7, in the

10th Range. He never made any speeches, and always voted with the minority, which was what he was sent to do. He made me and himself a great many good friends, some of whom I did not afterwards recognize as quickly as Dennis did my parishioners. On one or two occasions, when there was wood to saw at home, I kept him at home; but I took those occasions to go to Augusta myself. Finding myself often in his vacant seat at these times, I watched the proceedings with a good deal of care; and once was so much excited that I delivered my somewhat celebrated speech on the Central School-District question, a speech of which the "State of Maine" printed some extra copies. I believe there is no formal rule permitting strangers to speak; but no one objected.

Dennis himself, as I have said, never spoke at all. But our experience this session led me to think that if, by some such "general understanding" as the reports speak of in legislation daily, every member of Congress might leave a double to sit through those deadly sessions and answer to roll-calls and do the legitimate party-voting, which appears stereotyped in the regular list of Ashe, Bocock, Black, etc., we should gain decidedly in working-power. As things stand, the saddest State prison I ever visit is that Representatives' Chamber in Washington. If a man leaves for an hour, twenty "correspondents" may be howling, "Where was Mr. Prendergast when the Oregon bill passed?" And if poor Prendergast stays there! Certainly, the worst use you can make of a man is to put him in prison!

I know, indeed, that public men of the highest rank have resorted to this expedient long ago. Dumas' novel of the *Iron Mask* turns on the brutal imprisonment of Louis the Fourteenth's double. There seems little doubt, in our own history, that it was the real General Pierce who shed tears when the delegate from Lawrence explained to him the sufferings of the people there,—and only General Pierce's double who had given the orders for the assault on that town, which was invaded the next day. My charming friend, George Withers, has, I am almost sure, a double, who preaches his afternoon sermons for him. This is the reason that the theology often varies so from that of the forenoon. But that double is almost as charming as the original. Some of the most well-defined men, who stand out most prominently on the background of history, are in this way stereoscopic men, who owe their distinct relief to the slight differences between the doubles. All this I know. My present suggestion is simply the great extension of the system, so that all public machine-work may be done by it.

But I see I loiter on my story, which is rushing to the plunge. Let me stop an instant more, however, to recall, were it only to myself, that charming year while all was yet well. After the double had become a matter of course, for nearly twelve months before he undid me, what a year it was. Full of active life, full of happy love, of the hardest work, of the sweetest sleep, and the fulfilment of so many of the fresh aspirations and dreams of boyhood! Dennis went to every school-committee meeting, and sat through all those late wranglings which used to keep me up till midnight and awake till morning. He attended all the lectures to which foreign exiles sent me tickets begging me to come for the love of Heaven and of Bohemia. He accepted and used all the tickets for charity concerts which were sent to me. He appeared everywhere it was specially desirable "our denomination," or "our party," or "our class," or "our family," or "our street," or "our town," or "our country," or "our State," should be fully represented. And I fell back to that charming life which in boyhood one dreams of, when he supposes he shall do his own duty and make his own sacrifices, without being tied up with those of other people. My rusty Sanskrit, Arabic, Hebrew, Greek, Latin, French, Italian, Spanish, German, and English began to take polish. Heavens! how little I had done with them while I attended to my *public* duties! My calls on my parishioners became the friendly, frequent, homelike sociabilities they were meant to be, instead of the hard work of a man goaded to desperation by the sight of his lists of arrears. And preaching! what a luxury preaching was when I had on Sunday the whole result of an individual, personal week, from which to speak to a people whom all that week I had been meeting as hand-to-hand friend. I never tired on Sunday, and was in condition to leave the sermon at home, if I chose, and preach it extempore, as all men should do always. Indeed, I wonder, when I think that a sensible people, like ours,— really more attached to their clergy than they were in the lost days, when the Mathers and Nortons were noblemen, —should choose to neutralize so much of their ministers' lives, and destroy so much of their early training, by this undefined passion for seeing them in public. It springs from our balancing of sects. If a spirited Episcopalian takes an interest in the almshouse, and is put on the Poor Board, every other denomination must have a minister there, lest the poorhouse be changed into St. Paul's Cathedral. If a Sandemanian is chosen president of the Young Men's Library, there must be a Methodist vice-president and a Baptist secretary. And if a Universalist Sunday-School Convention collects five hundred delegates, the next Congregationalist Sabbath-School Conference must be as large, "lest 'they'—whoever *they* may be—should think 'we'— whoever *we* may be—are going down."

Freed from these necessities, that happy year I began to know my wife by sight. We saw each other sometimes. In those long mornings, when Dennis was in the study explaining to map-peddlers that I had eleven maps of Jerusalem already, and to school-book agents that I would see them hanged before I would be bribed to introduce their text-books into the schools,—she and I were at work together, as in those old dreaming days,—and in these of our log-cabin again. But all this could not last,—and at length poor Dennis, my double, overtasked in turn, undid me.

It was thus it happened.—There is an excellent fellow,— once a minister,—I will call him Isaacs,—who deserves well of the world till he dies, and after,—because he once, in a real exigency, did the right thing, in the right way, at the right time, as no other man could do it. In the world's great football match, the ball by chance found him loitering on the outside of the field; he closed with it, "camped" it, charged it home,—yes, right through the other side,—not disturbed, not frightened by his own success,—and, breathless, found himself a great man,—as the Great Delta rang applause. But he did not find himself a rich man; and the football has never come in his way again. From that moment to this moment he has been of no use, that one can see at all. Still, for that great act we speak of Isaacs gratefully and remember him kindly; and he forges on, hoping to meet the football somewhere again. In that vague hope, he had arranged a "movement" for a general organization of the human family into Debating Clubs, County Societies, State Unions, etc., etc., with a view of inducing all children to take hold of the handles of their knives and forks, instead of the metal. Children have bad habits in that way. The movement, of course, was absurd; but we all did our best to forward, not it, but him. It came time for the annual county-meeting on this subject to be held at Naguadavick. Isaacs came round, good fellow! to arrange for it,—got the town-hall, got the Governor to preside (the saint!—he ought to have triplet doubles provided him by law), and then came to get me to speak. "No," I said, "I would not speak, if ten Governors presided. I do not believe in the enterprise. If I spoke, it should be to say children should take hold of the prongs of the forks and the blades of the knives. I would subscribe ten dollars, but I would not speak a mill." So poor Isaacs went his way, sadly, to coax Auchmuty to speak, and Delafield. I went out. Not long after, he came back, and told Polly that they had promised to speak,—the Governor would speak,—and he himself would close with the quarterly report, and some interesting anecdotes regarding Miss Biffin's way of handling her knife and Mr. Nellis's way of footing his fork. "Now, if Mr. Ingham will only come and sit on the platform, he need not say one word; but it will show well in the paper,—it will show that the Sandemanians take as much interest in the movement as the Armenians or the Mesopotamians, and will be a great favor to me." Polly, good soul! was tempted, and she promised. She knew Mrs. Isaacs was starving, and the babies,—she knew Dennis was at home,—and she promised! Night came, and I returned. I heard her story. I was sorry. I doubted. But Polly had promised to beg me, and I dared all! I told Dennis to hold his peace, under all circumstances, and sent him down.

It was not half an hour more before he returned, wild with excitement,—in a perfect Irish fury,—which it was long before I understood. But I knew at once that he had undone me!

What happened was this. The audience got together, attracted by Governor Gorges' name. There were a thousand people. Poor Gorges was late from Augusta. They became impatient. He came in direct from the train at last, really ignorant of the object of the meeting. He opened it in the fewest possible words, and said other gentlemen were present who would entertain them better than he. The audience were disappointed, but waited. The Governor, prompted by Isaacs, said, "The Honorable Mr. Delafield will address you." Delafield had forgotten the knives and forks, and was playing the Ruy Lopez opening at the chess-club. "The Rev. Mr. Auchmuty will address you." Auchmuty had promised to speak late, and was at the school-committee. "I see Dr. Stearns in the hall; perhaps he will say a word." Dr. Stearns said he had come to listen and not to speak. The Governor and Isaacs whispered. The Governor looked at Dennis, who was resplendent on the platform; but Isaacs, to give him his due, shook his head. But the look was enough. A miserable lad, ill-bred, who had once been in Boston, thought it would sound well to call for me, and peeped out, "Ingham!" A few more wretches cried, "Ingham! Ingham!" Still Isaacs was firm; but the Governor, anxious, indeed, to prevent a row, knew I would say something, and said, "Our friend

Mr. Ingham is always prepared,—and though we had not relied upon him, he will say a word, perhaps." Applause followed, which turned Dennis's head. He rose, fluttered, and tried No. 3: "There has been so much said, and, on the whole, so well said, that I will not longer occupy the time!" and sat down, looking for his hat; for things seemed squally. But the people cried, "Go on! go on!" and some applauded. Dennis, still confused, but flattered by the applause, to which neither he nor I are used, rose again, and this time tried No. 2: "I am very glad you liked it!" in a sonorous, clear delivery. My best friends stared. All the people who did not know me personally yelled with delight at the aspect of the evening; the Governor was beside himself, and poor Isaacs thought he was undone! Alas, it was I! A boy in the gallery cried in a loud tone, "It's all an infernal humbug," just as Dennis, waving his hand, commanded silence, and tried No. 4: "I agree, in general, with my friend the other side of the room." The poor Governor doubted his senses, and crossed to stop him,—not in time, however. The same gallery-boy shouted, "How's your mother?"—and Dennis, now completely lost, tried, as his last shot, No. 1 vainly: "Very well, thank you; and you?"

I think I must have been undone already. But Dennis, like another Lockhard, chose "to make sicker." The audience rose in a whirl of amazement, rage, and sorrow. Some other impertinence, aimed at Dennis, broke all restraint, and, in pure Irish, he delivered himself of an address to the gallery, inviting any person who wished to fight to come down and do so,—stating, that they were all dogs and cowards and the sons of dogs and cowards,—that he would take any five of them single-handed. "Shure, I have said all his Riverence and the Mishtress bade me say," cried he, in defiance; and, seizing the Governor's cane from his hand, brandished it, quarter-staff fashion, above his head. He was, indeed, got from the hall only with the greatest difficulty by the Governor, the City Marshal, who had been called in, and the Superintendent of my Sunday-School.

The universal impression, of course, was, that the Rev. Frederic Ingham had lost all command of himself in some of those haunts of intoxication which for fifteen years I have been laboring to destroy. Till this moment, indeed, that is the impression in Naguadavick. This number of the *Atlantic* will relieve from it a hundred friends of mine who have been sadly wounded by that notion now for years;— but I shall not be likely ever to show my head there again.

No! My double has undone me.

We left town at seven the next morning. I came to No. 9 in the Third Range, and settled on the Minister's Lot. In the new towns in Maine, the first settled minister has a gift of a hundred acres of land. I am the first settled minister in No. 9. My wife and little Paulina are my parish. We raise corn enough to live on in summer. We kill bear's meat enough to carbonize it in winter. I work on steadily on my "Traces of Sandemanianism in the Sixth and Seventh Centuries," which I hope to persuade some publisher to publish next year. We are very happy, but the world thinks we are undone.

THE PHANTOM 'RICKSHAW

By Rudyard Kipling

May no ill dreams disturb my rest,
Nor Powers of Darkness me molest.
Evening Hymn.

ONE of the few advantages that India has over England is a great Knowability. After five years' service a man is directly or indirectly acquainted with the two or three hundred Civilians in his Province, all the Messes of ten or twelve Regiments and Batteries, and some fifteen hundred other people of the non-official caste. In ten years his knowledge should be doubled, and at the end of twenty he knows, or knows something about, every Englishman in the Empire, and may travel anywhere and everywhere without paying hotel-bills.

Globe-trotters who expect entertainment as a right have, even within my memory, blunted this open-heartedness, but none the less today, if you belong to the Inner Circle and are neither a Bear nor a Black Sheep, all houses are open to you, and our small world is very, very kind and helpful. Rickett of Kamartha stayed with Polder of Kumaon some fifteen years ago. He meant to stay two nights, but was knocked down by rheumatic fever, and for six weeks disorganized Polder's establishment, stopped Polder's work, and nearly died in Polder's bedroom. Polder behaves as though he had been placed under eternal obligation by Rickett, and yearly sends the little Ricketts a box of presents and toys. It is the same everywhere. The men who do not take the trouble to conceal from you their opinion that you are an incompetent ass, and the women who blacken your character and misunderstand your wife's amusements, will work themselves to the bone in your behalf if you fall sick or into serious trouble.

Heatherlegh, the Doctor, kept, in addition to his regular practice, a hospital on his private account—an arrangement of loose boxes for Incurables, his friend called it—but it was really a sort of fitting-up shed for craft that had been damaged by stress of weather. The weather in India is often sultry, and since the tale of bricks is always a fixed quantity, and the only liberty allowed is permission to work overtime and get no thanks, men occasionally break down and become as mixed as the metaphors in this sentence.

Heatherlegh is the dearest doctor that ever was, and his invariable prescription to all his patients is, "lie low, go slow, and keep cool." He says that more men are killed by overwork than the importance of this world justifies. He maintains that overwork slew Pansay, who died under his hands about three years ago. He has, of course, the right to speak authoritatively, and he laughs at my theory that there was a crack in Pansay's head and a little bit of the Dark World came through and pressed him to death. "Pansay went off the handle," says Heatherlegh, "after the stimulus of long leave at Home. He may or he may not have behaved like a blackguard to Mrs. Keith-Wessington. My notion is that the work of the Katabundi Settlement ran him off his legs, and that he took to brooding and making much of an ordinary P. & O. flirtation. He certainly was engaged to Miss Mannering, and she certainly broke off the engagement. Then he took a feverish chill and all that nonsense about ghosts developed. Overwork started his illness, kept it alight, and killed him, poor devil. Write him off to the System—one man to take the work of two and a half men."

I do not believe this. I used to sit up with Pansay sometimes when Heatherlegh was called out to patients, and I happened to be within claim. The man would make me most unhappy by describing in a low, even voice, the procession that was always passing at the bottom of his bed. He had a sick man's command of language. When he recovered I suggested that he should write out the whole affair from beginning to end, knowing that ink might assist him to ease his mind. When little boys have learned a new bad word they are never happy till they have chalked it up on a door. And this also is Literature.

He was in a high fever while he was writing, and the blood-and-thunder Magazine diction he adopted did not calm him. Two months afterwards he was reported fit for duty, but, in spite of the fact that he was urgently needed to help an undermanned Commission stagger through a deficit, he preferred to die; vowing at the last that he was hag-ridden. I got his manuscript before he died, and this is his version of the affair, dated 1885:—

My doctor tells me that I need rest and change of air. It is not improbable that I shall get both ere long—rest that neither the red-coated messenger nor the midday gun can break, and change of air far beyond that which any home-ward-bound steamer can give me. In the meantime I am resolved to stay where I am; and, in flat defiance of my doctor's orders, to take all the world into my confidence. You shall learn for yourselves the precise nature of my malady; and shall, too, judge for yourselves whether any man born of woman on this weary earth was ever so tormented as I.

Speaking now as a condemned criminal might speak ere the drop-bolts are drawn, my story, wild and hideously improbable, as it may appear, demands at least attention. That it will ever receive credence I utterly disbelieve. Two months ago I should have scouted as mad or drunk the man who had dared tell me the like. Two months ago I was the happiest man in India. To-day, from Peshawar to the sea, there is no one more wretched. My doctor and I are the only two who know this. His explanation is, that my brain, digestion, and eyesight are all slightly affected; giving rise to my frequent and persistent "delusions." Delusions, indeed! I call him a fool; but he attends me still with the same unwearied smile, the same bland professional manner, the same neatly-trimmed red whiskers, till I begin to suspect that I am an ungrateful, evil-tempered invalid. But you shall judge for yourselves.

Three years ago it was my fortune—my great misfortune—to sail from Gravesend to Bombay, on return from long leave, with one Agnes Keith-Wessington, wife of an officer on the Bombay side. It does not in the least concern you to know what manner of woman she was. Be content with the knowledge that, ere the voyage had ended, both she and I were desperately and unreasoningly in love with one another. Heaven knows that I can make the admission now without one particle of vanity. In matters of this sort there is always one who gives and another who accepts. From the first day of our ill-omened attachment, I was conscious that Agnes's passion was a stronger, a more dominant, and—if I may use the expression—a purer sentiment than mine. Whether she recognized the fact then, I do not know. Afterwards it was bitterly plain to both of us.

Arrived at Bombay in the spring of the year, we went our respective ways, to meet no more for the next three or four months, when my leave and her love took us both to Simla. There we spent the season together; and there my fire of straw burnt itself out to a pitiful end with the closing year. I attempt no excuse. I make no apology. Mrs. Wessington had given up much for my sake, and was prepared to give up all. From my own lips, in August, 1882, she learnt that I was sick of her presence, tired of her company, and weary of the sound of her voice. Ninety-nine women out of a hundred would have wearied of me as I wearied of them; seventy-five of that number would have promptly avenged themselves by active and obtrusive flirtation with other men. Mrs. Wessington was the hundredth. On her neither my openly expressed aversion nor the cutting brutalities with which I garnished our interviews had the least effect.

"Jack, darling!" was her one eternal cuckoo cry: "I'm sure it's all a mistake—a hideous mistake; and we'll be good friends again some day. *Please* forgive me, Jack, dear."

I was the offender, and I knew it. That knowledge transformed my pity into passive endurance, and, eventually, into blind hate—the same instinct, I suppose, which prompts a man to savagely stamp on the spider he has but half killed. And with this hate in my bosom the season of 1882 came to an end.

Next year we met again at Simla—she with her monotonous face and timid attempts at reconciliation, and I with loathing of her in every fiber of my frame. Several times I could not avoid meeting her alone; and on each occasion her words were identically the same. Still the unreasoning wail that it was all a "mistake;" and still the hope of eventually "making friends." I might have seen, had I cared to look, that that hope only was keeping her alive. She grew more wan and thin month by month. You will agree with me, at least, that such conduct would have driven any one to despair. It was uncalled for; childish; unwomanly. I maintain that she was much to blame. And again, sometimes, in the black, fever-stricken night watches, I have begun to think that I might have been a little kinder to her. But that really *is* a "delusion." I could not have continued pretending to love her when I didn't; could I? It would have been unfair to us both.

Last year we met again—on the same terms as before. The same weary appeals, and the same curt answers from my lips. At least I would make her see how wholly wrong and hopeless were her attempts at resuming the old relationship. As the season wore on, we fell apart—that is to say, she found it difficult to meet me, for I had other and more absorbing interests to attend to. When I think it over quietly in my sick-room, the season of 1884 seems a confused nightmare wherein light and shade were fantastically intermingled—my courtship of little Kitty Mannering; my hopes, doubts, and fears; our long rides together; my trembling avowal of attachment; her reply; and now and again a vision of a white face flitting by in the 'rickshaw with the black and white liveries I once watched for so earnestly; the wave of Mrs. Wessington's gloved hand; and, when she met me alone, which was but seldom, the irksome monotony of her appeal. I loved Kitty Mannering; honestly, heartily loved her, and with my love for her grew my hatred for Agnes. In August, Kitty and I were engaged. The next day I met those accursed "magpie" *jhampanies* at the back of Jakko, and, moved by some passing sentiment of pity, stopped to tell Mrs. Wessington everything. She knew it already.

"So I hear you're engaged, Jack dear." Then, without a moment's pause:—"I'm sure it's all a mistake—a hideous mistake. We shall be as good friends some day, Jack, as we ever were."

My answer might have made even a man wince. It cut the dying woman before me like the blow of a whip.

"Please forgive me, Jack; I didn't mean to make you angry; but it's true, it's true!"

And Mrs. Wessington broke down completely. I turned away and left her to finish her journey in peace, feeling, but only for a moment or two, that I had been an unutterably mean hound. I looked back, and saw that she had turned her 'rickshaw with the idea, I suppose, of overtaking me.

The scene and its surroundings were photographed on my memory. The rain-swept sky (we were at the end of the wet weather), the sodden, dingy pines, the muddy road, and the black powder-riven cliffs formed a gloomy background against which the black and white liveries of the *jhampanies,* the yellow-paneled 'rickshaw and Mrs. Wessington's down-bowed golden head stood out clearly. She was holding her handkerchief in her left hand and was leaning back exhausted against the 'rickshaw cushions. I turned my horse up a by-path near the Sanjowlie Reservoir and literally ran away. Once I fancied I heard a faint call of "Jack!" This may have been imagination. I never stopped to verify it. Ten minutes later I came across Kitty on horseback; and, in the delight of a long ride with her, forgot all about the interview.

A week later Mrs. Wessington died, and the inexpressible burden of her existence was removed from my life. I went Plainsward perfectly happy. Before three months were over I had forgotten all about her, except that at times the discovery of some of her old letters reminded me unpleasantly of our bygone relationship. By January I had disinterred what was left of our correspondence from among my scattered belongings and had burnt it. At the beginning of April of this year, 1885, I was at Simla—semi-deserted Simla—once more, and was deep in lover's talks and walks with Kitty. It was decided that we should be married at the end of June. You will understand, therefore, that, loving Kitty as I did, I am not saying too much when I pronounce myself to have been, at that time, the happiest man in India.

Fourteen delightful days passed almost before I noticed their flight. Then, aroused to the sense of what was proper among mortals circumstanced as we were, I pointed out to Kitty that an engagement ring was the outward and visible sign of her dignity as an engaged girl; and that she must forthwith come to Hamilton's to be measured for one. Up to that moment, I give you my word, we had completely forgotten so trivial a matter. To Hamilton's we accordingly went on the 15th of April, 1885. Remember that—whatever my doctor may say to the contrary—I was then in perfect health, enjoying a well-balanced mind and an *absolutely* tranquil spirit. Kitty and I entered Hamilton's shop together, and there, regardless of the order of affairs, I measured Kitty for the ring in the presence of the amused assistant. The ring was a sapphire with two diamonds. We then rode out down the slope that leads to the Combermere Bridge and Peliti's shop.

While my Waler was cautiously feeling his way over the loose shale, and Kitty was laughing and chattering at my

side—while all Simla, that is to say as much of it as had
then come from the Plains, was grouped round the Reading-
room and Peliti's veranda,—I was aware that some one,
apparently at a vast distance, was calling me by my Christian name. It struck me that I had heard the voice
before, but when and where I could not at once determine.
In the short space it took to cover the road between the
path from Hamilton's shop and the first plank of the Combermere Bridge I had thought over half a dozen people who
might have committed such a solecism, and had eventually
decided that it must have been some singing in my ears.
Immediately opposite Peliti's shop my eye was arrested by
the sight of four *jhampanies* in "magpie" livery, pulling a
yellow-paneled, cheap, bazar 'rickshaw. In a moment my
mind flew back to the previous season and Mrs. Wessington with a sense of irritation and disgust. Was it not
enough that the woman was dead and done with, without
her black and white servitors reappearing to spoil the day's
happiness? Whoever employed them now I thought I
would call upon, and ask as a personal favor to change
her *jhampanies'* livery. I would hire the men myself, and,
if necessary, buy their coats from off their backs. It is
impossible to say here what a flood of undesirable memories
their presence evoked.

"Kitty," I cried, "there are poor Mrs. Wessington's
jhampanies turned up again! I wonder who has them now?"

Kitty had known Mrs. Wessington slightly last season,
and had always been interested in the sickly woman.

"What? Where?" she asked. "I can't see them anywhere."

Even as she spoke, her horse, swerving from a laden
mule, threw himself directly in front of the advancing
'rickshaw. I had scarcely time to utter a word of warning,
when, to my unutterable horror, horse and rider passed
through men and carriage as if they had been thin air.

"What's the matter?" cried Kitty; "what made you call
out so foolishly, Jack? If I *am* engaged I don't want all

creation to know about it. There was lots of space between the mule and the veranda, and, if you think I can't ride ——There!"

Whereupon wilful Kitty set off, her dainty little head in the air, at a hand-gallop in the direction of the Band-stand; fully expecting, as she herself afterwards told me, that I should follow her. What was the matter? Nothing indeed. Either that I was mad or drunk, or that Simla was haunted with devils. I reined in my impatient cob, and turned round. The 'rickshaw had turned too, and now stood immediately facing me, near the left railing of the Combermere Bridge.

"Jack! Jack, darling!" There was no mistake about the words this time: they rang through my brain as if they had been shouted in my ear. "It's some hideous mistake, I'm sure. *Please* forgive me, Jack, and let's be friends again."

The 'rickshaw-hood had fallen back, and inside, as I hope and pray daily for the death I dread by night, sat Mrs. Keith-Wessington, handkerchief in hand, and golden head bowed on her breast.

How long I stared motionless I do not know. Finally, I was aroused by my syce taking the Waler's bridle and asking whether I was ill. From the horrible to the commonplace is but a step. I tumbled off my horse and dashed, half fainting, into Peliti's for a glass of cherry-brandy. There two or three couples were gathered round the coffee-tables discussing the gossip of the day. Their trivialities were more comforting to me just then than the consolations of religion could have been. I plunged into the midst of the conversation at once; chatted, laughed, and jested with a face (when I caught a glimpse of it in a mirror) as white and drawn as that of a corpse. Three or four men noticed my condition; and, evidently setting it down to the results of over-many pegs, charitably endeavored to draw me apart from the rest of the loungers. But I refused to be led away. I wanted the company of my kind—as a child rushes into thȩ midst of the dinner-party after a fright in the dark. I must have talked for about ten minutes or so, though it seemed an eternity to me, when I heard Kitty's clear voice outside inquiring for me. In another minute she had entered the shop, prepared to roundly upbraid me for failing so signally in my duties. Something in my face stopped her. "Why, Jack," she cried, "what *have* you been doing? What *has* happened? Are you ill?" Thus driven into a direct lie, I said that the sun had been a little too much for me. It was close upon five o'clock of a cloudy April afternoon, and the sun had been hidden all day. I saw my mistake as soon as the words were out of my mouth; attempted to recover it; blundered hopelessly and followed Kitty in a regal rage, out of doors, amid the smiles of my acquaintances. I made some excuse (I have forgotten what) on the score of my feeling faint; and cantered away to my hotel, leaving Kitty to finish the ride by herself.

In my room I sat down and tried calmly to reason out the matter. Here was I, Theobald Jack Pansay, a well-educated Bengal Civilian in the year of grace 1885, presumably sane, certainly healthy, driven in terror from my sweetheart's side by the apparition of a woman who had been dead and buried eight months ago. These were facts that I could not blink. Nothing was further from my thought than any memory of Mrs. Wessington when Kitty and I left Hamilton's shop. Nothing was more utterly commonplace than the stretch of wall opposite Peliti's. It was broad daylight. The road was full of people; and yet here, look you, in defiance of every law of probability, in direct outrage of Nature's ordinance, there had appeared to me a face from the grave.

Kitty's Arab had gone *through* the 'rickshaw: so that my first hope that some woman marvelously like Mrs. Wessington had hired the carriage and the coolies with their old livery was lost. Again and again I went round this treadmill of thought; and again and again gave up baffled and in despair. The voice was as inexplicable as the apparition. I had originally some wild notion of confiding it all to Kitty; of begging her to marry me at once; and in her arms defying the ghostly occupant of the 'rickshaw. "After all," I argued, "the presence of the 'rickshaw is in itself enough to prove the existence of a spectral illusion. One may see ghosts of men and women, but surely never of coolies and carriages. The whole thing is absurd. Fancy the ghost of a hillman!"

Next morning I sent a penitent note to Kitty, imploring her to overlook my strange conduct of the previous afternoon. My Divinity was still very wroth, and a personal apology was necessary. I explained, with a fluency born of night-long pondering over a falsehood, that I had been attacked with a sudden palpitation of the heart—the result of indigestion. This eminently practical solution had its effect; and Kitty and I rode out that afternoon with the shadow of my first lie dividing us.

Nothing would please her save a canter round Jakko. With my nerves still unstrung from the previous night, I feebly protested against the notion, suggesting Observatory Hill, Jutogh, the Boileaugunge road—anything rather than the Jakko round. Kitty was angry and a little hurt: so I yielded from fear of provoking further misunderstanding, and we set out together towards Chota Simla. We walked the greater part of the way, and according to our custom, cantered from a mile or so below the convent to a stretch of level road by the Sanjowlie Reservoir. The wretched horses appeared to fly, and my heart beat quicker and quicker as we neared the crest of the ascent. My mind had been full of Mrs. Wessington all the afternoon; and every inch of the Jakko road bore witness to our old-time walks and talks. The bowlders were full of it; the pines sang it aloud overhead; the rain-fed torrents giggled and chuckled unseen over the shameful story; and the wind in my ears chanted the iniquity aloud.

As a fitting climax, in the middle of the level men call the Ladies' Mile the Horror was awaiting me. No other 'rickshaw was in sight—only the four black and white *jham-panies,* the yellow-paneled carriage, and the golden head of the woman within—all apparently just as I had left them eight months and one fortnight ago! For an instant I fancied that Kitty *must* see what I saw—we were so marvelously sympathetic in all things. Her next words undeceived me—"Not a soul in sight! Come along, Jack, and I'll race you to the Reservoir buildings!" Her wiry little Arab was off like a bird, my Waler following close behind, and in this order we dashed under the cliffs. Half a minute brought us within fifty yards of the 'rickshaw. I pulled my Waler and fell back a little. The 'rickshaw was directly in the middle of the road; and once more the Arab passed through it, my horse following. "Jack! Jack dear! *Please* forgive me," rang with a wail in my ears, and, after an interval:—"It's all a mistake, a hideous mistake!"

I spurred my horse like a man possessed. When I turned my head at the Reservoir works, the black and white liveries were still waiting—patiently waiting—under the gray hillside, and the wind brought me a mocking echo of the words I had just heard. Kitty bantered me a good deal on my silence throughout the remainder of the ride. I had been talking up till then wildly and at random. To save my life I could not speak afterwards naturally, and from Sanjowlie to the Church wisely held my tongue.

I was to dine with the Mannerings that night, and had barely time to canter home to dress. On the road to Elysium Hill I overheard two men talking together in the dusk.— "It's a curious thing," said one, "how completely all trace of it disappeared. You know my wife was insanely fond of the woman (never could see anything in her myself), and wanted me to pick up her old 'rickshaw and coolies if they were to be got for love or money. Morbid sort of fancy I call it; but I've got to do what the *Memsahib* tells me. Would you believe that the man she hired it from tells me that all four of the men—they were brothers—died of cholera on the way to Hardwar, poor devils; and the 'rickshaw has been broken up by the man himself. 'Told me he never used a dead *Memsahib's* 'rickshaw. 'Spoilt his luck. Queer notion, wasn't it? Fancy poor little Mrs. Wessington spoiling any one's luck except her own!" I laughed aloud at this point; and my laugh jarred on me as I uttered it. So there *were* ghosts of 'rickshaws after all, and ghostly employments in the other world! How much did Mrs. Wessington give her men? What were their hours? Where did they go?

And for visible answer to my last question I saw the infernal Thing blocking my path in the twilight. The dead travel fast, and by short cuts unknown to ordinary coolies. I laughed aloud a second time, and checked my laughter suddenly, for I was afraid I was going mad. Mad to a certain extent I must have been, for I recollect that I reined in my horse at the head of the 'rickshaw, and politely wished Mrs. Wessington "Good evening." Her answer was one I knew only too well. I listened to the end; and replied that I had heard it all before, but should be delighted if she had anything further to say. Some malignant devil stronger than I must have entered into me that evening, for I have a dim recollection of talking the commonplaces of the day for five minutes to the Thing in front of me.

"Mad as a hatter, poor devil—or drunk. Max, try and get him to come home."

Surely *that* was not Mrs. Wessington's voice! The two men had overheard me speaking to the empty air, and had returned to look after me. They were very kind and considerate, and from their words evidently gathered that I was extremely drunk. I thanked them confusedly and cantered away to my hotel, there changed, and arrived at the Mannerings' ten minutes late. I pleaded the darkness of the night as an excuse; was rebuked by Kitty for my unloverlike tardiness; and sat down.

The conversation had already become general; and under cover of it, I was addressing some tender small talk to my sweetheart, when I was aware that at the further end of the table a short red-whiskered man was describing, with much broidery, his encounter with a mad unknown that evening.

A few sentences convinced me that he was repeating the incident of half an hour ago. In the middle of the story he looked round for applause, as professional story-tellers do, caught my eye, and straightway collapsed. There was a moment's awkward silence, and the red-whiskered man muttered something to the effect that he had "forgotten the rest," thereby sacrificing a reputation as a good story-teller which he had built up for six seasons past. I blessed him from the bottom of my heart, and—went on with my fish.

In the fulness of time that dinner came to an end; and with genuine regret I tore myself away from Kitty—as certain as I was of my own existence that It would be waiting for me outside the door. The red-whiskered man, who had been introduced to me as Dr. Heatherlegh of Simla, volunteered to bear me company as far as our roads lay together. I accepted his offer with gratitude.

My instinct had not deceived me. It lay in readiness in the Mall, and, in what seemed devilish mockery of our ways, with a lighted head-lamp. The red-whiskered man went to the point at once, in a manner that showed he had been thinking over it all dinner time.

"I say, Pansay, what the deuce was the matter with you this evening on the Elysium road?" The suddenness of the question wrenched an answer from me before I was aware.

"That!" said I, pointing to It.

"*That,* may be either *D. T.* or Eyes for aught I know. Now you don't liquor. I saw as much at dinner, so it can't be *D. T.* There's nothing whatever where you're pointing, though you're sweating and trembling with fright like a scared pony. Therefore, I conclude that it's Eyes. And I ought to understand all about them. Come along home with me. I'm on the Blessington lower road."

To my intense delight the 'rickshaw, instead of waiting for us, kept about twenty yards ahead—and this, too, whether we walked, trotted, or cantered. In the course of that long night ride I had told my companion almost as much as I have told you here.

"Well, you've spoilt one of the best tales I've ever laid tongue to," said he, "but I'll forgive you for the sake of what you've gone through. Now come home and do what I tell you; and when I've cured you, young man, let this be a lesson to you to steer clear of women and indigestible food till the day of your death."

The 'rickshaw kept steady in front; and my red-whiskered friend seemed to derive great pleasure from my account of its exact whereabouts.

"Eyes, Pansay—all Eyes, Brain, and Stomach. And the greatest of these three is Stomach. You've too much conceited Brain, too little Stomach, and thoroughly unhealthy Eyes. Get your Stomach straight and the rest follows. And all that's French for a liver pill. I'll take sole medical charge of you from this hour! for you're too interesting a phenomenon to be passed over."

By this time we were deep in the shadow of the Blessington lower road and the 'rickshaw came to a dead stop under a pine-clad, overhanging shale cliff. Instinctively I halted too, giving my reason, Heatherlegh rapped out an oath.

"Now, if you think I'm going to spend a cold night on the hillside for the sake of a Stomach *cum*-Brain-*cum*-Eye illusion . . . Lord, ha' mercy! What's that?"

There was a muffled report, a blinding smother of dust just in front of us, a crack, the noise of rent boughs, and about ten yards of the cliff-side—pines, undergrowth, and all—slid down into the road below, completely blocking it up. The uprooted trees swayed and tottered for a moment like drunken giants in the gloom, and then fell prone among their fellows with a thunderous crash. Our two horses stood motionless and sweating with fear. As soon as the rattle of falling earth and stone had subsided, my companion muttered:—"Man if we'd gone forward we should have been ten feet deep in our graves by now. 'There are more things in heaven and earth' . . . Come home, Pansay, and thank God. I want a peg badly."

We retraced our way over the Church Ridge, and I arrived at Dr. Heatherlegh's house shortly after midnight.

His attempts towards my cure commenced almost immediately, and for a week I never left his side. Many a time in the course of that week did I bless the good-fortune which had thrown me in contact with Simla's best and kindest doctor. Day by day my spirits grew lighter and more equable. Day by day, too, I became more and more inclined to fall in with Heatherlegh's "spectral illusion" theory, implicating eyes, brain, and stomach. I wrote to Kitty, telling her that a slight sprain caused by a fall from my horse kept me indoors for a few days; and that I should be recovered before she had time to regret my absence.

Heatherlegh's treatment was simple to a degree. It consisted of liver pills, cold-water baths, and strong exercise, taken in the dusk or at early dawn—for, as he sagely observed:—"A man with a sprained ankle doesn't walk a dozen miles a day, and your young woman might be wondering if she saw you."

At the end of the week, after much examination of pupil and pulse, and strict injunctions as to diet and pedestrianism, Heatherlegh dismissed me as brusquely as he had taken charge of me. Here is his parting benediction:—"Man, I certify to your mental cure, and that's as much as to say I've cured most of your bodily ailments. Now, get your traps out of this as soon as you can; and be off to make love to Miss Kitty."

I was endeavoring to express my thanks for his kindness. He cut me short.

"Don't think I did this because I like you. I gather that you've behaved like a blackguard all through. But, all the same, you're a phenomenon, and as queer a phenomenon as you are a blackguard. No!"—checking me a second time—"not a rupee, please. Go out and see if you can find the eyes-brain-and-stomach business again. I'll give you a lakh for each time you see it."

Half an hour later I was in the Mannerings' drawing-room with Kitty—drunk, with the intoxication of present happiness and the foreknowledge that I should never more be troubled with Its hideous presence. Strong in the sense of my new-found security, I proposed a ride at once; and, by preference, a canter round Jakko.

Never had I felt so well, so overladen with vitality and mere animal spirits, as I did on the afternoon of the 30th of April. Kitty was delighted at the change in my appearance, and complimented me on it in her delightfully frank and outspoken manner. We left the Mannerings' house together, laughing and talking, and cantered along the Chota Simla road as of old.

I was in haste to reach the Sanjowlie Reservoir and there make my assurance doubly sure. The horses did their best, but seemed all too slow to my impatient mind. Kitty was astonished at my boisterousness. "Why, Jack!" she cried at last, "you are behaving like a child. What are you doing?"

We were just below the Convent, and from sheer wantonness I was making my Waler plunge and curvet across the road as I tickled it with the loop of my riding-whip.

"Doing?" I answered: "nothing, dear. That's just it. If you'd been doing nothing for a week except lie up, you'd be as riotous as I.

> "'Singing and murmuring in your feastful mirth,
>   Joying to feel yourself alive;
> Lord over Nature, Lord of the visible Earth,
>   Lord of the senses five.'"

My quotation was hardly out of my lips before we had rounded the corner above the Convent; and a few yards further on could see across to Sanjowlie. In the center of the level road stood the black and white liveries, the yellow-paneled 'rickshaw, and Mrs. Keith-Wessington. I pulled up, looked, rubbed my eyes, and, I believe, must have said something. The next thing I knew was that I was lying face downward on the road, with Kitty kneeling above me in tears.

"Has It gone, child?" I gasped. Kitty only wept more bitterly.

"Has what gone, Jack dear? What does it all mean? There must be a mistake somewhere, Jack. A hideous mistake." Her last words brought me to my feet—mad—raving for the time being.

"Yes, there *is* a mistake somewhere," I repeated, "a hideous mistake. Come and look at It."

I have an indistinct idea that I dragged Kitty by the wrist along the road up to where It stood, and implored her for pity's sake to speak to It; to tell It that we were betrothed; that neither Death nor Hell could break the tie between us; and Kitty only knows how much more to the same effect. Now and again I appealed passionately to the Terror in the 'rickshaw to bear witness to all I had said, and to release me from a torture that was killing me. As I talked I suppose I must have told Kitty of my old relations with Mrs. Wessington, for I saw her listen intently with white face and blazing eyes.

"Thank you, Mr. Pansay," she said, "that's *quite* enough. *Syce ghora láo.*"

The syces, impassive as Orientals always are, had come up with the recaptured horses; and as Kitty sprang into her saddle I caught hold of the bridle, entreating her to hear me out and forgive. My answer was the cut of her riding-whip across my face from mouth to eye, and a word or two of farewell that even now I cannot write down. So I judged, and judged rightly, that Kitty knew all; and I staggered back to the side of the 'rickshaw. My face was cut and bleeding, and the blow of the riding-whip had raised a livid blue weal on it. I had no self-respect. Just then, Heatherlegh, who must have been following Kitty and me at a distance, cantered up.

"Doctor," I said, pointing to my face, "here's Miss

Mannering's signature to my order of dismissal and . . . I'll thank you for that lakh as soon as convenient."

Heatherlegh's face, even in my abject misery, moved me to laughter.

"I'll stake my professional reputation"—he began.

"Don't be a fool," I whispered. "I've lost my life's happiness and you'd better take me home."

As I spoke the 'rickshaw was gone. Then I lost all knowledge of what was passing. The crest of Jakko seemed to heave and roll like the crest of a cloud and fall in upon me.

Seven days later (on the 7th of May, that is to say) I was aware that I was lying in Heatherlegh's room as weak as a little child. Heatherlegh was watching me intently from behind the papers on his writing-table. His first words were not encouraging; but I was too far spent to be much moved by them.

"Here's Miss Kitty has sent back your letters. You correspond a good deal, you young people. Here's a packet that looks like a ring, and a cheerful sort of a note from Mannering Papa, which I've taken the liberty of reading and burning. The old gentleman's not pleased with you."

"And Kitty?" I asked dully.

"Rather more drawn than her father, from what she says. By the same token you must have been letting out any number of queer reminiscences just before I met you. 'Says that a man who would have behaved to a woman as you did to Mrs. Wessington ought to kill himself out of sheer pity for his kind. She is a hot-headed little virago, your mash. 'Will have it too that you were suffering from $D. T.$ when that row on the Jakko road turned up. 'Says she'll die before she ever speaks to you again."

I groaned and turned over on the other side.

"Now you've got your choice, my friend. This engagement has to be broken off; and the Mannerings don't want to be too hard on you. Was it broken through $D. T.$ or epileptic fits? Sorry I can't offer you a better exchange unless you'd prefer hereditary insanity. Say the word and

I'll tell 'em it's fits. All Simla knows about that scene on the Ladies' Mile. Come! I'll give you five minutes to think over it."

During those five minutes I believe that I explored thoroughly the lowest circles of the Inferno which it is permitted man to tread on earth. And at the same time I myself was watching myself faltering through the dark labyrinths of doubt, misery, and utter despair. I wondered, as Heatherlegh in his chair might have wondered, which dreadful alternative I should adopt. Presently I heard myself answering in a voice that I hardly recognized,—

"They're confoundedly particular about morality in these parts. Give 'em fits, Heatherlegh, and my love. Now let me sleep a bit longer."

Then my two selves joined, and it was only I (half crazed, devil-driven I) that tossed in my bed, tracing step by step the history of the past month.

"But I am in Simla," I kept repeating to myself. "I, Jack Pansay, am in Simla, and there are no ghosts here. It's unreasonable of that woman to pretend there are. Why couldn't Agnes have left me alone? I never did her any harm. It might just as well have been me as Agnes. Only I'd never have come back on purpose to kill *her*. Why can't I be left alone—left alone and happy?"

It was high noon when I first awoke: and the sun was low in the sky before I slept—slept as the tortured criminal sleeps on his rack, too worn to feel further pain.

Next day I could not leave my bed. Heatherlegh told me in the morning that he had received an answer from Mr. Mannering, and that, thanks to his (Heatherlegh's) friendly offices, the story of my affliction had traveled through the length and breadth of Simla, where I was on all sides much pitied.

"And that's rather more than you deserve," he concluded pleasantly, "though the Lord knows you've been going through a pretty severe mill. Never mind; we'll cure you yet, you perverse phenomenon."

I declined firmly to be cured. "You've been much too good to me already, old man," said I; "but I don't think I need trouble you further."

In my heart I knew that nothing Heatherlegh could do would lighten the burden that had been laid upon me.

With that knowledge came also a sense of hopeless, impotent rebellion against the unreasonableness of it all. There were scores of men no better than I whose punishments had at least been reserved for another world; and I felt that it was bitterly, cruelly unfair that I alone should have been singled out for so hideous a fate. This mood would in time give place to another where it seemed that the 'rickshaw and I were the only realities in a world of shadows; that Kitty was a ghost; that Mannering, Heatherlegh, and all the other men and women I knew were all ghosts; and the great, gray hills themselves but vain shadows devised to torture me. From mood to mood I tossed backwards and forwards for seven weary days; my body growing daily stronger and stronger, until the bedroom looking-glass told me that I had returned to everyday life, and was as other men once more. Curiously enough my face showed no signs of the struggle I had gone through. It was pale indeed, but as expressionless and commonplace as ever. I had expected some permanent alteration—visible evidence of the disease that was eating me away. I found nothing.

On the 15th of May I left Heatherlegh's house at eleven o'clock in the morning; and the instinct of the bachelor drove me to the Club. There I found that every man knew my story as told by Heatherlegh, and was, in clumsy fashion, abnormally kind and attentive. Nevertheless I recognized that for the rest of my natural life I should be among but not of my fellows; and I envied very bitterly indeed the laughing coolies on the Mall below. I lunched at the Club, and at four o'clock wandered aimlessly down the Mall in the vague hope of meeting Kitty. Close to the Bandstand the black and white liveries joined me; and I heard Mrs. Wessington's old appeal at my side. I had been expecting this ever since I came out; and was only surprised at her delay. The phantom 'rickshaw and I went side by side along the Chota Simla road in silence. Close to the bazar, Kitty and a man on horseback overtook and passed us. For any sign she gave I might have been a dog in the road. She did not even pay me the compliment of quickening her pace; though the rainy afternoon had served for an excuse.

So Kitty and her companion, and I and my ghostly Light-o'-Love, crept round Jakko in couples. The road was streaming with water; the pines dripped like roof-pipes on the rocks below, and the air was full of fine, driving rain. Two or three times I found myself saying to myself almost aloud:—"I'm Jack Pansay on leave at Simla—*at Simla!* Everyday, ordinary Simla. I mustn't forget that— I mustn't forget that." Then I would try to recollect some of the gossip I had heard at the Club; the prices of So-and-So's horses—anything, in fact, that related to the work-a-day Anglo-Indian world I knew so well. I even repeated the multiplication-table rapidly to myself, to make quite sure that I was not taking leave of my senses. It gave me much comfort; and must have prevented my hearing Mrs. Wessington for a time.

Once more I wearily climbed the Convent slope and entered the level road. Here Kitty and the man started off at a canter, and I was left alone with Mrs. Wessington. "Agnes," said I, "will you put back your hood and tell me what it all means?" The hood dropped noiselessly, and I was face to face with my dead and buried mistress. She was wearing the dress in which I had last seen her alive; carried the same tiny handkerchief in her right hand; and the same card-case in her left. (A woman eight months dead with a card-case?) I had to pin myself down to the multiplication-table, and to set both hands on the stone parapet of the road, to assure myself that that at least was real.

"Agnes," I repeated, "for pity's sake tell me what it all

means." Mrs. Wessington leant forward with that odd, quick turn of the head I used to know so well, and spoke.

If my story had not already so madly overleaped the bounds of all human belief I should apologize to you now. As I know that no one—no, not even Kitty, for whom it is written as some sort of justification of my conduct—will believe me, I will go on. Mrs. Wessington spoke and I walked with her from the Sanjowlie road to the turning below the Commander-in-chief's house as I might walk by the side of any living woman's 'rickshaw, deep in conversation. The second and most tormenting of my moods of sickness had suddenly laid hold upon me, and like the Prince in Tennyson's poem, "I seemed to move amid a world of ghosts." There had been a garden-party at the Commander-in-chief's, and we two joined the crowd of homeward-bound folk. As I saw them then it seemed that *they* were the shadows—impalpable fantastic shadows—that divided for Mrs. Wessington's 'rickshaw to pass through. What we said during the course of that weird interview I cannot —indeed, I dare not—tell. Heatherlegh's comment would have been a short laugh and a remark that I had been "mashing a brain-eye-and-stomach chimera." It was a ghastly and yet in some indefinable way a marvelously dear experience. Could it be possible, I wondered, that I was in this life to woo a second time the woman I had killed by my own neglect and cruelty?

I met Kitty on the homeward road—a shadow among shadows.

If I were to describe all the incidents of the next fort-night in their order, my story would never come to an end; and your patience would be exhausted. Morning after morning and evening after evening the ghostly 'rickshaw and I used to wander through Simla together. Wherever I went there the four black and white liveries followed me and bore me company to and from my hotel. At the Theater I found them amid the crowd of yelling *jhampanies;* outside the Club veranda, after a long evening of whist; at the

Birthday Ball, waiting patiently for my reappearance; and in broad daylight when I went calling. Save that it cast no shadow, the 'rickshaw was in every respect as real to look upon as one of wood and iron. More than once, indeed, I have had to check myself from warning some hard-riding friend against cantering over it. More than once I have walked down the Mall deep in conversation with Mrs. Wessington to the unspeakable amazement of the passers-by.

Before I had been out and about a week I learned that the "fit" theory had been discarded in favor of insanity. However, I made no change in my mode of life, I called, rode, and dined out as freely as ever. I had a passion for the society of my kind which I had never felt before; I hungered to be among the realities of life; and at the same time I felt vaguely unhappy when I had been separated too long from my ghostly companion. It would be almost impossible to describe my varying moods from the 15th of May up to to-day.

The presence of the 'rickshaw filled me by turns with horror, blind fear, a dim sort of pleasure, and utter despair. I dared not leave Simla; and I knew that my stay there was killing me. I knew, moreover, that it was my destiny to die slowly and a little every day. My only anxiety was to get the penance over as quietly as might be. Alternately I hungered for a sight of Kitty and watched her outrageous flirtations with my successor—to speak more accurately, my successors—with amused interest. She was as much out of my life as I was out of hers. By day I wandered with Mrs. Wessington almost content. By night I implored Heaven to let me return to the world as I used to know it. Above all these varying moods lay the sensation of dull, numbing wonder that the Seen and the Unseen should mingle so strangely on this earth to hound one poor soul to its grave.

*   *   *   *   *   *

August 27.—Heatherlegh has been indefatigable in his attendance on me; and only yesterday told me that I ought to send in an application for sick leave. An application to escape the company of a phantom! A request that the Government would graciously permit me to get rid of five ghosts and an airy 'rickshaw by going to England! Heatherlegh's proposition moved me almost to hysterical laughter. I told him that I should await the end quietly at Simla; and I am sure that the end is not far off. Believe me that I dread its advent more than any word can say; and I torture myself nightly with a thousand speculations as to the manner of my death.

Shall I die in my bed decently and as an English gentleman should die; or, in one last walk on the Mall, will my soul be wrenched from me to take its place forever and ever by the side of that ghastly phantasm? Shall I return to my old lost allegiance in the next world, or shall I meet Agnes, loathing her and bound to her side through all eternity? Shall we two hover over the scene of our lives till the end of Time? As the day of my death draws nearer, the intense horror that all living flesh feels towards escaped spirits from beyond the grave grows more and more powerful. It is an awful thing to go down quick among the dead with scarcely one-half of your life completed. It is a thousand times more awful to wait as I do in your midst, for I know not what unimaginable terror. Pity me, at least on the score of my "delusion," for I know you will never believe what I have written here. Yet as surely as ever a man was done to death by the Powers of Darkness I am that man.

In justice, too, pity her. For as surely as ever woman was killed by man, I killed Mrs. Wessington. And the last portion of my punishment is even now upon me.

THE BEDFORD-ROW CONSPIRACY

By William Makepeace Thackeray

PART ONE

OF THE LOVES OF MR. PERKINS AND MISS GORGON, AND OF THE TWO GREAT FACTIONS IN THE TOWN OF OLDBOROUGH

"My dear, John," cried Lucy, with a very wise look indeed, "it must and shall be so. As for Doughty-street, with our means, a house is out of the question. We must keep three servants, and aunt Biggs says the taxes are one-and-twenty pounds a year."

"I have seen a sweet place at Chelsea," remarked John; "Paradise-row, No. 17, — garden — greenhouse — fifty pounds a year — omnibus to town within a mile."

"What, that I may be left alone all day, and you spend a fortune in driving backward and forward in those horrid breakneck cabs? My darling, I should die there—die of fright, I know I should. Did you not say yourself that the road was not as yet lighted, and that the place swarmed with public-houses and dreadful tipsy Irish bricklayers? Would you kill me, John?"

"My da—arling," said John, with tremendous fondness, clutching Miss Lucy suddenly round the waist, and rapping the hand of that young person violently against his waistcoat,—"my da—arling, don't say such things, even in joke. If I objected to the chambers, it is only because you, my love, with your birth and connexions, ought to have a house of

75

your own.   The chambers are quite large enough, and certainly quite good enough for me." And so after some more sweet parley on the part of these young people, it was agreed that they should take up their abode, when married, in a part of the house, number one hundred and something, Bedford-row.

It will be necessary to explain to the reader, that John was no other than John Perkins, Esq., of the Middle Temple, barrister at law, and that Miss Lucy was the daughter of the late Captain Gorgon, and Marianne Biggs, his wife. The captain, being of noble connexions, younger son of a baronet, cousin to Lord X., and related to the Y. family, had angered all his relatives, by marrying a very silly pretty young woman, who kept a lady's school at Canterbury.   She had six hundred pounds to her fortune, which the captain laid out in the purchase of a sweet travelling-carriage and dressing-case for himself; and going abroad with his lady, spent several years in the principal prisons of Europe, in one of which he died.   His wife and daughter were meantime supported by the contributions of Mrs. Jemima Biggs, who still kept the lady's school.

At last a dear old relative—such a one as one reads of in romances—died and left seven thousand pounds apiece to the two sisters, whereupon the elder gave up schooling and retired to London, and the younger managed to live with some comfort and decency at Brussels, upon two hundred and ten pounds per annum. Mrs. Gorgon never touched a shilling of her capital, for the very good reason that it was placed entirely out of her reach; so that when she died, her daughter found herself in possession of a sum of money that is not always to be met with in this world.

Her aunt, the baronet's lady, and her aunt, the ex-schoolmistress, both wrote very pressing invitations to her, and she resided with each for six months after her arrival in England.   Now for a second time she had come to Mrs. Biggs, Caroline-place, Mecklenburgh-square.   It was under the roof of that respectable old lady, that John Perkins, Esq., being invited to take tea, wooed and won Miss Gorgon.

Having thus described the circumstances of Miss Gorgon's life, let us pass for a moment from that young lady, and lift up the veil of mystery which envelops the deeds and character of Perkins.

Perkins, too, was an orphan; and he and his Lucy, of summer evenings, when Sol descending lingered fondly yet about the minarets of the Foundling, and gilded the grassplots of Mecklenburgh-square—Perkins, I say, and Lucy, would often sit together in the summer-house of that pleasure-ground, and muse upon the strange coincidences of their life. Lucy was motherless and fatherless, so too was Perkins. If Perkins was brotherless and sisterless, was not Lucy likewise an only child? Perkins was twenty-three—his age and Lucy's united, amounted to forty-six; and it was to be remarked as a fact still more extraordinary, that while Lucy's relatives were *aunts,* John's were *uncles.* Mysterious spirit of love!—let us treat thee with respect and whisper not too many of thy secrets. The fact is, John and Lucy were a pair of fools (as every young couple *ought* to be who have hearts that are worth a farthing), and were ready to find coincidences, sympathies, hidden gushes of feeling, mystic unions of the soul and what not, in every single circumstance that occurred from the rising of the sun to the going down thereof, and in the intervals. Bedford-row where Perkins lived, is not very far from Mecklenburghsquare; and John used to say, that he felt a comfort that his house and Lucy's were served by the same muffin-man.

Further comment is needless. A more honest, simple, clever, warm-hearted, soft, whimsical, romantical, highspirited young fellow than John Perkins did not exist. When his father, Dr. Perkins, died, this, his only son, was placed under the care of John Perkins, Esq., of the house of Perkins, Scully, and Perkins, those celebrated attorneys in the trading town of Oldborough, which the second partner,

William Pitt Scully, Esq., represented in parliament and in London.

All John's fortune was the house in Bedford-row, which, at his father's death, was let out into chambers, and brought in a clear hundred a year. Under his uncle's roof at Old-borough, where he lived with thirteen red-haired male and female cousins, he was only charged fifty pounds for board, clothes, and pocket-money, and the remainder of his rents was carefully put by for him until his majority. When he approached that period—when he came to belong to two spouting clubs at Oldborough, among the young merchants and lawyers'-clerks—to blow the flute nicely, and play a good game at billiards—to have written one or two smart things in the Oldborough *Sentinel*—to be fond of smoking (in which act he was discovered by his fainting aunt at three o'clock one morning)—in one word when John Per-kins arrived at manhood, he discovered that he was quite unfit to be an attorney, that he detested all the ways of his uncle's stern, dull, vulgar, regular, red-headed family, and vowed that he would go to London and make his fortune. Thither he went, his aunt and cousins, who were all "seri-ous," vowing that he was a lost boy. When this history opens, John had been two years in the metropolis, inhabiting his own garrets; and a very nice compact set of apartments, looking into the back-garden, at this moment falling vacant, the prudent Lucy Gorgon had visited them, and vowed that she and her John should there commence housekeeping.

All these explanations are tedious but necessary; and furthermore, it must be said, that as John's uncle's partner was the liberal member for Oldborough, so Lucy's uncle was its ministerial representative.

This gentleman, the brother of the deceased Captain Gorgon, lived at the paternal mansion of Gorgon Castle, and rejoiced in the name and title of Sir George Grimsby Gorgon. He, too, like his younger brother, had married a lady beneath his own rank in life: having espoused the daughter and heiress of Mr. Hicks, the great brewer at

Oldborough, who held numerous mortgages on the Gorgon property, all of which he yielded up, together with his daughter Juliana, to the care of the baronet.

What Lady Gorgon was in character, this history will show. In person, if she may be compared to any vulgar animal, one of her father's heavy, healthy, broad-flanked, Roman-nosed, white dray-horses might, to the poetic mind, appear to resemble her. At twenty she was a splendid creature, and though not at her full growth, yet remarkable for strength and sinew: at forty-five she was as fine a woman as any in his Majesty's dominions. Five feet seven in height, thirteen stone, her own teeth and hair. She looked as if she were the mother of a regiment of grenadier-guards. She had three daughters of her own size, and at length, ten years after the birth of the last of the young ladies, a son—one son—George Augustus Frederic Grimsby Gorgon, the godson of a royal duke, whose steady officer in waiting Sir George had been for many years.

It is needless to say after entering so largely into a description of Lady Gorgon, that her husband was a little, shrivelled, weazon-faced creature, eight inches shorter than her ladyship. This is the way of the world, as every single reader of this periodical must have remarked; for frolic, love delights to join giants and pigmies of different sexes into bonds of matrimony. When you saw her ladyship in flame-coloured satin, and gorgeous toque and feathers, entering the drawing-room, as footmen along the stairs shouted melodiously, SIR GEORGE AND LADY GORGON, you beheld in her company a small withered old gentleman, with powder and large royal household buttons, who tripped at her elbow as a little weak-legged colt does at the side of a stout mare.

The little General had been present at about a hundred and twenty pitch-battles on Hounslow Heath and Wormwood Scrubs, but had never drawn his sword against an enemy. As might be expected, therefore, his talk and *tenue* were outrageously military. He had the whole army-list by heart—that is, as far as the field officers—all below them he scorned. A bugle at Gorgon Castle always sounded to breakfast and dinner: a gun announced sunset. He clung to his pigtail for many years after the army had forsaken that ornament, and could never be brought to think much of the Peninsula men for giving it up. When he spoke of the duke, he used to call him *"My Lord Wellington—I recollect him as Captain Wesley."* He swore fearfully in conversation—was most regular at church, and regularly read to his family and domestics the morning and evening prayer; he bullied his daughters, *seemed* to bully his wife, who led him whither she chose; gave grand entertainments, and never asked a friend by chance; had splendid liveries, and starved his people; and was as dull, stingy, pompous, insolent, cringing, ill-tempered a little creature as ever was known.

With such qualities you may fancy that he was generally admired in society and by his country. So he was: and I never knew a man so endowed whose way through life was not safe—who had fewer pangs of conscience—more positive enjoyments—more respect shown to him—more favours granted to him, than such a one as my friend the general.

Her ladyship was just suited to him, and they did in reality admire each other hugely. Previously to her marriage with the baronet, many love-passages had passed between her and William Pitt Scully, Esq., the attorney, and there was especially one story *apropos* of certain syllabubs and Sally-Lunn cakes, which seemed to show that matters had gone very far. Be this as it may, no sooner did the general (Major Gorgon he was then) cast an eye on her, than Scully's five years' fabric of love was instantly dashed to the ground. She cut him pitiously, cut Sally Scully, his sister, her dearest friend and confidant, and bestowed her big person upon the little aide-de-camp at the end of a fortnight's wooing. In the course of time, their mutual fathers died; the Gorgon estates were unencumbered: patron of both the seats in the borough of Oldborough, and occupant of one, Sir George Grimsby Gorgon, baronet, was a personage of no small importance.

He was—must we confess it?—a Tory; and this was the reason why William Pitt Scully, Esq., of the firm of Perkins and Scully, deserted those principles in which he had been bred and christened; deserted that church which he had frequented, for he could not bear to see Sir George and my lady flaunting in their grand pew;—deserted, I say, the church, adopted the conventicle, and became one of the most zealous and eloquent supporters that Freedom has known in our time. Scully, of the house of Scully and Perkins, was a dangerous enemy—in five years from that marriage, which snatched from the jilted solicitor his heart's young affections, Sir George Gorgon found that he must actually spend seven hundred pounds to keep his two seats. At the next election a liberal was set up against his man, and actually ran him hard; and finally at the end of eighteen years, the rejected Scully—the mean attorney—was actually the *first* member for Oldborough, Sir George Grimsby Gorgon, baronet, being only the second!

The agony of that day cannot be imagined—the dreadful curses of Sir George, who saw fifteen hundred a year robbed from under his very nose—the religious resignation of my lady—the hideous window-smashing that took place at the Gorgon Arms, and the discomfiture of the pelted mayor and corporation. The very next Sunday, Scully was reconciled to the church (or attended it in the morning, and the meeting twice in the afternoon) and as Doctor Shorter uttered the prayer for the high court of parliament, his eye—the eye of his whole party—turned towards Lady Gorgon and Sir George in a most unholy triumph. Sir George (who always stood during prayers, like a military man) fairly sunk down among the hassocks, and Lady Gorgon was heard to sob as audibly as ever did little beadle-belaboured urchin.

Scully, when at Oldborough, came from that day forth to church. "What," said he, "was it to him? Were we not all brethren?" Old Perkins, however, kept religiously to the Squaretoes congregation. In fact, to tell the truth, this subject had been debated between the partners, who saw the advantage of courting both the establishment and the dissenters—a manœuvre which, I need not say, is repeated in almost every country-town in England, where a solicitor's house has this kind of power and connexion.

Three months after this election came the races at Oldborough, and the race-ball. Gorgon was so infuriated by his defeat, that he gave "the Gorgon cup-and-cover," a matter of fifteen pounds. Scully, "although anxious," as he wrote from town, "anxious beyond measure to preserve the breed of horses for which our beloved country has ever been famous, could attend no such sports as these, which but too often degenerated into vice."—It was voted a shabby excuse. Lady Gorgon was radiant in her barouche and four, and gladly became the patroness of the ball that was to ensue; and which all the gentry and townspeople, Tory and Whig, were in the custom of attending. The ball took place on the last day of the races—on that day, the walls of the market-house, the principal public buildings, and the Gorgon Arms hotel itself, were plastered with the following

Letter from our distinguished representative William P. Scully, Esq., &c., &c.

"House of Commons, June 4, 18—.

"My dear Heeltap,
"You know my opinion about horse-racing, and though I blame neither you, nor any brother Englishman, who enjoys that manly sport, you will, I am sure, appreciate the conscientious motives which induce me not to appear among my friends and constituents on the festival of the 3d, 4th, and 5th instant. If *I,* however, cannot allow my name to appear among your list of stewards, *one* at least of the representatives of Oldborough, has no such scruples: Sir George Gorgon is among you, and though I differ from that honourable baronet on more than *one vital point,* I am glad to think that he is with you—a gentleman, a soldier, a man of property in the county, how can he be better employed than in forwarding the county's amusements, and in forwarding the happiness of all?

"Had I no such scruples as those to which I have just alluded, I must still have refrained from coming among you. Your great Old-borough common-drainage and enclosure bill comes on to-night, and I shall be *at my post*. I am sure, if Sir George Gorgon were here, he and I should on this occasion, vote side by side, and that party strife would be forgotten in the object of our common interest—*our dear native town.*

"There is, however, another occasion at hand, in which I shall be proud to meet him. Your ball is on the night of the 6th. Party for-gotten—brotherly union—innocent mirth—beauty, *our dear town's beauty,* our daughters in the joy of their expanding loveliness, our matrons in the exquisite contemplation of their children's bliss—can you, can I, can Whig or Tory, can any Briton be indifferent to a scene like this, or refuse to join in this heart-stirring festival? If there *be such,* let them pardon me. I, for one, my dear Heeltap, will be among you on Friday night—ay, and hereby invite all pretty Tory misses, who are in want of a partner.

"I am here in the very midst of good things, you know, and we old folks like *a supper* after a dance. Please to accept a brace of bucks and a turtle, which come herewith. My worthy colleague, who was so liberal last year of his soup to the poor, will not, I trust, refuse to taste a little of Alderman Birch's—'tis offered on my part with hearty good will. Hey for the 6th, and *vive la joie!*

"Ever, my dear Heeltap, your faithful,

"W. Pitt Scully.

"P. S. Of course this letter is *strictly private*. Say that the venison, &c., came from a *well-wisher to Oldborough."*

This amazing letter was published, in defiance of Mr. Scully's injunctions by the enthusiastic Heeltap, who said bluntly in a preface, "That he saw no reason why Mr. Scully should be ashamed of his action, and he, for his part, was glad to let all friends at Oldborough know of it."

The allusion about the Gorgon soup was killing—thirteen paupers in Oldborough had, it was confidently asserted, died of it. Lady Gorgon on the reading of this letter was struck completely dumb—Sir George Gorgon was wild—ten dozen of champagne was he obliged to send down to the Gorgon Arms, to be added to the festival. He would have staid away if he could, but he dared not.

At nine o'clock, he in general's uniform, his wife in blue satin and diamonds, his daughters in blue crape and white roses, his niece, Lucy Gorgon, in white muslin, his son, George Augustus Frederic Grimsby Gorgon, in a blue velvet jacket, sugar-loaf buttons, and nankeens, entered the north door of the ball-room to much cheering, and the sound of "God save the King!"

At that very same moment, and from the south door issued William Pitt Scully, Esq., M.P., and his staff. Mr. Scully had a bran-new blue coat and brass buttons, buff waistcoat, white kerseymere tights, pumps with large rosettes, and pink silk stockings.

"This wool," said he to a friend, "was grown on Old-borough sheep, this cloth was spun in Oldborough looms, these buttons were cast in an Oldborough manufactory, these shoes were made by an Oldborough tradesman, this *heart* first beat in Oldborough town, and pray Heaven may be buried there."

Could anything resist a man like this? John Perkins who had come down as one of Scully's aides-de-camp, in a fit of generous enthusiasm, leaped on a whist-table, flung up a pocket-handkerchief, and shrieked SCULLY FOR EVER!

Heeltap, who was generally drunk, fairly burst into tears, and the grave tradesmen and Whig gentry, who had dined with the member at his inn, and accompanied him thence to the Gorgon Arms, lifted their deep voices and shouted, "Hear! Good! Bravo! Noble! Scully for ever! God bless him! and Hurra!"

The scene was tumultuously affecting, and when young Perkins sprung down from the table, and came blushing up to the member, that gentleman said,

"Thank you, Jack! *thank* you, my boy! THANK you," in a way which made Perkins think that his supreme cup of bliss was quaffed, that he had but to die; for that life had no other such joy in store for him. Scully was Perkins's Napoleon—he yielded himself up to the attorney, body and soul.

Whilst this scene was going on under one chandelier of the ball-room, beneath the other, scarlet little General Gorgon, sumptuous Lady Gorgon, the daughter and niece Gorgons were standing surrounded by their Tory court, who affected to sneer and titter at the Whig demonstrations which were taking place.

"What a howwid thmell of whithkey!" lisped Cornet Fitch of the dragoons to Miss Lucy, confidentially; "and thethe are what they call Whigth, are they? he! he!"

"They are drunk, —— me—drunk by ——!" said the general to the mayor.

"*Which* is Scully?" said Lady Gorgon, lifting her glass gravely (she was at that very moment thinking of the syllabubs). "Is it that tipsy man in the green coat, or that vulgar creature in the blue one?"

"Law, my lady!" said the mayoress; "have you forgotten him? Why that's him in blue and buff."

"And a monthous fine man, too," said Cornet Fitch; "I wish we had him in our twoop—he'th thix feet thwee, if he'th an inch, ain't he, genewal?"

No reply.

"And Heavens! mamma," shrieked the three Gorgons, in a breath; "see one creature is on the whist-table. Oh, the wretch!"

"Im sure he's very good-looking," said Lucy simply.

Lady Gorgon darted at her an angry look, and was about to say something very contemptuous, when, at that instant, John Perkins's shout taking effect, Master George Augustus Frederic Grimsby Gorgon, not knowing better, incontinently raised a small shout on his side.

"Hear! good! bravo!" exclaimed he! "Scully for ever? Hurra-a-a-ay!" and fell skipping about like the Whigs opposite.

"Silence, you brute, you!" groaned Lady Gorgon; and seizing him by the shirt-frill, and coat-collar, carried him away to his nurse, who with many other maids of the Whig and Tory parties, stood giggling and peeping at the landing-place.

Fancy how all these small incidents augmented the heap of Lady Gorgon's anger and injuries. She was a dull, phlegmatic woman, for the most part, and contented herself generally with merely despising her neighbours, but oh! what a fine active hatred raged in her bosom for victorious Scully! At this moment Mr. Perkins had finished shaking hands with his Napoleon—Napoleon seemed bent upon some tremendous enterprise. He was looking at Lady Gorgon very hard.

"She's a fine woman," said Scully, thoughtfully; he was still holding the hand of Perkins. And then, after a pause, "Gad! I think I'll try."

"Try what, sir?"

"She's a *deuced* fine woman!" burst out again the tender solicitor. "I *will* go.—Springer, tell the fiddlers to strike up."

Springer scuttled across the room, and gave the leader of the band a knowing nod. Suddenly, "God save the King" ceased, and "Sir Roger de Coverley" began. The rival forces eyed each other; Mr. Scully, accompanied by his friend, came forward, looking very red, and fumbling two large kid gloves.

"He's going to ask me to dance," hissed out Lady Gorgon, with a dreadful intuition, and she drew back behind her lord.

"D—— it, madam, *then dance* with him!" said the general. "Don't you see that the scoundrel is carrying it all his own way; — him, and——him, and——him." (All of which dashes the reader may fill up with oaths of such strength as may be requisite.)

"General!" cried Lady Gorgon, but could say no more. Scully was before her.

"Madam!" exclaimed the liberal member for Oldborough, "in a moment like this—I say—that is—that on the present occasion—your ladyship—unaccustomed as I am—pooh, psha—*will* your ladyship give me the distinguished honour and pleasure of going down the country-dance with your ladyship?"

An immense heave of her ladyship's ample chest was perceptible. Yards of blonde-lace, which might be compared to a foam of the sea, were agitated at the same moment, and by the same mighty emotion. The river of diamonds which flowed round her ladyship's neck, seemed to swell and to shine more than ever. The tall plumes on her ambrosial head, bowed down beneath the storm. In other words, Lady Gorgon, in a furious rage, which she was compelled to restrain, trembled, drew up, and bowing majestically said,

"Sir, I shall have much pleasure." With this she extended her hand. Scully, trembling, thrust forward one of his huge kid gloves, and led her to the head of the country-dance. John Perkins, who I presume had been drinking pretty freely so as to have forgotten his ordinary bashfulness, looked at the three Gorgons in blue, then at the pretty smiling one in white, and stepping up to her without the smallest hesitation, asked her, if she would dance with him. The young lady smilingly agreed. The great example of Scully and Lady Gorgon, was followed by all dancing men and women. Political enmities were forgotten. Whig voters invited Tory voters' wives to the dance. The daughters of Reform accepted the hands of the sons of Conservatism. The reconciliation of the Romans and Sabines was not more touching than this sweet fusion. Whack! whack! Mr. Springer clapped his hands: and the fiddlers, adroitly obeying the cheerful signal, began playing "Sir Roger de Coverley" louder than ever.

I do not know by what extraordinary charm (*nescio quà praeter solitum, &c.*); but young Perkins, who all his life had hated country-dances, was delighted with this one, and skipped, and laughed, poussetting, crossing down-the-midling, with his merry little partner, till every one of the bettermost sort of the thirty-nine couples had dropped panting away, and till the youngest Miss Gorgon, coming up to his partner, said, in a loud hissing, scornful whisper, "Lucy, mamma thinks you have danced quite enough with this—this person." And Lucy, blushing, starting back, and looking at Perkins in a very melancholy way, made him a little courtesy, and went off to the Gorgonian party with her cousin. Perkins was too frightened to lead her back to her place—too frightened at first, and then too angry. "Person!" said he; his soul swelled with a desperate republicanism: he went back to his patron more of a radical than ever.

He found that gentleman in the solitary tea-room, pacing up and down before the observant landlady and handmaidens of the Gorgon Arms, wiping his brows, gnawing his fingers—his ears looming over his stiff white shirt-collar, as red as fire. Once more the great man seized John Perkins's hand as the latter came up.

"D—— the aristocrats!" roared the ex-follower of Square-toes.

"And so say I; but what's the matter, sir?"

"What's the matter? Why, that woman—that infernal, haughty, strait-laced, cold-blooded, brewer's daughter! I loved that woman, sir—I *kissed* that woman, sir, twenty years ago—we were all but engaged, sir—we've walked for hours and hours, sir, us and the governess—I've got a lock of her hair, sir, among my papers now—and to-night, would you believe it?—as soon as she got to the bottom of the set, away she went—not one word would she speak to me all the way down: and, when I wanted to lead her to her place, and asked her if she would have a glass of negus, 'Sir,' says she, 'I have done my duty; I bear no malice; but I consider you a traitor to Sir George Gorgon's family—a traitor and an upstart! I consider your speaking to me as a piece of insolent vulgarity, and beg you will leave me to myself!' There's her speech, sir. Twenty people heard it, and all of her Tory set, too. I'll tell you what, Jack, at the next election I'll put *you* up. Oh! that woman! that woman!—and to think that I love her still!" Here Mr. Scully paused, and fiercely consoled himself by swallowing three cups of Mrs. Rincer's green tea.

The fact is, that Lady Gorgon's passion had completely got the better of her reason. Her ladyship was naturally cold and artificially extremely squeamish; and when this great red-faced enemy of hers looked tenderly at her through his red little eyes, and squeezed her hand, and attempted to renew old acquaintance, she felt such an intolerable disgust at his triumph, at his familiarity, and at the remembrance of her own former liking for him, that she gave utterance to the speech above correctly reported. The Tories were delighted with her spirit, and Cornet Fitch, with much glee, told the story to the general; but that officer, who was at whist with some of his friends, flung down his cards, and coming up to his lady, said briefly,

"Madam, you are a fool!"

"I will *not* stay here to be bearded by that disgusting man!—Mr. Fitch, call my people.—Henrietta, bring Miss Lucy from that linendraper with whom she is dancing.—I will not stay, general, once for all."

Henrietta ran—she hated her cousin; Cornet Fitch was departing. "Stop, Fitch," said Sir George, seizing him by the arm.—"You are a fool, Lady Gorgon," said he, "and I repeat it—a —— fool. This fellow, Scully, is carrying all before him; he has talked with everybody, laughed with everybody—and you, with your infernal airs—a brewer's daughter, by ——, must sit like a queen, and not speak to a soul! You've lost me one seat of my borough, with your infernal pride—fifteen hundred a year, by Jove!—and you think you will bully me out of another. No, madam, you *shall* stay, and stay to supper too—and the girls shall dance with every cursed chimneysweep and butcher in the room: they shall, confound me!"

Her ladyship saw that it was necessary to submit; and Mr. Springer, the master of the ceremonies, was called, and requested to point out some eligible partners for the young ladies. One went off with a whig auctionman; another figured in a quadrille with a very liberal apothecary; and the third, Miss Henrietta, remained.

"Hallo! you sir!" roared the little general to John Perkins, who was passing by. John turned round and faced him.

"You were dancing with my niece just now—show us your skill now, and dance with one of my daughters. Stand up, Miss Henrietta Gorgon—Mr. What's-your-name."

"My name," said John, with marked and majestic emphasis, is PERKINS," and he looked towards Lucy who dared not look again.

"Miss Gorgon—Mr. Perkins. There, now go and dance."

"Mr. Perkins regrets, madam," said John, making a bow to Miss Henrietta, "that he is not able to dance this evening. I am this moment obliged to look to the supper; but you will find, no doubt, some other PERSON who will have much pleasure."

"Go to ——, sir!" screamed the general, starting up and shaking his cane.

"Calm yourself, dearest George," said Lady Gorgon, clinging fondly to him. Fitch twiddled his moustaches. Miss Henrietta Gorgon stared with open mouth. The silks of the surrounding dowagers rustled—the countenances of all looked grave.

"I will follow you, sir, wherever you please; and you may hear of me whenever you like," said Mr. Perkins, bowing and retiring. He heard little Lucy sobbing in a corner. He was lost at once—lost in love; he felt as if he could combat fifty generals! he never was so happy in his life!

The supper came; but as that meal cost five shillings a head, General Gorgon dismissed the four spinsters of his family homewards in the carriage, and so saved himself a pound. This added to Jack Perkins's wrath, he had hoped to have seen Miss Lucy once more. He was a steward, and, in the general's teeth, would have done his duty. He was thinking how he would have helped her to the most delicate chicken-wings and *blanc-manges,* how he *would* have made her take champagne. Under the noses of indignant aunt and uncle, what glorious fun it would have been!

Out of place as Mr. Scully's present was, and though Lady Gorgon and her party sneered at the vulgar notion of venison and turtle for supper, all the world at Oldborough ate very greedily of those two substantial dishes; and the mayor's wife became from that day forth a mortal enemy of the Gorgons; for sitting near her ladyship, who refused the proffered soup and meat, the mayoress thought herself obliged to follow this disagreeable example. She sent away the plate of turtle with a sigh, saying, however, to the baronet's lady, "I thought, mem, that the *Lord Mayor of London* always had turtle to his supper."

"And what if he didn't, Biddy?" said his honour the mayor; "a good thing's a good thing, and here goes!" wherewith he plunged his spoon into the savoury mess. The mayoress, as we have said, dared not; but she hated Lady Gorgon, and remembered it at the next election.

The pride, in fact, and insolence of the Gorgon party rendered every person in the room hostile to them; so soon as, gorged with meat, they began to find that courage which Britons invariably derive from their victuals. The show of the Gorgon plate seemed to offend the people. The Gorgon champagne was a long time, too, in making its appearance. Arrive, however, it did; the people were waiting for it. The young ladies not accustomed to that drink, declined pledging their admirers until it was produced; the men, too, despised the bucellas and sherry and were looking continually towards the door. At last Mr. Rincer, the landlord, Mr. Hock, Sir George's butler, and sundry others entered the room. Bang went the corks—fizz the foamy liquor sparkled into all sorts of glasses that were held out for its reception. Mr. Hock helped Sir George and his party, who drank with great gusto: the wine which was administered to the persons immediately around Mr. Scully, was likewise pronounced to be good. But Mr. Perkins, who had taken his seat among the humbler individuals, and in the very middle of the table, observed that all these persons after drinking, made to each other very wry and ominous faces, and whispered much. He tasted his wine—it was a villainous compound of sugar, vitriol, soda, water, and green gooseberries. At this moment a great clatter of forks was made by the president's and vice-president's party. Silence for a toast—'twas silence all.

"Landlord," said Mr. Perkins starting up, (the rogue, where did his impudence come from?) "have you any champagne of *your own?*"

"Silence! down!" roared the Tories, the ladies looking aghast. "Silence! sit down you!" shrieked the well-known voice of the general.

"I beg your pardon, general," said young John Perkins; "but where *could* you have bought this champagne? My worthy friend I know is going to propose the ladies, let us at any rate drink such a toast in good wine." (Hear, hear.) "Drink her ladyship's health in *this* stuff? I declare to goodness I would sooner drink it in beer!"

No pen can describe the uproar which arose; the anguish of the Gorgonites—the shrieks, jeers, cheers, ironic cries of "Swipes, &c.!" which proceeded from the less genteel, but more enthusiastic Scullyites.

"This vulgarity is too much," said Lady Gorgon, rising; and Mrs. Mayoress, and the ladies of the party did so too.

The general, two squires, the clergyman, the Gorgon apothecary and attorney, with their respective ladies followed her—they were plainly beaten from the field. Such of the Tories as dared, remained, and in inglorious compromise shared the jovial Whig feast.

"Gentlemen and ladies," hiccupped Mr. Heeltap, "I'll give you a toast, 'Champagne to our real—hic—friends,' no, 'Real champagne to our friend,' and—hic—pooh! 'Champagne to our friends, and real pain to our enemies,'—huzzay!"

The Scully faction on this day bore the victory away, and if the polite reader has been shocked by certain vulgarities on the part of Mr. Scully and his friends, he must remember *imprimis* that Oldborough was an inconsiderable place— that the inhabitants thereof were chiefly tradespeople, not of refined habits—that Mr. Scully himself, had only for three months mingled among the aristocracy—that his young friend, Perkins, was violently angry—and finally, and to conclude, that the proud vulgarity of the great Sir George Gorgon and his family, were infinitely more odious and contemptible, than the mean vulgarity of the Scullyites and their leader.

Immediately after this event, Mr. Scully and his young friend, Perkins, returned to town; the latter to his garrets in Bedford-row—the former to his apartments on the first floor of the same house. He lived here to superintend his legal business, his London agents, Messrs. Higgs, Biggs, and Blatherwick, occupying the ground floor; the junior partner, Mr. Gustavus Blatherwick, the second-flat of the house. Scully made no secret of his profession or residence —he was an attorney, and proud of it—he was the grandson of a labourer, and thanked God for it—he had made his fortune by his own honest labour, and why should he be ashamed of it?

And now having explained at full length, who the several heroes and heroines of this history were, and how they conducted themselves in the country, let us describe their behaviour in London, and the great events which occurred there.

You must know that Mr. Perkins bore away the tenderest recollections of the young lady with whom he had danced at the Oldborough ball, and, having taken particular care to find out where she dwelt when in the metropolis, managed soon to become acquainted with Aunt Biggs, and made himself so amiable to that lady, that she begged he would pass all his disengaged evenings at her lodgings in Caroline-place. Mrs. Biggs was perfectly aware that the young gentleman did not come for her bohea and muffins, so much as for the sweeter conversation of her niece, Miss Gorgon;

but seeing that these two young people were of an age when ideas of love and marriage will spring up, do what you will; seeing that her niece had a fortune, and Mr. Perkins had the prospect of a place, and was moreover a very amiable and well-disposed young fellow, she thought her niece could not do better than marry him; and Miss Gorgon thought so too. Now the public will be able to understand the meaning of that important conversation which is recorded at the very commencement of this history.

Lady Gorgon and her family were likewise in town; but when in the metropolis, they never took notice of their relative, Miss Lucy; the idea of acknowledging an ex-schoolmistress living in Mecklenburgh-square being much too preposterous for a person of my Lady Gorgon's breeding and fashion. She did not, therefore, know of the progress which sly Perkins was making all this while; for Lucy Gorgon did not think it was at all necessary to inform her ladyship how deeply she was smitten by the wicked young gentleman, who had made all the disturbance at the Oldborough ball.

The intimacy of these young persons had in fact become so close, that on a certain sunshiny Sunday in December, after having accompanied aunt Biggs to church, they had pursued their walk as far as that rendezvous of lovers—the Regent's Park, and were talking of their coming marriage with much confidential tenderness, before the bears in the Zoological Gardens.

Miss Lucy was ever and anon feeding those interesting animals with buns; to perform which act of charity, she had clambered up on the parapet which surrounds their den. Mr. Perkins was below, and Miss Lucy, having distributed her buns, was on the point of following; but whether from timidity, or whether from a desire to do young Perkins an essential service, I know not; however, she found herself quite unwilling to jump down unaided.

"My dearest John," said she, "I never can jump that."

Whereupon, John stepped up, put one hand round Lucy's

waist; and as one of hers gently fell upon his shoulder, Mr. Perkins took the other and said,

"Now jump."

Hoop! jump she did, and so excessively active and clever was Mr. John Perkins, that he jumped Miss Lucy plump into the middle of a group formed of

Lady Gorgon,

The Misses Gorgon,

Master George Augustus Frederic Grimsby Gorgon,

And a footman, poodle, and French governess, who had all been, for two or three minutes, listening to the billings and cooings of these imprudent young lovers.

PART TWO

CHAPTER I

"Miss Lucy!"

"Upon my word!"

"I'm hanged if it arn't Lucy! How do, Lucy?" uttered Lady, the Misses, and Master Gorgon in a breath.

Lucy came forward, bending down her ambrosial curls, and blushing as a modest young woman should; for in truth the scrape was very awkward—and as for John Perkins, he made a start, and then a step forwards, and then two backwards, and then began laying hands upon his black satin stock—in short, the sun did not shine at that moment upon a man who looked so exquisitely foolish.

"Miss Lucy Gorgon, is your aunt, is Mrs. Briggs here?" said Lady Gorgon, drawing herself up with much state.

"Mrs. Biggs, aunt," said Lucy, demurely.

"Biggs or Briggs, madam, it is not of the slightest consequence. I presume that persons in my rank of life are not expected to know everybody's name in Magdeburg-square? (Lady Gorgon had a house in Baker-street, and a dismal house it was.) *Not* here," continued she, rightly interpreting Lucy's silence, "NOT here?—and may I ask how long it is that young ladies have been allowed to walk abroad without chaperons; and to—to take a part in such scenes, as that which we have just seen acted?"

To this question—and indeed it was rather difficult to

96

answer—Miss Gorgon had no reply. There were the six grey eyes of her cousins glowering at her: and there was George Augustus Frederic examining her with an air of extreme wonder, Mademoiselle the governess turning her looks demurely away, and awful Lady Gorgon glancing fiercely at her in front. Not mentioning the footman and poodle, what could a poor, modest, timid girl plead before such an inquisition, especially when she was clearly guilty? Add to this, that as Lady Gorgon, that majestic woman, always remarkable for her size and insolence of demeanour, had planted herself in the middle of the path, and spoke at the extreme pitch of her voice, many persons walking in the neighbourhood, had heard her ladyship's speech, and stopped, and seemed disposed to await the rejoinder.

"For Heaven's sake, aunt, don't draw a crowd around us," said Lucy, who indeed was glad of the only escape that lay in her power. "I will tell you of the—of the circumstances of—of my engagement with this gentleman—with Mr. Perkins," added she in a softer tone—so soft that the *'erkins* was quite inaudible.

"A Mr. What? An engagement without consulting your guardians!" screamed her ladyship, "this must be looked to! Jerningham, call round my carriage. Mademoiselle, you will have the goodness to walk home with Master Gorgon, and carry him if you please, where there is wet, and, girls, as the day is fine, you will do likewise. Jerningham, you will attend the young ladies. Miss Gorgon, I will thank you to follow me immediately;" and so saying, and looking at the crowd with ineffable scorn, and at Mr. Perkins not at all, the lady bustled away forwards, the files of Gorgon daughters and governess closing round and enveloping poor Lucy, who found herself carried forward against her will, and in a minute seated in her aunt's coach, along with that tremendous person.

Her case was bad enough, but what was it to Perkins's? Fancy his blank surprise and rage at having his love thus suddenly ravished from him, and his delicious *tête-à-tête* interrupted. He managed, in an inconceivably short space of time, to conjure up half a million obstacles to his union. What should he do? He would rush on to Baker-street, and wait there until his Lucy left Lady Gorgon's house.

He could find no vehicle for him in the Regent's Park, and was in consequence obliged to make his journey on foot. Of course, he nearly killed himself with running, and ran so quick, that he was just in time to see the two ladies step out of Lady Gorgon's carriage at her own house, and to hear Jerningham's fellow-footman roar to the Gorgonian coachman, "Half-past seven;" at which hour we are, to this day, convinced that Lady Gorgon was going out to dine. Mr. Jerningham's associate having banged-to the door, with an insolent look towards Perkins, who was prying in with a most suspicious and indecent curiosity, retired exclaiming, "That chap has a hi to our great-coats, I reckon," and left John Perkins to pace the street and be miserable.

John Perkins then walked resolutely up and down dismal Baker-street, determined on an *éclaircissement*. He was for some time occupied in thinking how it was that the Gorgons were not at church, they who made such a parade of piety: and John Perkins smiled as he passed the chapel, and saw that two *charity-sermons* were to be preached that day—and therefore it was that General Gorgon read prayers to his family at home in the morning.

Perkins at last saw that little general, in blue frock-coat and spotless buff gloves, saunter scowling home; and half an hour before his arrival, had witnessed the entrance of Jerningham, and the three gaunt Miss Gorgons, poodle, son-and-heir, and French governess, protected by him, into Sir George's mansion.

"Can she be going to stay all night?" mused poor John, after being on the watch for three hours, "that footman is the only person who has left the house," when presently, to his inexpressible delight, he saw a very dirty hackney-coach clatter up to the Gorgon door, out of which first issued the ruby plush breeches and stalwart calves of Mr. Jerningham; these were followed by his body, and then the gentleman, ringing modestly, was admitted.

Again the door opened—a lady came out, nor was she followed by the footman, who crossed his legs at the doorpost, and allowed her to mount the jingling vehicle as best she might. Mr. Jerningham had witnessed the scene in the Park-gardens, had listened to the altercation, through the library keyhole, and had been mighty sulky at being ordered to call a coach for this young woman. He did not therefore deign to assist her to mount.

But there was *one* who did! Perkins was by the side of his Lucy: he had seen her start back, and cry, "La, John!" had felt her squeeze his arm—had mounted with her into the coach, and then shouted with a voice of thunder to the coachman,

"Caroline-place, Mecklenburgh-square."

But Mr. Jerningham would have been much more surprised and puzzled if he had waited one minute longer, and seen this Mr. Perkins, who had so gallantly escaladed the hackney-coach, step out of it with the most mortified, miserable, chapfallen countenance possible.

The fact is, he had found poor Lucy sobbing fit to break her heart, and instead of consoling her as he expected, he only seemed to irritate her further: for she said, "Mr. Perkins—I beg—I insist, that you leave the carriage;" and when Perkins made some movement (which, not being in the vehicle at the time, we have never been able to comprehend), she suddenly sprang from the back-seat and began pulling at a large piece of cord, which communicated with the wrist of the gentleman driving, and, screaming to him at the top of her voice, bade him immediately stop.

This Mr. Coachman did, with a curious, puzzled, grinning air.

Perkins descended, and on being asked, "Vere ham I to drive the young 'oman, sir?" I am sorry to say muttered something like an oath, and uttered the above-mentioned words, "Caroline-place, Mecklenburgh-square," in a tone which I should be inclined to describe as both dogged and sheepish—very different from that cheery voice, which he had used when he first gave the order.

Poor Lucy in the course of those fatal three hours, which had passed while Mr. Perkins was pacing up and down Baker-street, had received a lecture which lasted exactly one hundred and eighty minutes: from her aunt first, then from her uncle, whom we have seen marching homewards, and often from both together.

Sir George Gorgon and his lady poured out such a flood of advice and abuse against the poor girl, that she came away from the interview quite timid and cowering; and when she saw John Perkins (the sly rogue! how well he thought he had managed the trick!) she shrunk from him as if he had been a demon of wickedness, ordered him out of the carriage and went home by herself, convinced that she had committed some tremendous sin.

While, then, her coach jingled away to Caroline-place, Perkins, once more alone, bent his steps in the same direction—a desperate, heart-stricken man—he passed by the beloved's door—saw lights in the front drawing-room—felt probably that she was there—but he could not go in. Moodily he paced down Doughty-street, and turning abruptly into Bedford-row, rushed into his own chambers, where Mrs. Snooks, the laundress, had prepared his humble sabbath meal.

A cheerful fire blazed in his garret, and Mrs. Snooks had prepared for him the favourite blade-bone he loved (blest four days' dinner for a bachelor, roast, cold, hashed, grilled blade-bone, the fourth being better than the first); but although he usually did rejoice in this meal, ordinarily, indeed, grumbling that there was not enough to satisfy him—he, on this occasion, after two mouthfuls, flung down his knife and fork, and buried his two claws in his hair.

"Snooks," said he at last, very moodily, "remove this d—— mutton, give me my writing things, and some hot brandy-and-water."

This was done without much alarm, for you must know that Perkins used to dabble in poetry, and ordinarily prepared himself for composition by this kind of stimulus.

He wrote hastily a few lines.

"Snooks, put on your bonnet," said he, "and carry this —*you know where?*" he added, in a hollow heart-breaking tone of voice, that affected poor Snooks almost to tears. She went, however, with the note, which was to this purpose:

> "Lucy! Lucy! my soul's love—what, what has happened? I am writing this (*a gulp of brandy-and-water*) in a state bordering on distraction—madness—insanity (*another*). Why did you send me out of the coach in that cruel, cruel way? Write to me a word, a line— tell me, tell me, I may come to you—and leave me not in this agonizing condition. Your faithful (*glog—glog—glog—the whole glass*)
> "J. P."

He never signed John Perkins in full—he couldn't, it was so unromantic.

Well, this missive was despatched by Mrs. Snooks, and Perkins in a fearful state of excitement, haggard, wild, and with more brandy-and-water, awaited the return of his messenger.

When at length, after about an absence of about forty years, as it seemed to him, the old lady returned with a large packet, Perkins seized it with a trembling hand, and was yet more frightened to see the handwriting of Mrs. or Miss Biggs.

> "My dear Mr. Perkins," she began, "although I am not your soul's adored, I performed her part for once, since I have read your letter: as I told her—you need not be very much alarmed, although Lucy is at this moment in bed and unwell, for the poor girl has had a sad scene at her grand uncle's house in Baker-street, and came home very much affected. Rest, however, will restore her, for she is not one of your nervous sort, and I hope when you come in the morning, you will see her as blooming as she was when you went out to-day on that unlucky walk.
> "See what Sir George Gorgon says of us all! You won't challenge

him I know, as he is to be your uncle, and so I may show you his letter.

"Good night, my dear John; do not go *quite* distracted before morning; and believe me your loving aunt,

"BARBARA BIGGS."

"Baker-street, 11 December.

"Major-general Sir George Gorgon has heard with the utmost disgust and surprise of the engagement which Miss Lucy Gorgon has thought fit to form.

"The major-general cannot conceal his indignation at the share which Miss Biggs has taken in this disgraceful transaction.

"Sir George Gorgon puts an absolute veto upon all further communication between his niece and the low-born adventurer who has been admitted into her society, and begs to say that Lieutenant Fitch, of the Life-guards, is the gentleman who he intends shall marry Miss Gorgon.

"It is the major-general's wish, that on the 28th Miss Gorgon should be ready to come to his house, in Baker-street, where she will be more safe from impertinent intrusions than she has been in Mucklebury-square.

"Mrs. Biggs,
    "Caroline-place,
        "Mecklenburgh-square."

When poor John Perkins read this epistle, blank rage and wonder filled his soul, at the audacity of the little general, who thus, without the smallest title in the world, pretended to dispose of the hand and fortune of his niece. The fact is, that Sir George had such a transcendent notion of his own dignity and station that it never for a moment entered his head that his niece, or any body else connected with him, should take a single step in life without previously receiving his orders, and Mr. Fitch, a baronet's son, having expressed an admiration of Lucy, Sir George had determined that his suit should be accepted, and really considered Lucy's preference of another as downright treason.

John Perkins determined on the death of Fitch as the very least reparation that should satisfy him; and vowed too that some of the general's blood should be shed for the words which he had dared to utter.

We have said that William Pitt Scully, Esq., M.P., occupied the first floor of Mr. Perkins's house, in Bedford-row;
and the reader is further to be informed that an immense
friendship had sprung up between these two gentlemen.
The fact is, that poor John was very much flattered by
Scully's notice, and began in a very short time to fancy
himself a political personage; for he had made several of
Scully's speeches, written more than one letter from him
to his constituents, and, in a word, acted as his gratis clerk.
At least a guinea a week did Mr. Perkins save to the pockets
of Mr. Scully, and with hearty good will too, for he adored
the great William Pitt, and believed every word that
dropped from the pompous lips of that gentleman.

Well, after having discussed Sir George Gorgon's letter,
poor Perkins, in the utmost fury of mind that his darling
should be slandered so, feeling a desire for fresh air, determined to descend to the garden, and smoke a cigar in
that rural quiet spot. The night was very calm. The moonbeams slept softly upon the herbage of Gray's Inn-gardens,
and bathed with silver splendour Tibbald's-row. A million
of little frisky twinkling stars attended their queen, who,
looked with bland round face upon their gambols, as they
peeped in and out from the azure heavens. Along Gray's
Inn wall a lazy row of cabs stood listlessly, for who would
call a cab on such a night? Meanwhile their drivers, at the
alehouse near, smoked the short pipe or quaffed the foaming
beer. Perhaps from Gray's Inn-lane some broken sounds
of Irish revelry might rise. Issuing perhaps from Raymond-
buildings-gate, six lawyers'-clerks might whoop a tipsy song
—or the loud watchman yell the passing hour—but beyond
this all was silence, and young Perkins as he sat in the
summer-house at the bottom of the garden, and contem-
plated the peaceful heaven, felt some influences of it entering into his soul, and almost forgetting revenge, thought
but of peace and love.

Presently he was aware there was some one else pacing
the garden. Who could it be?—not Blatherwick, for he

passed the sabbath with his grandmamma at Clapham—not
Scully surely, for he always went to Bethesda chapel, and to
a select prayer-meeting afterwards. Alas! it *was* Scully—
for though that gentleman said that he went to chapel, we
have it for a fact that he did not always keep his promise,
and was at this moment employed in rehearsing an extempore speech which he proposed to deliver at St. Stephen's.

"Had I, sir," spouted he, with folded arms, slowly pacing
to and fro, "had I, sir, entertained the smallest possible
intention of addressing the House on the present occasion
—hum, on the present occasion—I would have endeavoured
to prepare myself in a way that should have at least shown
my sense of the greatness of the subject before the House's
consideration, and the nature of the distinguished audience
I have the honour to address. I am, sir, a plain man—
born of the people—myself one of the people, having won,
thank Heaven, an honourable fortune and position by my
own honest labour; and standing here as I do—"

* * * * * *

Here Mr. Scully (it may be said that he never made a
speech without bragging about himself, and an excellent
plan it is, for people cannot help believing you at last)—
here, I say, Mr. Scully, who had one arm raised, felt himself
suddenly tipped on the shoulder; and heard a voice saying,
"Your money or your life!"

The honourable gentleman twirled round as if he had
been shot—the papers on which a great part of this impromptu was written dropped from his lifted hand, and
some of them were actually borne on the air into neighbour-
ing gardens—the man was, in fact, in the direst fright.

"It's only I," said Perkins, with rather a forced laugh,
when he saw the effect that his wit had produced.

"Only you! And pray what the dev——what right have
you to—to come upon a man of my rank in that way, and
disturb me in the midst of very important meditations?"
asked Mr. Scully, beginning to grow fierce.

"I want your advice," said Perkins, "on a matter of the very greatest importance to me. You know my idea of marrying?"

"Marry!" said Scully, "I thought you had given up that silly scheme. And how, pray, do you intend to live?"

"Why, my intended has a couple of hundreds a year, and my clerkship in the Tape-and-Sealing-Wax Office, will be as much more."

"Clerkship—Tape-and-Sealing-Wax Office—government sinecure—why, good Heavens! John Perkins, you don't tell *me* that you are going to accept any such thing?"

"It *is* a very small salary, certainly," said John, who had a decent notion of his own merits, "but consider, six months' vacation, two hours in the day, and those spent over the newspapers. After all it's——"

"After all, it's a swindle," roared out Mr. Scully, "a swindle upon the country; an infamous tax upon the people, who starve that you may fatten in idleness. But take this clerkship in the Tape-and-Sealing-Wax Office," continued the patriot, his bosom heaving with noble indignation, and his eye flashing the purest fire,—"*Take* this clerkship, John Perkins, and sanction tyranny by becoming one of its agents; sanction dishonesty by sharing in its plunder—do this, BUT never more be friend of mine. Had I a child," said the patriot, clasping his hands and raising his eyes to heaven, "I would rather see him—dead, sir—dead, dead at my feet, than the servant of a government which all honest men despise;" and here giving a searching glance at Perkins, Mr. Scully began tramping up and down the garden in a perfect fury.

"Good Heavens!" exclaimed the timid John Perkins—"don't say *so*. My dear Mr. Scully, I'm not the dishonest character you suppose me to be—I never looked at the matter in this light. I'll—I'll consider of it. I'll tell Crampton that I will give up the place—but, for heaven's sake, don't let me forfeit *your* friendship, which is dearer to me than any place in the world."

Mr. Scully pressed his hand and said nothing; and though their interview lasted a full half-hour longer, during which they paced up and down the gravel-walk, we shall not breathe a single syllable of their conversation, as it has nothing to do with our tale.

The next morning, after an interview with Miss Lucy, John Perkins, Esq., was seen to issue from Mrs. Biggs's house, looking particularly pale, melancholy, and thoughtful; and he did not stop until he reached a certain door in Downing-street, where was the office of a certain great minister, and the offices of the clerks in his lordship's department.

The head of them was Mr. Josiah Crampton, who has now to be introduced to the public. He was a little old gentleman, some sixty years of age, maternal uncle to John Perkins; a bachelor, who had been about forty-two years employed in the department of which he was now the head.

After waiting four hours in an ante-room, where a number of Irishmen, some newspaper-editors, many pompous-looking, political personages asking for the "first lord;" a few sauntering clerks, and numbers of swift active messengers passed to and fro—after waiting for four hours, making drawings on the blotting-book, and reading the *Morning Post* for that day week, Mr. Perkins was informed that he might go into his uncle's room, and did so accordingly.

He found a little hard old gentleman seated at a table covered with every variety of sealing-wax, blotting-paper, envelops, despatch-boxes, green-tapers, &c., &c. An immense fire was blazing in the grate, an immense sheet-almanac hung over that, a screen, three or four chairs, and a faded Turkey carpet, formed the rest of the furniture of this remarkable room, which I have described thus particularly, because in the course of a long official life, I have remarked that such is the invariable decoration of political rooms.

"Well, John," said the little hard old gentleman, pointing to an armchair, "I'm told you've been here since eleven. Why the deuce do you come so early?"

"I had important business," answered Mr. Perkins, stoutly, and as his uncle looked up with a comical expression of wonder, John began in a solemn tone to deliver a little speech which he had composed, and which proved him to be a very worthy, easy, silly fellow.

"Sir," said Mr. Perkins, "you have known for some time past the nature of my political opinions, and the intimacy which I have had the honour to form with one—with some of the leading members of the liberal party (a grin from Mr. Crampton), when first, by your kindness, I was promised the clerkship in the Tape-and-Sealing-Wax Office, my opinions were not formed as they are now; and having taken the advice of the gentlemen with whom I act (an enormous grin)—the advice I say of the gentlemen with whom I act, and the council likewise of my own conscience, I am compelled, with the deepest grief to say, my dear uncle, that I—that I——"

"That you what, sir!" exclaimed little Mr. Crampton, bouncing off his chair. "You don't mean to say that you are such a fool as to decline the place?"

"I do decline the place," said Perkins, whose blood rose at the word fool; "as a man of honour I cannot take it."

"Not take it, and how are you to live? on the rent of that house of yours; for by gad, sir, if you give up the clerkship, I never will give you a shilling."

"It cannot be helped," said Mr. Perkins, looking as much like a martyr as he possibly could, and thinking himself a very fine fellow. "I have talents, sir, which I hope to cultivate, and am member of a profession by which a man may hope to rise to the very highest offices of the state."

"Profession, talents, offices of the state! are you mad, John Perkins, that you come to me with such insufferable twaddle as this? Why, do you think if you *had* been capable of rising at the bar, I would have taken so much trouble about getting you a place? No, sir, you are too fond of

pleasure, and bed, and tea-parties, and small-talk, and reading novels, and playing the flute, and writing sonnets. You
would no more rise at the bar than my messenger, sir; it
was because I knew your disposition—that hopeless, careless, irresolute good-humour of yours, that I had determined
to keep you out of danger, by placing you in a snug shelter,
where the storms of the world would not come near you.
You must have principles, forsooth! and you must marry
Miss Gorgon of course; and by the time you have gone ten
circuits, and had six children, you will have eaten up every
shilling of your wife's fortune, and be as briefless as you are
now. Who the deuce has put all this nonsense into your
head? I think I know."

Mr. Perkins's ears tingled as these hard words saluted
them; and he scarcely knew whether he ought to knock his
uncle down, or fall at his feet and say, "Uncle, I have been
a fool and I know it." The fact is, that in his interview
with Miss Gorgon and her aunt, in the morning, when he
came to tell them of the resolution he had formed to give
up the place, both the ladies and John himself had agreed,
with a thousand rapturous tears and exclamations, that he
was one of the noblest young men that ever lived, had acted
as became himself, and might with perfect propriety give up
the place, his talents being so prodigious that no power on
earth could hinder him from being lord chancellor. Indeed
John and Lucy had always thought the clerkship quite beneath him, and were not a little glad, perhaps, at finding a
pretext for decently refusing it. But as Perkins was a young
gentleman, whose candour was such that he was always
swayed by the opinions of the last speaker, he did begin to
feel now the truth of his uncle's statements, however disagreeable they might be.

Mr. Crampton continued—

"I think I know the cause of your patriotism;—has not
William Pitt Scully, Esq., had something to do with it?"

Mr. Perkins *could* not turn any redder than he was, but

confessed with deep humiliation that "he *had* consulted Mr. Scully among other friends."

Mr. Crampton smiled—drew a letter from a heap before him, and tearing off the signature handed over the document to his nephew. It contained the following paragraphs:—

"Hawxby has sounded Scully: we can have him any day we want him. He talks very big at present, and says he would not take anything under a * * * ; this is absurd. He has a Yorkshire nephew coming up to town, and wants a place for him. There is one vacant in the Tape-office he says: have you not a promise of it?"

"I can't—I can't believe it," said John; "this, sir, is some weak invention of the enemy. Scully is the most honourable man breathing."

"Mr. Scully is a gentleman in a very fair way to make a fortune," answered Mr. Crampton. "Look you, John,—it is just as well for your sake that I should give you the news a few weeks before the papers, for I don't want you to be ruined if I can help it, as I don't wish to have you on my hands. We know all the particulars of Scully's history: he was a tory attorney at Oldborough; he was jilted by the present Lady Gorgon: turned radical, and fought Sir George in his own borough. Sir George would have had the peerage he is dying for had he not lost that second seat (by the by, my lady will be here in five minutes), and Scully is now quite firm there. Well, my dear lad, we have bought your incorruptible Scully. Look here," and Mr. Crampton produced three *Morning Posts*.

"'THE HONOURABLE HENRY HAWXBY'S DINNER-PARTY. —Lord So-and-So.—Duke of So-and-So.—W. Pitt Scully, Esq., M.P.'

"Hawxby is our neutral, our dinner-giver.

"'LADY DIANA DOLDRUM'S ROUT.—W. Pitt Scully, Esq., again.'

"'THE EARL OF MANTRAP'S GRAND DINNER.—A duke— four lords—'Mr. Scully, and *Sir George Gorgon*.'"

"Well, but I don't see how you have bought him: look at his votes."

"My dear John," said Mr. Crampton, jingling his watch-seals very complacently, "I am letting you into fearful secrets. The great common end of party is to buy your opponents—the great statesman buys them for nothing."

Here the attendant genius of Mr. Crampton made his appearance, and whispered something, to which the little gentleman said, "Show her ladyship in," when the attendant disappeared.

"John," said Mr. Crampton, with a very queer smile, "you can't stay in this room while Lady Gorgon is with me; but there is a little clerk's room behind the screen there, where you can wait until I call you."

John retired, and as he closed the door of communication, strange to say, little Mr. Crampton sprang up and said, "Confound the young ninny, he has shut the door."

Mr. Crampton then remembering that he wanted a map in the next room, sprang into it; left the door half-open in coming out, and was in time to receive her ladyship with smiling face as she, ushered by Mr. Strongitharm, majestically sailed in.

CHAPTER II

BEHIND THE SCENES

IN issuing from, and leaving open, the door of the inner room, Mr. Crampton had bestowed upon Mr. Perkins a look so peculiarly arch, that even he, simple as he was, began to imagine that some mystery was about to be cleared up, or some mighty matter to be discussed. Presently he heard the well-known voice of Lady Gorgon in conversation with his uncle. What could their talk be about? Mr. Perkins was dying to know, and, shall we say it? advanced to the door on tiptoe and listened with all his might.

Her ladyship, that Juno of a woman, if she had not borrowed Venus's girdle to render herself irresistible, at least had adopted a tender, coaxing, wheedling, frisky tone, quite different from her ordinary dignified style of conversation. She called Mr. Crampton a naughty man for neglecting his old friends, vowed that Sir George was quite hurt at his not coming to dine—nor fixing a day when he would come— and added with a most engaging ogle, that she had three fine girls at home, who would perhaps make an evening pass pleasantly, even to such a gay bachelor as Mr. Crampton.

"Madam," said he with much gravity, "the daughters of such a mother must be charming, but I who have seen your ladyship, am, alas! proof against even them."

Both parties here heaved tremendous sighs, and affected to be wonderfully unhappy about something.

"I wish," after a pause, said Lady Gorgon, "I wish, dear Mr. Crampton, you would not use that odious title 'my ladyship,' you know it always makes me melancholy."

"Melancholy, my dear Lady Gorgon, and why?"

"Because I think of another title that ought to have been mine—ours (I speak for dear Sir George's and my darling boy's sake, heaven knows, not mine). What a sad disappointment it has been to my husband, that after all his services, all the promises he has had, they have never given him his peerage. As for me, you know——"

"For you, my dear madam, I know quite well that you care for no such bauble as a coronet, except in so far as it may confer honour upon those most dear to you—excellent wife and noble mother as you are. Heigh-ho! what a happy man is Sir George!"

Here there was another pause, and if Mr. Perkins could have seen what was taking place behind the screen, he would have beheld little Mr. Crampton looking into Lady Gorgon's face, with as lovesick a Romeo-gaze as he could possibly counterfeit, while her ladyship blushing somewhat and turning her own gray gogglers up to heaven received all his words for gospel, and sat fancying herself to be the best, most meritorious, and most beautiful creature in the three kingdoms.

"You men are terrible flatterers," continued she, "but you say right, for myself I value not these empty distinctions. I am growing old, Mr. Crampton—yes, indeed I am, although you smile so incredulously—and let me add, that *my* thoughts are fixed upon *higher* things than earthly crowns; but tell me, you who are all-in-all with Lord Bagwig, are we never to have our peerage? His majesty, I know, is not averse, the services of dear Sir George to a member of his majesty's august family, I know, have been appreciated in the highest quarter. Ever since the peace we have had a promise—four hundred pounds has Sir George spent at the herald's-office (I, myself, am one of the most ancient families in the kingdom, Mr. Crampton) and the poor dear man's health is really ruined by the anxious sickening feeling of hope so long delayed."

Mr. Crampton now assumed an air of much solemnity.

"My dear Lady Gorgon," said he, "will you let me be frank with you and will you promise solemnly that what I am going to tell you shall never be repeated to a single soul?"

Lady Gorgon promised.

"Well then, since the truth you must know,—you yourselves have been in part the cause of the delay of which you complain. You gave us two votes five years ago, you now only give us one. If Sir George were to go up to the Peers we should lose even that one vote; and would it be common sense in us to incur such a loss? Mr. Scully, the Liberal, would return another member of his own way of thinking, and as for the Lords, we have you know a majority there."

"Oh, that horrid man!" said Lady Gorgon, cursing Mr. Scully in her heart, and beginning to play a rapid tattoo with her feet, "that miscreant, that traitor, that—that attorney has been our ruin!"

"Horrid man, if you please, but give me leave to tell you that the horrid man is not the sole cause of your ruin—if ruin you will call it. I am sorry to say that I do candidly think—ministers think—that Sir George Gorgon has lost his influence in Oldborough as much through his own fault, as through Mr. Scully's cleverness."

"Our own fault! Good heavens, have we not done every thing—every thing that persons of our station in the county could do, to keep those misguided men? Have we not remonstrated, threatened? Taken away our custom from the mayor, established a Conservative apothecary, in fact, done all that gentlemen could do? but these are such times, Mr. Crampton, the spirit of revolution is abroad, and the great families of England are menaced by democratic insolence."

This was Sir George Gorgon's speech always after dinner, and was delivered by his lady with a great deal of stateliness. Somewhat perhaps to her annoyance, Mr. Crampton only smiled, shook his head, and said,

"Nonsense, my dear Lady Gorgon—pardon the phrase, but I am a plain old man, and call things by their names. Now will you let me whisper in your ear one word of truth? You have tried all sorts of remonstrances, and exerted yourself to maintain your influence in every way, except the right one, and that is——"

"What, in Heaven's name?"

"Conciliation. We know your situation in the borough. Mr. Scully's whole history, and, pardon me for saying so (but we men in office know every thing), yours——"

Lady Gorgon's ears and cheeks now assumed the hottest hue of crimson. She thought of her former passages with Scully, and of the days when—but never mind when, for she suffered her veil to fall, and buried her head in the folds of her handkerchief. Vain folds! The wily little Mr. Crampton could see all that passed behind the cambric, and continued,

"Yes, madam, we know the absurd hopes that were formed by a certain attorney twenty years since. We know how up to this moment he boasts of certain walks——"

"With the governess, we were always with the governess," shrieked out Lady Gorgon, clasping her hands; "she was not the wisest of women."

"With the governess!—of course," said Mr. Crampton firmly, "do you suppose that any man dare breathe a syllable against your spotless reputation? Never, my dear madam; but what I would urge is this—you have treated your disappointed admirer too cruelly."

"What! the traitor, who has robbed us of our rights?"

"He never would have robbed you of your rights if you had been more kind to him. You should be gentle, madam, you should forgive him—you should be friends with him."

"With a traitor, never!"

"Think what made him a traitor, Lady Gorgon; look in your glass, and say if there be not some excuse for him. Think of the feelings of the man, who saw beauty such as yours (I am a plain man, and must speak), virtue such as yours, in the possession of a rival. By heavens! madam, I think he was *right* to hate Sir George Gorgon; would you have him allow such a prize to be ravished from him without a pang on his part?"

"He was I believe very much attached to me," said Lady Gorgon quite delighted; "but you must be aware that a young man of his station in life, could not look up to a person of my rank."

"Surely not; it was monstrous pride and arrogance in Mr. Scully; but *que voulez-vous?* such is the world's way—Scully could not help loving you—who that knows you can (I am a plain man and say what I think)—he loves you still. Why make an enemy of him, who would at a word be at your feet? Dearest Lady Gorgon, listen to me—Sir George Gorgon and Mr. Scully have already met—their meeting was our contrivance, it is for our interest, for yours, that they should be friends; if there were two ministerial members for Oldborough, do you think your husband's peerage would be less secure? I am not at liberty to tell you all I know on this subject; but do, I entreat you, do be reconciled to him."

And after a little more conversation which was carried on by Mr. Crampton in the same tender way, this important interview closed, and Lady Gorgon folding her shawl round her, threaded certain mysterious passages, and found her way to her carriage in Whitehall.

"I hope you have not been listening, you rogue," said Mr. Crampton to his nephew, who blushed most absurdly by way of answer. "You would have heard great state secrets, if you had dared to do so—that woman is perpetually here, and if peerages are to be had for the asking, she ought to have been a duchess by this time. I would not have admitted her but for a reason that I have. Go you now and ponder upon what you have heard and seen—be on good terms with Scully, and above all, speak not a word concerning our interview—no, not a word even to your mistress. By the way, I presume, sir, you will recall your resignation?"

The bewildered Perkins was about to stammer out a speech, when his uncle cutting it short, pushed him gently out of the door.

*   *   *   *   *   *

At the period when the important events occurred which have been recorded here, parties ran very high, and a mighty struggle, for the vacant speakership was about to come on. The Right Honourable Robert Pincher was the ministerial candidate, and Sir Charles Macabaw was patronised by the opposition. The two members for Oldborough of course took different sides, the baronet being of the Pincher faction, while Mr. William Pitt Scully strongly supported the Macabaw party.

It was Mr. Scully's intention to deliver an impromptu speech upon the occasion of the election, and he and his faithful Perkins prepared it between them for the latter gentleman had wisely kept his uncle's counsel and his own, and Mr. Scully was quite ignorant of the conspiracy that was brooding, indeed, so artfully had that young Machiavel of a Perkins conducted himself, that when asked by his patron, whether he had given up his place in the Tape-and-Sealing-Wax Office, he replied that "he *had* tendered his resignation," but did not say one word about having recalled it.

"You were right, my boy, quite right," said Mr. Scully, "a man of uncompromising principles should make no compromise;" and herewith he sat down and wrote off a couple of letters, one to Mr. Ringwood, telling him that the place in the Sealing-Wax Office was, as he had reason to know, vacant; and the other to his nephew stating that it was to be his. "Under the rose, my dear Bob," added Mr. Scully, "it will cost you five hundred pounds, but you cannot invest your money better."

It is needless to state that the affair was to be conducted "with the strictest secrecy and honour," and that the money was to pass through Mr. Scully's hands.

While, however, the great Pincher and Macabaw question was yet undecided, an event occurred to Mr. Scully which had a great influence upon his afterlife. A second grand banquet was given at the Earl of Mantrap's, Lady Mantrap requested him to conduct Lady Gorgon to dinner, and the latter with a charming timidity, and a gracious melancholy look into his face (after which her veined eyelids veiled her azure eyes), put her hand into the trembling one of Mr. Scully and said as much as looks could say, "Forgive and forget."

Down went Scully to dinner, there were dukes on his right hand and earls on his left, there were but two persons without title in the midst of that glittering assemblage, the very servants look like noblemen, the cook had done wonders, the wines were cool and rich, and Lady Gorgon was splendid! What attention did every body pay to her and to him! Why *would* she go on gazing into his face with that tender imploring look? in other words, Scully after partaking of soup and fish (he, during their discussion had been thinking over all the former love and hate passages between himself and Lady Gorgon) turned very red, and began talking to her.

"Were you not at the opera on Tuesday," began he, assuming at once the airs of a man of fashion; "I thought I caught a glimpse of you in the Duchess of Diddlebury's box?"

"Opera! Mr. Scully" (pronouncing the word "Scully" with the utmost softness). "Ah, no! we seldom go, and yet too often. For serious persons the enchantments of that place are too dangerous—I am so nervous, so—so delicate; the smallest trifle so agitates, depresses, or irritates me, that I dare not yield myself up to the excitement of music. I am too passionately attached to it; and shall I tell you, it has such a strange influence upon me, that the smallest false note almost drives me to distraction, and for that very reason I hardly ever go to a concert or a ball."

"Egad," thought Scully, "I recollect when she would dance down a matter of five-and-forty couple, and jingle away at the battle of Prague all day."

She continued, "Don't you recollect, I do with, oh, what regret! that day at Oldborough race-ball, when I behaved with such sad rudeness to you, you will scarcely believe me, and yet I assure you 'tis the fact, the music had made me almost mad; do let me ask your pardon for my conduct, I was not myself. Oh! Mr. Scully! I am no worldly woman; I know my duties, and I feel my wrongs. Nights and nights have I lain awake weeping and thinking of that unhappy day. That I should ever speak so to an old friend, for we *were* old friends, were we not?"

Scully did not speak, but his eyes were bursting out of his head, and his face was the exact colour of a deputy-lieutenant's uniform.

"That I should ever forget myself and you so! How I have been longing for this opportunity to ask you to forgive me! I asked Lady Mantrap, when I heard you were to be here, to invite me to her party. Come, I know you will forgive me—your eyes say you will. You used to look so in

old days, and forgive me my caprices *then*. Do give me a
little wine, we will drink to the memory of old days."

Her eyes filled with tears, and poor Scully's hand caused
such a rattling and trembling of the glass and the decanter,
that the Duke of Doldrum who had been, during the course
of this whispered sentimentality, describing a famous run
with the queen's hounds at the top of his voice, stopped
at the jingling of the glass, and his tale was lost for ever.
Scully hastily drank his wine, and Lady Gorgon turned
round to her next neighbour, a little gentleman in black,
between whom and herself certain conscious looks passed.

"I am glad poor Sir George is not here," said he, smiling.

Lady Gorgon said, "Pooh, for shame!" The little gentleman was no other than Josiah Crampton, Esq., that eminent
financier, and he was now going through the curious calculation which we mentioned in our last, and by which you *buy*
a man for nothing. He intended to pay the very same price
for Sir George Gorgon too, but there was no need to tell the
baronet so; only of this the reader must be made aware.

While Mr. Crampton was conducting this intrigue, which
was to bring a new recruit to the ministerial ranks, his
mighty spirit condescended to ponder upon subjects of
infinitely less importance, and to arrange plans for the welfare of his nephew and the young woman to whom he had
made a present of his heart. These young persons as we
said before, had arranged to live in Mr. Perkins's own house
in Bedford-row. It was of a peculiar construction, and
might more properly be called a house and a half; for a snug
little tenement of four chambers protruded from the back
of the house into the garden. These rooms communicated
with the drawing-rooms occupied by Mr. Scully; and
Perkins who acted as his friend and secretary, used frequently to sit in the one nearest the member's study, in order
that he might be close at hand to confer with that great man.
The rooms had a private entrance too, were newly decorated,
and in them the young couple proposed to live; the kitchen
and garrets being theirs likewise. What more could they

need? We are obliged to be particular in describing these apartments, for extraordinary events occurred therein.

To say the truth, until the present period, Mr. Crampton had taken no great interest in his nephew's marriage, or indeed in the young man himself. The old gentleman was of a saturnine turn, and inclined to undervalue the qualities of Mr. Perkins, which were idleness, simplicity, enthusiasm, and easy good-nature.

"Such fellows never do any thing in the world," he would say, and for such he had accordingly the most profound contempt. But when, after John Perkins's repeated entreaties, he had been induced to make the acquaintance of Miss Gorgon—he became instantly charmed with her, and warmly espoused her cause against her overbearing relations.

At his suggestion she wrote back to decline Sir George Gorgon's peremptory invitation, and hinted at the same time that she had attained an age and a position which enabled her to be the mistress of her own actions. To this letter there came an answer from Lady Gorgon, which we shall not copy, but which simply stated that Miss Lucy Gorgon's conduct was unchristian, ungrateful, unladylike, and immodest; that the Gorgon family disowned her for the future, and left her at liberty to form whatever base connexions she pleased.

"A pretty world this," said Mr. Crampton, in a great rage, when the letter was shown to him. "This same fellow, Scully, dissuades my nephew from taking a place, because Scully wants it for himself. This prude of a Lady Gorgon cries out shame, and disowns an innocent amiable girl; she, a heartless jilt herself once, and a heartless flirt now. The Pharisees, the Pharisees!—and to call mine a base family too!"

Now Lady Gorgon did not in the least know Mr. Crampton's connexions with Mr. Perkins, or she would have been much more guarded in her language; but whether she knew it or not, the old gentleman felt a huge indignation, and determined to have his revenge.

"That's right, uncle, *shall* I call Gorgon out?" said the impetuous young Perkins, who was all for blood.

"John, you are a fool," said his uncle. "You shall have a better revenge; you shall be married from Sir George Gorgon's house, and you shall see Mr. William Pitt Scully sold for nothing." This to the veteran diplomatist, seemed to be the highest triumph which man could possibly enjoy.

It was very soon to take place: and as has been the case ever since the world began, woman, lovely woman, was to be the cause of his fall. The tender scene at Lord Mantrap's, was followed by many others equally sentimental. Sir George Gorgon called upon his colleague the very next day, and brought with him a card from Lady Gorgon, inviting Mr. Scully to dinner. The attorney eagerly accepted the invitation, was received in Baker-street by the whole amiable family with much respectful cordiality, and was pressed to repeat his visits as country neighbours should. More than once did he call, and somehow always at the hour when Sir George was away at his club, or riding in the park, or elsewhere engaged. Sir George Gorgon was very old, very feeble, very much shattered in constitution. Lady Gorgon used to impart her fears to Mr. Scully every time he called there, and the sympathizing attorney used to console her as best he might. Sir George's country agent neglected the property, his lady consulted Mr. Scully concerning it; he knew to a fraction how large her jointure was; how she was to have Gorgon Castle for her life; and how, in the event of the young baronet's death (he, too, was a sickly poor boy), the chief part of the estates, bought by her money, would be at her absolute disposal.

"What a pity these odious politics prevent me from having you for our agent," would Lady Gorgon say, and indeed Scully thought it was a pity too. Ambitious Scully! what wild notions filled his brain. He used to take leave of Lady Gorgon and ruminate upon these things and when he was gone, Sir George and her ladyship used to laugh.

"If we can but commit him—if we can but make him

vote for Pincher," said the general, "my peerage is secure
—Hawxby and Crampton as good as told me so."

The point had been urged upon Mr. Scully repeatedly and
adroitly. "Is not Pincher a more experienced man than
Macabaw?" would Sir George say to his guest over their
wine. Scully allowed it. "Can't you vote for him on personal grounds, and say so in the house?" Scully wished he
could—how he wished he could! Every time the general
coughed Scully saw his friend's desperate situation more
and more, and thought how pleasant it would be to be Lord
of Gorgon Castle. "Knowing my property," cried Sir
George, "as you do, and with your talents and integrity,
what a comfort it would be could I leave you as guardian
to my boy! But these cursed politics prevent it, my dear
fellow. Why *will* you be a Radical?" And Scully cursed
politics too. "Hang the low-bred rogue," added Sir George,
when William Pitt Scully, Esq., left the house, "he will do
every thing but promise."

"My dear general," said Lady Gorgon, sidling up to him
and patting him on his old yellow cheek. "My dear Georgy,
tell me one thing,—are you jealous?"

"Jealous, my dear! and jealous of *that* fellow—pshaw!"

"Well then, give me leave, and you shall have the promise
to-morrow."

*   *   *   *   *   *

To-morrow arrived. It was a remarkably fine day, and
in the forenoon Mr. Perkins gave his accustomed knock at
Scully's study, which was only separated from his own sit-
ting-room by a double-door. John had wisely followed his
uncle's advice, and was on the best terms with the honourable member.

"Here are a few sentences," said he, "which I think may
suit your purpose. Great public services—undeniable merit
—years of integrity—cause of reform, and Macabaw for
ever." He put down the paper. It was, in fact, a speech
in favour of Mr. Macabaw.

"Hush," said Scully, rather surlily, for he was thinking how disagreeable it was to support Macabaw, and besides there were clerks in the room, whom the thoughtless Perkins had not at first perceived. As soon as that gentleman saw them, "You are busy, I see," continued he in a lower tone. "I came to say, that I must be off duty to-day, for I am engaged to take a walk with some ladies of my acquaintance."

So saying, the light-hearted young man placed his hat unceremoniously on his head, and went off through his own door humming a song—he was in such high spirits, that he did not even think of closing the doors of communication, and Scully looked after him with a sneer.

"Ladies forsooth," thought he, "I know who they are—this precious girl that he is fooling with, for one I suppose." He was right, Perkins was off on the wings of love to see Miss Lucy; and she and aunt Biggs and uncle Crampton had promised this very day to come and look at the apartments, which Mrs. John Perkins was to occupy with her happy husband.

"Poor devil," so continued Mr. Scully's meditations, "it is almost too bad to do him out of his place, but my Bob wants it, and John's girl has, I hear, seven thousand pounds. His uncle will get him another place before all that money is spent;" and herewith Mr. Scully began conning the speech which Perkins had made for him.

He had not read it more than six times, in truth, he was getting it by heart, when his head-clerk came to him from the front room, bearing a card; a footman had brought it, who said his lady was waiting below. Lady Gorgon's name was on the card!—to seize his hat and rush downstairs was, with Mr. Scully, the work of an infinitesimal portion of time.

It was indeed Lady Gorgon, in her Gorgonian chariot.

"Mr. Scully," said she, popping her head out of window and smiling in a most engaging way, "I want to speak to you on something very particular *indeed,*" and she held him

out her hand. Scully pressed it most tenderly, he hoped all
the heads in Bedford-row were at the windows to see him.
"I can't ask you into the carriage for you see the governess
is with me, and I want to talk secrets to you."

"Shall I go and make a little promenade?" said mademoiselle innocently; and her mistress hated her for that
speech.

"No. Mr. Scully I am sure will let me come in for five
minutes."

Mr. Scully was only too happy. My lady descended and
walked upstairs, leaning on the happy solicitor's arm. But
how should he manage? The front room was consecrated
to clerks—there were clerks too, as ill luck would have it, in
his private room. "Perkins is out for the day," thought
Scully; "I will take her into his room;" and into Perkins's
room he took her—ay, and he shut the double doors after
him too, and trembled as he thought of his own happiness.

"What a charming little study," said Lady Gorgon, seating herself. And indeed it was very pretty, for Perkins
had furnished it beautifully, and laid out a neat tray with
cakes, a cold fowl, and sherry, to entertain his party withal.
"And do you bachelors always live so well?" continued she,
pointing to the little cold collation.

Mr. Scully looked rather blank when he saw it, and a
dreadful suspicion crossed his soul; but there was no need
to trouble Lady Gorgon with explanations, therefore at
once, and with much presence of mind, he asked her to
partake of his bachelor's fare (she would refuse Mr. Scully
nothing that day). A pretty sight would it have been for
young Perkins to see strangers so unceremoniously devouring his feast. She drank, Mr. Scully drank, and so imbold-
ened was he by the draught, that he actually seated
himself by the side of Lady Gorgon, on John Perkins's new
sofa!

Her ladyship had of course something to say to him. She
was a pious woman, and had suddenly conceived a violent
wish for building a chapel of ease at Oldborough, to which

she entreated him to subscribe. She enlarged upon the bene-
fits that the town would derive from it, spoke of Sunday-
schools, sweet spiritual instruction, and the duty of all
well-minded persons to give aid to the scheme.

"I will subscribe a hundred pounds," said Scully, at the
end of her ladyship's harangue, "would I not do any thing
for you?"

"Thank you, thank you, dear Mr. Scully," said the enthusiastic woman. (How the "dear" went burning through his
soul!) "Ah!" added she, "if you *would* but do any thing
for me: if you, who are so eminently, so truly distinguished,
in a religious point of view, would but see the truth in politics too; and if I could see your name among those of the
true patriot party in this empire, how blest—oh! how blest,
should I be! Poor Sir George often says he should go to
his grave happy, could he but see you the guardian of his
boy, and I, your old friend (for we *were* friends, William),
how have I wept to think of you, as one of those who are
bringing our monarchy to ruin. Do, do, promise me this
too!" And she took his hand and pressed it between hers.

The heart of William Pitt Scully during this speech was
thumping up and down with a frightful velocity and
strength. His old love, the agency of the Gorgon property—
the dear widow—five thousand a year clear—a thousand
delicious hopes rushed madly through his brain, and almost
took away his reason. And there she sat, she the loved one,
pressing his hand and looking softly into his eyes.

Down, down, he plumped on his knees.

"Juliana," shrieked he, "don't take away your hand. My
love—my only love! Speak but those blessed words again!
Call me William once more, and do with me what you will."

Juliana cast down her eyes and said, in the very smallest
type,

"William!"

*   *   *   *   *   *

when the door opened, and in walked Mr. Crampton, leading

Mrs. Biggs, who could hardly contain herself for laughing, and Mr. John Perkins, who was squeezing the arm of Miss Lucy. They had heard every word of the two last speeches.

For at the very moment when Lady Gorgon had stopped at Mr. Scully's door, the four above-named individuals had issued from Great James-street into Bedford-row. Lucy cried out that it was her aunt's carriage, and they all saw Mr. Scully come out, bare-headed, in the sunshine, and my lady descend, and the pair go into the house. They meanwhile entered by Mr. Perkins's own private door, and had been occupied in examining the delightful rooms on the ground floor, which were to be his dining-room and library, from which they ascended a stair to visit the other two rooms, which were to form Mrs. John Perkins's drawing-room and bedroom. Now whether it was that they trod softly, or that the stairs were covered with a grand new carpet and drugget, as was the case, or that the party within were too much occupied in themselves to heed any outward disturbances, I know not; but Lucy, who was advancing with John (he was saying something about one of the apartments, the rogue!), Lucy suddenly started and whispered, "There is somebody in the rooms!" and at that instant began the speech already reported, *"Thank you, thank you, dear Mr. Scully,"* &c., &c., which was delivered by Lady Gorgon, in a full, clear voice, for to do her ladyship justice, *she* had not one single grain of love for Mr. Scully, and during the delivery of her little oration was as cool as the coolest cucumber.

Then began the impassioned rejoinder to which the four listened on the landing-place, and then the little *William* as narrated above, at which juncture Mr. Crampton thought proper to rattle at the door, and, after a brief pause, to enter with his party.

"William" had had time to bounce off his knees, and was on a chair at the other end of the room.

"What, Lady Gorgon!" said Mr. Crampton, with excellent surprise, "how delighted I am to see you! Always, I see, employed in works of charity (the chapel-of-ease paper was on her knees), and on such an occasion too—it is really the most wonderful coincidence! My dear madam, here is a silly fellow, a nephew of mine, who is going to marry a silly girl, a niece of your own."

"Sir, I——" began Lady Gorgon, rising.

"They heard every word," whispered Mr. Crampton, eagerly. "Come forward, Mr. Perkins, and show yourself." Mr. Perkins made a genteel bow. "Miss Lucy, please to shake hands with your aunt; and this, my dear madam, is Mrs. Biggs of Mecklenburgh-square, who, if she were not too old, might marry a gentleman in the treasury, who is your very humble servant," and with this gallant speech old Mr. Crampton began helping every body to sherry and cake.

As for William Pitt Scully he had disappeared, evaporated, in the most absurd, sneaking way imaginable. Lady Gorgon made good her retreat presently, with much dignity, her countenance undismayed, and her face turned resolutely to the foe.

*   *   *   *   *   *

About five days afterwards, that memorable contest took place in the House of Commons, in which the partisans of Mr. Macabaw were so very nearly getting him the speaker-ship. On the day that the report of the debate appeared in the *Times,* there appeared also an announcement in the *Gazette* as follows:

"The king has been pleased to appoint John Perkins, Esq., to be Deputy-subcomptroller of his majesty's Tape-office and Custos of the Sealing-wax Department."

Mr. Crampton showed this to his nephew with great glee, and was chuckling to think how Mr. William Pitt Scully would be annoyed, who had expected the place, when Perkins burst out laughing and said, "By Heavens, here is my own speech; Scully has spoken every word of it, he has

only put in Mr. Pincher's name in the place of Mr.
Macabaw's."

"He is ours now," responded his uncle, "and I told you
we would have him for nothing. I told you, too, that
you should be married from Sir George Gorgon's, and here
is proof of it."

It was a letter from Lady Gorgon, in which she said that,
"Had she known Mr. Perkins to be a nephew of her friend
Mr. Crampton, she never for a moment would have opposed
his marriage with her niece, and she had written that morning to her dear Lucy, begging that the marriage breakfast
should take place in Baker-street."

"It shall be in Mecklenburgh-square," said John Perkins,
stoutly, and in Mecklenburgh-square it was.

William Pitt Scully, Esq., was, as Mr. Crampton said,
hugely annoyed at the loss of the place for his nephew. He
had still, however, his hopes to look forward to, but these
were unluckily dashed by the coming in of the whigs. As
for Sir George Gorgon, when he came to ask about his peerage, Hawxby told him that they could not afford to lose him
in the Commons, for a liberal member would infallibly fill
his place.

And now that the Tories are out and the Whigs are in,
strange to say a Liberal does fill his place. This Liberal is
no other than Sir George Gorgon himself, who is still longing to be a lord, and his lady is still devout and intriguing.
So that the members for Oldborough have changed sides,
and taunt each other with apostacy, and hate each other
cordially. Mr. Crampton still chuckles over the manner in
which he tricked them both, and talks of those five minutes
during which he stood on the landing-place, and hatched and
executed his "Bedford-row Conspiracy."

THE CASE OF GENERAL OPLE
AND LADY CAMPER

By George Meredith

CHAPTER I

An excursion beyond the immediate suburbs of London,
projected long before his pony-carriage was hired to conduct him, in fact ever since his retirement from active
service, led General Ople across a famous common, with
which he fell in love at once, to a lofty highway along the
borders of a park, for which he promptly exchanged his
heart, and so gradually within a stone's-throw or so of the
river-side, where he determined not solely to bestow his
affections but to settle for life. It may be seen that he was
of an impulsive temperament, though he had thought fit to
loosen his sword-belt. The pony-carriage, however, had
been hired for the very special purpose of helping him to
pass in review the lines of what he called country houses,
cottages, or even sites for building, not too remote from
sweet London; and as when Cœlebs goes forth intending to
pursue and obtain, there is no doubt of his bringing home a
wife, the circumstance that there stood a house to let, in an
airy situation, at a certain distance in hail of the metropolis
he worshipped, was enough to kindle the General's enthusiasm. He would have taken the first he saw, had it not been
for his daughter, who accompanied him, and at the age of

eighteen was about to undertake the management of his house. Fortune, under Elizabeth Ople's guiding restraint, directed him to an epitome of the comforts. The place he fell upon is only to be described in the tongue of auctioneers, and for the first week after taking it he modestly followed them by terming it bijou. In time, when his own imagination, instigated by a state of something more than mere contentment, had been at work on it, he chose the happy phrase, "a gentlemanly residence." For it was, he declared, a small estate. There was a lodge to it, resembling two sentry-boxes forced into union, where in one half an old couple sat bent, in the other half lay compressed; there was a back-drive to discoverable stables; there was a bit of grass that would have appeared a meadow if magnified; and there was a wall round the kitchen-garden and a strip of wood round the flower-garden. The prying of the outside world was impossible. Comfort, fortification, and gentlemanliness made the place, as the General said, an ideal English home.

The compass of the estate was half an acre, and perhaps a perch or two, just the size for the hugging love General Ople was happiest in giving. He wisely decided to retain the old couple at the lodge, whose members were used to restriction, and also not to purchase a cow, that would have wanted pasture. With the old man, while the old woman attended to the bell at the handsome front entrance with its gilt-spiked gates, he undertook to do the gardening; a business he delighted in, so long as he could perform it in a gentlemanly manner, that is to say, so long as he was not overlooked. He was perfectly concealed from the road. Only one house, and curiously indeed, only one window of the house, and further to show the protection extended to Douro Lodge, that window an attic, overlooked him. And the house was empty.

The house (for who can hope, and who should desire a commodious house with conservatories, aviaries, pond and boat-shed, and other joys of wealth, to remain unoccupied) was taken two seasons later by a lady, of whom Fame, rolling like a dust-cloud from the place she had left, reported that she was eccentric. The word is uninstructive: it does not frighten. In a lady of a certain age, it is rather a characteristic of aristocracy in retirement. And at least it implies wealth.

General Ople was very anxious to see her. He had the sentiment of humble respectfulness toward aristocracy, and there was that in riches which roused his admiration. London, for instance, he was not afraid to say he thought the wonder of the world. He remarked, in addition, that the sacking of London would suffice to make every common soldier of the foreign army of occupation an independent gentleman for the term of his natural days. But this is a nightmare! said he, startling himself with an abhorrent dream of envy of those enriched invading officers: for Booty is the one lovely thing which the military mind can contemplate in the abstract. His habit was to go off in an explosion of heavy sighs when he had delivered himself so far, like a man at war with himself.

The lady arrived in time: she received the cards of the neighbourhood, and signalized her eccentricity by paying no attention to them, excepting the card of a Mrs. Baerens, who had audience of her at once. By express arrangement, the card of General Wilson Ople, as her nearest neighbour, followed the card of the rector, the social head of the district; and the rector was granted an interview, but Lady Camper was not at home to General Ople. She is of superior station to me, and may not wish to associate with me, the General modestly said. Nevertheless he was wounded: for in spite of himself, and without the slightest wish to obtrude his own person, as he explained the meaning that he had in him, his rank in the British army forced him to be the representative of it, in the absence of any one of a superior rank. So that he was professionally hurt, and his heart being in his profession, it may be honestly stated that he was wounded in his feelings, though he said no, and insisted on the distinction. Once a day his walk for constitutional exercise compelled him to pass before Lady Camper's windows, which were not bashfully withdrawn, as he said humorously of Douro Lodge, in the seclusion of half-pay, but bowed out imperiously, militarily, like a generalissimo on horseback, and had full command of the road and levels up to the swelling park-foliage. He went by at a smart stride, with a delicate depression of his upright bearing, as though hastening to greet a friend in view, whose hand was getting ready for the shake. This much would have been observed by a housemaid; and considering his fine figure and the peculiar shining silveriness of his hair, the acceleration of his gait was noticeable. When he drove by, the pony's right ear was flicked, to the extreme indignation of a mettlesome little animal. It ensued in consequence that the General was borne flying under the eyes of Lady Camper, and such pace displeasing him, he reduced it invariably at a step or two beyond the corner of her grounds.

But neither he nor his daughter Elizabeth attached importance to so trivial a circumstance. The General punctiliously avoided glancing at the windows during the passage past them, whether in his wild career or on foot. Elizabeth took a side-shot, as one looks at a wayside tree. Their speech concerning Lady Camper was an exchange of commonplaces over her loneliness: and this condition of hers was the more perplexing to General Ople on his hearing from his daughter that the lady was very fine-looking, and not so very old, as he had fancied eccentric ladies must be. The rector's account of her, too, excited the mind. She had informed him bluntly that she now and then went to church to save appearances, but was not a church-goer, finding it impossible to support the length of the service; might, however, be reckoned in subscriptions for all the charities, and left her pew open to poor people, and none but the poor. She had travelled over Europe, and knew the East. Sketches in water-colours of the scenes she had visited adorned her walls, and a pair of pistols, that she had found useful, she affirmed, lay on the writing-desk in her drawing-room. General Ople gathered from the rector that she had a great contempt for men: yet it was curiously varied with lamentations over the weakness of women. "Really she cannot possibly be an example of that," said the General, thinking of the pistols.

Now we learn from those who have studied women on the chess-board, and know what ebony or ivory will do along particular lines, or hopping, that men much talked about will take possession of their thoughts: and certainly the fact may be accepted for one of their moves. But the whole fabric of our knowledge of them, which we are taught to build on this originally acute perception, is shattered when we hear that it is exactly the same, in the same degree, in proportion to the amount of work they have to do, exactly the same with men and their thoughts in the case of women much talked about. So it was with General Ople, and nothing is left for me to say except that there is broader ground than the chess-board. I am earnest in protesting the similarity of the singular couples on common earth, because otherwise the General is in peril of the accusation that he is a feminine character; and not simply was he a gallant officer, and a veteran in gunpowder strife, he was also (and it is an extraordinary thing that a genuine humility did not prevent it, and did survive it) a lord and conqueror of the sex. He had done his pretty bit of mischief, all in the way of honour, of course, but hearts had knocked. And now, with his bright white hair, his close-brushed white whiskers on a face burnt brown, his clear-cut features, and a winning droop of his eyelids, there was powder in him still, if not shot.

There was a lamentable susceptibility to ladies' charms. On the other hand, for the protection of the sex, a remainder of shyness kept him from active enterprise, and in the state of suffering, so long as indications of encouragement were wanting. He had killed the soft ones, who came to him, attracted by the softness in him, to be killed: but clever women alarmed and paralyzed him. Their aptitude to ques-

tion and require immediate sparkling answers; their demand
for fresh wit, of a kind that is not furnished by publications
which strike it into heads with a hammer, and supply it
wholesale; their various reading; their power of ridicule
too; made them awful in his contemplation.

Supposing (for the inflammable officer was now thinking,
and deeply thinking, of a clever woman), supposing that
Lady Camper's pistols were needed in her defence one
night: at the first report proclaiming her extremity, valour
might gain an introduction to her upon easy terms, and
would not be expected to be witty. She would, perhaps,
after the excitement, admit his masculine superiority, in
the beautiful old fashion, by fainting in his arms. Such
was the reverie he passingly indulged, and only so could he
venture to hope for an acquaintance with the formidable
lady who was his next neighbour. But the proud society
of the burglarious denied him opportunity.

Meanwhile, he learnt that Lady Camper had a nephew,
and the young gentleman was in a cavalry regiment. General Ople met him outside his gates, received and returned a
polite salute, liked his appearance and manners, and talked
of him to Elizabeth, asking her if by chance she had seen
him. She replied that she believed she had, and praised his
horsemanship. The General discovered that he was an excellent sculler. His daughter was rowing him up the river
when the young gentleman shot by, with a splendid stroke,
in an outrigger, backed, and floating alongside presumed to
enter into conversation, during which he managed to express regrets at his aunt's turn for solitariness. As they
belonged to sister branches of the same service, the General
and Mr. Reginald Rolles had a theme in common, and a
passion. Elizabeth told her father that nothing afforded
her so much pleasure as to hear him talk with Mr. Rolles
on military matters. General Ople assured her that it pleased
him likewise. He began to spy about for Mr. Rolles, and it
sometimes occurred that they conversed across the wall; it
could hardly be avoided. A hint or two, an undefinable

flying allusion, gave the General to understand that Lady Camper had not been happy in her marriage. He was pained to think of her misfortune; but as she was not over forty, the disaster was, perhaps, not irremediable; that is to say, if she could be taught to extend her forgiveness to men, and abandon her solitude. "If," he said to his daughter, "Lady Camper should by any chance be induced to contract a second alliance, she would, one might expect, be humanized, and we should have highly agreeable neighbours." Elizabeth artlessly hoped for such an event to take place.

She rarely differed with her father, up to whom, taking example from the world around him, she looked as the pattern of a man of wise conduct.

And he was one; and though modest, he was in good humour with himself, approved himself, and could say that without boasting of success, he was a satisfied man, until he met his touchstone in Lady Camper.

CHAPTER II

THIS is the pathetic matter of my story, and it requires pointing out, because he never could explain what it was that seemed to him so cruel in it, for he was no brilliant son of fortune, he was no great pretender, none of those who are logically displaced from the heights they have been raised to, manifestly created to show the moral in providence. He was modest, retiring, humbly contented; a gentlemanly residence appeased his ambition. Popular, he could own that he was, but not meteorically; rather by reason of his willingness to receive light than to shed it. Why, then, was the terrible test brought to bear upon him, of all men? He was one of us; no worse, and not strikingly or perilously better; and he could not but feel, in the bitterness of his reflections upon an inexplicable destiny, that the punishment befalling him, unmerited as it was, looked like absence of Design in the scheme of things above. It looked as if the blow had been dealt him by reckless chance. And to believe that, was for the mind of General Ople the having to return to his alphabet and recommence the ascent of the laborious mountain of understanding.

To proceed, the General's introduction to Lady Camper was owing to a message she sent him by her gardener, with a request that he would cut down a branch of a wych-elm, obscuring her view across his grounds toward the river. The General consulted with his daughter, and came to the conclusion that, as he could hardly despatch a written reply to a verbal message, yet greatly wished to subscribe to the wishes of Lady Camper, the best thing for him to do was to apply for an interview. He sent word that he would wait on Lady Camper immediately, and betook himself forthwith to his toilette. She was the niece of an earl.

Elizabeth commended his appearance, "passed him," as he would have said; and well she might, for his hat, surtout, trousers and boots, were worthy of an introduction to Royalty. A touch of scarlet silk round the neck gave him bloom, and better than that, the blooming consciousness of it.

"You are not to be nervous, papa," Elizabeth said.

"Not at all," replied the General. "I say, not at all, my dear," he repeated, and so betrayed that he had fallen into the nervous mood. "I was saying, I have known worse mornings than this." He turned to her and smiled brightly, nodded, and set his face to meet the future.

He was absent an hour and a half.

He came back with his radiance a little subdued, by no means eclipsed; as, when experience has afforded us matter for thought, we cease to shine dazzlingly, yet are not clouded; the rays have merely grown serener. The sum of his impressions was conveyed in the reflective utterance— "It only shows, my dear, how different the reality is from our anticipation of it!"

Lady Camper had been charming; full of condescension, neighbourly, friendly, willing to be satisfied with the sacrifice of the smallest branch of the wych-elm, and only requiring that much for complimentary reasons.

Elizabeth wished to hear what they were, and she thought the request rather singular; but the General begged her to bear in mind that they were dealing with a very extraordinary woman; "highly accomplished, really exceedingly handsome," he said to himself, aloud.

The reasons were, her liking for air and view, and desire to see into her neighbour's grounds without having to mount to the attic.

Elizabeth gave a slight exclamation, and blushed.

"So, my dear, we are objects of interest to her ladyship," said the General.

He assured her that Lady Camper's manners were delightful. Strange to tell, she knew a great deal of his antecedent history, things he had not supposed were known; "little matters," he remarked, by which his daughter faintly conceived a reference to the conquests of his dashing days. Lady Camper had deigned to impart some of her own, incidentally; that she was of Welsh blood, and born among the mountains. "She has a romantic look," was the General's comment; and that her husband had been an insatiable traveller before he became an invalid, and had never cared for art. "Quite an extraordinary circumstance, with such a wife!" the General said.

He fell upon the wych-elm with his own hands, under cover of the leafage, and the next day he paid his respects to Lady Camper, to inquire if her ladyship saw any further obstruction to the view.

"None," she replied. "And now we shall see what the two birds will do."

Apparently, then, she entertained an animosity to a pair of birds in the tree.

"Yes, yes; I say they chirp early in the morning," said General Ople.

"At all hours."

"The song of birds? . . ." he pleaded softly for nature.

"If the nest is provided for them; but I don't like vaga-bond chirping."

The General perfectly acquiesced. This, in an engage-ment with a clever woman, is what you should do, or else you are likely to find yourself planted unawares in a high wind, your hat blown off, and your coat-tails anywhere; in other words, you will stand ridiculous in your bewilder-ment; and General Ople ever footed with the utmost caution to avoid that quagmire of the riciduous. The extremer quags he had hitherto escaped; the smaller, into which he fell in his agile evasions of the big, he had hitherto been blest in finding none to notice.

He requested her ladyship's permission to present his daughter. Lady Camper sent in her card.

Elizabeth Ople beheld a tall handsomely-mannered lady, with good features and penetrating dark eyes, an easy car-riage of her person and an agreeable voice, but (the vision of her age flashed out under the compelling eyes of youth) fifty if a day. The rich colouring confessed to it. But she was very pleasing, and Elizabeth's perception dwelt on it only because her father's manly chivalry had defended the lady against one year more than forty.

The richness of the colouring, Elizabeth feared, was arti-ficial, and it caused her ingenuous young blood a shudder. For we are so devoted to nature when the dame is flattering us with her gifts, that we loathe the substitute, omitting to think how much less it is an imposition than a form of prac-tical adoration of the genuine.

Our young detective, however, concealed her emotion of childish horror.

Lady Camper remarked of her, "She seems honest, and that is the most we can hope of girls."

"She is a jewel for an honest man," the General sighed, "some day!"

"Let us hope it will be a distant day."

"Yet," said the General, "girls expect to marry."

Lady Camper fixed her black eyes on him, but did not speak.

He told Elizabeth that her ladyship's eyes were exceedingly searching: "Only," said he, "as I have nothing to hide, I am able to submit to inspection;" and he laughed slightly up to an arresting cough, and made the mantelpiece ornaments pass muster.

General Ople was the hero to champion a lady whose airs of haughtiness caused her to be somewhat backbitten. He assured everybody that Lady Camper was much misunderstood; she was a most remarkable woman; she was a most affable and highly intelligent lady. Building up her attributes to a splendid climax, he declared she was pious, charitable, witty, and really an extraordinary artist. He laid particular stress on her artistic qualities, describing her power with the brush, her water-colour sketches, and also some immensely clever caricatures. As he talked of no one else, his friends heard enough of Lady Camper, who was anything but a favourite. The Pollingtons, the Wilders, the Wardens, the Baerens, the Goslings, and others of his acquaintance, talked of Lady Camper and General Ople rather maliciously. They were all City people, and they admired the General, but mourned that he should so abjectly have fallen at the feet of a lady as red with rouge as a railway bill. His not seeing it showed the state he was in. The sister of Mrs. Pollington, an amiable widow, relict of a large City warehouse, named Barcop, was chilled by a falling off in his attentions. His apology for not appearing at garden parties was, that he was engaged to wait on Lady Camper.

And at one time, her not condescending to exchange visits with the obsequious General was a topic fertile in irony. But she did condescend.

Lady Camper came to his gate unexpectedly, rang the bell, and was let in like an ordinary visitor. It happened that the General was gardening—not the pretty occupation of pruning, he was digging—and of necessity his coat was off, and he was hot, dusty, unpresentable. From adoring

earth as the mother of roses, you may pass into a lady's
presence without purification; you cannot (or so the General
thought) when you are caught in the act of adoring the
mother of cabbages. And though he himself loved the cabbage equally with the rose, in his heart respected the vegetable yet more than he esteemed the flower, for he gloried
in his kitchen garden, this was not a secret for the world to
know, and he almost heeled over on his beam ends when
word was brought of the extreme honour Lady Camper had
done him. He worked his arms hurriedly into his fatigue
jacket, trusting to get away to the house and spend a couple
of minutes on his adornment; and with any other visitor it
might have been accomplished, but Lady Camper disliked
sitting alone in a room. She was on the square of lawn as
the General stole along the walk. Had she kept her back to
him, he might have rounded her like a shadow of a dial,
undetected. She was frightfully acute of hearing. She
turned while he was in the agony of hesitation, in a queer
attitude, one leg on the march, projected by a frenzied tiptoe
of the hinder leg, the very fatallest moment she could have
possibly selected for unveiling him.

Of course there was no choice but to surrender on the
spot.

He began to squander his dizzy wits in profuse apologies.
Lady Camper simply spoke of the nice little nest of a garden,
smelt the flowers, accepted a Niel rose and a Rohan, a
Céline, a Falcot, and La France.

"A beautiful rose indeed," she said of the latter, "only
it smells of macassar oil."

"Really, it never struck me, I say it never struck me before," rejoined the General, smelling it as at a pinch of
snuff. "I was saying, I always . . ." And he tacitly, with
the absurdest of smiles, begged permission to leave untermi-
nated a sentence not in itself particularly difficult.

"I have a nose," observed Lady Camper.

Like the nobly-bred person she was, according to General
Ople's version of the interview on his estate, when he stood

before her in his gardening costume, she put him at his ease, or she exerted herself to do so; and if he underwent considerable anguish, it was the fault of his excessive scrupulousness regarding dress, propriety, appearance.

He conducted her at her request to the kitchen garden and the handful of paddock, the stables and coach-house, then back to the lawn.

"It is the home for a young couple," she said.

"I am no longer young," the General bowed, with the sigh peculiar to this confession. "I say, I am no longer young, but I call the place a gentlemanly residence. I was saying, I . . ."

"Yes, yes!" Lady Camper tossed her head, half closing her eyes, with a contraction of the brows as if in pain.

He perceived a similar expression whenever he spoke of his residence.

Perhaps it recalled happier days to enter such a nest. Perhaps it had been such a home for a young couple that she had entered on her marriage with Sir Scrope Camper, before he inherited his title and estates.

The General was at a loss to conceive what it was.

It recurred at another mention of his idea of the nature of the residence. It was almost a paroxysm. He determined not to vex her reminiscences again; and as this resolution directed his mind to his residence, thinking it pre-eminently gentlemanly, his tongue committed the error of repeating it, with "gentlemanlike" for a variation.

Elizabeth was out—he knew not where. The housemaid informed him that Miss Elizabeth was out rowing on the water.

"Is she alone?" Lady Camper inquired of him.

"I fancy so," the General replied.

"The poor child has no mother."

"It has been a sad loss to us both, Lady Camper."

"No doubt. She is too pretty to go out alone."

"I can trust her."

"Girls!"

"She has the spirit of a man."

"That is well. She has a spirit; it will be tried."

The General modestly furnished an instance or two of her spiritedness.

Lady Camper seemed to like this theme; she looked graciously interested.

"Still, you should not suffer her to go out alone," she said.

"I place implicit confidence in her," said the General; and Lady Camper gave it up.

She proposed to walk down the lanes to the river-side, to meet Elizabeth returning.

The General manifested alacrity checked by reluctance. Lady Camper had told him she objected to sit in a strange room by herself; after that, he could hardly leave her to dash upstairs to change his clothes; yet how, attired as he was, in a fatigue jacket, that warned him not to imagine his back view, and held him constantly a little to the rear of Lady Camper, lest she should be troubled by it;—and he knew the habit of the second rank to criticise the front— how consent to face the outer world in such style side by side with the lady he admired?

"Come," said she; and he shot forward a step, looking as if he had missed fire.

"Are you not coming, General?"

He advanced mechanically.

Not a soul met them down the lanes, except a little one, to whom Lady Camper gave a small silver-piece, because she was a picture.

The act of charity sank into the General's heart, as any pretty performance will do upon a warm waxen bed.

Lady Camper surprised him by answering his thoughts. "No; it's for my own pleasure."

Presently she said, "Here they are."

General Ople beheld his daughter by the river-side at the end of the lane, under escort of Mr. Reginald Rolles.

It was another picture, and a pleasing one. The young lady and the young gentleman wore boating hats, and were both dressed in white, and standing by or just turning from the outrigger and light skiff they were about to leave in charge of a waterman. Elizabeth stretched a finger at arm's-length, issuing directions, which Mr. Rolles took up and worded further to the man, for the sake of emphasis; and he, rather than Elizabeth, was guilty of the half-start at sight of the persons who were approaching.

"My nephew, you should know, is intended for a working soldier," said Lady Camper; "I like that sort of soldier best."

General Ople drooped his shoulders at the personal compliment.

She resumed. "His pay is a matter of importance to him. You are aware of the smallness of a subaltern's pay."

"I," said the General, "I say I feel my poor half-pay, having always been a working soldier myself, very important, I was saying, very important to me."

"Why did you retire?"

Her interest in him seemed promising. He replied conscientiously, "Beyond the duties of General of Brigade, I could not, I say I could not, dare to aspire; I can accept and execute orders; I shrink from responsibility."

"It is a pity," said she, "that you were not, like my nephew Reginald, entirely dependent on your profession."

She laid such stress on her remark, that the General, who had just expressed a very modest estimate of his abilities, was unable to reject the flattery of her assuming him to be a man of some fortune. He coughed, and said, "Very little." The thought came to him that he might have to make a statement to her in time, and he emphasized, "Very little indeed. Sufficient," he assured her, "for a gentlemanly appearance."

"I have given you your warning," was her inscrutable rejoinder, uttered within earshot of the young people, to whom, especially to Elizabeth, she was gracious. The damsel's boating uniform was praised, and her sunny flush of exercise and exposure.

Lady Camper regretted that she could not abandon her parasol: "I freckle so easily."

The General, puzzling over her strange words about a warning, gazed at the red rose of art on her cheek with an air of profound abstraction.

"I freckle so easily," she repeated, dropping her parasol to defend her face from the calculating scrutiny.

"I burn brown," said Elizabeth.

Lady Camper laid the bud of a Falcot rose against the young girl's cheek, but fetched streams of colour that overwhelmed the momentary comparison of the sun-swarthed skin with the rich dusky yellow of the rose in its deeping inward to soft brown.

Reginald stretched his hand for the privileged flower, and she let him take it; then she looked at the General; but the General was looking, with his usual air of satisfaction, nowhere.

CHAPTER III

"LADY CAMPER is no common enigma," General Ople observed to his daughter.

Elizabeth inclined to be pleased with her, for at her suggestion the General had bought a couple of horses, that she might ride in the park, accompanied by her father or the little groom. Still, the great lady was hard to read. She tested the resources of his income by all sorts of instigation to expenditure, which his gallantry could not withstand; she encouraged him to talk of his deeds in arms; she was friendly, almost affectionate, and most bountiful in the presents of fruit, peaches, nectarines, grapes, and hot-house wonders that she showered on his table; but she was an enigma in her evident dissatisfaction with him for something he seemed to have left unsaid. And what could that be?

At their last interview she had asked him, "Are you sure, General, you have nothing more to tell me?"

And as he remarked, when relating it to Elizabeth, "One

might really be tempted to misapprehend her ladyship's . . .
I say one might commit oneself beyond recovery. Now, my
dear, what do you think she intended?"

Elizabeth was "burning brown," or darkly blushing, as
her manner was.

She answered, "I am certain you know of nothing that
would interest her; nothing unless . . ."

"Well?" the General urged her.

"How can I speak it, papa?"

"You really can't mean . . ."

"Papa, what could I mean?"

"If I were fool enough!" he murmured. "No, no, I am an
old man. I was saying, I am past the age of folly."

One day Elizabeth came home from her ride in a thoughtful mood. She had not, further than has been mentioned,
incited her father to think of the age of folly; but volun-
tarily or not, Lady Camper had, by an excess of gracious-
ness amounting to downright invitation; as thus, "Will you
persist in withholding your confidence from me, General?"
She added, "I am not so difficult a person." These prompt-
ing speeches occurred on the morning of the day when
Elizabeth sat at his table, after a long ride into the country,
profoundly meditative.

A note was handed to General Ople, with the request that
he would step in to speak with Lady Camper in the course
of the evening, or next morning. Elizabeth waited till his
hat was on, then said, "Papa, on my ride to-day, I met Mr.
Rolles."

"I am glad you had an agreeable escort, my dear."

"I could not refuse his company."

"Certainly not. And where did you ride?"

"To a beautiful valley; and there we met . . ."

"Her ladyship?"

"Yes."

"She always admires you on horseback."

"So you know it, papa, if she should speak of it."

"And I am bound to tell you, my child," said the General,

"that this morning Lady Camper's manner to me was . . .
if I were a fool . . . I say, this morning I beat a retreat,
but apparently she . . . I see no way out of it, supposing
she . . ."

"I am sure she esteems you, dear papa," said Elizabeth.

"You take to her, my dear?" the General inquired, anx-
iously; "a little? A little afraid of her?"

"A little," Elizabeth replied, "only a little."

"Don't be agitated about me."

"No, papa; you are sure to do right."

"But you are trembling."

"Oh! no. I wish you success."

General Ople was overjoyed to be reinforced by his
daughter's good wishes. He kissed her to thank her. He
turned back to her to kiss her again. She had greatly lightened the difficulty at least of a delicate position.

It was just like the imperious nature of Lady Camper to
summon him in the evening to terminate the conversation
of the morning, from the visible pitfall of which he had
beaten a rather precipitate retreat. But if his daughter cordially wished him success, and Lady Camper offered him
the crown of it, why then he had only to pluck up spirit, like
a good commander who has to pass a fordable river in the
enemy's presence; a dash, a splash, a rattling volley or
two, and you are over, established on the opposite bank.
But you must be positive of victory, otherwise, with the
river behind you, your new position is likely to be ticklish.
So the General entered Lady Camper's drawing-room
warily, watching the fair enemy. He knew he was capti-
vating, his old conquests whispered in his ears, and her reception of him all but pointed to a footstool at her feet. He
might have fallen there at once, had he not remembered a
hint that Mr. Reginald Rolles had dropped concerning Lady
Camper's amazing variability.

Lady Camper began.

"General, you ran away from me this morning. Let me
speak. And, by the way, I must reproach you; you should

not have left it to me. Things have now gone so far that I cannot pretend to be blind. I know your feelings as a father. Your daughter's happiness . . ."

"My lady," the General interposed, "I have her distinct assurance that it is, I say it is wrapt up in mine."

"Let me speak. Young people will say anything. Well, they have a certain excuse for selfishness; we have not. I am in some degree bound to my nephew; he is my sister's son."

"Assuredly, my lady. I would not stand in his light, be quite assured. If I am, I was saying if I am not mistaken, I . . . and he is, or has the making of an excellent soldier in him, and is likely to be a distinguished cavalry officer."

"He has to carve his own way in the world, General."

"All good soldiers have, my lady. And if my position is not, after a considerable term of service, I say if . . ."

"To continue," said Lady Camper: "I never have liked early marriages. I was married in my teens before I knew men. Now I do know them, and now . . ."

The General plunged forward: "The honour you do us now:—a mature experience is worth:—my dear Lady Camper, I have admired you:—and your objection to early marriages cannot apply to . . . indeed, madam, vigour, they say . . . though youth, of course . . . yet young people, as you observe . . . and I have, though perhaps my reputation is against it, I was saying I have a natural timidity with your sex, and I am grey-headed, white-headed, but happily without a single malady."

Lady Camper's brows showed a trifling bewilderment. "I am speaking of these young people, General Ople."

"I consent to everything beforehand, my dear lady. He should be, I say Mr. Rolles should be provided for."

"So should she, General, so should Elizabeth."

"She shall be, she will, dear madam. What I have, with your permission, if—good heavens! Lady Camper, I scarcely know where I am. She would . . . I shall not like

to lose her: you would not wish it. In time she will . . .
she has every quality of a good wife."

"There, stay there, and be intelligible," said Lady
Camper. "She has every quality. Money should be one of
them. Has she money?"

"Oh! my lady," the General exclaimed, "we shall not
come upon your purse when her time comes."

"Has she ten thousand pounds?"

"Elizabeth? She will have, at her father's death . . . but
as for my income, it is moderate, and only sufficient to maintain a gentlemanly appearance in proper self-respect. I
make no show. I say I make no show. A wealthy marriage
is the last thing on earth I should have aimed at. I prefer
quiet and retirement. Personally, I mean. That is my personal taste. But if the lady: I say if it should happen that
the lady . . . and indeed I am not one to press a suit: but if
she who distinguishes and honours me should chance to be
wealthy, all I can do is to leave her wealth at her disposal,
and that I do: I do that unreservedly. I feel I am very confused, alarmingly confused. Your ladyship merits a superior
. . . I trust I have not . . . I am entirely at your ladyship's
mercy."

"Are you prepared, if your daughter is asked in marriage, to settle ten thousand pounds on her, General Ople?"

The General collected himself. In his heart he thoroughly
appreciated the moral beauty of Lady Camper's extreme
solicitude on behalf of his daughter's provision; but he
would have desired a postponement of that and other material questions belonging to a distant future until his own
fate was decided.

So he said: "Your ladyship's generosity is very marked.
I say it is very marked."

"How, my good General Ople! how is it marked in any
degree?" cried Lady Camper. "I am not generous. I don't
pretend to be; and certainly I don't want the young people
to think me so. I want to be just. I have assumed that you

intend to be the same. Then will you do me the favour to reply to me?"

The General smiled winningly and intently, to show her that he prized her, and would not let her escape his eulogies.

"Marked, in this way, dear madam, that you think of my daughter's future more than I. I say more than her father himself does. I know I ought to speak more warmly, I feel warmly. I was never an eloquent man, and if you take me as a soldier, I am, as I have ever been in the service, I was saying I am Wilson Ople, of the grade of General, to be relied on for executing orders; and, madam, you are Lady Camper, and you command me. I cannot be more precise. In fact, it is the feeling of the necessity for keeping close to the business that destroys what I would say. I am in fact lamentably incompetent to conduct my own case."

Lady Camper left her chair.

"Dear me, this is very strange, unless I am singularly in error," she said.

The General now faintly guessed that he might be in error, for his part.

But he had burned his ships, blown up his bridges; retreat could not be thought of.

He stood up, his head bent and appealing to her side-face, like one pleadingly in pursuit, and very deferentially, with a courteous vehemence, he entreated first her ladyship's pardon for his presumption, and then the gift of her ladyship's hand.

As for his language, it was the tongue of General Ople. But his bearing was fine. If his clipped white silken hair spoke of age, his figure breathed manliness. He was a picture, and she loved pictures.

For his own sake, she begged him to cease. She dreaded to hear of something "gentlemanly."

"This is a new idea to me, my dear General," she said. "You must give me time. People at our age have to think of fitness. Of course, in a sense, we are both free to do as we like. Perhaps I may be of some aid to you. My preference is for absolute independence. And I wished to talk of a different affair. Come to me to-morrow. Do not be hurt if I decide that we had better remain as we are."

The General bowed. His efforts, and the wavering of the fair enemy's flag, had inspired him with a positive re-awakening of masculine passion to gain this fortress. He said well: "I have, then, the happiness, madam, of being allowed to hope until to-morrow?"

She replied, "I would not deprive you of a moment of happiness. Bring good sense with you when you do come."

The General asked eagerly, "I have your ladyship's permission to come early?"

"Consult your happiness," she answered; and if to his mind she seemed returning to the state of enigma, it was on the whole deliciously. She restored him his youth. He told Elizabeth that night, he really must begin to think of marrying her to some worthy young fellow. "Though," said he, with an air of frank intoxication, "my opinion is, the young ones are not so lively as the old in these days, or I should have been besieged before now."

The exact substance of the interview he forbore to relate to his inquisitive daughter, with a very honourable discretion.

CHAPTER IV

ELIZABETH came riding home to breakfast from a gallop round the park, and passing Lady Camper's gates, received the salutation of her parasol. Lady Camper talked with her through the bars. There was not a sign to tell of a change or twist in her neighbourly affability. She remarked simply enough that it was her nephew's habit to take early gallops, and possibly Elizabeth might have seen him, for his quarters were proximate; but she did not demand an answer. She had passed a rather restless night, she said. "How is the General?"

"Papa must have slept soundly, for he usually calls to me

through his door when he hears I am up," said Elizabeth.

Lady Camper nodded kindly and walked on.

At seven in the morning General Ople was ready for battle. His forces were, the anticipation of victory, a carefully arranged toilette, and an unaccustomed spirit of enterprise in the realms of speech; for he was no longer in such awe of Lady Camper.

"You have slept well?" she inquired.

"Excellently, my lady."

"Yes, your daughter tells me she heard you, as she went by your door in the morning for a ride to meet my nephew. You are, I shall assume, prepared for business."

"Elizabeth? . . . to meet? . . ." General Ople's impression of anything extraneous to his emotion was feeble and passed instantly. "Prepared! Oh, certainly;" and he struck in a compliment on her ladyship's fresh morning bloom.

"It can hardly be visible," she responded; "I have not painted yet."

"Does your ladyship proceed to your painting in the very early morning?"

"Rouge. I rouge."

"Dear me! I should not have supposed it."

"You have speculated on it very openly, General. I remember your trying to see a freckle through the rouge; but the truth is, I am of a supernatural paleness if I do not rouge, so I do. You understand, therefore, I have a false complexion. Now to business."

"If your ladyship insists on calling it business. I have little to offer—myself!"

"You have a gentlemanly residence."

"It is, my lady, it is. It is a bijou."

"Ah!" Lady Camper sighed dejectedly.

"It is a perfect bijou!"

"Oblige me, General, by not pronouncing the French word as if you were swearing by something in English, like a trooper."

General Ople started, admitted that the word was French,

and apologized for his pronunciation. Her variability was now visible over a corner of the battlefield like a thunder-cloud.

"The business we have to discuss concerns the young people, General."

"Yes," brightened by this, he assented: "Yes, dear Lady Camper; it is a part of the business; it is a secondary part; it has to be discussed; I say I subscribe beforehand. I may say that honouring, esteeming you as I do, and hoping ardently for your consent . . ."

"They must have a home and an income, General."

"I presume, dearest lady, that Elizabeth will be welcome in your home. I certainly shall never chase Reginald out of mine."

Lady Camper threw back her head. "Then you are not yet awake, or you practise the art of sleeping with open eyes! Now listen to me. I rouge, I have told you. I like colour, and I do not like to see wrinkles or have them seen. Therefore I rouge. I do not expect to deceive the world so flagrantly as to my age, and you I would not deceive for a moment. I am seventy."

The effect of this noble frankness on the General, was to raise him from his chair in a sitting posture as if he had been blown up.

Her countenance was inexorably imperturbable under his alternate blinking and gazing that drew her close and shot her distant, like a mysterious toy.

"But," said she, "I am an artist; I dislike the look of extreme age, so I conceal it as well as I can. You are very kind to fall in with the deception: an innocent and, I think, a proper one, before the world, though not to the gentleman who does me the honour to propose to me for my hand. You desire to settle our business first. You esteem me, I suppose you mean as much as young people mean when they say they love. Do you? Let us come to an understanding."

"I can," the melancholy General gasped, "I say I can—I cannot—I cannot credit your ladyship's . . ."

"You are at liberty to call me Angela."

"Ange . . ." he tried it, and in shame relapsed. "Madam, yes. Thanks."

"Ah," cried Lady Camper, "do not use these vulgar contractions of decent speech in my presence. I abhor the word 'thanks.' It is fit for fribbles."

"Dear me, I have used it all my life," groaned the General.

"Then for the remainder, be it understood that you renounce it. To continue, my age is . . ."

"Oh, impossible, impossible," the General almost wailed; there was really a crack in his voice.

"Advancing to seventy. But, like you, I am happy to say I have not a malady. I bring no invalid frame to a union that necessitates the leaving of the front door open day and night to the doctor. My belief is, I could follow my husband still on a campaign, if he were a warrior instead of a pensioner."

General Ople winced.

He was about to say humbly, "As General of Brigade . . ."

"Yes, yes, you want a commanding officer, and that I have seen, and that has caused me to meditate on your proposal," she interrupted him; while he, studying her countenance hard, with the painful aspect of a youth who lashes a donkey memory in an examination by word of mouth, attempted to marshal her signs of younger years against her awful confession of the extremely ancient, the witheringly ancient. But for the manifest rouge, manifest in spite of her declaration that she had not yet that morning proceeded to her paint-brush, he would have thrown down his glove to challenge her on the subject of her age. She had actually charms. Her mouth had a charm; her eyes were lively; her figure, mature if you like, was at least full and good; she stood upright, she had a queenly seat. His mental ejaculation was, "What a wonderful constitution!"

By a lapse of politeness, he repeated it to himself half aloud; he was shockingly nervous.

"Yes, I have finer health than many a younger woman," she said. "An ordinary calculation would give me twenty good years to come. I am a widow, as you know. And, by the way, you have a leaning for widows. Have you not? I thought I had heard of a widow Barcop in this parish. Do not protest. I assure you I am a stranger to jealousy. My income . . ."

The General raised his hands.

"Well, then," said the cool and self-contained lady, "before I go farther, I may ask you, knowing what you have forced me to confess, are you still of the same mind as to marriage? And one moment, General. I promise you most sincerely that your withdrawing a step shall not, as far as it touches me, affect my neighbourly and friendly sentiments; not in any degree. Shall we be as we were?"

Lady Camper extended her delicate hand to him.

He took it respectfully, inspected the aristocratic and unshrunken fingers, and kissing them said, "I never withdraw from a position, unless I am beaten back. Lady Camper, I . . ."

"My name is Angela."

The General tried again: he could not utter the name.

To call a lady of seventy Angela is difficult in itself. It is, it seems, thrice difficult in the way of courtship.

"Angela!" said she.

"Yes. I say, there is not a more beautiful female name, dear Lady Camper."

"Spare me that word 'female' as long as you live. Address me by that name, if you please."

The General smiled. The smile was meant for propitiation and sweetness. It became a brazen smile.

"Unless you wish to step back," said she.

"Indeed, no. I am happy, Lady Camper. My life is yours. I say, my life is devoted to you, dear madam."

"Angela!"

General Ople was blushingly delivered of the name.

"That will do," said she. "And as I think it possible one may be admired too much as an artist, I must request you to keep my number of years a secret."

"To the death, madam," said the General.

"And now we will take a turn in the garden, Wilson Ople. And beware of one thing, for a commencement, for you are full of weeds, and I mean to pluck out a few: never call any place a gentlemanly residence in my hearing, nor let it come to my ears that you have been using the phrase elsewhere. Don't express astonishment. At present it is enough that I dislike it. But this only," Lady Camper added, "this only if it is not your intention to withdrawn from your position."

"Madam, my lady, I was saying—hem!—Angela, I *could* not wish to withdraw."

Lady Camper leaned with some pressure on his arm, observing, "You have a curious attachment to antiquities."

"My dear lady, it is your mind; I say it is your mind: I was saying I am in love with your mind," the General endeavoured to assure her, and himself too.

"Or is it my powers as an artist?"

"Your mind, your extraordinary powers of mind."

"Well," said Lady Camper, "a veteran General of Brigade is as good a crutch as a childless old grannam can have."

And such, as a crutch, General Ople, parading her grounds with the aged woman, found himself used and treated.

The accuracy of his perceptions might be questioned. He was like a man stunned by some great tropical fruit, which responds to the longing of his eyes by falling on his head; but it appeared to him that she increased in bitterness at every step they took, as if determined to make him realize her wrinkles.

He was even so inconsequent, or so little recognized his position, as to object in his heart to hear himself called Wilson.

It is true that she uttered Wilsonople as if the names formed one word. And on a second occasion (when he inclined to feel hurt) she remarked, "I fear me, Wilsonople, if we are to speak plainly, thou art but a fool." He, perhaps, naturally objected to that. He was, however, giddy, and barely knew.

Yet once more the magical woman changed. All semblance of harshness, and harridan-like spike-tonguedness vanished when she said adieu.

The astronomer, looking at the crusty jag and scoria of the magnified moon through his telescope, and again with naked eyes at the soft-beaming moon, when the crater-ridges are faint as eyebrow-pencillings, has a similar sharp alternation of prospect to that which mystified General Ople.

But between watching an orb that is only variable at our caprice, and contemplating a woman who shifts and quivers ever at her own, how vast the difference!

And consider that this woman is about to be one's wife!

He could have believed (if he had not known full surely that such things are not) he was in the hands of a witch.

Lady Camper's "adieu" was perfectly beautiful—a kind, cordial, intimate, above all, to satisfy his present craving, it was a lady-like adieu—the adieu of a delicate and elegant woman, who had hardly left her anchorage by forty to sail into the fifties.

Alas! he had her word for it that she was not less than seventy. And, worse, she had betrayed most melancholy signs of sourness and agedness as soon as he had sworn himself to her fast and fixed.

"The road is open to you to retreat," were her last words.

"My road," he answered gallantly, "is forward."

He was drawing backward as he said it, and something provoked her to smile.

CHAPTER V

IT is a noble thing to say that your road is forward, and
it befits a man of battles. General Ople was too loyal a
gentleman to think of any other road. Still, albeit not gifted
with imagination, he could not avoid the feeling that he had
set his face to winter. He found himself suddenly walking
straight into the heart of winter, and a nipping winter. For
her ladyship had proved acutely nipping. His little customary phrases, to which Lady Camper objected, he could
see no harm in whatever. Conversing with her in the pri-
vacy of domestic life would never be the flowing business
that it is for other men. It would demand perpetual vigi-
lance, hop, skip, jump, flounderings, and apologies.

This was not a pleasing prospect.

On the other hand, she was the niece of an earl. She was
wealthy. She might be an excellent friend to Elizabeth; and
she could be, when she liked, both commandingly and be-
witchingly lady-like.

Good! But he was a General Officer of not more than
fifty-five, in his full vigour, and she a woman of seventy!

The prospect was bleak. It resembled an outlook on the
steppes. In point of the discipline he was to expect, he might
be compared to a raw recruit, and in his own home!

However, she was a woman of mind. One would be proud
of her.

But did he know the worst of her? A dreadful presentiment that he did not know the worst of her rolled an ocean
of gloom upon General Ople, striking out one solitary
thought in the obscurity, namely, that he was about to receive punishment for retiring from active service to a life
of ease at a comparatively early age, when still in marching
trim. And the shadow of the thought was, that he deserved
the punishment!

He was in his garden with the dawn. Hard exercise is
the best of opiates for dismal reflections. The General dis-

composed his daughter by offering to accompany her on her morning ride before breakfast. She considered that it would fatigue him. "I am not a man of eighty!" he cried. He could have wished that he had been.

He led the way to the park, where they soon had sight of young Rolles, who checked his horse, and spied them like a vedette, but, perceiving that he had been seen, came cantering, and hailing the General with hearty wonderment.

"And what's this the world says, General?" said he. "But we all applaud your taste. My aunt Angela was the handsomest woman of her time."

The General murmured in confusion, "Dear me!" and looked at the young man, thinking that he could not have known the time.

"Is all arranged, my dear General?"

"Nothing is arranged, and I beg—I say I beg . . . I came out for fresh air and peace."

The General rode frantically.

In spite of the fresh air, he was unable to eat at breakfast. He was bound, of course, to present himself to Lady Camper, in common civility, immediately after it.

And first, what were the phrases he had to avoid uttering in her presence? He could remember only the "gentlemanly residence." And it was a gentlemanly residence, he thought as he took leave of it. It was one, neatly named to fit the place. Lady Camper is indeed a most eccentric person! he decided from his experience of her.

He was rather astonished that young Rolles should have spoken so coolly of his aunt's leaning to matrimony; but perhaps her exact age was unknown to the younger members of her family.

This idea refreshed him by suggesting the extremely honourable nature of Lady Camper's uncomfortable confession.

He himself had an uncomfortable confession to make. He would have to speak of his income. He was living up to the edges of it.

"She is an upright woman, and I must be the same!" he said, fortunately not in her hearing.

The subject was disagreeable to a man sensitive on the topic of money, and feeling that his prudence had recently been misled to keep up appearances.

Lady Camper was in her garden, reclining under her parasol. A chair was beside her, to which, acknowledging the salutation of her suitor, she waved him.

"You have met my nephew Reginald this morning, General?"

"Curiously, in the park, this morning, before breakfast, I did, yes. Hem! I, I say I did meet him. Has your ladyship seen him?"

"No. The park is very pretty in the early morning."

"Sweetly pretty."

Lady Camper raised her head, and with the mildness of assured dictatorship, pronounced: "Never say that before me."

"I submit, my lady," said the poor scourged man.

"Why, naturally you do. Vulgar phrases have to be endured, except when our intimates are guilty, and then we are not merely offended, we are compromised by them. You are still of the mind in which you left me yesterday? You are one day older. But I warn you, so am I."

"Yes, my lady, we cannot, I say we cannot check time. Decidedly of the same mind. Quite so."

"Oblige me by never saying 'Quite so.' My lawyer says it. It reeks of the City of London. And do not look so miserable."

"I, madam? my dear lady!" the General flashed out in a radiance that dulled instantly.

"Well," said she, cheerfully, "and you're for the old woman?"

"For Lady Camper."

"You are seductive in your flatteries, General. Well, then, we have to speak of business."

"My affairs——" General Ople was beginning, with perturbed forehead; but Lady Camper held up her finger.

"We will touch on your affairs incidentally. Now listen to me, and do not exclaim until I have finished. You know that these two young ones have been whispering over the wall for some months. They have been meeting on the river and in the park habitually, apparently with your consent."

"My lady!"

"I did not say with your connivance."

"You mean my daughter Elizabeth?"

"And my nephew Reginald. We have named them, if that advances us. Now, the end of such meetings is marriage, and the sooner the better, if they are to continue. I would rather they should not; I do not hold it good for young soldiers to marry. But if they do, it is very certain that their pay will not support a family; and in a marriage of two healthy young people, we have to assume the existence of the family. You have allowed matters to go so far that the boy is hot in love; I suppose the girl is, too. She is a nice girl. I do not object to her personally. But I insist that a settlement be made on her before I give my nephew one penny. Hear me out, for I am not fond of business, and shall be glad to have done with these explanations. Reginald has nothing of his own. He is my sister's son, and I loved her, and rather like the boy. He has at present four hundred a-year from me. I will double it, on the condition that you at once make over ten thousand—not less; and let it be yes or no!—to be settled on your daughter and go to her children, independent of the husband—*cela va sans dire*. Now you may speak, General."

The General spoke, with breath fetched from the deeps:

"Ten thousand pounds! Hem! Ten! Hem, frankly—ten, my lady! One's income—I am quite taken by surprise. I say Elizabeth's conduct—though, poor child! it is natural to her to seek a mate, I mean, to accept a mate and an establishment, and Reginald is a very hopeful fellow—I was saying, they jump on me out of an ambush, and I wish them every happiness. And she is an ardent soldier, and a soldier she must marry. But ten thousand!"

"It is to secure the happiness of your daughter, General."

"Pounds! my lady. It would rather cripple me."

"You would have my house, General; you would have the moiety, as the lawyers say, of my purse; you would have horses, carriages, servants; I do not divine what more you would wish to have."

"But, madam—a pensioner on the Government! I can look back on past services, I say old services, and I accept my position. But, madam, a pensioner on my wife, bringing next to nothing to the common estate! I fear my self-respect would, I say would . . ."

"Well, and what would it do, General Ople?"

"I was saying, my self-respect as my wife's pensioner, my lady. I could not come to her empty-handed."

"Do you expect that I should be the person to settle money on your daughter, to save her from mischances? A rakish husband, for example, for Reginald is young, and no one can guess what will be made of him."

"Undoubtedly your ladyship is correct. We might try absence for the poor girl. I have no female relation, but I could send her to the sea-side to a lady-friend."

"General Ople, I forbid you, as you value my esteem, ever —and I repeat, I forbid you ever—to afflict my ears with that phrase, 'lady-friend!' "

The General blinked in a state of insurgent humility.

These incessant whippings could not but sting the humblest of men; and "lady-friend," he was sure, was a very common term, used, he was sure, in the very best society. He had never heard Her Majesty speak at levées of a lady-friend, but he was quite sure that she had one; and if so, what could be the objection to her subjects mentioning it as a term to suit their own circumstances?

He was harassed and perplexed by old Lady Camper's

treatment of him, and he resolved not to call her Angela even upon supplication—not that day, at least.

She said, "You will not need to bring property of any kind to the common estate; I neither look for it nor desire it. The generous thing for you to do would be to give your daughter all you have, and come to me."

"But, Lady Camper, if I denude myself or curtail my income—a man at his wife's discretion, I was saying a man at his wife's mercy! . . ."

General Ople was really forced, by his manly dignity, to make this protest on its behalf. He did not see how he could have escaped doing so; he was more an agent than a principal. "My wife's mercy," he said again, but simply as a herald proclaiming superior orders.

Lady Camper's brows were wrathful. A deep blood-crimson overcame the rouge, and gave her a terrible stormy look.

"The congress now ceases to sit, and the treaty is not concluded," was all she said.

She rose, bowed to him, "Good morning, General," and turned her back.

He sighed. He was a free man. But this could not be denied—whatever the lady's age, she was a grand woman in her carriage, and when looking angry, she had a queen-like aspect that raised her out of the reckoning of time.

So now he knew there was a worse behind what he had previously known. He was precipitate in calling it the worst. "Now," said he to himself, "I know the worst!"

No man should ever say it. Least of all, one who has entered into relations with an eccentric lady.

CHAPTER VI

POLITENESS required that General Ople should not appear to rejoice in his dismissal as a suitor, and should at least make some show of holding himself at the beck of a reconsidering mind. He was guilty of running up to London early next day, and remaining absent until nightfall; and he did the same on the two following days. When he presented himself at Lady Camper's lodge-gates, the astonishing intelligence that her ladyship had departed for the Continent and Egypt gave him qualms of remorse, which assumed a more definite shape in something like awe of her triumphant constitution. He forbore to mention her age, for he was the most honourable of men, but a habit of tea-table talkativeness impelled him to say and repeat an idea that had visited him, to the effect that Lady Camper was one of those wonderful women who are comparable to brilliant generals, and defend themselves from the siege of Time by various aggressive movements. Fearful of not being understood, owing to the rarity of the occasions when the squat plain squad of honest Saxon regulars at his command were called upon to explain an idea, he re-cast the sentence. But, as it happened that the regulars of his vocabulary were not numerous, and not accustomed to work upon thoughts and images, his repetitions rather succeeded in exposing the piece of knowledge he had recently acquired than in making his meaning plainer. So we need not marvel that his acquaintances should suppose him to be secretly aware of an extreme degree in which Lady Camper was a veteran.

General Ople entered into the gaieties of the neighbourhood once more, and passed through the winter cheerfully. In justice to him, however, it should be said that to the intent dwelling of his mind upon Lady Camper, and not to the festive life he led, was due his entire ignorance of his daughter's unhappiness. She lived with him, and yet it was in other houses he learnt that she was unhappy. After his last interview with Lady Camper, he had informed Elizabeth of the ruinous and preposterous amount of money demanded of him for a settlement upon her: and Elizabeth, like the girl of good sense that she was, had replied immediately, "It could not be thought of, papa." He had spoken to Reginald likewise. The young man fell into a dramatic tearing-of-hair and long-stride fury, not ill becoming an enamoured dragoon. But he maintained that his aunt, though an eccentric, was a cordially kind woman. He seemed to feel, if he did not partly hint, that the General might have accepted Lady Camper's terms. The young officer could no longer be welcome at Douro Lodge, so the General paid him a morning call at his quarters, and was distressed to find him breakfasting very late, tapping eggs that he forgot to open—one of the surest signs of a young man downright and deep in love, as the General knew from experience—and surrounded by uncut sporting journals of past weeks, which dated from the day when his blow had struck him, as accurately as the watch of the drowned man marks his minute. Lady Camper had gone to Italy, and was in communication with her nephew: Reginald was not further explicit. His legs were very prominent in his despair, and his fingers frequently performed the part of blunt combs, consequently the General was impressed by his passion for Elizabeth. The girl who, if she was often meditative, always met his eyes with a smile, and quietly said "Yes, papa," and "No, papa," gave him little concern as to the state of her feelings. Yet everybody said now that she was unhappy. Mrs. Barcop, the widow, raised her voice above the rest. So attentive was she to Elizabeth that the General had it kindly suggested to him that someone was courting him through his daughter. He gazed at the widow. Now she was not much past thirty; and it was really singular— he could have laughed—thinking of Mrs. Barcop set him persistently thinking of Lady Camper. That is to say, his mad fancy reverted from the lady of perhaps thirty-five to the lady of seventy! Such, thought he, is genius in a woman! Of his neighbours generally, Mrs. Baerens, the wife of a German merchant, an exquisite player on the pianoforte, was the most inclined to lead him to speak of Lady Camper. She was a kind prattling woman, and was known to have been a governess before her charms withdrew the gastronomic Gottfried Baerens from his devotion to the well-served City club, where, as he exclaimed (ever turning fondly to his wife as he vocalized the compliment), he had found every necessity, every luxury, in life, "as you cannot have dem out of London—all save de female!" Mrs. Baerens, a lady of Teutonic extraction, was distinguishable as of that sex; at least she was not masculine. She spoke with great respect of Lady Camper and her family, and seemed to agree in the General's eulogies of Lady Camper's constitution. Still he thought she eyed him strangely.

One April morning the General received a letter with the Italian postmark. Opening it with his usual calm and happy curiosity, he perceived that it was composed of pen-and-ink drawings. And suddenly his heart sank like a scuttled ship. He saw himself the victim of a caricature.

The first sketch had merely seemed picturesque, and he supposed it a clever play of fancy by some travelling friend, or perhaps an actual scene slightly exaggerated. Even on reading, "A distant view of the city of Wilsonople," he was only slightly enlightened. His heart beat still with befitting regularity. But the second and the third sketches betrayed the terrible hand. The distant view of the city of Wilsonople was fair with glittering domes, which, in the succeeding near view, proved to have been soap-bubbles, for a place of extreme flatness, begirt with crazy old-fashioned fortifications, was shown; and in the third view, representing the interior, stood for sole place of habitation, a sentry-box.

Most minutely drawn, and, alas! with fearful accuracy, a military gentleman in undress occupied the box. Not a doubt could exist as to the person it was meant to be.

The General tried hard to remain incredulous. He remembered too well who had called him Wilsonople.

But here was the extraordinary thing that sent him over the neighbourhood canvassing for exclamations: on the fourth page was the outline of a lovely feminine hand, holding a pen, as in the act of shading, and under it was written these words: *"What I say is, I say I think it exceedingly unladylike."*

Now consider the General's feelings when, turning to this fourth page, having these very words in his mouth, as the accurate expression of his thoughts, he discovered them written!

An enemy who anticipates the actions of our mind, has a quality of the malignant divine that may well inspire terror. The senses of General Ople were struck by the aspect of a Black Goddess, who penetrated him, read him through, and had both power and will to expose and make him ridiculous forever.

The loveliness of the hand, too, in a perplexing manner contested his denunciation of her conduct. It was ladylike eminently, and it involved him in a confused mixture of the moral and material, as great as young people are known to feel when they make the attempt to separate them, in one of their frenzies.

With a petty bitter laugh he folded the letter, put it in his breast-pocket, and sallied forth for a walk, chiefly to talk to himself about it. But as it absorbed him entirely, he showed it to the rector, whom he met, and what the rector said is of no consequence, for General Ople listened to no remarks, calling in succession on the Pollingtons, the Goslings, the Baerens', and others, early though it was, and the lords of those houses absent amassing hoards; and to the ladies everywhere he displayed the sketches he had received, observing that Wilsonople meant himself; and there he was, he said, pointing at the capped fellow in the sentry-box, done unmistakably. The likeness indeed was remarkable. "She is a woman of genius," he ejaculated, with utter melancholy. Mrs. Baerens, by the aid of a magnifying glass, assisted him to read a line under the sentry-box, that he had taken for a mere trembling dash; it ran, *A gentlemanly residence.*

"What eyes she has!" the General exclaimed; "I say it is miraculous what eyes she has at her time of . . . I was saying I should never have known it was writing."

He sighed heavily. His shuddering sensitiveness to caricature was increased by a certain evident dread of the hand which struck; the knowing that he was absolutely bare to this woman, defenceless, open to exposure in his little whims, foibles, tricks, incompetencies, in what lay in his heart, and the words that would come to his tongue. He felt like a man haunted.

So deeply did he feel the blow, that people asked how it was that he could be so foolish as to dance about assisting Lady Camper in her efforts to make him ridiculous; he acted the parts of publisher and agent for the fearful caricaturist. In truth, there was a strangely double reason for his conduct; he danced about for sympathy, he had the intensest craving for sympathy, but more than this, or quite as much, he desired to have the powers of his enemy widely appreciated; in the first place, that he might be excused to himself for wincing under them, and secondly, because an awful admiration of her, that should be deepened by a corresponding sentiment around him, helped him to enjoy luxurious recollections of an hour when he was near making her his own—his own, in the holy abstract contemplation of marriage, without realizing their probable relative conditions after the ceremony.

"I say, that is the very image of her ladyship's hand," he was especially fond of remarking, "I say it is a beautiful hand."

He carried the letter in his pocket-book; and beginning to fancy that she had done her worst, for he could not imagine an inventive malignity capable of pursuing the theme, he spoke of her treatment of him with compassionate regret, not badly assumed from being partly sincere.

Two letters dated in France, the one Dijon, the other Fontainebleau, arrived together; and as the General knew Lady Camper to be returning to England, he expected that she was anxious to excuse herself to him. His fingers were not so confident, for he tore one of the letters to open it.

The City of Wilsonople was recognisable immediately. So likewise was the sole inhabitant.

General Ople's petty bitter laugh recurred, like a weak-chested patient's cough in the shifting of our winds eastward.

A faceless woman's shadow kneels on the ground near the sentry-box, weeping. A faceless shadow of a young man on horseback is beheld galloping toward a gulf. The sole inhabitant contemplates his largely substantial full fleshed face and figure in a glass.

Next, we see the standard of Great Britain furled; next, unfurled and borne by a troop of shadows to the sentry-box. The officer within says, "I say I should be very happy to carry it, but I cannot quit this gentlemanly residence."

Next, the standard is shown assailed by popguns. Several of the shadows are prostrate. "I was saying, I assure you that nothing but this gentlemanly residence prevents me from heading you," says the gallant officer.

General Ople trembled with protestant indignation when he saw himself reclining in a magnified sentry-box, while detachments of shadows hurry to him to show him the standard of his country trailing in the dust; and he is maliciously made to say, "I dislike responsibility. I say I am a fervent patriot, and very fond of my comforts, but I shun responsibility."

The second letter contained scenes between Wilsonople and the Moon.

He addresses her as his neighbour, and tells her of his triumphs over the sex.

He requests her to inform him whether she is a "female," that she may be triumphed over.

He hastens past her window on foot, with his head bent, just as the General had been in the habit of walking.

He drives a mouse-pony furiously by.

He cuts down a tree, that she may peep through.

Then, from the Moon's point of view, Wilsonople, a Silenus, is discerned in an arm-chair winking at a couple too plainly pouting their lips for a doubt of their intentions to be entertained.

A fourth letter arrived, bearing date of Paris. This one illustrated Wilsonople's courtship of the Moon, and ended with his "saying," in his peculiar manner, *"In spite of her paint I could not have conceived her age to be so enormous."*

How break off his engagement with the Lady Moon? Consent to none of her terms!

Little used as he was to read behind a veil, acuteness of suffering sharpened the General's intelligence to a degree that sustained him in animated dialogue with each succeeding sketch, or poisoned arrow whirring at him from the moment his eyes rested on it; and here are a few samples:—

"Wilsonople informs the Moon that she is 'sweetly pretty.'

"He thanks her with 'thanks' for a handsome piece of lunar green cheese.

"He points to her, apparently telling some one, 'my lady friend.'

"He sneezes, 'Bijou! bijou! bijou!' "

They were trifles, but they attacked his habits of speech; and he began to grow more and more alarmingly absurd in each fresh caricature of his person.

He looked at himself as the malicious woman's hand had shaped him. It was unjust; it was no resemblance—and yet it was! There was a corner of likeness left that leavened the lump; henceforth he must walk abroad with this distressing image of himself before his eyes, instead of the satisfactory reflex of the man who had, and was happy in thinking that he had, done mischief in his time. Such an end for a conquering man was too pathetic.

The General surprised himself talking to himself in something louder than a hum at neighbours' dinner-tables. He looked about and noticed that people were silently watching him.

CHAPTER VII

LADY CAMPER'S return was the subject of speculation in the neighbourhood, for most people thought she would cease to persecute the General with her preposterous and unwarrantable pen-and-ink sketches when living so closely proximate; and how he would behave was the question. Those who made a hero of him were sure he would treat her with disdain. Others were uncertain. He had been so severely hit that it seemed possible he would not show much spirit.

He, for his part, had come to entertain such dread of the post, that Lady Camper's return relieved him of his morning apprehensions; and he would have forgiven her, though he feared to see her, if only she had promised to leave him in peace for the future. He feared to see her, because of the too probable furnishing of fresh matter for her ladyship's hand. Of course he could not avoid being seen by her, and that was a particular misery. A gentlemanly humility, or demureness of aspect, when seen, would, he hoped, disarm his enemy. It should, he thought. He had borne unheard-of things. No one of his friends and acquaintances knew, they could not know, what he had endured. It had caused him fits of stammering. It had destroyed the composure of his gait. Elizabeth had informed him that he talked to himself incessantly, and aloud. She, poor child, looked pale too. She was evidently anxious about him.

Young Rolles, whom he had met now and then, persisted in praising his aunt's good heart. So, perhaps, having satiated her revenge, she might now be inclined for peace, on the terms of distant civility.

"Yes! poor Elizabeth!" sighed the General, in pity of the poor girl's disappointment; "poor Elizabeth! she little guesses what her father has gone through. Poor child! I say, she hasn't an idea of my sufferings."

General Ople delivered his card at Lady Camper's lodge gates, and escaped to his residence in a state of prickly heat that required the brushing of his hair with hard brushes for ten minutes to comfort and re-establish him.

He fell to working in his garden, when Lady Camper's card was brought to him an hour after the delivery of his own, a pleasing promptitude, showing signs of repentance, and suggesting to the General instantly some sharp sarcasms upon women, which he had come upon in quotations in the papers and the pulpit, his two main sources of information.

Instead of handing back the card to the maid, he stuck it in his hat and went on digging.

The first of a series of letters containing shameless realistic caricatures was handed to him the afternoon following. They came fast and thick. Not a day's interval of grace was allowed. Niobe under the shafts of Diana was hardly less violently and mortally assailed. The deadliness of the attack lay in the ridicule of the daily habits of one of the most sensitive of men, as to his personal appearance, and the opinion of the world. He might have concealed the sketches, but he could not have concealed the bruises, and people were perpetually asking the unhappy General what he was saying, for he spoke to himself as if he were repeating something to them for the tenth time.

"I say," said he, "I say that for a lady, really an educated lady, to sit, as she must—I was saying, she must have sat in an attic to have the right view of me. And there you see this is what she has done. This is the last, this is the afternoon's delivery. Her ladyship has me correctly as to costume, but I could not exhibit such a sketch to ladies."

A back view of the General was displayed in his act of digging.

"I say I could not allow ladies to see it," he informed the gentlemen, who were suffered to inspect it freely.

"But you see I have no means of escape; I am at her mercy from morning to night," the General said, with a quivering tongue, "unless I stay at home inside the house; and that is death to me, or unless I abandon the place, and my lease; and I shall—I say, I shall find nowhere in England for anything like the money or conveniences such a gent—a residence you would call fit for a gentleman. I call it a bi . . . it is, in short, a gem. But I shall have to go."

Young Rolles offered to expostulate with his aunt Angela. The General said, "Tha . . . I thank you very much. I would not have her ladyship suppose I am so susceptible. I hardly know," he confessed pitiably, "what it is right to say, and what not—what not. I—I—I never know when I am not looking a fool. I hurry from tree to tree to shun the light. I am seriously affected in my appetite. I say, I shall have to go."

Reginald gave him to understand that if he flew, the shafts would follow him, for Lady Camper would never forgive his running away, and was quite equal to publishing a book of the adventures of Wilsonople.

Sunday afternoon, walking in the park with his daughter on his arm, General Ople met Mr. Rolles. He saw that the young man and Elizabeth were mortally pale, and as the very idea of wretchedness directed his attention to himself, he addressed them conjointly on the subject of his persecution, giving neither of them a chance of speaking until they were constrained to part.

A sketch was the consequence, in which a withered Cupid and a fading Psyche were seen divided by Wilsonople, who keeps them forcibly asunder with policeman's fists, while courteously and elegantly entreating them to hear him. "Meet," he tells them, "as often as you like, in my company, so long as you listen to me;" and the pathos of his aspect makes hungry demand for a sympathetic audience.

Now, this, and not the series representing the martyrdom of the old couple at Douro Lodge Gates, whose rigid frames bore witness to the close packing of a gentlemanly residence, this was the sketch General Ople, in his madness from the pursuing bite of the gadfly, handed about at Mrs. Pollington's lawn-party. Some have said that he would not have betrayed his daughter; but it is reasonable to suppose he had no idea of his daughter's being the Psyche. Or if he had, it was indistinct, owing to the violence of his personal emotion. Assuming this to have been the very sketch; he handed it to two or three ladies in turn, and was heard to deliver himself at intervals in the following snatches: "As you like, my lady, as you like; strike, I say strike; I bear it; I say I bear it. ... If her ladyship is unforgiving, I say I am enduring ... I may go, I was saying I may go mad, but while I have my reason I walk upright, I walk upright."

Mr. Pollington and certain city gentlemen hearing the poor General's renewed soliloquies, were seized with disgust of Lady Camper's conduct, and stoutly advised an application to the Law Courts.

He gave ear to them abstractedly, but after pulling out the whole chapter of the caricatures (which it seemed that he kept in a case of morocco leather in his breast-pocket), showing them, with comments on them, and observing, "There will be more, there must be more, I say I am sure there are things I do that her ladyship will discover and expose," he declined to seek redress or simple protection; and the miserable spectacle was exhibited soon after of this courtly man listening to Mrs. Barcop on the weather, and replying in acquiescence: "It is hot.—If your ladyship will only abstain from colours. Very hot as you say, madam,— I do not complain of pen and ink, but I would rather escape colours. And I dare say you find it hot too?"

Mrs. Barcop shut her eyes and sighed over the wreck of a handsome military officer.

She asked him: "What is your objection to colours?"

His hand was at his breast-pocket immediately, as he said: "Have you not seen?"—though but a few minutes back he had shown her the contents of the packet including a hurried glance of the famous digging scene.

By this time the entire district was in fervid sympathy with General Ople. The ladies did not, as their lords did, proclaim astonishment that a man should suffer a woman to goad him to a state of semi-lunacy; but one or two confessed

to their husbands, that it required a great admiration of
General Ople not to despise him, both for his susceptibility
and his patience. As for the men, they knew him to have
faced the balls in bellowing battle-strife; they knew him to
have endured privation, not only cold but downright want of
food and drink—an almost unimaginable horror to these
brave daily feasters; so they could not quite look on him in
contempt; but his want of sense was offensive, and still more
so his submission to a scourging by a woman. Not one of
them would have deigned to feel it. Would they have allowed
her to see that she could sting them? They would have
laughed at her. Or they would have dragged her before a
magistrate.

It was a Sunday in early summer when General Ople
walked to morning service, unaccompanied by Elizabeth,
who was unwell. The church was of the considerate old-
fashioned order, with deaf square pews, permitting the mind
to abstract itself from the sermon, or wrestle at leisure with
the difficulties presented by the preacher, as General Ople
often did, feeling not a little in love with his sincere attentiveness for grappling with the knotty point, and partially
allowing the struggle to be seen.

The Church was, besides, a sanctuary for him. Hither
his enemy did not come. He had this one place of refuge,
and he almost looked a happy man again.

He had passed into his hat and out of it, which he habitually did standing, when who should walk up to within a
couple of yards of him but Lady Camper. Her pew was full
of poor people, who made signs of retiring. She signified to
them that they were to sit, then quietly took her seat among
them, fronting the General across the aisle.

During the sermon a low voice, sharp in contradistinction
to the monotone of the preacher's, was heard to repeat these
words: "I say I am not sure I shall survive it." Considerable muttering in the same quarter was heard besides.

After the customary ceremonious game, when all were
free to move, of nobody liking to move first, Lady Camper

and a charity boy were the persons who took the lead. But Lady Camper could not quit her pew, owing to the sticking of the door. She smiled as with her pretty hand she twice or thrice essayed to shake it open. General Ople strode to her aid. He pulled the door, gave the shadow of a respectful bow, and no doubt he would have withdrawn, had not Lady Camper, while acknowledging the civility, placed her Prayer-book in his hands to carry at her heels. There was no choice for him. He made a sort of slipping dance back for his hat, and followed her ladyship. All present being eager to witness the spectacle, the passage of Lady Camper dragging the victim General behind her was observed without a stir of the well-dressed members of the congregation, until a desire overcame them to see how Lady Camper would behave to her fish when she had him outside the sacred edifice.

None could have imagined such a scene. Lady Camper was in her carriage; General Ople was hat in hand at the carriage step, and he looked as if he were toasting before the bars of a furnace; for while he stood there, Lady Camper was rapidly pencilling outlines in a small pocket sketch-book. There are dogs whose shyness is put to it to endure human observation and a direct address to them, even on the part of their masters; and these dear simple dogs wag tail and turn their heads aside waveringly, as though to entreat you not to eye them and talk to them so. General Ople, in the presence of the sketch-book, was much like the nervous animal. He would fain have run away. He glanced at it, and round about, and again at it, and at the heavens. Her ladyship's cruelty, and his inexplicable submission to it, were witnessed of the multitude.

The General's friends walked very slowly. Lady Camper's carriage whirled by, and the General came up with them, accosting them and himself alternately. They asked him where Elizabeth was, and he replied, "Poor child, yes! I am told she is pale, but I cannot believe I am so perfectly, I say so perfectly ridiculous when I join the responses." He drew

forth half-a-dozen sheets, and showed them sketches that
Lady Camper had taken in church, caricaturing him in the
sitting down and the standing up. She had torn them out of
the book, and presented them to him when driving off. "I
was saying, worship in the ordinary sense will be interdicted
to me if her ladyship . . . ," said the General, woefully shuffling the sketch-paper sheets in which he figured.

He made the following odd confession to Mr. and Mrs.
Gosling on the road:—that he had gone to his chest, and
taken out his sword-belt to measure his girth, and found
himself thinner than when he left the service, which had not
been the case before his attendance at the last levée of the
foregoing season. So the deduction was obvious, that Lady
Camper had reduced him. She had reduced him as effectually as a harassing siege.

"But why do you pay attention to her? Why! . . ," exclaimed Mr. Gosling, a gentleman of the City, whose round-
ness would have turned a rifle-shot.

"To allow her to wound you so seriously!" exclaimed
Mrs. Gosling.

"Madam, if she were my wife," the General explained, "I
should feel it. I say it is the fact of it; I feel it, if I appear
so extremely ridiculous to a human eye, to any one eye."

"To Lady Camper's eye!"

He admitted it might be that. He had not thought of
ascribing the acuteness of his pain to the miserable image he
presented in this particular lady's eye. No; it really was
true, curiously true: another lady's eye might have transformed him to a pumpkin shape, exaggerated all his foibles
fifty fold, and he though not liking it, of course not, would
yet have preserved a certain manly equanimity. How was it
Lady Camper had such power over him?—a lady concealing
seventy years with a rouge-box or paint-pot! It was witch-
craft in its worst character. He had for six months at her
bidding been actually living the life of a beast, degraded in
his own esteem; scorched by every laugh he heard; running,

pursued, overtaken, and as it were scored or branded, and then let go for the process to be repeated.

CHAPTER VIII

OUR young barbarians have it all their own way with us when they fall into love-liking; they lead us whither they please, and interest us in their wishings, their weepings, and that fine performance, their kissings. But when we see our veterans tottering to their fall, we scarcely consent to their having a wish; as for a kiss, we halloo at them if we discover them on a byway to the sacred grove where such things are supposed to be done by the venerable. And this piece of rank injustice, not to say impoliteness, is entirely because of an unsound opinion that Nature is not in it, as though it were our esteem for Nature which caused us to disrespect them. They, in truth, show her to us discreet, civilized, in a decent moral aspect: vistas of real life, views of the mind's eye, are opened by their touching little emotions; whereas those bully youngsters who come bellowing at us and catch us by the senses plainly prove either that we are no better than they, or that we give our attention to Nature only when she makes us afraid of her. If we cared for her, we should be up and after her reverentially in her sedater steps, deeply studying her in her slower paces. Whirling she teaches nothing. Our closest instructors, the true philosophers— the story-tellers, in short—will learn in time that Nature is not of necessity always roaring, and as soon as they do, the world may be said to be enlightened. Meantime, in the contemplation of a pair of white whiskers fluttering round a pair of manifestly painted cheeks, be assured that Nature is in it, very Nature, domesticated Nature, the Nature of gradations, Nature with a perspective. Art in days to come will dote on the theme. It is Nature calling to Nature, Nature amazed with brains, and pursuing the direction of their index; not that hectoring wanton—but let the young have their fun. Let the superior interest of the passions of the aged be conceded, and not a word shall be said against the young. They are young, and haply they cannot clothe themselves.

If, then, Nature is in it, with a couple properly attired, how has she been made active? The reason of her launch upon this last adventure is, that she has perceived the person who can supply the virtue known to her by experience to be wanting. Thus, in the broader instance, many who have journeyed far down the road, turn back to the worship of youth, which they have lost. Some are for the graceful worldliness of wit, which they have just enough share of to admire it. Some are captivated by hands that can wield the rod, which in earlier days they escaped to their cost. In the case of General Ople, it was partly her whippings of him, partly her penetration: her ability, that sat so finely on a wealthy woman, her indifference to conventional manners, that so well beseemed a nobly-born one, and more than all, her correction of his little weaknesses and incompetencies, in spite of his dislike of it, won him. He began to feel a sort of nibbling pleasure in her grotesque sketches of his person; a tendency to recur to the old ones while dreading the arrival of the new. You hear old gentlemen speak fondly of the swish; and they are not attached to pain, but the instrument revives their feeling of youth; and General Ople half enjoyed, while shrinking, Lady Camper's foregone outlines of him. For in the distance, the whip's-end may look like a clinging caress instead of a stinging flick. But this craven melting in his heart was rebuked by a very worthy pride, that flew for support to the injury she had done to his devotions, and the offence to the sacred edifice. After thinking over it, he decided that he must quit his residence; and as it appeared to him in the light of a duty, he, with an unspoken anguish, commissioned the house-agent of his town to sell his lease or let the house furnished, without further parley.

From the house-agent's shop he turned into the chemist's,

for a tonic—a foolish proceeding, for he had received brac-
ing enough in the blow he had just dealt himself, but he had
been cogitating on tonics recently, imagining certain valiant
effects of them, with visions of a former careless happiness
that they were likely to restore. So he requested to have the
tonic strong, and he took one glass of it over the counter.

Fifteen minutes after the draught, he came in sight of his
house, and beholding it, he could have called it a gentlemanly
residence aloud under Lady Camper's windows, his insur-
gency was of such violence. He talked of it incessantly, but
forbore to tell Elizabeth, as she was looking pale, the reason
why its modest merits touched him so. He longed for the
hour of his next dose, and for a caricature to follow, that he
might drink and defy it. A caricature was really due to him,
he thought; otherwise why had he abandoned his bijou
dwelling. Lady Camper, however, sent none. He had to
wait a fortnight before one came, and that was rather a likeness, and a handsome likeness, except as regarded a certain
disorderliness in his dress, which he knew to be very unlike
him. Still it despatched him to the looking-glass, to bring
that verifier of facts in evidence against the sketch. While
sitting there he heard the housemaid's knock at the door,
and the strange intelligence that his daughter was with Lady
Camper, and had left word that she hoped he would not forget his engagement to go to Mrs. Baerens' lawn-party.

The General jumped away from the glass, shouting at the
absent Elizabeth in a fit of wrath so foreign to him, that he
returned hurriedly to have another look at himself, and
exclaimed at the pitch of his voice, "I say I attribute it to an
indigestion of that tonic. Do you hear?" The housemaid
faintly answered outside the door that she did, alarming
him, for there seemed to be confusion somewhere. His hope
was that no one would mention Lady Camper's name, for
the mere thought of her caused a rush to his head. "I believe I am in for a touch of apoplexy," he said to the rector,
who greeted him, in advance of the ladies, on Mrs. Baerens'
lawn. He said it smilingly, but wanting some show of sym-

pathy, instead of the whisper and meaningless hand at his clerical band, with which the rector responded, he cried, "Apoplexy," and his friend seemed then to understand, and disappeared among the ladies.

Several of them surrounded the General, and one inquired whether the series was being continued. He drew forth his pocket-book, handed her the latest, and remarked on the gross injustice of it; for, as he requested them to take note, her ladyship now sketched him as a person inattentive to his dress, and he begged them to observe that she had drawn him with his necktie hanging loose. "And that, I say that has never been known of me since I first entered society."

The ladies exchanged looks of profound concern; for the fact was, the General had come without any necktie and any collar, and he appeared to be unaware of the circumstance. The rector had told them that in answer to a hint he had dropped on the subject of neckties, General Ople expressed a slight apprehension of apoplexy; but his careless or merely partial observance of the laws of buttonment could have nothing to do with such fears. They signified rather a disorder of the intelligence. Elizabeth was condemned for leaving him to go about alone. The situation was really most painful, for a word to so sensitive a man would drive him away in shame and for good; and still, to let him parade the ground in the state, compared with his natural self, of scarecrow, and with the dreadful habit of talking to himself quite raging, was a horrible alternative. Mrs. Baerens at last directed her husband upon the General, trembling as though she watched for the operations of a fish torpedo; and other ladies shared her excessive anxiousness, for Mr. Baerens had the manner and the look of artillery, and on this occasion carried a surcharge of powder.

The General bent his ear to Mr. Baerens, whose German-English and repeated remark, "I am to do it wid delicassy," did not assist his comprehension, and when he might have been enlightened, he was petrified by seeing Lady Camper walk on the lawn with Elizabeth. The great lady stood a moment beside Mrs. Baerens; she came straight over to him, contemplating him in silence.

Then she said, "Your arm, General Ople," and she made one circuit of the lawn with him, barely speaking.

At her request he conducted her to her carriage. He took a seat beside her, obediently. He felt that he was being sketched, and comported himself like a child's flat man, that jumps at the pulling of a string.

"Where have you left your girl, General?"

Before he could rally his wits to answer the question, he was asked:

"And what have you done with your necktie and collar?"

He touched his throat.

"I am rather nervous to-day, I forgot Elizabeth," he said, sending his fingers in a dotting run of wonderment round his neck.

Lady Camper smiled with a triumphing humour on her close-drawn lips.

The verified absence of necktie and collar seemed to be choking him.

"Never mind, you have been abroad without them," said Lady Camper, "and that is a victory for me. And you thought of Elizabeth first when I drew your attention to it, and that is a victory for you. It is a very great victory. Pray do not be dismayed, General. You have a handsome campaigning air. And no apologies, if you please; I like you well enough as you are. There is my hand."

General Ople understood her last remark. He pressed the lady's hand in silence, very nervously.

"But do not shrug your head into your shoulders as if there were any possibility of concealing the thunderingly evident," said Lady Camper, electrifying him, what with her cordial squeeze, her kind eyes, and her singular language. "You have omitted the collar. Well? The collar is the fatal finishing touch in men's dress; it would make Apollo look bourgeois."

Her hand was in his; and watching the play of her features, a spark entered General Ople's brain, causing him, in forgetfulness of collar and caricatures, to ejaculate, "Seventy? Did your ladyship say seventy? Utterly impossible! You trifled with me."

"We will talk when we are free of this accompaniment of carriage-wheels, General," said Lady Camper.

"I will beg permission to go and fetch Elizabeth, madam."

"Rightly thought of. Fetch her in my carriage. And, by the way, Mrs. Baerens was my old music-mistress, and is, I think, one year older than I. She can tell you on which side of seventy I am."

"I shall not require to ask, my lady," he said, sighing.

"Then we will send the carriage for Elizabeth, and have it out together at once. I am impatient; yes, General, impatient: for what?—forgiveness."

"Of me, my lady?" The General breathed profoundly.

"Of whom else? Do you know what it is?—I don't think you do. You English have the smallest experience of humanity. I mean this: to strike so hard that, in the end, you soften your heart to the victim. Well, that is my weakness. And we of our blood put no restraint on the blows we strike, so we are always overdoing it."

General Ople assisted Lady Camper to alight from the carriage, which was forthwith despatched for Elizabeth.

He prepared to listen to her with a disconnected smile of acute attentiveness.

She had changed. She spoke of money. Ten thousand pounds must be settled on his daughter. "And now," said she, "you will remember that you are wanting a collar."

He acquiesced. He craved permission to retire for ten minutes.

"Simplest of men! what will cover you?" she exclaimed, and peremptorily bidding him sit down in the drawing-room, she took one of the famous pair of pistols in her hand, and said, "If I put myself in a similar position, and make myself *décolletée* too, will that satisfy you? You see these murderous weapons. Well, I am a coward. I dread fire-arms. They are laid there to impose on the world, and I believe they do. They have imposed on you. Now you would never think of pretending to a moral quality you do not possess. But, silly, simple man that you are! You can give yourself the airs of wealth, buy horses to conceal your nakedness, and when you are taken upon the standard of your apparent income, you would rather seem to be beating a miserly retreat than behave frankly and honestly. I have a little overstated it, but I am near the mark."

"Your ladyship wanting courage!" cried the General.

"Refresh yourself by meditating on it," said she. "And to prove it to you, I was glad to take this house when I knew I was to have a gallant gentleman for a neighbour. No visitors will be admitted, General Ople, so you are barethroated only to me: sit quietly. One day you speculated on the paint in my cheeks for the space of a minute and a half: —I had said that I freckled easily. Your look signified that you really could not detect a single freckle for the paint. I forgave you, or I did not. But when I found you, on closer acquaintance, as indifferent to your daughter's happiness as you had been to her reputation . . ."

"My daughter! her reputation! her happiness!" General Ople raised his eyes under a wave, half uttering the outcries.

"So indifferent to her reputation that you allowed a young man to talk with her over the wall, and meet her by appointment: so reckless of the girl's happiness that when I tried to bring you to a treaty, on her behalf, you could not be dragged from thinking of yourself and your own affair. When I found that, perhaps I was predisposed to give you some of what my sisters used to call my spice. You would not honestly state the proportions of your income, and you affected to be faithful to the woman of seventy. Most preposterous! Could any caricature of mine exceed in grotesqueness your sketch of yourself? You are a brave and a generous man all the same: and I suspect it is more hoodwinking than egotism—or extreme egotism—that blinds you. A certain amount you must have to be a man. You did not like my paint, still less did you like my sincerity; you were annoyed by my corrections of your habits of speech; you were horrified by the age of seventy, and you were credulous—General Ople, listen to me, and remember that you have no collar on!—you were credulous of my statement of my great age, or you chose to be so, or chose to seem so, because I had brushed your cat's coat against the fur. And then, full of yourself, not thinking of Elizabeth, but to withdraw in the chivalrous attitude of the man true to his word to the old woman, only stickling to bring a certain independence to the common stock, because—I quote you! and you have no collar on, mind—'*you could not be at your wife's mercy*,' you broke from your proposal on the money question. Where was your consideration for Elizabeth, then?

"Well, General, you were fond of thinking of yourself, and I thought I would assist you. I gave you plenty of subject matter. I will not say I meant to work a homœopathic cure. But if I drive you to forget your collar, is it or is it not a triumph?

"No," added Lady Camper, "it is no triumph for me, but it is one for you, if you like to make the most of it. Your fault has been to quit active service, General, and love your ease too well. It is the fault of your countrymen. You must get a militia regiment, or inspectorship of militia. You are ten times the man in exercise. Why, do you mean to tell me that you would have cared for those drawings of mine when marching?"

"I think so, I say I think so," remarked the General, seriously.

"I doubt it," said she. "But to the point; here comes Elizabeth. If you have not much money to spare for her, according to your prudent calculations, reflect how this money has enfeebled you and reduced you to the level of the people round about us here—who are what? Inhabitants of gentlemanly residences, yes! But what kind of creatures? They have no mental standard, no moral aim, no native chivalry. You were rapidly becoming one of them, only, fortunately for you, you were sensitive to ridicule."

"Elizabeth shall have half my money settled on her," said the General; "though I fear it is not much. And if I can find occupation, my lady . . ."

"Something worthier than *that*," said Lady Camper, pencilling outlines rapidly on the margin of a book, and he saw himself lashing a pony; "or *that*," and he was plucking at a cabbage; "or *that*," and he was bowing to three petticoated posts.

"The likeness is exact," General Ople groaned.

"So you may suppose I have studied you," said she. "But there is no real likeness. Slight exaggerations do more harm to truth than reckless violations of it. You would not have cared one bit for a caricature, if you had not nursed the absurd idea of being one of our conquerors. It is the very tragedy of modesty for a man like you to have such notions, my poor dear good friend. The modest are the most easily intoxicated when they sip at vanity. And reflect whether you have not been intoxicated, for these young people have been wretched, and you have not observed it, though one of them was living with you, and is the child you love. There, I have done. Pray show a good face to Elizabeth."

The General obeyed as well as he could. He felt very like a sheep that has come from a shearing, and when released he wished to run away. But hardly had he escaped before he had a desire for the renewal of the operation. "She sees me through, she sees me through," he was heard saying to himself, and in the end he taught himself to say it with a secret exultation, for as it was on her part an extraordinary piece of insight to see him through, it struck him that in acknowledging the truth of it, he made a discovery of new powers in human nature.

General Ople studied Lady Camper diligently for fresh proofs of her penetration of the mysteries in his bosom; by which means, as it happened that she was diligently observ-

ing the two betrothed young ones, he began to watch them
likewise, and took a pleasure in the sight. Their meetings,
their partings, their rides out and home, furnished him
themes of converse. He soon had enough to talk of, and
previously, as he remembered, he had never sustained a conversation of any length with composure and the beneficent
sense of fulness. Five thousand pounds, to which sum Lady
Camper reduced her stipulation for Elizabeth's dowry, he
signed over to his dear girl gladly, and came out with the
confession to her ladyship that a well-invested twelve thousand comprised his fortune. She shrugged: she had left off
pulling him this way and that, so his chains were enjoyable,
and he said to himself: "If ever she should in the dead of
night want a man to defend her!" He mentioned it to Reginald, who had been the repository of Elizabeth's lamentations about her father being left alone, forsaken, and the
young man conceived a scheme for causing his aunt's great
bell to be rung at midnight, which would certainly have led
to a dramatic issue and the happy re-establishment of our
masculine ascendancy at the close of this history. But he
forgot it in his bridegroom's delight, until he was making
his miserable official speech at the wedding-breakfast, and
set Elizabeth winking over a tear. As she stood in the hall
ready to depart, a great van was observed in the road at the
gates of Douro Lodge; and this, the men in custody declared
to contain the goods and knick-knacks of the people who had
taken the house furnished for a year, and were coming in
that very afternoon.

"I remember, I say now I remember, I had a notice," the
General said cheerily to his troubled daughter.

"But where are you to go, papa?" the poor girl cried, close
on sobbing.

"I shall get employment of some sort," said he. "I was
saying I want it, I need it, I require it."

"You are saying three times what once would have suf-
ficed for," said Lady Camper, and she asked him a few ques-

tions, frowned with a smile, and offered him a lodgement in his neighbour's house.

"Really, dearest Aunt Angela?" said Elizabeth.

"What else can I do, child? I have, it seems, driven him out of a gentlemanly residence, and I must give him a lady-like one. True, I would rather have had him at call, but as I have always wished for a policeman in the house, I may as well be satisfied with a soldier."

"But if you lose your character, my lady?" said Reginald.

"Then I must look to the General to restore it."

General Ople immediately bowed his head over Lady Camper's fingers.

"An odd thing to happen to a woman of forty-one!" she said to her great people, and they submitted with the best grace in the world, while the General's ears tingled till he felt younger than Reginald. This, his reflections ran, or it would be more correct to say waltzed, this is the result of painting!—that you can believe a woman to be any age when her cheeks are tinted!"

As for Lady Camper, she had been floated accidentally over the ridicule of the bruit of a marriage at a time of life as terrible to her as her fiction of seventy had been to General Ople; she resigned herself to let things go with the tide. She had not been blissful in her first marriage, she had abandoned the chase of an ideal man, and she had found one who was tuneable so as not to offend her ears, likely ever to be a fund of amusement for her humour, good, impressible, and above all, very picturesque. There is the secret of her, and of how it came to pass that a simple man and a complex woman fell to union after the strangest division.

THE PAVILION ON THE LINKS

By Robert Louis Stevenson

CHAPTER I

TELLS HOW I CAMPED IN GRADEN SEA-WOOD, AND BEHELD A LIGHT IN THE PAVILION

I WAS a great solitary when I was young. I made it my pride to keep aloof and suffice for my own entertainment; and I may say that I had neither friends nor acquaintances until I met that friend who became my wife and the mother of my children. With one man only was I on private terms; this was R. Northmour, Esquire, of Graden Easter, in Scotland. We had met at college; and though there was not much liking between us, nor even much intimacy, we were so nearly of a humor that we could associate with ease to both. Misanthropes, we believed ourselves to be; but I have thought since that we were only sulky fellows. It was scarcely a companionship, but a co-existence in unsociability. Northmour's exceptional violence of temper made it no easy affair for him to keep the peace with any one but me; and as he respected my silent ways, and let me come and go as I pleased, I could tolerate his presence without concern. I think we called each other friends.

When Northmour took his degree and I decided to leave the university without one, he invited me on a long visit to Graden Easter; and it was thus that I first became acquainted with the scene of my adventures. The mansion house of Graden stood in a bleak stretch of country some three miles from the shore of the German Ocean. It was as

187

large as a barrack; and as it had been built of a soft stone, liable to consume in the eager air of the seaside, it was damp and drafty within and half ruinous without.   It was impossible for two young men to lodge with comfort in such a dwelling.   But there stood in the northern part of the estate, in a wilderness of links and blowing sand-hills, and between a plantation and the sea, a small Pavilion or Belvedere, of modern design, which was exactly suited to our wants; and in this hermitage, speaking little, reading much, and rarely associating except at meals, Northmour and I spent four tempestuous winter months.   I might have stayed longer; but one March night there sprang up between us a dispute, which rendered my departure necessary.   Northmour spoke hotly, I remember, and I suppose I must have made some tart rejoinder.   He leaped from his chair and grappled me; I had to fight, without exaggeration, for my life; and it was only with a great effort that I mastered him, for he was near as strong in body as myself, and seemed filled with the devil.   The next morning, we met on our usual terms; but I judged it more delicate to withdraw; nor did he attempt to dissuade me.

It was nine years before I revisited the neighborhood.   I traveled at that time with a tilt cart, a tent, and a cooking-stove, tramping all day beside the wagon, and at night, whenever it was possible, gipsying in a cove of the hills, or by the side of a wood.   I believe I visited in this manner most of the wild and desolate regions both in England and Scotland; and, as I had neither friends nor relations, I was troubled with no correspondence, and had nothing in the nature of headquarters, unless it was the office of my solicitors, from whom I drew my income twice a year.   It was a life in which I delighted; and I fully thought to have grown old upon the march, and at last die in a ditch.

It was my whole business to find desolate corners, where I could camp without the fear of interruption; and hence, being in another part of the same shire, I bethought me suddenly of the Pavilion on the Links.   No thoroughfare

passed within three miles of it.   The nearest town, and that
was but a fisher village, was at a distance of six or seven.
For ten miles of length, and from a depth varying from
three miles to half a mile, this belt of barren country lay
along the sea.   The beach, which was the natural approach,
was full of quicksands.   Indeed I may say there is hardly a
better place of concealment in the United Kingdom.   I determined to pass a week in the Sea-Wood of Graden Easter,
and making a long stage, reached it about sundown on a
wild September day.

The country, I have said, was mixed sand-hill and links;
links being a Scottish name for sand which has ceased drift-
ing and become more or less solidly covered with turf.   The
pavilion stood on an even space; a little behind it, the wood
began in a hedge of elders huddled together by the wind;
in front, a few tumbled sand-hills stood between it and the
sea.   An outcropping of rock had formed a bastion for the
sand, so that there was here a promontory in the coast-line
between two shallow bays; and just beyond the tides, the
rock again cropped out and formed an islet of small dimen-
sions but strikingly designed.   The quicksands were of great
extent at low water, and had an infamous reputation in the
country.   Close inshore, between the islet and the promontory, it was said they would swallow a man in four minutes
and a half; but there may have been little ground for this
precision.   The district was alive with rabbits, and haunted
by gulls which made a continual piping about the pavilion.
On summer days the outlook was bright and even gladsome;
but at sundown in September, with a high wind, and a heavy
surf rolling in close along the links, the place told of nothing
but dead mariners and sea disaster.   A ship beating to windward on the horizon, and a huge truncheon of wreck half
buried in the sands at my feet, completed the innuendo of
the scene.

The pavilion—it had been built by the last proprietor,
Northmour's uncle, a silly and prodigal virtuoso—presented
little signs of age.   It was two stories in height, Italian in

design, surrounded by a patch of garden in which nothing
had prospered but a few coarse flowers; and looked, with its
shuttered windows, not like a house that had been deserted,
but like one that had never been tenanted by man. Northmour was plainly from home; whether, as usual, sulking in
the cabin of his yacht, or in one of his fitful and extravagant
appearances in the world of society, I had, of course, no
means of guessing. The place had an air of solitude that
daunted even a solitary like myself; the wind cried in the
chimneys with a strange and wailing note; and it was with
a sense of escape, as if I were going indoors, that I turned
away and, driving my cart before me, entered the skirts of
the wood.

The Sea-Wood of Graden had been planted to shelter the
cultivated fields behind, and check the encroachments of the
blowing sand. As you advanced into it from coastward,
elders were succeeded by other hardy shrubs; but the timber
was all stunted and bushy; it led a life of conflict; the trees
were accustomed to swing there all night long in fierce winter tempests; and even in early spring, the leaves were
already flying, and autumn was beginning, in this exposed
plantation. Inland the ground rose into a little hill, which,
along with the islet, served as a sailing mark for seamen.
When the hill was open of the islet to the north, vessels
must bear well to the eastward to clear Graden Ness and the
Graden Bullers. In the lower ground, a streamlet ran
among the trees, and, being dammed with dead leaves and
clay of its own carrying, spread out every here and there,
and lay in stagnant pools. One or two ruined cottages were
dotted about the wood; and, according to Northmour, these
were ecclesiastical foundations, and in their time had sheltered pious hermits.

I found a den, or small hollow, where there was a spring
of pure water; and there, clearing away the brambles, I
pitched the tent, and made a fire to cook my supper. My
horse I picketed further in the wood where there was a
patch of sward. The banks of the den not only concealed

the light of my fire, but sheltered me from the wind, which was cold as well as high.

The life I was leading made me both hardy and frugal. I never drank but water, and rarely ate anything more costly than oatmeal; and I required so little sleep, that, although I rose with the peep of day, I would often lie long awake in the dark or starry watches of the night. Thus in Graden Sea-Wood, although I fell thankfully asleep by eight in the evening I was awake again before eleven with a full possession of my faculties, and no sense of drowsiness or fatigue. I rose and sat by the fire, watching the trees and clouds tumultuously tossing and fleeing overhead, and hearkening to the wind and the rollers along the shore; till at length, growing weary of inaction, I quitted the den, and strolled toward the borders of the wood. A young moon, buried in mist, gave a faint illumination to my steps; and the light grew brighter as I walked forth into the links. At the same moment, the wind, smelling salt of the open ocean and carrying particles of sand, struck me with its full force, so that I had to bow my head.

When I raised it again to look about me, I was aware of a light in the pavilion. It was not stationary; but passed from one window to another, as though some one were reviewing the different apartments with a lamp or candle. I watched it for some seconds in great surprise. When I had arrived in the afternoon the house had been plainly deserted; now it was as plainly occupied. It was my first idea that a gang of thieves might have broken in and be now ransacking Northmour's cupboards, which were many and not ill supplied. But what should bring thieves to Graden Easter? And, again, all the shutters had been thrown open, and it would have been more in the character of such gentry to close them. I dismissed the notion, and fell back upon another. Northmour himself must have arrived, and was now airing and inspecting the pavilion.

I have said that there was no real affection between this man and me; but, had I loved him like a brother, I was then so much more in love with solitude that I should none the less have shunned his company. As it was, I turned and ran for it; and it was with genuine satisfaction that I found myself safely back beside the fire. I had escaped an acquaintance; I should have one more night in comfort. In the morning I might either slip away before Northmour was abroad or pay him as short a visit as I chose.

But when morning came I thought the situation so diverting that I forgot my shyness. Northmour was at my mercy; I arranged a good practical jest, though I knew well that my neighbor was not the man to jest with in security; and, chuckling beforehand over its success, took my place among the elders at the edge of the wood, whence I could command the door of the pavilion. The shutters were all once more closed, which I remember thinking odd; and the house, with its white walls and green venetians, looked spruce and habitable in the morning light. Hour after hour passed, and still no sign of Northmour. I knew him for a sluggard in the morning; but, as it drew on toward noon, I lost my patience. To say the truth, I had promised myself to break my fast in the pavilion, and hunger began to prick me sharply. It was a pity to let the opportunity go by without some cause for mirth; but the grosser appetite prevailed, and I relinquished my jest with regret, and sallied from the wood.

The appearance of the house affected me, as I drew near, with disquietude. It seemed unchanged since last evening; and I had expected it, I scarce knew why, to wear some external signs of habitation. But no: the windows were all closely shuttered, the chimneys breathed no smoke, and the front door itself was closely padlocked. Northmour, therefore, had entered by the back; this was the natural, and, indeed, the necessary conclusion; and you may judge of my surprise when, on turning the house, I found the back door similarly secured.

My mind at once reverted to the original theory of thieves; and I blamed myself sharply for my last night's inaction. I examined all the windows on the lower story, but none of them had been tampered with; I tried the padlocks, but they were both secure. It thus became a problem how the thieves, if thieves they were, had managed to enter the house. They must have got, I reasoned, upon the roof of the outhouse where Northmour used to keep his photographic battery; and from thence, either by the window of the study or that of my old bedroom, completed their burglarious entry.

I followed what I supposed was their example; and, getting on the roof, tried the shutters of each room. Both were secure; but I was not to be beaten; and, with a little force, one of them flew open, grazing, as it did so, the back of my hand. I remember, I put the wound to my mouth, and stood for perhaps half a minute licking it like a dog, and mechanically gazing behind me over the waste links and the sea; and, in that space of time, my eye made note of a large schooner yacht some miles to the northeast. Then I threw up the window and climbed in.

I went over the house, and nothing can express my mystification. There was no sign of disorder, but, on the contrary, the rooms were unusually clean and pleasant. I found fires laid, ready for lighting; three bedrooms prepared with a luxury quite foreign to Northmour's habits, and with water in the ewers and the beds turned down; a table set for three in the dining-room; and an ample supply of cold meats, game, and vegetables on the pantry shelves. There were guests expected, that was plain; but why guests, when Northmour hated society? And, above all, why was the house thus stealthily prepared at dead of night? and why were the shutters closed and the doors padlocked?

I effaced all traces of my visit, and came forth from the window feeling sobered and concerned.

The schooner yacht was still in the same place; and it flashed for a moment through my mind that this might be the "Red Earl" bringing the owner of the pavilion and his guests. But the vessel's head was set the other way.

CHAPTER II

TELLS OF THE NOCTURNAL LANDING FROM THE YACHT

I RETURNED to the den to cook myself a meal, of which I stood in great need, as well as to care for my horse, whom I had somewhat neglected in the morning. From time to time I went down to the edge of the wood; but there was no change in the pavilion, and not a human creature was seen all day upon the links. The schooner in the offing was the one touch of life within my range of vision. She, apparently with no set object, stood off and on or lay to, hour after hour; but as the evening deepened, she drew steadily nearer. I became more convinced that she carried Northmour and his friends, and that they would probably come ashore after dark; not only because that was of a piece with the secrecy of the preparations, but because the tide would not have flowed sufficiently before eleven to cover Graden Floe and the other sea-quags that fortified the shore against invaders.

All day the wind had been going down, and the sea along with it; but there was a return toward sunset of the heavy weather of the day before. The night set in pitch dark. The wind came off the sea in squalls, like the firing of a battery of cannon; now and then there was a flaw of rain, and the surf rolled heavier with the rising tide. I was down at my observatory among the elders, when a light was run up to the masthead of the schooner, and showed she was closer in than when I had last seen her by the dying daylight. I concluded that this must be a signal to Northmour's associates on shore; and, stepping forth into the links, looked around me for something in response.

A small footpath ran along the margin of the wood, and formed the most direct communication between the pavilion and the mansion-house; and, as I cast my eyes to that side, I saw a spark of light, not a quarter of a mile away, and rapidly approaching. From its uneven course it appeared to be the light of a lantern carried by a person who followed the windings of the path, and was often staggered and taken aback by the more violent squalls. I concealed myself once more among the elders, and waited eagerly for the new-comer's advance. It proved to be a woman; and, as she passed within half a rod of my ambush, I was able to recognize the features. The deaf and silent old dame, who had nursed Northmour in his chlidhood, was his associate in this underhand affair.

I followed her at a little distance, taking advantage of the innumerable heights and hollows, concealed by the darkness, and favored not only by the nurse's deafness, but by the uproar of the wind and surf. She entered the pavilion, and, going at once to the upper story, opened and set a light in one of the windows that looked toward the sea. Immediately afterward the light at the schooner's masthead was run down and extinguished. Its purpose had been attained, and those on board were sure that they were expected. The old woman resumed her preparations; although the other shutters remained closed, I could see a glimmer going to and fro about the house; and a gush of sparks from one chimney after another soon told me that the fires were being kindled.

Northmour and his guests, I was now persuaded, would come ashore as soon as there was water on the floe. It was a wild night for boat service; and I felt some alarm mingle with my curiosity as I reflected on the danger of the landing. My old acquaintance, it was true, was the most eccentric of men; but the present eccentricity was both disquieting and lugubrious to consider. A variety of feelings thus led me toward the beach, where I lay flat on my face in a hollow within six feet of the track that led to the pavilion. Thence, I should have the satisfaction of recognizing the arrivals, and, if they should prove to be acquaintances, greeting them as soon as they had landed.

Some time before eleven, while the tide was still danger-ously low, a boat's lantern appeared close inshore; and, my attention being thus awakened, I could perceive another still far to seaward, violently tossed, and sometimes hidden by the billows. The weather, which was getting dirtier as the night went on, and the perilous situation of the yacht upon a lee-shore, had probably driven them to attempt a landing at the earliest possible moment.

A little afterward, four yachtsmen carrying a very heavy chest, and guided by a fifth with a lantern, passed close in front of me as I lay, and were admitted to the pavilion by the nurse. They returned to the beach, and passed me a second time with another chest, larger but apparently not so heavy as the first. A third time they made the transit; and on this occasion one of the yachtsmen carried a leather portmanteau, and the others a lady's trunk and carriage bag. My curiosity was sharply excited. If a woman were among the guests of Northmour, it would show a change in his habits and an apostasy from his pet theories of life well calculated to fill me with surprise. When he and I dwelt there together, the pavilion had been a temple of misogyny. And now, one of the detested sex was to be installed under its roof. I remembered one or two particulars, a few notes of daintiness and almost of coquetry which had struck me the day before as I surveyed the preparations in the house; their purpose was now clear, and I thought myself dull not to have perceived it from the first.

While I was thus reflecting, a second lantern drew near me from the beach. It was carried by a yachtsman whom I had not yet seen, and who was conducting two other persons to the pavilion. These two persons were unquestionably the guests for whom the house was made ready; and, straining eye and ear, I set myself to watch them as they passed. One was an unusually tall man, in a traveling hat slouched over his eyes, and a highland cape closely buttoned and turned up so as to conceal his face. You could make out no more of him than that he was, as I have said, unusually tall, and walked feebly with a heavy stoop. By his side, and either clinging to him or giving him support—I could not make out which—was a young, tall, and slender figure of a woman. She was extremely pale; but in the light of the lantern her face was so marred by strong and changing shadows that she might equally well have been as ugly as sin or as beautiful as I afterward found her to be.

When they were just abreast of me, the girl made some remark which was drowned by the noise of the wind.

"Hush!" said her companion; and there was something in the tone with which the word was uttered that thrilled and rather shook my spirits. It seemed to breathe from a bosom laboring under the deadliest terror; I have never heard another syllable so expressive; and I still hear it again when I am feverish at night, and my mind runs upon old times. The man turned toward the girl as he spoke; I had a glimpse of much red beard and a nose which seemed to have been broken in youth; and his light eyes seemed shining in his face with some strong and unpleasant emotion.

But these two passed on and were admitted in their turn to the pavilion.

One by one, or in groups, the seamen returned to the beach. The wind brought me the sound of a rough voice crying, "Shove off!" Then, after a pause, another lantern drew near. It was Northmour alone.

My wife and I, a man and a woman, have often agreed to wonder how a person could be, at the same time, so handsome and so repulsive as Northmour. He had the appearance of a finished gentleman; his face bore every mark of intelligence and courage; but you had only to look at him, even in his most amiable moment, to see that he had the temper of a slaver captain. I never knew a character that was both explosive and revengeful to the same degree; he combined the vivacity of the south with the sustained and deadly hatreds of the north; and both traits were plainly written on his face, which was a sort of danger signal. In person, he was tall, strong, and active; his hair and complexion very dark; his features handsomely designed, but spoiled by a menacing expression.

At that moment he was somewhat paler than by nature; he wore a heavy frown; and his lips worked, and he looked sharply round him as he walked, like a man besieged with apprehensions. And yet I thought he had a look of triumph underlying all, as though he had already done much, and was near the end of an achievement.

Partly from a scruple of delicacy—which I dare say came too late—partly from the pleasure of startling an acquaintance, I desired to make my presence known to him without delay.

I got suddenly to my feet, and stepped forward.

"Northmour!" said I.

I have never had so shocking a surprise in all my days. He leaped on me without a word; something shone in his hand; and he struck for my heart with a dagger. At the same moment I knocked him head over heels. Whether it was my quickness, or his own uncertainty, I know not; but the blade only grazed my shoulder, while the hilt and his fist struck me violently on the mouth.

I fled, but not far. I had often and often observed the capabilities of the sand-hills for protracted ambush or stealthy advances and retreats; and, not ten yards from the scene of the scuffle, plumped down again upon the grass. The lantern had fallen and gone out. But what was my astonishment to see Northmour slip at a bound into the pavilion, and hear him bar the door behind him with a clang of iron!

He had not pursued me. He had run away. Northmour, whom I knew for the most implacable and daring of men, had run away! I could scarce believe my reason; and yet in this strange business, where all was incredible, there was nothing to make a work about in an incredibility more or less. For why was the pavilion secretly prepared? Why had Northmour landed with his guests at dead of night, in half a gale of wind, and with the floe scarce covered? Why had he sought to kill me? Had he not recognized my voice? I wondered. And, above all, how had he come to have a dagger ready in his hand? A dagger, or even a sharp knife, seemed out of keeping with the age in which we lived; and a gentleman landing from his yacht on the shore of his own estate, even although it was at night and with some mysterious circumstances, does not usually, as a matter of fact, walk thus prepared for deadly onslaught. The more I reflected, the further I felt at sea. I recapitulated the elements of mystery, counting them on my fingers: the pavilion secretly prepared for guests; the guests landed at the risk of their lives and to the imminent peril of the yacht; the guests, or at least one of them, in undisguised and seemingly causeless terror; Northmour with a naked weapon; Northmour stabbing his most intimate acquaintance at a word; last, and not least strange, Northmour fleeing from the man whom he had sought to murder, and barricading himself, like a hunted creature, behind the door of the pavilion. Here were at least six separate causes for extreme surprise; each part and parcel with the others, and forming all together one consistent story. I felt almost ashamed to believe my own senses.

As I thus stood, transfixed with wonder, I began to grow painfully conscious of the injuries I had received in the scuffle; skulked round among the sand-hills; and, by a devious path, regained the shelter of the wood. On the way, the old nurse passed again within several yards of me, still carrying her lantern, on the return journey to the mansion-house of Graden. This made a seventh suspicious feature in the case. Northmour and his guests, it appeared, were to cook and do the cleaning for themselves, while the old woman continued to inhabit the big empty barrack among the policies. There must surely be great cause for secrecy, when so many inconveniences were confronted to preserve it.

So thinking, I made my way to the den. For greater security, I trod out the embers of the fire, and lighted my lantern to examine the wound upon my shoulder. It was a trifling hurt, although it bled somewhat freely, and I dressed it as well as I could (for its position made it difficult to reach) with some rag and cold water from the spring. While I was thus busied, I mentally declared war against Northmour and his mystery. I am not an angry man by nature, and I believe there was more curiosity than resentment in my heart. But war I certainly declared; and, by way of preparation, I got out my revolver, and, having drawn the charges, cleaned and reloaded it with scrupulous care. Next I became preoccupied about my horse. It might break loose, or fall to neighing, and so betray my camp in the Sea-Wood. I determined to rid myself of its neighborhood; and long before dawn I was leading it over the links in the direction of the fisher village.

CHAPTER III

TELLS HOW I BECAME ACQUAINTED WITH MY WIFE

For two days I skulked round the pavilion, profiting by the uneven surface of the links. I became an adept in the necessary tactics. These low hillocks and shallow dells, running one into another, became a kind of cloak of darkness for my enthralling, but perhaps dishonourable, pursuit. Yet, in spite of this advantage, I could learn but little of Northmour or his guests.

Fresh provisions were brought under cover of darkness by the old woman from the mansion-house. Northmour, and the young lady, sometimes together, but more often singly, would walk for an hour or two at a time on the beach beside the quicksand. I could not but conclude that this promenade was chosen with an eye to secrecy; for the spot was open only to the seaward. But it suited me not less excellently; the highest and most accidented of the sand-hills immediately adjoined; and from these, lying flat in a hollow, I could overlook Northmour or the young lady as they walked.

The tall man seemed to have disappeared. Not only did

he never cross the threshold, but he never so much as showed face at a window; or, at least, not so far as I could see; for I dared not creep forward beyond a certain distance in the day, since the upper floor commanded the bottoms of the links; and at night, when I could venture further, the lower windows were barricaded as if to stand a siege. Sometimes I thought the tall man must be confined to bed, for I remembered the feebleness of his gait; and sometimes I thought he must have gone clear away, and that Northmour and the young lady remained alone together in the pavilion. The idea, even then, displeased me.

Whether or not this pair were man and wife, I had seen abundant reason to doubt the friendliness of their relation. Although I could hear nothing of what they said, and rarely so much as glean a decided expression on the face of either, there was a distance, almost a stiffness, in their bearing which showed them to be either unfamiliar or at enmity. The girl walked faster when she was with Northmour than when she was alone; and I conceived that any inclination between a man and a woman would rather delay than accelerate the step. Moreover, she kept a good yard free of him, and trailed her umbrella, as if it were a barrier, on the side between them. Northmour kept sidling closer; and, as the girl retired from his advance, their course lay at a sort of diagonal across the beach, and would have landed them in the surf had it been long enough continued. But, when this was imminent, the girl would unostentatiously change sides and put Northmour between her and the sea. I watched these maneuvres, for my part, with high enjoyment and approval, and chuckled to myself at every move.

On the morning of the third day, she walked alone for some time, and I perceived to my great concern, that she was more than once in tear   You will see that my heart was already interested more than I supposed. She had a firm yet airy motion of the body, and carried her head with unimaginable grace; every step was a thing to look at, and she seemed in my eyes to breathe sweetness and distinction.

The day was so agreeable, being calm and sunshiny, with a tranquil sea, and yet with a healthful piquancy and vigor in the air, that, contrary to custom, she was tempted forth a second time to walk. On this occasion she was accompanied by Northmour, and they had been but a short while on the beach when I saw him take forcible possession of her hand. She struggled, and uttered a cry that was almost a scream. I sprang to my feet, unmindful of my strange position; but, ere I had taken a step, I saw Northmour bareheaded and bowing very low, as if to apologize; and dropped again at once into my ambush. A few words were interchanged; and then, with another bow, he left the beach to return to the pavilion. He passed not far from me, and I could see him, flushed and lowering, and cutting savagely with his cane among the grass. It was not without satisfaction that I recognized my own handiwork in a great cut under his right eye, and a considerable discoloration round the socket.

For some time the girl remained where he had left her, looking out past the islet and over the bright sea. Then with a start, as one who throws off preoccupation and puts energy again upon its mettle, she broke into a rapid and decisive walk. She also was much incensed by what had passed. She had forgotten where she was. And I beheld her walk straight into the borders of the quicksand where it is most abrupt and dangerous. Two or three steps further and her life would have been in serious jeopardy, when I slid down the face of the sand-hill, which is there precipitous, and, running half-way forward, called to her to stop.

She did so, and turned round. There was not a tremor of fear in her behavior, and she marched directly up to me like a queen. I was barefoot, and clad like a common sailor, save for an Egyptian scarf round my waist; and she probably took me at first for some one from the fisher village, straying after bait. As for her, when I thus saw her face to face, her eyes set steadily and imperiously upon mine, I was

filled with admiration and astonishment, and thought her
even more beautiful than I had looked to find her. Nor could
I think enough of one who, acting with so much boldness,
yet preserved a maidenly air that was both quaint and engaging; for my wife kept an old-fashioned precision of manner through all her admirable life—an excellent thing in
woman, since it sets another value on her sweet familiarities.

"What does this mean?" she asked.

"You were walking," I told her, "directly into Graden
Floe."

"You do not belong to these parts," she said again. "You
speak like an educated man."

"I believe I have right to that name," said I, "although
in this disguise."

But her woman's eye had already detected the sash.

"Oh!" she said; "your sash betrays you."

"You have said the word *betray*," I resumed. "May I
ask you not to betray me? I was obliged to disclose myself
in your interest; but if Northmour learned my presence it
might be worse than disagreeable for me."

"Do you know," she asked, "to whom you are speaking?"

"Not to Mr. Northmour's wife?" I asked, by way of
answer.

She shook her head. All this while she was studying my
face with an embarrassing intentness. Then she broke out:

"You have an honest face. Be honest like your face, sir,
and tell me what you want and what you are afraid of.
Do you think I could hurt you? I believe you have far more
power to injure me! And yet you do not look unkind. What
do you mean—you, a gentleman—by skulking like a spy
about this desolate place? Tell me," she said, "who is it
you hate?"

"I hate no one," I answered; "and I fear no one face to
face. My name is Cassilis—Frank Cassilis. I lead the life
of a vagabond for my own good pleasure. I am one of
Northmour's oldest friends; and three nights ago, when I

addressed him on these links, he stabbed me in the shoulder with a knife."

"It was you!" she said.

"Why he did so," I continued, disregarding the interruption, "is more than I can guess, and more than I care to know. I have not many friends, nor am I very susceptible to friendship; but no man shall drive me from a place by terror. I had camped in Graden Sea-Wood ere he came; I camp in it still. If you think I mean harm to you or yours, madam, the remedy is in your hand. Tell him that my camp is in the Hemlock Den, and to-night he can stab me in safety while I sleep."

With this I doffed my cap to her, and scrambled up once more among the sand-hills. I do not know why, but I felt a prodigious sense of injustice, and felt like a hero and a martyr; while, as a matter of fact, I had not a word to say in my defense, nor so much as one plausible reason to offer for my conduct. I had stayed at Graden out of a curiosity natural enough, but undignified; and though there was another motive growing in along with the first, it was not one which, at that period, I could have properly explained to the lady of my heart.

Certainly, that night, I thought of no one else; and, though her whole conduct and position seemed suspicious, I could not find it in my heart to entertain a doubt of her integrity. I could have staked my life that she was clear of blame, and, though all was dark at the present, that the explanation of the mystery would show her part in these events to be both right and needful. It was true, let me cudgel my imagination as I pleased, that I could invent no theory of her relations to Northmour; but I felt none the less sure of my conclusion because it was founded on instinct in place of reason, and, as I may say, went to sleep that night with the thought of her under my pillow.

Next day she came out about the same hour alone, and, as soon as the sand-hills concealed her from the pavilion, drew nearer to the edge, and called me by name in guarded

tones. I was astonished to observe that she was deadly
pale, and seemingly under the influence of strong emotion.

"Mr. Cassilis!" she cried; "Mr. Cassilis!"

I appeared at once, and leaped down upon the beach. A
remarkable air of relief overspread her countenance as soon
as she saw me.

"Oh!" she cried, with a hoarse sound, like one whose
bosom has been lightened of a weight. And then, "Thank
God you are still safe!" she added; "I knew, if you were, you
would be here." (Was not this strange? So swiftly and
wisely does Nature prepare our hearts for these great life-
long intimacies, that both my wife and I had been given a
presentiment on this the second day of our acquaintance. I
had even then hoped that she would seek me; she had felt
sure that she would find me.) "Do not," she went on swiftly,
"do not stay in this place. Promise me that you will sleep
no longer in that wood. You do not know how I suffer; all
last night I could not sleep for thinking of your peril."

"Peril?" I repeated. "Peril from whom? From Northmour?"

"Not so," she said. "Did you think I would tell him after
what you said?"

"Not from Northmour?" I repeated. "Then how? From
whom? I see none to be afraid of."

"You must not ask me," was her reply, "for I am not
free to tell you. Only believe me, and go hence—believe
me, and go away quickly, quickly for your life!"

An appeal to his alarm is never a good plan to rid one's
self of a spirited young man. My obstinacy was but increased by what she said, and I made it a point of honor to
remain. And her solicitude for my safety still more con-
firmed me in the resolve.

"You must not think me inquisitive, madam," I replied;
"but, if Graden is so dangerous a place, you yourself perhaps remain here at some risk."

She only looked at me reproachfully.

"You and your father——" I resumed; but she interrupted me almost with a gasp.

"My father! How do you know that?" she cried.

"I saw you together when you landed," was my answer; and I do not know why, but it seemed satisfactory to both of us, as indeed it was the truth. "But," I continued, "you need have no fear from me. I see you have some reason to be secret, and, you may believe me, your secret is as safe with me as if I were in Graden Floe. I have scarce spoken to any one for years; my horse is my only companion, and even he, poor beast, is not beside me. You see, then, you may count on me for silence. So tell me the truth, my dear young lady, are you not in danger?"

"Mr. Northmour says you are an honorable man," she returned, "and I believe it when I see you. I will tell you so much; you are right; we are in dreadful, dreadful danger, and you share it by remaining where you are."

"Ah!" said I; "you have heard of me from Northmour? And he gives me a good character?"

"I asked him about you last night," was her reply. "I pretended," she hesitated, "I pretended to have met you long ago, and spoken to you of him. It was not true; but I could not help myself without betraying you, and you had put me in a difficulty. He praised you highly."

"And—you may permit me one question—does this danger come from Northmour?" I asked.

"From Mr. Northmour?" she cried. "Oh, no; he stays with us to share it."

"While you propose that I should run away?" I said. "You do not rate me very high."

"Why should you stay?" she asked. "You are no friend of ours."

I know not what came over me, for I had not been conscious of a similiar weakness since I was a child, but I was so mortified by this retort that my eyes pricked and filled with tears, as I continued to gaze upon her face.

"No, no," she said, in a changed voice; "I did not mean the words unkindly."

"It was I who offended," I said; and I held out my hand with a look of appeal that somehow touched her, for she gave me hers at once, and even eagerly. I held it for a while in mine, and gazed into her eyes. It was she who first tore her hand away, and, forgetting all about her request and the promise she had sought to extort, ran at the top of her speed, and without turning, till she was out of sight. And then I knew that I loved her, and thought in my glad heart that she—she herself—was not indifferent to my suit. Many a time she has denied it in after days, but it was with a smiling and not a serious denial. For my part, I am sure our hands would not have lain so closely in each other if she had not begun to melt to me already. And, when all is said, it is no great contention, since, by her own avowal, she began to love me on the morrow.

And yet on the morrow very little took place. She came and called me down as on the day before, upbraided me for lingering at Graden, and, when she found I was still obdurate, began to ask me more particularly as to my arrival. I told her by what series of accidents I had come to witness their disembarkation, and how I had determined to remain, partly from the interest which had been wakened in me by Northmour's guests, and partly because of his own murderous attack. As to the former, I fear I was disingenuous, and led her to regard herself as having been an attraction to me from the first moment that I saw her on the links. It relieves my heart to make this confession even now, when my wife is with God, and already knows all things, and the honesty of my purpose even in this; for while she lived, although it often pricked my conscience, I had never the hardihood to undeceive her. Even a little secret, in such a married life as ours, is like the rose-leaf which kept the Princess from her sleep.

From this the talk branched into other subjects, and I told her much about my lonely and wandering existence;

she, for her part, giving ear, and saying little. Although we spoke very naturally, and latterly on topics that might seem indifferent, we were both sweetly agitated. Too soon it was time for her to go; and we separated, as if by mutual consent, without shaking hands, for both knew that, between us, it was no idle ceremony.

The next, and that was the fourth day of our acquaintance, we met in the same spot, but early in the morning, with much familiarity and yet much timidity on either side. When she had once more spoken about my danger—and that, I understood, was her excuse for coming—I, who had prepared a great deal of talk during the night, began to tell her how highly I valued her kind interest, and how no one had ever cared to hear about my life, nor had I ever cared to relate it, before yesterday. Suddenly she interrupted me, saying with vehemence:

"And yet, if you knew who I was, you would not so much as speak to me!"

I told her such a thought was madness, and, little as we had met, I counted her already a dear friend; but my protestations seemed only to make her more desperate.

"My father is in hiding!" she cried.

"My dear," I said, forgetting for the first time to add "young lady," "what do I care? If he were in hiding twenty times over, would it make one thought of change in you?"

"Ah, but the cause!" she cried, "the cause! It is"—she faltered for a second—"it is disgraceful to us!"

CHAPTER IV

TELLS IN WHAT A STARTLING MANNER I LEARNED THAT I WAS NOT ALONE IN GRADEN SEA-WOOD

THIS was my wife's story, as I drew it from her among tears and sobs. Her name was Clara Huddlestone: it sounded very beautiful in my ears; but not so beautiful as that other name of Clara Cassilis, which she wore during the longer and, I thank God, the happier portion of her life. Her father, Bernard Huddlestone, had been a private banker in a very large way of business. Many years before, his affairs becoming disordered, he had been led to try dangerous, and at last criminal, expedients to retrieve himself from ruin. All was in vain; he became more and more cruelly involved, and found his honor lost at the same moment with his fortune. About this period, Northmour had been courting his daughter with great assiduity, though with small encouragement; and to him, knowing him thus disposed in his favor, Bernard Huddlestone turned for help in his extremity. It was not merely ruin and dishonor, nor merely a legal condemnation, that the unhappy man had brought upon his head. It seems he could have gone to prison with a light heart. What he feared, what kept him awake at night or recalled him from slumber into frenzy, was some secret, sudden, and unlawful attempt upon his life. Hence, he desired to bury his existence and escape to one of the islands in the South Pacific, and it was in Northmour's yacht, the "Red Earl," that he designed to go. The yacht picked them up clandestinely upon the coast of Wales, and had once more deposited them at Graden, till she could be refitted and provisioned for the longer voyage. Nor could Clara doubt that her hand had been stipulated as the price of passage. For, although Northmour was neither unkind nor even discourteous, he had shown himself in several instances somewhat overbold in speech and manner.

I listened, I need not say, with fixed attention, and put many questions as to the more mysterious part. It was in vain. She had no clear idea of what the blow was, nor of how it was expected to fall. Her father's alarm was unfeigned and physically prostrating, and he had thought more than once of making an unconditional surrender to the police. But the scheme was finally abandoned, for he was convinced that not even the strength of our English prisons could shelter him from his pursuers. He had had many affairs with Italy, and with Italians resident in London, in the later years of his business; and these last, as Clara fancied, were somehow connected with the doom that threatened him. He had shown great terror at the presence of an Italian seaman on board the "Red Earl," and had bitterly and repeatedly accused Northmour in consequence. The latter had protested that Beppo (that was the seaman's name) was a capital fellow, and could be trusted to the death; but Mr. Huddlestone had continued ever since to declare that all was lost, that it was only a question of days, and that Beppo would be the ruin of him yet.

I regarded the whole story as the hallucination of a mind shaken by calamity. He had suffered heavy loss by his Italian transactions; and hence the sight of an Italian was hateful to him, and the principal part in his nightmare would naturally enough be played by one of that nation.

"What your father wants," I said, "is a good doctor and some calming medicine."

"But Mr. Northmour?" objected Clara. "He is untroubled by losses, and yet he shares in this terror."

I could not help laughing at what I considered her simplicity.

"My dear," said I, "you have told me yourself what reward he has to look for. All is fair in love, you must remember; and if Northmour foments your father's terrors, it is not at all because he is afraid of any Italian man, but simply because he is infatuated with a charming Englishwoman."

She reminded me of his attack upon myself on the night of the disembarkation, and this I was unable to explain. In short, and from one thing to another, it was agreed between us that I should set out at once for the fisher village, Graden Wester, as it was called, look up all the newspapers I could find, and see for myself if there seemed any basis of fact for these continued alarms. The next morning, at the same hour and place, I was to make my report to Clara. She said no more on that occasion about my departure; nor, indeed, did she make it a secret that she clung to the thought of my proximity as something helpful and pleasant; and, for my part, I could not have left her, if she had gone upon her knees to ask it.

I reached Graden Wester before ten in the forenoon; for in those days I was an excellent pedestrian, and the distance, as I think I have said, was little over seven miles; fine walking all the way upon the springy turf. The village is one of the bleakest on that coast, which is saying much: there is a church in a hollow; a miserable haven in the rocks, where many boats have been lost as they returned from fishing; two or three score of stone houses arranged along the beach and in two streets, one leading from the harbor, and another striking out from it at right angles; and, at the corner of these two, a very dark and cheerless tavern, by way of principal hotel.

I had dressed myself somewhat more suitably to my station in life, and at once called upon the minister in his little manse beside the graveyard. He knew me, although it was more than nine years since we had met; and when I told him that I had been long upon a walking tour, and was behind with the news, readily lent me an armful of newspapers, dating from a month back to the day before. With these I sought the tavern, and, ordering some breakfast, sat down to study the "Huddlestone Failure."

It had been, it appeared, a very flagrant case. Thousands of persons were reduced to poverty; and one in particular had blown out his brains as soon as payment was suspended. It was strange to myself that, while I read these details, I continued rather to sympathize with Mr. Huddlestone than with his victims; so complete already was the empire of my love for Clara. A price was naturally set upon the banker's head; and, as the case was inexcusable and the public indignation thoroughly aroused, the unusual figure of 750*l.* was offered for his capture. He was reported to have large sums of money in his possession. One day, he had been heard of in Spain; the next, there was sure intelligence that he was still lurking between Manchester and Liverpool, or along the border of Wales; and the day after, a telegram would announce his arrival in Cuba or Yucatan. But in all this there was no word of an Italian, nor any sign of mystery.

In the very last paper, however, there was one item not so clear. The accountants who were charged to verify the failure had, it seemed, come upon the traces of a very large number of thousands, which figured for some time in the transactions of the house of Huddlestone; but which came from nowhere, and disappeared in the same mysterious fashion. It was only once referred to by name, and then under the initials "X. X."; but it had plainly been floated for the first time into the business at a period of great depression some six years ago. The name of a distinguished royal personage had been mentioned by rumor in connection with this sum. "The cowardly desperado"—such, I remember, was the editorial expression—was supposed to have escaped with a large part of this mysterious fund still in his possession.

I was still brooding over the fact, and trying to torture it into some connection with Mr. Huddlestone's danger, when a man entered the tavern and asked for some bread and cheese with a decided foreign accent.

"*Siete Italiano?*" said I.

"*Si, Signor,*" was his reply.

I said it was unusually far north to find one of his compatriots; at which he shrugged his shoulders, and replied that a man would go anywhere to find work. What work he could hope to find at Graden Wester, I was totally unable to conceive; and the incident struck so unpleasantly upon my mind that I asked the landlord, while he was counting me some change, whether he had ever before seen an Italian in the village. He said he had once seen some Norwegians, who had been shipwrecked on the other side of Graden Ness and rescued by the lifeboat from Cauld-haven.

"No!" said I; "but an Italian, like the man who has just had bread and cheese."

"What?" cried he, "yon black-avised fellow wi' the teeth?

Was he an I-talian? Weel, yon's the first that ever I saw,
an' I daresay he's like to be the last."

Even as he was speaking, I raised my eyes, and, casting
a glance into the street, beheld three men in earnest conversation together, and not thirty yards away. One of them
was my recent companion in the tavern parlor; the other
two, by their handsome, sallow features and soft hats,
should evidently belong to the same race. A crowd of village
children stood around them, gesticulating and talking gib-
berish in imitation. The trio looked singularly foreign to
the bleak dirty street in which they were standing, and the
dark gray heaven that overspread them; and I confess my
incredulity received at that moment a shock from which it
never recovered. I might reason with myself as I pleased,
but I could not argue down the effect of what I had seen and
I began to share in the Italian terror.

It was already drawing toward the close of the day before
I had returned the newspapers at the manse, and got well
forward on to the links on my way home. I shall never
forget that walk. It grew very cold and boisterous; the wind
sang in the short grass about my feet; thin rain showers
came running on the gusts; and an immense mountain range
of clouds began to arise out of the bosom of the sea. It
would be hard to imagine a more dismal evening; and
whether it was from these external influences, or because my
nerves were already affected by what I had heard and seen,
my thoughts were as gloomy as the weather.

The upper windows of the pavilion commanded a considerable spread of links in the direction of Graden Wester. To
avoid observation, it was necessary to hug the beach until I
had gained cover from the higher sand-hills on the little
headland, when I might strike across, through the hollows,
for the margin of the wood. The sun was about setting; the
tide was low, and all the quicksands uncovered; and I was
moving along, lost in unpleasant thought, when I was suddenly thunderstruck to perceive the prints of human feet.
They ran parallel to my own course, but low down upon the

beach instead of along the border of the turf; and, when I examined them, I saw at once, by the size and coarseness of the impression, that it was a stranger to me and to those in the pavilion who had recently passed that way. Not only so; but from the recklessness of the course which he had followed, steering near to the most formidable portions of the sand, he was as evidently a stranger to the country and to the ill-repute of Graden beach.

Step by step I followed the prints; until, a quarter of a mile further, I beheld them die away into the southeastern boundary of Graden Floe. There, whoever he was, the miserable man had perished. One or two gulls, who had, perhaps, seen him disappear, wheeled over his sepulchre with their usual melancholy piping. The sun had broken through the clouds by a last effort, and colored the wide level of quicksands with a dusky purple. I stood for some time gazing at the spot, chilled and disheartened by my own reflections, and with a strong and commanding consciousness of death. I remember wondering how long the tragedy had taken, and whether his screams had been audible at the pavilion. And then, making a strong resolution, I was about to tear myself away, when a gust fiercer than usual fell upon this quarter of the beach, and I saw, now whirling high in air, now skimming lightly across the surface of the sands, a soft black felt hat, somewhat conical in shape, such as I had remarked already on the heads of the Italians.

I believe, but I am not sure, that I uttered a cry. The wind was driving the hat shoreward, and I ran round the border of the floe to be ready against its arrival. The gust fell, dropping the hat for a while upon the quicksand, and then, once more freshening, landed it a few yards from where I stood. I seized it with the interest you may imagine. It had seen some service; indeed, it was rustier than either of those I had seen that day upon the street. The lining was red, stamped with the name of the maker, which I have forgotten, and that of the place of manufacture, Venedig. This (it is not yet forgotten) was the name given by the Austrians to the beautiful city of Venice, then, and for long after, a part of their dominions.

The shock was complete. I saw imaginary Italians upon every side; and for the first and, I may say, for the last time in my experience became overpowered by what is called a panic terror. I knew nothing, that is, to be afraid of, and yet I admit that I was heartily afraid; and it was with a sensible reluctance that I returned to my exposed and solitary camp in the Sea-Wood.

There I ate some cold porridge which had been left over from the night before, for I was disinclined to make a fire; and, feeling strengthened and reassured, dismissed all these fanciful terrors from my mind, and lay down to sleep with composure.

How long I may have slept it is impossible for me to guess; but I was awakened at last by a sudden, blinding flash of light into my face. It woke me like a blow. In an instant I was upon my knees. But the light had gone as suddenly as it came. The darkness was intense. And, as it was blowing great guns from the sea and pouring with rain, the noises of the storm effectually concealed all others.

It was, I dare say, half a minute before I regained my self-possession. But for two circumstances, I should have thought I had been awakened by some new and vivid form of nightmare. First, the flap of my tent, which I had shut carefully when I retired, was now unfastened; and, second, I could still perceive, with a sharpness that excluded any theory of hallucination, the smell of hot metal and of burning oil. The conclusion was obvious. I had been wakened by some one flashing a bull's-eye lantern in my face. It had been but a flash, and away. He had seen my face, and then gone. I asked myself the object of so strange a proceeding, and the answer came pat. The man, whoever he was, had thought to recognize me, and he had not. There was yet another question unresolved; and to this, I may say, I feared to give an answer; if he had recognized me, what would he have done?

My fears were immediately diverted from myself, for I saw that I had been visited in a mistake; and I became persuaded that some dreadful danger threatened the pavilion. It required some nerve to issue forth into the black and intricate thicket which surrounded and overhung the den; but I groped my way to the links, drenched with rain, beaten upon and deafened by the gusts, and fearing at every step to lay my hand upon some lurking adversary. The darkness was so complete that I might have been surrounded by an army and yet none the wiser, and the uproar of the gale so loud that my hearing was as useless as my sight.

For the rest of that night, which seemed interminably long, I patrolled the vicinity of the pavilion, without seeing a living creature or hearing any noise but the concert of the wind, the sea, and the rain. A light in the upper story filtered through a cranny of the shutter, and kept me company till the approach of dawn.

CHAPTER V

TELLS OF AN INTERVIEW BETWEEN NORTHMOUR, CLARA, AND MYSELF

WITH the first peep of day, I retired from the open to my old lair among the sand-hills, there to await the coming of my wife. The morning was gray, wild, and melancholy; the wind moderated before sunrise, and then went about, and blew in puffs from the shore; the sea began to go down, but the rain still fell without mercy. Over all the wilderness of links there was not a creature to be seen. Yet I felt sure the neighborhood was alive with skulking foes. The light that had been so suddenly and surprisingly flashed upon my face as I lay sleeping, and the hat that had been blown ashore by the wind from over Graden Floe, were two speaking signals of the peril that environed Clara and the party in the pavilion.

It was, perhaps, half-past seven, or nearer eight, before

I saw the door open, and that dear figure come toward me in the rain. I was waiting for her on the beach before she had crossed the sand-hills.

"I have had such trouble to come!" she cried. "They did not wish me to go walking in the rain."

"Clara," I said, "you are not frightened?"

"No," said she, with a simplicity that filled my heart with confidence. For my wife was the bravest as well as the best of women; in my experience I have not found the two go always together, but with her they did; and she combined the extreme of fortitude with the most endearing and beautiful virtues.

I told her what had happened; and, though her cheek grew visibly paler, she retained perfect control over her senses.

"You see now that I am safe," said I, in conclusion. "They do not mean to harm me; for, had they chosen, I was a dead man last night."

She laid her hand upon my arm.

"And I had no presentiment!" she cried.

Her accent thrilled me with delight. I put my arm about her, and strained her to my side; and, before either of us was aware, her hands were on my shoulders and my lips upon her mouth. Yet up to that moment no word of love had passed between us. To this day I remember the touch of her cheek, which was wet and cold with the rain; and many a time since, when she has been washing her face, I have kissed it again for the sake of that morning on the beach. Now that she is taken from me, and I finish my pilgrimage alone, I recall our old lovingkindnesses and the deep honesty and affection which united us, and my present loss seems but a trifle in comparison.

We may have thus stood for some seconds—for time passes quickly with lovers—before we were startled by a peal of laughter close at hand. It was not natural mirth, but seemed to be affected in order to conceal an angrier feeling. We both turned, though I still kept my left arm about Clara's waist; nor did she seek to withdraw herself; and there, a few paces off upon the beach, stood Northmour, his head lowered, his hands behind his back, his nostrils white with passion.

"Ah! Cassilis!" he said, as I disclosed my face.

"That same," said I; for I was not at all put about.

"And so, Miss Huddlestone," he continued slowly but savagely, "this is how you keep your faith to your father and to me? This is the value you set upon your father's life? And you are so infatuated with this young gentleman that you must brave ruin, and decency, and common human caution—"

"Miss Huddlestone—" I was beginning to interrupt him, when he, in his turn, cut in brutally—

"You hold your tongue," said he; "I am speaking to that girl."

"That girl, as you call her, is my wife," said I; and my wife only leaned a little nearer, so that I knew she had affirmed my words.

"Your what?" he cried. "You lie!"

"Northmour," I said, "we all know you have a bad temper, and I am the last man to be irritated by words. For all that, I propose that you speak lower, for I am convinced that we are not alone."

He looked round him, and it was plain my remark had in some degree sobered his passion. "What do you mean?" he asked.

I only said one word: "Italians."

He swore a round oath, and looked at us, from one to the other.

"Mr. Cassilis knows all that I know," said my wife.

"What I want to know," he broke out, "is where the devil Mr. Cassilis comes from, and what the devil Mr. Cassilis is doing here. You say you are married; that I do not believe. If you were, Graden Floe would soon divorce you; four minutes and a half, Cassilis. I keep my private cemetery for my friends."

"It took somewhat longer," said I, "for that Italian."

He looked at me for a moment half daunted, and then, almost civilly, asked me to tell my story. "You have too much the advantage of me, Cassilis," he added. I complied of course; and he listened, with several ejaculations, while I told him how I had come to Graden; that it was I whom he had tried to murder on the night of landing; and what I had subsequently seen and heard of the Italians.

"Well," said he, when I had done, "it is here at last; there is no mistake about that. And what, may I ask, do you propose to do?"

"I propose to stay with you and lend a hand," said I.

"You are a brave man," he returned, with a peculiar intonation.

"I am not afraid," said I.

"And so," he continued, "I am to understand that you two are married? And you stand up to it before my face, Miss Huddlestone?"

"We are not yet married," said Clara; "but we shall be as soon as we can."

"Bravo!" cried Northmour. "And the bargain? D—n it, you're not a fool, young woman; I may call a spade a spade with you. How about the bargain? You know as well as I do what your father's life depends upon. I have only to put my hands under my coat-tails and walk away, and his throat would be cut before the evening."

"Yes, Mr. Northmour," returned Clara, with great spirit; "but that is what you will never do. You made a bargain that was unworthy of a gentleman; but you are a gentleman for all that, and you will never desert a man whom you have begun to help."

"Aha!" said he. "You think I will give my yacht for nothing? You think I will risk my life and liberty for love of the old gentleman; and then, I suppose, be best man at the wedding, to wind up? Well," he added, with an old smile, "perhaps you are not altogether wrong. But ask

Cassilis here. *He* knows me. Am I a man to trust? Am I safe and scrupulous? Am I kind?"

"I know you talk a great deal, and sometimes, I think, very foolishly," replied Clara, "but I know you are a gentleman, and I am not the least afraid."

He looked at her with a peculiar approval and admiration; then, turning to me, "Do you think I would give her up without a struggle, Frank?" said he. "I tell you plainly, you look out. The next time we come to blows—"

"Will make the third," I interrupted, smiling.

"Ay, true; so it will," he said. "I had forgotten. Well, the third time's lucky."

"The third time, you mean, you will have the crew of the 'Red Earl' to help," I said.

"Do you hear him?" he asked, turning to my wife.

"I hear two men speaking like cowards," said she. "I should despise myself either to think or speak like that. And neither of you believe one word that you are saying, which makes it the more wicked and silly."

"She's a trump!" cried Northmour. "But she's not yet Mrs. Cassilis. I say no more. The present is not for me."

Then my wife surprised me.

"I leave you here," she said suddenly. "My father has been too long alone. But remember this: you are to be friends, for you are both good friends to me."

She has since told me her reason for this step. As long as she remained, she declares that we two would have continued to quarrel; and I suppose that she was right, for when she was gone we fell at once into a sort of confidentiality.

Northmour stared after her as she went away over the sand-hill.

"She is the only woman in the world!" he exclaimed with an oath. "Look at her action."

I, for my part, leaped at this opportunity for a little further light.

"See here, Northmour," said I; "we are all in a tight place, are we not?"

"I believe you, my boy," he answered, looking me in the eyes, and with great emphasis. "We have all hell upon us, that's the truth. You may believe me or not, but I'm afraid of my life."

"Tell me one thing," said I. "What are they after, these Italians? What do they want with Mr. Huddlestone?"

"Don't you know?" he cried. "The black old scamp had Carbonaro funds on a deposit—two hundred and eighty thousand; and of course he gambled it away on stocks. There was to have been a revolution in the Tridentino, or Parma; but the revolution is off, and the whole wasps' nest is after Huddlestone. We shall all be lucky if we can save our skins."

"The Carbonari!" I exclaimed; "God help him indeed!"

"Amen!" said Northmour. "And now, look here: I have said that we are in a fix; and, frankly, I shall be glad of your help. If I can't save Huddlestone, I want at least to save the girl. Come and stay in the pavilion; and, there's my hand on it, I shall act as your friend until the old man is either clear or dead. But," he added, "once that is settled, you become my rival once again, and I warn you—mind yourself."

"Done!" said I; and we shook hands.

"And now let us go directly to the fort," said Northmour; and he began to lead the way through the rain.

CHAPTER VI

TELLS OF MY INTRODUCTION TO THE TALL MAN

WE were admitted to the pavilion by Clara, and I was surprised by the completeness and security of the defenses. A barricade of great strength, and yet easy to displace, supported the door against any violence from without; and the shutters of the dining-room, into which I was led directly, and which was feebly illuminated by a lamp, were even more elaborately fortified. The panels were strengthened by bars and cross-bars; and these, in their turn, were kept in position by a system of braces and struts, some abutting on the floor, some on the roof, and others, in fine, against the opposite wall of the apartment. It was at once a solid and well-designed piece of carpentry; and I did not seek to conceal my admiration.

"I am the engineer," said Northmour. "You remember the planks in the garden? Behold them!"

"I did not know you had so many talents," said I.

"Are you armed?" he continued, pointing to an array of guns and pistols, all in admirable order, which stood in line against the wall or were displayed upon the sideboard.

"Thank you," I returned; "I have gone armed since our last encounter. But, to tell you the truth, I have had nothing to eat since early yesterday evening."

Northmour produced some cold meat, to which I eagerly set myself, and a bottle of good Burgundy, by which, wet as I was, I did not scruple to profit. I have always been an extreme temperance man on principle; but it is useless to push principle to excess, and on this occasion I believe that I finished three-quarters of the bottle. As I ate, I still continued to admire the preparations for defense.

"We could stand a siege," I said at length.

"Ye—es," drawled Northmour; "a very little one, perhaps. It is not so much the strength of the pavilion I misdoubt; it is the double danger that kills me. If we get to shooting, wild as the country is, some one is sure to hear it, and then—why then it's the same thing, only different, as they say: caged by law, or killed by Carbonari. There's the choice. It is a devilish bad thing to have the law against you in this world, and so I tell the old gentleman upstairs. He is quite of my way of thinking."

"Speaking of that," said I, "what kind of person is he?"

"Oh, he!" cried the other; "he's a rancid fellow, as far as he goes. I should like to have his neck wrung to-morrow

by all the devils in Italy. I am not in this affair for him.
You take me? I made a bargain for Missy's hand, and I
mean to have it, too."

"That, by the way," said I. "I understand. But how will
Mr. Huddlestone take my intrusion?"

"Leave that to Clara," returned Northmour.

I could have struck him in the face for this coarse familiarity; but I respected the truce, as, I am bound to say,
did Northmour, and so long as the danger continued not
a cloud arose in our relation. I bear him this testimony with
the most unfeigned satisfaction; nor am I without pride
when I look back upon my own behavior. For surely no
two men were ever left in a position so invidious and
irritating.

As soon as I had done eating, we proceeded to inspect
the lower floor. Window by window we tried the different
supports, now and then making an inconsiderable change;
and the strokes of the hammer sounded with startling loud-
ness through the house. I proposed, I remember, to make
loopholes; but he told me they were already made in the
windows of the upper story. It was an anxious business
this inspection, and left me down-hearted. There were two
doors and five windows to protect, and, counting Clara, only
four of us to defend them against an unknown number of
foes. I communicated my doubts to Northmour, who assured
me, with unmoved composure, that he entirely shared them.

"Before morning," said he, "we shall all be butchered and
buried in Graden Floe. For me, that is written."

I could not help shuddering at the mention of the quicksands, but reminded Northmour that our enemies had
spared me in the wood.

"Do not flatter yourself," said he. "Then you were not
in the same boat with the old gentleman; now you are. It's
the floe for all of us, mark my words."

I trembled for Clara; and just then her dear voice was
heard calling us to come upstairs. Northmour showed me
the way, and, when he had reached the landing, knocked

at the door of what used to be called *My Uncle's Bedroom,* as the founder of the pavilion had designed it especially for himself.

"Come in, Northmour; come in, dear Mr. Cassilis," said a voice from within.

Pushing open the door, Northmour admitted me before him into the apartment. As I came in I could see the daughter slipping out by the side door into the study, which had been prepared as her bedroom. In the bed, which was drawn back against the wall, instead of standing, as I had last seen it, boldly across the window, sat Bernard Huddlestone, the defaulting banker. Little as I had seen of him by the shifting light of the lantern on the links, I had no difficulty in recognizing him for the same. He had a long and sallow countenance, surrounded by a long red beard and side-whiskers. His broken nose and high cheekbones gave him somewhat the air of a Kalmuck, and his light eyes shone with the excitement of a high fever. He wore a skull-cap of black silk; a huge Bible lay open before him on the bed, with a pair of gold spectacles in the place, and a pile of other books lay on the stand by his side. The green curtains lent a cadaverous shade to his cheek; and, as he sat propped on pillows, his great stature was painfully hunched, and his head protruded till it overhung his knees. I believe if he had not died otherwise, he must have fallen a victim to consumption in the course of but a very few weeks.

He held out to me a hand, long, thin, and disagreeably hairy.

"Come in, come in, Mr. Cassilis," said he. "Another protector—ahem!—another protector. Always welcome as a friend of my daughter's, Mr. Cassilis. How they have rallied about me, my daughter's friends! May God in heaven bless and reward them for it!"

I gave him my hand, of course, because I could not help it; but the sympathy I had been prepared to feel for Clara's father was immediately soured by his appearance, and the wheedling, unreal tones in which he spoke.

"Cassilis is a good man," said Northmour; "worth ten."

"So I hear," cried Mr. Huddlestone eagerly; "so my girl tells me. Ah, Mr. Cassilis, my sin has found me out, you see! I am very low, very low; but I hope equally penitent. We must all come to the throne of grace at last, Mr. Cassilis. For my part, I come late indeed; but with unfeigned humility, I trust."

"Fiddle-de-dee!" said Northmour roughly.

"No, no, dear Northmour!" cried the banker. "You must not say that; you must not try to shake me. You forget, my dear, good boy, you forget I may be called this very night before my Maker."

His excitement was pitiful to behold; and I felt myself grow indignant with Northmour, whose infidel opinions I well knew and heartily derided, as he continued to taunt the poor sinner out of his humor of repentance.

"Pooh, my dear Huddlestone!" said he. "You do yourself injustice. You are a man of the world inside and out, and were up to all kinds of mischief before I was born. Your conscience is tanned like South American leather—only you forgot to tan your liver, and that, if you will believe me, is the seat of the annoyance."

"Rogue, rogue! bad boy!" said Mr. Huddlestone, shaking his finger. "I am no precisian, if you come to that; I always hated a precisian; but I never lost hold of something better through it all. I have been a bad boy, Mr. Cassilis; I do not seek to deny that; but it was after my wife's death, and you know, with a widower, it's a different thing: sinful —I won't say no; but there is a gradation, we shall hope. And talking of that—Hark!" he broke out suddenly, his hand raised, his fingers spread, his face racked with interest and terror. "Only the rain, bless God!" he added, after a pause, and with indescribable relief.

For some seconds he lay back among the pillows like a man near to fainting; then he gathered himself together, and, in somewhat tremulous tones, began once more to thank me for the share I was prepared to take in his defense.

"One question, sir," said I, when he had paused. "Is it true that you have money with you?"

He seemed annoyed by the question, but admitted with reluctance that he had a little.

"Well," I continued, "it is their money they are after, is it not? Why not give it up to them?"

"Ah!" replied he, shaking his head, "I have tried that already, Mr. Cassilis; and alas that it should be so! but it is blood they want."

"Huddlestone, that's a little less than fair," said Northmour. "You should mention that what you offered them was upward of two hundred thousand short. The deficit is worth a reference; it is for what they call a cool sum, Frank. Then, you see, the fellows reason in their clear Italian way; and it seems to them, as indeed it seems to me, that they may just as well have both while they're about it—money and blood together, by George, and no more trouble for the extra pleasure."

"Is it in the pavilion." I asked.

"It is; and I wish it were in the bottom of the sea instead," said Northmour; and then suddenly—"What are you making faces at me for?" he cried to Mr. Huddlestone, on whom I had unconsciously turned my back. "Do you think Cassilis would sell you?"

Mr. Huddlestone protested that nothing had been further from his mind.

"It is a good thing," retorted Northmour in his ugliest manner. "You might end by wearying us. What were you going to say?" he added, turning to me.

"I was going to propose an occupation for the afternoon," said I. "Let us carry that money out, piece by piece, and lay it down before the pavilion door. If the Carbonari come, why, it's theirs at any rate."

"No, no," cried Mr. Huddlestone; "it does not, it can not belong to them! It should be distributed *pro rata* among all my creditors."

"Come now, Huddlestone," said Northmour, "none of that."

"Well, but my daughter," moaned the wretched man.

"Your daughter will do well enough. Here are two suitors, Cassilis and I, neither of us beggars, between whom she has to choose. And as for yourself, to make an end of arguments, you have no right to a farthing, and, unless I'm much mistaken, you are going to die."

It was certainly very cruelly said; but Mr. Huddlestone was a man who attracted little sympathy; and, although I saw him wince and shudder, I mentally indorsed the rebuke; nay, I added a contribution of my own.

"Northmour and I," I said, "are willing enough to help you to save your life, but not to escape with stolen property."

He struggled for a while with himself, as though he were on the point of giving way to anger, but prudence had the best of the controversy.

"My dear boys," he said, "do with me or my money what you will. I leave all in your hands. Let me compose myself."

And so we left him, gladly enough I am sure. The last that I saw, he had once more taken up his great Bible, and with tremulous hands was adjusting his spectacles to read.

CHAPTER VII

TELLS HOW A WORD WAS CRIED THROUGH THE PAVILION WINDOW

The recollection of that afternoon will always be graven on my mind. Northmour and I were persuaded that an attack was imminent; and if it had been in our power to alter in any way the order of events, that power would have been used to precipitate rather than delay the critical moment. The worst was to be anticipated, yet we could conceive no extremity so miserable as the suspense we were now suffering. I have never been an eager, though always a great, reader; but I never knew books so insipid as those which I took up and cast aside that afternoon in the pavilion. Even talk became impossible, as the hours went on. One or other was always listening for some sound or peering from an upstairs' window over the links. And yet not a sign indicated the presence of our foes.

We debated over and over again my proposal with regard to the money; and had we been in complete possession of our faculties, I am sure we should have condemned it as unwise; but we were flustered with alarm, grasped at a straw, and determined, although it was as much as advertising Mr. Huddlestone's presence in the pavilion, to carry my proposal into effect.

The sum was part in specie, part in bank paper, and part in circular notes payable to the name of James Gregory. We took it out, counted it, enclosed it once more in a despatch-box belonging to Northmour, and prepared a letter in Italian which he tied to the handle. It was signed by both of us under oath, and declared that this was all the money which had escaped the failure of the house of Huddlestone. This was, perhaps, the maddest action ever perpetrated by two persons professing to be sane. Had the despatch-box fallen into other hands than those for which it was intended, we stood criminally convicted on our own written testimony; but, as I have said, we were neither of us in a condition to judge soberly, and had a thirst for action that drove us to do something, right or wrong, rather than endure the agony of waiting. Moreover, as we were both convinced that the hollows of the links were alive with hidden spies upon our movements, we hoped that our appearance with the box might lead to a parley, and, perhaps, a compromise.

It was nearly three when we issued from the pavilion. The rain had taken off; the sun shone quite cheerfully. I have never seen the gulls fly so close about the house or approach so fearlessly to human beings. On the very doorstep one flapped heavily past our heads, and uttered its wild cry in my very ear.

"There is an omen for you," said Northmour, who like all freethinkers was much under the influence of superstition. "They think we are already dead."

I made some light rejoinder, but it was with half my heart; for the circumstance had impressed me.

A yard or two before the gate, on a patch of smooth turf, we set down the despatch-box; and Northmour waved a white handkerchief over his head. Nothing replied. We raised our voices, and cried aloud in Italian that we were there as ambassadors to arrange the quarrel; but the stillness remained unbroken save by the sea-gulls and the surf. I had a weight at my heart when we desisted; and I saw that even Northmour was unusually pale. He looked over his shoulder nervously, as though he feared that some one had crept between him and the pavilion door.

"By God," he said in a whisper, "this is too much for me!"

I replied in the same key: "Suppose there should be none, after all!"

"Look there," he returned, nodding with his head, as though he had been afraid to point.

I glanced in the direction indicated; and there, from the northern quarter of the Sea-Wood, beheld a thin column of smoke rising steadily against the now cloudless sky.

"Northmour," I said (we still continued to talk in whispers), "it is not possible to endure this suspense. I prefer death fifty times over. Stay you here to watch the pavilion; I will go forward and make sure, if I have to walk right into their camp."

He looked once again all around him with puckered eyes, and then nodded assentingly to my proposal.

My heart beat like a sledge-hammer as I set out walking rapidly in the direction of the smoke; and, though up to that moment I had felt chill and shivering, I was suddenly conscious of a glow of heat over all my body. The ground in this direction was very uneven; a hundred men might have lain hidden in as many square yards about my path.

But I had not practised the business in vain, chose such routes as cut at the very root of concealment, and, by keeping along the most convenient ridges, commanded several hollows at a time. It was not long before I was rewarded for my caution. Coming suddenly on to a mound somewhat more elevated than the surrounding hummocks, I saw, not thirty yards away, a man bent almost double, and running as fast as his attitude permitted, along the bottom of a gully. I had dislodged one of the spies from his ambush. As soon as I sighted him, I called loudly both in English and Italian; and he, seeing concealment was no longer possible, straightened himself out, leaped from the gully, and made off as straight as an arrow for the borders of the wood.

It was none of my business to pursue; I had learned what I wanted—that we were beleaguered and watched in the pavilion; and I returned at once, walking as nearly as possible in my old footsteps, to where Northmour awaited me beside the despatch-box. He was even paler than when I had left him, and his voice shook a little.

"Could you see what he was like?" he asked.

"He kept his back turned," I replied.

"Let us get into the house, Frank. I don't think I'm a coward, but I can stand no more of this," he whispered.

All was still and sunshiny about the pavilion as we turned to re-enter it; even the gulls had flown in a wider circuit, and were seen flickering along the beach and sand-hills; and this loneliness terrified me more than a regiment under arms. It was not until the door was barricaded that I could draw a full inspiration and relieve the weight that lay upon my bosom. Northmour and I exchanged a steady glance; and I suppose each made his own reflections on the white and startled aspect of the other.

"You were right," I said. "All is over. Shake hands, old man, for the last time."

"Yes," replied he, "I will shake hands; for, as sure as I am here, I bear no malice. But, remember, if, by some im-

possible accident, we should give the slip to these blackguards, I'll take the upper hand of you by fair or foul."

"Oh," said I, "you weary me!"

He seemed hurt, and walked away in silence to the foot
of the stairs, where he paused.

"You do not understand," said he. "I am not a swindler,
and I guard myself; that is all. It may weary you or not,
Mr. Cassilis, I do not care a rush; I speak for my own satisfaction, and not for your amusement. You had better go
upstairs and court the girl; for my part, I stay here."

"And I stay with you," I returned. "Do you think I
would steal a march, even with your permission?"

"Frank," he said, smiling, "it's a pity you are an ass, for
you have the makings of a man. I think I must be *fey* to-
day; you can not irritate me even when you try. Do you
know," he continued softly, "I think we are the two most
miserable men in England, you and I? we have got on to
thirty without wife or child, or so much as a shop to look
after—poor, pitiful, lost devils, both! And now we clash
about a girl! As if there were not several millions in the
United Kingdom! Ah, Frank, Frank, the one who loses
this throw, be it you or me, he has my pity! It were better
for him—how does the Bible say?—that a millstone were
hanged about his neck and he were cast into the depths of
the sea. Let us take a drink," he concluded suddenly, but
without any levity of tone.

I was touched by his words, and consented. He sat down
on the table in the dining-room, and held up the glass of
sherry to his eye.

"If you beat me, Frank," he said, "I shall take to drink.
What will you do, if it goes the other way?"

"God knows," I returned.

"Well," said he, "here is a toast in the meantime: *'Italia
irredenta!'* "

The remainder of the day was passed in the same dreadful tedium and suspense. I laid the table for dinner, while
Northmour and Clara prepared the meal together in the

kitchen. I could hear their talk as I went to and fro, and was surprised to find it ran all the time upon myself. North-mour again bracketed us together, and rallied Clara on a choice of husbands; but he continued to speak of me with some feeling, and uttered nothing to my prejudice unless he included himself in the condemnation. This awakened a sense of gratitude in my heart, which combined with the immediateness of our peril to fill my eyes with tears. After all, I thought—and perhaps the thought was laughably vain —we were here, three very noble human beings to perish in defense of a thieving banker.

Before we sat down to table, I looked forth from an upstairs window. The day was beginning to decline; the links were utterly deserted; the despatch-box still lay un-touched where we had left it hours before.

Mr. Huddlestone, in a long yellow dressing-gown, took one end of the table, Clara the other; while Northmour and I faced each other from the sides. The lamp was brightly trimmed; the wine was good; the viands, although mostly cold, excellent of their sort. We seemed to have agreed tacitly; all reference to the impending catastrophe was care-fully avoided; and, considering our tragic circumstances, we made a merrier party than could have been expected. From time to time, it is true, Northmour or I would rise from the table and make a round of the defenses; and, on each of these occasions, Mr. Huddlestone was recalled to a sense of his tragic predicament, glanced up with ghastly eyes, and bore for an instant on his countenance the stamp of terror. But he hastened to empty his glass, wiped his forehead with his handkerchief, and joined again in the conversation.

I was astonished at the wit and information he displayed. Mr. Huddlestone's was certainly no ordinary character; he had read and observed for himself; his gifts were sound; and, though I could never have learned to love the man, I began to understand his success in business, and the great respect in which he had been held before his failure. He had, above all, the talent of society; and though I never heard him speak but on this one and most unfavorable occasion, I set him down among the most brilliant conversationalists I ever met.

He was relating with great gusto, and seemingly no feeling of shame, the maneuvres of a scoundrelly commission merchant whom he had known and studied in his youth, and we were all listening with an odd mixture of mirth and embarrassment, when our little party was brought abruptly to an end in the most startling manner.

A noise like that of a wet finger on the window-pane interrupted Mr. Huddlestone's tale; and in an instant we were all four as white as paper, and sat tongue-tied and motionless around the table.

"A snail," I said at last; for I had heard that these animals make a noise somewhat similar in character.

"Snail be d——d!" said Northmour. "Hush!"

The same sound was repeated twice at regular intervals; and then a formidable voice shouted through the shutters the Italian word *"Traditore!"*

Mr. Huddlestone threw his head in the air; his eyelids quivered; next moment he fell insensible below the table. Northmour and I had each run to the armory and seized a gun. Clara was on her feet with her hand at her throat.

So we stood waiting, for we thought the hour of attack was certainly come; but second passed after second, and all but the surf remained silent in the neighborhood of the pavilion.

"Quick," said Northmour; "upstairs with him before they come."

CHAPTER VIII

TELLS THE LAST OF THE TALL MAN

SOMEHOW or other, by hook and crook, and between the three of us, we got Bernard Huddlestone bundled upstairs and laid upon the bed in My Uncle's Room. During the whole process, which was rough enough, he gave no sign of consciousness, and he remained, as we had thrown him, without changing the position of a finger. His daughter opened his shirt and began to wet his head and bosom; while Northmour and I ran to the window. The weather continued clear; the moon, which was now about full, had risen and shed a very clear light upon the links; yet, strain our eyes as we might, we could distinguish nothing moving. A few dark spots, more or less, on the uneven expanse were not to be identified; they might be crouching men, they might be shadows; it was impossible to be sure.

"Thank God," said Northmour, "Aggie is not coming to-night."

Aggie was the name of the old nurse; he had not thought of her till now; but that he should think of her at all was a trait that surprised me in the man.

We were again reduced to waiting. Northmour went to the fireplace and spread his hands before the red embers, as if he were cold. I followed him mechanically with my eyes, and in so doing turned my back upon the window. At that moment a very faint report was audible from without, and a ball shivered a pane of glass, and buried itself in the shutter two inches from my head. I heard Clara scream; and though I whipped instantly out of range and into a corner, she was there, so to speak, before me, beseeching to know if I were hurt. I felt that I could stand to be shot at every day and all day long, with such marks of solicitude for a reward; and I continued to reassure her with the tenderest caresses and in complete forgetfulness of our situation till the voice of Northmour recalled me to myself.

"An air-gun," he said. "They wish to make no noise."

I put Clara aside and looked at him. He was standing with his back to the fire and his hands clasped behind him; and I knew by the black look on his face that passion was boiling within. I had seen just such a look before he attacked me, that March night, in the adjoining chamber; and, though I could make every allowance for his anger, I confess I trembled for the consequences. He gazed straight before him; but he could see us with the tail of his eye, and his temper kept rising like a gale of wind. With regular battle awaiting us outside, this prospect of an internecine strife within the walls began to daunt me.

Suddenly, as I was thus closely watching his expression and prepared against the worst, I saw a change, a flash, a look of relief, upon his face. He took up the lamp which stood beside him on the table, and turned to us with an air of some excitement.

"There is one point that we must know," said he. "Are they going to butcher the lot of us, or only Huddlestone? Did they take you for him, or fire at you for your own *beaux yeux?*"

"They took me for him, for certain," I replied. "I am near as tall, and my head is fair."

"I am going to make sure," returned Northmour; and he stepped up to the window, holding the lamp above his head, and stood there, quietly affronting death, for half a minute.

Clara sought to rush forward and pull him from the place of danger; but I had the pardonable selfishness to hold her back by force.

"Yes," said Northmour, turning coolly from the window; "it's only Huddlestone they want."

"Oh, Mr. Northmour!" cried Clara; but found no more to add; the temerity she had just witnessed seeming beyond the reach of words.

He, on his part, looked at me, cocking his head with a fire of triumph in his eyes; and I understood at once that he had thus hazarded his life merely to attract Clara's notice, and depose me from my position as the hero of the hour. He snapped his fingers.

"The fire is only beginning," said he. "When they warm up to their work, they won't be so particular."

A voice was now heard hailing us from the entrance. From the window we could see the figure of a man in the moonlight; he stood motionless, his face uplifted to ours, and a rag of something white on his extended arm; and as we looked right down upon him, though he was a good many yards distant on the links, we could see the moonlight glitter on his eyes.

He opened his lips again, and spoke for some minutes on end, in a key so loud that he might have been heard in every corner of the pavilion, and as far away as the borders of the wood. It was the same voice that had already shouted *"Traditore!"* through the shutters of the dining-room; this time it made a complete and clear statement. If the traitor "Oddlestone" were given up, all others should be spared; if not, no one should escape to tell the tale.

"Well, Huddlestone, what do you say to that?" asked Northmour, turning to the bed.

Up to that moment the banker had given no sign of life, and I, at least, had supposed him to be still lying in a faint; but he replied at once, and in such tones as I have never heard elsewhere, save from a delirious patient, adjured and besought us not to desert him. It was the most hideous and abject performance that my imagination can conceive.

"Enough," cried Northmour; and then he threw open the window, leaned out into the night, and in a tone of exultation, and with a total forgetfulness of what was due to the presence of a lady, poured out upon the ambassador a string of the most abominable raillery both in English and Italian, and bade him begone where he had come from. I believe that nothing so delighted Northmour at that moment as the thought that we must all infallibly perish before the night was out.

Meantime the Italian put his flag of truce into his pocket, and disappeared, at a leisurely pace, among the sand-hills.

"They make honorable war," said Northmour. "They are all gentlemen and soldiers. For the credit of the thing, I wish we could change sides—you and I, Frank, and you too, Missy, my darling—and leave that being on the bed to some one else. Tut! Don't look shocked! We are all going post to what they call eternity, and may as well be aboveboard while there's time. As far as I'm concerned, if I could first strangle Huddlestone and then get Clara in my arms, I could die with some pride and satisfaction. And as it is, by God, I'll have a kiss!"

Before I could do anything to interfere, he had rudely embraced and repeatedly kissed the resisting girl. Next moment I had pulled him away with fury, and flung him heavily against the wall. He laughed loud and long, and I feared his wits had given way under the strain; for even in the best of days he had been a sparing and a quiet laugher.

"Now, Frank," said he, when his mirth was somewhat appeased, "it's your turn. Here's my hand. Good-by; farewell!" Then, seeing me stand rigid and indignant, and holding Clara to my side—"Man!" he broke out, "are you angry? Did you think we were going to die with all the airs and graces of society? I took a kiss; I'm glad I had it; and now you can take another if you like, and square accounts."

I turned from him with a feeling of contempt which I did not seek to dissemble.

"As you please," said he. "You've ben a prig in life; a prig you'll die."

And with that he sat down in a chair, a rifle over his knee, and amused himself with snapping the lock; but I could see that his ebullition of light spirits (the only one I ever knew him to display) had already come to an end, and was succeeded by a sullen, scowling humor.

All this time our assailants might have been entering the house, and we been none the wiser; we had in truth almost forgotten the danger that so imminently overhung our days. But just then Mr. Huddlestone uttered a cry, and leaped from the bed.

I asked him what was wrong.

"Fire!" he cried. "They have set the house on fire!"

Northmour was on his feet in an instant, and he and I ran through the door of communication with the study. The room was illuminated by a red and angry light. Almost at the moment of our entrance, a tower of flame arose in front of the window, and, with a tingling report, a pane fell inward on the carpet. They had set fire to the lean-to outhouse, where Northmour used to nurse his negatives.

"Hot work," said Northmour. "Let us try in your old room."

We ran thither in a breath, threw up the casement, and looked forth. Along the whole back wall of the pavilion piles of fuel had been arranged and kindled; and it is probable they had been drenched with mineral oil, for, in spite of the morning's rain, they all burned bravely. The fire had taken a firm hold already on the outhouse, which blazed higher and higher every moment; the back door was in the centre of a red-hot bonfire; the eaves we could see, as we looked upward, were already smoldering, for the roof overhung, and was supported by considerable beams of wood. At the same time, hot, pungent, and choking volumes of smoke began to fill the house. There was not a human being to be seen to right or left.

"Ah, well?" said Northmour, "here's the end, thank God."

And we returned to My Uncle's Room. Mr. Huddlestone was putting on his boots, still violently trembling, but with an air of determination such as I had not hitherto observed. Clara stood close by him, with her cloak in both hands ready to throw about her shoulders, and a strange look in her eyes, as if she were half hopeful, half doubtful of her father.

"Well, boys and girl," said Northmour, "how about a sally? The oven is heating; it is not good to stay here and be baked; and, for my part, I want to come to my hands with them, and be done."

"There is nothing else left," I replied.

And both Clara and Mr. Huddlestone, though with a very different intonation, added, "Nothing."

As we went downstairs the heat was excessive, and the roaring of the fire filled our ears; and we had scarce reached the passage before the stairs window fell in, a branch of flame shot brandishing through the aperture, and the interior of the pavilion became lighted up with that dreadful and fluctuating glare. At the same moment we heard the fall of something heavy and inelastic in the upper story. The whole pavilion, it was plain, had gone alight like a box of matches, and now not only flamed sky-high to land and sea, but threatened with every moment to crumble and fall in about our ears.

Northmour and I cocked our revolvers. Mr. Huddlestone, who had already refused a firearm, put us behind him with a manner of command.

"Let Clara open the door," said he. "So, if they fire a volley, she will be protected. In the meantime stand behind me. I am the scapegoat; my sins have found me out."

I heard him, as I stood breathless by his shoulder, with my pistol ready, pattering off prayers in a tremulous, rapid whisper; and I confess, horrid as the thought may seem, I despised him for thinking of supplications in a moment so critical and thrilling. In the meantime, Clara, who was dead white but still possessed her faculties, had displaced the barricade from the front door. Another moment, and she had pulled it open. Firelight and moonlight illuminated the links with confused and changeful lustre, and far away against the sky we could see a long trail of glowing smoke.

Mr. Huddlestone, filled for the moment with a strength greater than his own, struck Northmour and myself a backhander in the chest; and while we were thus for the moment incapacitated from action, lifting his arms above his head like one about to dive, he ran straight forward out of the pavilion.

"Here am I!" he cried—"Huddlestone! Kill me, and spare the others!"

His sudden appearance daunted, I suppose, our hidden enemies; for Northmour and I had time to recover, to seize Clara between us, one by each arm, and to rush forth to his assistance, ere anything further had taken place. But scarce had we passed the threshold when there came near a dozen reports and flashes from every direction among the hollows of the links. Mr. Huddlestone staggered, uttered a weird and freezing cry, threw up his arms over his head, and fell backward on the turf.

"*Traditore! Traditore!*" cried the invisible avengers.

And just then, a part of the roof of the pavilion fell in, so rapid was the progress of the fire. A loud, vague, and horrible noise accompanied the collapse, and a vast volume of flame went soaring up to heaven. It must have been visible at that moment from twenty miles out to sea, from the shore at Graden Wester, and far inland from the peak of Graystiel, the most eastern summit of the Caulder Hills. Bernard Huddlestone, although God knows what were his obsequies, had a fine pyre at the moment of his death.

CHAPTER IX

TELLS HOW NORTHMOUR CARRIED OUT HIS THREAT

I SHOULD have the greatest difficulty to tell you what followed next after this tragic circumstance. It is all to me, as I look back upon it, mixed, strenuous, and ineffectual, like the struggles of a sleeper in a nightmare. Clara, I remember, uttered a broken sigh and would have fallen forward to earth, had not Northmour and I supported her insensible body. I do not think we were attacked; I do not remember even to have seen an assailant; and I believe we deserted Mr. Huddlestone without a glance. I only remember running like a man in a panic, now carrying Clara altogether in my own arms, now sharing her weight with Northmour, now scuffling confusedly for the possession of that dear burden. Why we should have made for my camp in the Hemlock Den, or how we reached it, are points lost forever to my recollection. The first moment at which I became definitely sure, Clara had been suffered to fall against the outside of my little tent, Northmour and I were tumbling together on the ground, and he, with contained ferocity, was striking for my head with the butt of his revolver. He had already twice wounded me on the scalp; and it is to the consequent loss of blood that I am tempted to attribute the sudden clearness of my mind.

I caught him by the wrist.

"Northmour," I remember saying, "you can kill me afterward. Let us first attend to Clara."

He was at that moment uppermost. Scarcely had the words passed my lips, when he had leaped to his feet and ran toward the tent; and the next moment, he was straining Clara to his heart and covering her unconscious hands and face with his caresses.

"Shame!" I cried. "Shame to you, Northmour!"

And, giddy though I still was, I struck him repeatedly upon the head and shoulders.

He relinquished his grasp, and faced me in the broken moonlight.

"I had you under, and I let you go," said he; "and now you strike me! Coward!"

"You are the coward," I retorted. "Did she wish your kisses while she was still sensible of what she wanted? Not she! And now she may be dying; and you waste this precious time, and abuse her helplessness. Stand aside, and let me help her."

He confronted me for a moment, white and menacing; then suddenly he stepped aside.

"Help her then," said he.

I threw myself on my knees beside her, and loosened, as well as I was able, her dress and corset; but while I was thus engaged, a grasp descended on my shoulder.

"Keep your hands off her," said Northmour fiercely. "Do you think I have no blood in my veins."

"Northmour," I cried, "if you will neither help her yourself, nor let me do so, do you know that I shall have to kill you?"

"That is better!" he cried. "Let her die also, where's the harm? Step aside from that girl! and stand up to fight."

"You will observe," said I, half rising, "that I have not kissed her yet."

"I dare you to," he cried.

I do not know what possessed me; it was one of the things I am most ashamed of in my life, though, as my wife used to say, I knew that my kisses would be always welcome were she dead or living; down I fell again upon my knees, parted the hair from her forehead, and, with the dearest respect, laid my lips for a moment on that cold brow. It was such a caress as a father might have given; it was such a one as was not unbecoming from a man soon to die to a woman already dead.

"And now," said I, "I am at your service, Mr. Northmour."

But I saw, to my surprise, that he had turned his back upon me.

"Do you hear?" I asked.

"Yes," said he, "I do. If you wish to fight, I am ready. If not, go on and save Clara. All is one to me."

I did not wait to be twice bidden; but, stooping again over Clara, continued my efforts to revive her. She still lay white and lifeless; I began to fear that her sweet spirit had indeed fled beyond recall, and horror and a sense of utter desolation seized upon my heart. I called her by name with the most endearing inflections; I chafed and beat her hands; and now I laid her head low, now supported it against my knee; but all seemed to be in vain, and the lids still lay heavy on her eyes.

"Northmour," I said, "there is my hat. For God's sake bring some water from the spring."

Almost in a moment he was by my side with the water.

"I have brought it in my own," he said. "You do not grudge me the privilege?"

"Northmour," I was beginning to say, as I laved her head and breast; but he interrupted me savagely.

"Oh, you hush up!" he said. "The best thing you can do is to say nothing."

I had certainly no desire to talk, my mind being swallowed up in concern for my dear love and her condition; so I continued in silence to do my best toward her recovery, and, when the hat was empty, returned it to him, with one word—"More." He had, perhaps, gone several times upon this errand, when Clara reopened her eyes.

"Now," said he, "since she is better, you can spare me, can you not? I wish you a good-night, Mr. Cassilis."

And with that he was gone among the thicket. I made a fire, for I had now no fear of the Italians, who had even spared all the little possessions left in my encampment; and, broken as she was by the excitement and the hideous catastrophe of the evening, I managed, in one way or another— by persuasion, encouragement, warmth, and such simple remedies as I could lay my hand on—to bring her back to some composure of mind and strength of body.

Day had already come, when a sharp "Hist!" sounded from the thicket. I started from the ground; but the voice of Northmour was heard adding, in the most tranquil tones: "Come here, Cassilis, and alone; I want to show you something."

I consulted Clara with my eyes, and, receiving her tacit permission, left her alone, and clambered out of the den. At some distance off I saw Northmour leaning against an elder; and, as soon as he perceived me, he began walking seaward. I had almost overtaken him as he reached the outskirts of the wood.

"Look," said he, pausing.

A couple of steps more brought me out of the foliage. The light of the morning lay cold and clear over that well-known scene. The pavilion was but a blackened wreck; the roof had fallen in, one of the gables had fallen out; and, far and near, the face of the links was cicatrized with little patches of burned furze. Thick smoke still went straight upward in the windless air of the morning, and a great pile of ardent cinders filled the bare walls of the house, like coals in an open grate. Close by the islet a schooner yacht lay to, and a well-manned boat was pulling vigorously for the shore.

"The 'Red Earl!' " I cried. "The 'Red Earl,' twelve hours too late!"

"Feel in your pocket, Frank. Are you armed?" asked Northmour.

I obeyed him, and I think I must have become deadly pale. My revolver had been taken from me.

"You see I have you in my power," he continued. "I disarmed you last night while you were nursing Clara; but this morning—here—take your pistol. No thanks!" he cried, holding up his hand. "I do not like them; that is the only way you can annoy me now."

He began to walk forward across the links to meet the boat, and I followed a step or two behind. In front of the pavilion I paused to see where Mr. Huddlestone had fallen; but there was no sign of him, nor so much as a trace of blood.

"Graden Floe," said Northmour.

He continued to advance till we had come to the head of the beach.

"No further, please," said he. "Would you like to take her to Graden House?"

"Thank you," replied I; "I shall try to get her to the minister's at Graden Wester."

The prow of the boat here grated on the beach, and a sailor jumped ashore with a line in his hand.

"Wait a minute, lads!" cried Northmour; and then lower and to my private ear: "You had better say nothing of all this to her," he added.

"On the contrary," I broke out, "she shall know everything that I can tell."

"You do not understand," he returned, with an air of great dignity. "It will be nothing to her; she expects it of me. Good-by!" he added, with a nod.

I offered him my hand.

"Excuse me," said he. "It's small, I know; but I can't

push things quite so far as that. I don't wish any sentimental business, to sit by your hearth a white-haired wanderer, and all that. Quite the contrary: I hope to God I shall never again clap eyes on either one of you."

"Well, God bless you, Northmour!" I said heartily.

"Oh, yes," he returned.

He walked down the beach; and the man who was ashore gave him an arm on board, and then shoved off and leaped into the bows himself. Northmour took the tiller; the boat rose to the waves, and the oars between the tholepins sounded crisp and measured in the morning air.

They were not yet half-way to the "Red Earl," and I was still watching their progress, when the sun rose out of the sea.

One word more, and my story is done. Years after, Northmour was killed fighting under the colors of Garibaldi for the liberation of the Tyrol.

A TERRIBLY STRANGE BED

By Wilkie Collins

SHORTLY after my education at college was finished, I happened to be staying at Paris with an English friend. We were both young men then, and lived, I am afraid, rather a wild life, in the delightful city of our sojourn. One night we were idling about the neighborhood of the Palais Royal, doubtful to what amusement we should next betake ourselves. My friend proposed a visit to Frascati's; but his suggestion was not to my taste. I knew Frascati's, as the French saying is, by heart; had lost and won plenty of five-franc pieces there, merely for amusement's sake, until it was amusement no longer, and was thoroughly tired, in fact, of all the ghastly respectabilities of such a social anomaly as a respectable gambling-house.

"For Heaven's sake," said I to my friend, "let us go somewhere where we can see a little genuine, blackguard, poverty-stricken gaming, with no false gingerbread glitter thrown over it at all. Let us get away from fashionable Frascati's, to a house where they don't mind letting in a man with a ragged coat, or a man with no coat, ragged or otherwise."

"Very well," said my friend, "we needn't go out of the Palais Royal to find the sort of company you want. Here's the place just before us; as blackguard a place, by all report, as you could possibly wish to see."

In another minute we arrived at the door, and entered the house.

When we got upstairs, and had left our hats and sticks with the doorkeeper, we were admitted into the chief gambling-room. We did not find many people assembled there. But, few as the men were who looked up at us on our entrance, they were all types—lamentably true types—of their respective classes.

We had come to see blackguards; but these men were something worse. There is a comic side, more or less appreciable, in all blackguardism: here there was nothing but tragedy—mute, weird tragedy. The quiet in the room was horrible. The thin, haggard, long-haired young man, whose sunken eyes fiercely watched the turning up of the cards, never spoke; the flabby, fat-faced, pimply player, who pricked his piece of pasteboard perseveringly, to register how often black won, and how often red, never spoke; the dirty, wrinkled old man, with the vulture eyes and the darned great-coat, who had lost his last sou, and still looked on desperately after he could play no longer, never spoke. Even the voice of the croupier sounded as if it were strangely dulled and thickened in the atmosphere of the room. I had entered the place to laugh, but the spectacle before me was something to weep over. I soon found it necessary to take refuge in excitement from the depression of spirits which was fast stealing on me. Unfortunately I sought the nearest excitement, by going to the table and beginning to play. Still more unfortunately, as the event will show, I won—won prodigiously; won incredibly; won at such a rate that the regular players at the table crowded round me; and staring at my stakes with hungry, superstitious eyes, whispered to one another that the English stranger was going to break the bank.

The game was Rouge et Noir. I had played at it in every city in Europe, without, however, the care or the wish to study the Theory of Chances—that philosopher's stone of all gamblers! And a gambler, in the strict sense of the word, I had never been. I was heart-whole from the corroding passion for play. My gaming was a mere idle amusement. I never resorted to it by necessity, because I never knew what it was to want money. I never practised it so incessantly as to lose more than I could afford, or to gain more than I could coolly pocket without being thrown off my balance by my good luck. In short, I had hitherto frequented gambling-tables—just as I frequented ball-rooms and opera-houses—because they amused me, and because I had nothing better to do with my leisure hours.

But on this occasion it was very different—now, for the first time in my life, I felt what the passion for play really was. My successes first bewildered, and then, in the most literal meaning of the word, intoxicated me. Incredible as it may appear, it is nevertheless true, that I only lost when I attempted to estimate chances, and played according to previous calculation. If I left everything to luck, and staked without any care or consideration, I was sure to win—to win in the face of every recognized probability in favor of the bank. At first some of the men present ventured their money safely enough on my color; but I speedily increased my stakes to sums which they dared not risk. One after another they left off playing, and breathlessly looked on at my game.

Still, time after time, I staked higher and higher, and still won. The excitement in the room rose to fever pitch. The silence was interrupted by a deep-muttered chorus of oaths and exclamations in different languages, every time the gold was shoveled across to my side of the table—even the imperturbable croupier dashed his rake on the floor in a (French) fury of astonishment at my success. But one man present preserved his self-possession, and that man was my friend. He came to my side, and whispering in English, begged me to leave the place, satisfied with what I had already gained. I must do him the justice to say that he repeated his warnings and entreaties several times, and only left me and went away, after I had rejected his advice (I was to all intents and purposes gambling drunk) in terms which rendered it impossible for him to address me again that night.

Shortly after he had gone, a hoarse voice behind me cried, "Permit me, my dear sir—permit me to restore to their proper place two napoleons which you have dropped. Wonderful luck, sir! I pledge you my word of honor, as an old soldier, in the course of my long experience in this sort of thing, I never saw such luck as yours—never! Go on, sir—*Sacre mille bombes!* Go on boldly, and break the bank!"

I turned round and saw, nodding and smiling at me with inveterate civility, a tall man, dressed in a frogged and braided surtout.

If I had been in my senses, I should have considered him, personally, as being rather a suspicious specimen of an old soldier. He had goggling, bloodshot eyes, mangy mustaches, and a broken nose. His voice betrayed a barrack-room intonation of the worst order, and he had the dirtiest pair of bands I ever saw—even in France. These little personal peculiarities exercised, however, no repelling influence on me. In the mad excitement, the reckless triumph of that moment, I was ready to "fraternize" with anybody who encouraged me in my game. I accepted the old soldier's offered pinch of snuff; clapped him on the back, and swore he was the honestest fellow in the world—the most glorious relic of the Grand Army that I had ever met with. "Go on!" cried my military friend, snapping his fingers in ecstasy—"Go on, and win! Break the bank—*Mille tonnerres!* my gallant English comrade, break the bank!"

And I *did* go on—went on at such a rate, that in another quarter of an hour the croupier called out, "Gentlemen, the bank has discontinued for to-night." All the notes, and all the gold in that "bank," now lay in a heap under my hands; the whole floating capital of the gambling-house was waiting to pour into my pockets!

"Tie up the money in your pocket-handkerchief, my worthy sir," said the old soldier, as I wildly plunged my hands into my heap of gold. "Tie it up, as we used to tie up a bit of dinner in the Grand Army; your winnings are too heavy for any breeches-pockets that ever were sewed. There! that's it—shovel them in, notes and all! *Credie!* what luck! Stop! another napoleon on the floor. *Ah! sacre petit polisson de Napoleon!* have I found thee at last? Now then, sir—two tight double knots each way with your honorable permission, and the money's safe. Feel it! feel it, fortunate sir! hard and round as a cannon-ball— *A bas* if they had only fired such cannon-balls at us at Austerlitz—*nom d'une pipe!* if they only had! And now, as an ancient grenadier, as an ex-brave of the French army, what remains for me to do? I ask what? Simply this, to entreat my valued English friend to drink a bottle of champagne with me, and toast the goddess Fortune in foaming goblets before we part!"

"Excellent ex-brave! Convivial ancient grenadier! Champagne by all means! An English cheer for an old soldier! Hurrah! hurrah! Another English cheer for the goddess Fortune! Hurrah! hurrah! hurrah!"

"Bravo! the Englishman; the amiable, gracious Englishman, in whose veins circulates the vivacious blood of France! Another glass? *A bas!*—the bottle is empty! Never mind! *Vive le vin!* I, the old soldier, order another bottle, and half a pound of *bonbons* with it!"

"No, no, ex-brave; never—ancient grenadier! *Your* bottle last time; *my* bottle this! Behold it! Toast away! The French Army! the great Napoleon! the present company! the croupier! the honest croupier's wife and daughters—if he has any! the ladies generally! everybody in the world!"

By the time the second bottle of champagne was emptied, I felt as if I had been drinking liquid fire—my brain seemed all aflame. No excess in wine had ever had this effect on me before in my life. Was it the result of a stimulant acting upon my system when I was in a highly excited state? Was my stomach in a particularly disordered condition? Or was the champagne amazingly strong?

"Ex-brave of the French Army!" cried I, in a mad state of exhilaration, *"I* am on fire! how are *you?* You have set

me on fire! Do you hear, my hero of Austerlitz? Let us
have a third bottle of champagne to put the flame out!"

The old soldier wagged his head, rolled his goggle-eyes,
until I expected to see them slip out of their sockets; placed
his dirty forefinger by the side of his broken nose; solemnly
ejaculated "Coffee!" and immediately ran off into an inner
room.

The word pronounced by the eccentric veteran seemed to
have a magical effect on the rest of the company present.
With one accord they all rose to depart. Probably they had
expected to profit by my intoxication; but finding that my
new friend was benevolently bent on preventing me from
getting dead drunk, had now abandoned all hope of thriving
pleasantly on my winnings. Whatever their motive might
be, at any rate they went away in a body. When the old
soldier returned, and sat down again opposite to me at the
table, we had the room to ourselves. I could see the croupier, in a sort of vestibule which opened out of it, eating his
supper in solitude. The silence was now deeper than ever.

A sudden change, too, had come over the "ex-brave." He
assumed a portentously solemn look; and when he spoke to
me again, his speech was ornamented by no oaths, enforced
by no finger-snapping, enlivened by no apostrophes or exclamations.

"Listen, my dear sir," said he, in mysteriously confidential tones—"listen to an old soldier's advice. I have been to
the mistress of the house (a very charming woman, with a
genius for cookery!) to impress on her the necessity of making us some particularly strong and good coffee. You must
drink this coffee in order to get rid of your little amiable
exaltation of spirits before you think of going home—you
must, my good and gracious friend! With all that money
to take home to-night, it is a sacred duty to yourself to have
your wits about you. You are known to be a winner to an
enormous extent by several gentleman present to-night,
who, in a certain point of view, are very worthy and excellent fellows; but they are mortal men, my dear sir, and they

have their amiable weaknesses! Need I say more? Ah, no, no! you understand me! Now, this is what you must do—send for a cabriolet when you feel quite well again—draw up all the windows when you get into it—and tell the driver to take you home only through the large and well-lighted thoroughfares. Do this; and you and your money will be safe. Do this; and to-morrow you will thank an old soldier for giving you a word of honest advice."

Just as the ex-brave ended his oration in very lachrymose tones, the coffee came in, ready poured out in two cups. My attentive friend handed me one of the cups with a bow. I was parched with thirst, and drank it off at a draft. Almost instantly afterward I was seized with a fit of giddiness, and felt more completely intoxicated than ever. The room whirled round and round furiously; the old soldier seemed to be regularly bobbing up and down before me like the piston of a steam-engine. I was half deafened by a violent singing in my ears; a feeling of utter bewilderment, help-lessness, idiocy, overcame me. I rose from my chair, holding on by the table to keep my balance; and stammered out that I felt dreadfully unwell—so unwell that I did not know how I was to get home.

"My dear friend," answered the old soldier—and even his voice seemed to be bobbing up and down as he spoke—"my dear friend, it would be madness to go home in *your* state; you would be sure to lose your money; you might be robbed and murdered with the greatest ease. *I* am going to sleep here: *do* you sleep here, too—they make up capital beds in this house—take one; sleep off the effects of the wine, and go home safely with your winnings to-morrow—to-morrow, in broad daylight."

I had but two ideas left: one, that I must never let go hold of my handkerchief full of money; the other, that I must lie down somewhere immediately, and fall off into a comfortable sleep. So I agreed to the proposal about the bed, and took the offered arm of the old soldier, carrying my money with my disengaged hand. Preceded by the croupier, we passed along some passages and up a flight of stairs into the bedroom which I was to occupy. The ex-brave shook me warmly by the hand, proposed that we should breakfast together, and then, followed by the croupier, left me for the night.

I ran to the wash-hand stand; drank some of the water in my jug; poured the rest out, and plunged my face into it; then sat down in a chair and tried to compose myself. I soon felt better. The change for my lungs, from the fetid atmosphere of the gambling-room to the cool air of the apartment I now occupied, the almost equally refreshing change for my eyes, from the glaring gaslights of the "salon" to the dim, quiet flicker of one bedroom-candle, aided wonderfully the restorative effects of cold water. The giddiness left me, and I began to feel a little like a reasonable being again. My first thought was of the risk of sleeping all night in a gambling-house; my second, of the still greater risk of trying to get out after the house was closed, and of going home alone at night through the streets of Paris with a large sum of money about me. I had slept in worse places than this on my travels; so I determined to lock, bolt, and barricade my door, and take my chance till the next morning.

Accordingly, I secured myself against all intrusion; looked under the bed, and into the cupboard; tried the fastening of the window; and then, satisfied that I had taken every proper precaution, pulled off my upper clothing, put my light, which was a dim one, on the hearth among a feathery litter of wood-ashes, and got into bed, with the handkerchief full of money under my pillow.

I soon felt not only that I could not go to sleep, but that I could not even close my eyes. I was wide awake, and in a high fever. Every nerve in my body trembled—every one of my senses seemed to be preternaturally sharpened. I tossed and rolled, and tried every kind of position, and perseveringly sought out the cold corners of the bed, and all to no purpose. Now I thrust my arms over the clothes; now I poked them under the clothes; now I violently shot my legs straight out down to the bottom of the bed; now I convulsively coiled them up as near my chin as they would go; now I shook out my crumpled pillow, changed it to the cool side, patted it flat, and lay down quietly on my back; now I fiercely doubled it in two, set it up on end, thrust it against the board of the bed, and tried a sitting posture. Every effort was in vain; I groaned with vexation as I felt that I was in for a sleepless night.

What could I do? I had no book to read. And yet, unless I found out some method of diverting my mind, I felt certain that I was in the condition to imagine all sorts of horrors; to rack my brain with forebodings of every possible and impossible danger; in short, to pass the night in suffering all conceivable varieties of nervous terror.

I raised myself on my elbow, and looked about the room —which was brightened by a lovely moonlight pouring straight through the window—to see if it contained any pictures or ornaments that I could at all clearly distinguish. While my eyes wandered from wall to wall, a remembrance of Le Maistre's delightful little book, "Voyage autour de ma Chambre," occurred to me. I resolved to imitate the French author, and find occupation and amusement enough to relieve the tedium of my wakefulness, by making a mental inventory of every article of furniture I could see, and by following up to their sources the multitude of associations which even a chair, a table, or a wash-hand stand may be made to call forth.

In the nervous, unsettled state of my mind at that moment, I found it much easier to make my inventory than to make my reflections, and thereupon soon gave up all hope of thinking in Le Maistre's fanciful track—or, indeed, of thinking at all. I looked about the room at the different articles of furniture, and did nothing more.

There was, first, the bed I was lying in; a four-post bed, of all things in the world to meet with in Paris—yes, a thorough clumsy British four-poster, with a regular top

lined with chintz—the regular fringed valance all round—
the regular stifling, unwholesome curtains, which I remembered having mechanically drawn back against the posts
without particularly noticing the bed when I first got into
the room. Then there was the marble-topped wash-hand
stand, from which the water I had spilled, in my hurry to
pour it out, was still dripping, slowly and more slowly, on to
the brick floor. Then two small chairs, with my coat, waistcoat, and trousers flung on them. Then a large elbow-chair
covered with dirty white dimity, with my cravat and shirt
collar thrown over the back. Then a chest of drawers with
two of the brass handles off, and a tawdry, broken china
inkstand placed on it by way of ornament for the top. Then
the dressing-table, adorned by a very small looking-glass,
and a very large pincushion. Then the window—an unusually large window. Then a dark old picture, which the feeble
candle dimly showed me. It was the picture of a fellow in
a high Spanish hat, crowned with a plume of towering
feathers. A swarthy, sinister ruffian, looking upward, shading his eyes with his hand, and looking intently upward—it
might be at some tall gallows on which he was going to be
hanged. At any rate, he had the appearance of thoroughly
deserving it.

This picture put a kind of constraint upon me to look upward too—at the top of the bed. It was a gloomy and not
an interesting object, and I looked back at the picture. I
counted the feathers in the man's hat—they stood out in
relief—three white, two green. I observed the crown of his
hat, which was of a conical shape, according to the fashion
supposed to have been favored by Guido Fawkes. I wondered what he was looking up at. It couldn't be at the stars;
such a desperado was neither astrologer nor astronomer. It
must be at the high gallows, and he was going to be hanged
presently. Would the executioner come into possession of
his conical crowned hat and plume of feathers? I counted
the feathers again—three white, two green.

While I still lingered over this very improving and intellectual employment, my thoughts insensibly began to wander. The moonlight shining into the room reminded me of a certain moonlight night in England—the night after a picnic party in a Welsh valley. Every incident of the drive homeward, through lovely scenery, which the moonlight made lovelier than ever, came back to my remembrance, though I had never given the picnic a thought for years; though, if I had *tried* to recollect it, I could certainly have recalled little or nothing of that scene long past. Of all the wonderful faculties that help to tell us we are immortal, which speaks the sublime truth more eloquently than memory? Here was I, in a strange house of the most suspicious character, in a situation of uncertainty, and even of peril, which might seem to make the cool exercise of my recollection almost out of the question; nevertheless, remembering, quite involuntarily, places, people, conversations, minute circumstances of every kind, which I had thought forgotten forever; which I could not possibly have recalled at will, even under the most favorable auspices. And what cause had produced in a moment the whole of this strange, complicated, mysterious effect? Nothing but some rays of moonlight shining in at my bedroom window.

I was still thinking of the picnic—of our merriment on the drive home—of the sentimental young lady who *would* quote "Childe Harold" because it was moonlight. I was absorbed by these past scenes and past amusements, when, in an instant, the thread on which my memories hung snapped asunder; my attention immediately came back to present things more vividly than ever, and I found myself, I neither knew why nor wherefore, looking hard at the picture again.

Looking for what?

Good God! the man had pulled his hat down on his brows! No! the hat itself was gone! Where was the conical crown? Where the feathers—three white, two green? Not there!

In place of the hat and feathers, what dusky object was it that now hid his forehead, his eyes, his shading hand?

Was the bed moving?

I turned on my back and looked up. Was I mad? drunk? dreaming? giddy again? or was the top of the bed really moving down—sinking slowly, regularly, silently, horribly, right down throughout the whole of its length and breadth —right down upon me, as I lay underneath?

My blood seemed to stand still. A deadly, paralyzing coldness stole all over me as I turned my head round on the pillow and determined to test whether the bed-top was really moving or not, by keeping my eye on the man in the picture.

The next look in that direction was enough. The dull, black, frowzy outline of the valance above me was within an inch of being parallel with his waist. I still looked breathlessly. And steadily and slowly—very slowly—I saw the figure, and the line of frame below the figure, vanish, as the valance moved down before it.

I am, constitutionally, anything but timid. I have been on more than one occasion in peril of my life, and have not lost my self-possession for an instant; but when the conviction first settled on my mind that the bed-top was really moving, was steadily and continuously sinking down upon me, I looked up shuddering, helpless, panic-stricken, beneath the hideous machinery for murder, which was advancing closer and closer to suffocate me where I lay.

I looked up, motionless, speechless, breathless. The candle, fully spent, went out; but the moonlight still brightened the room. Down and down, without pausing and without sounding, came the bed-top, and still my panic terror seemed to bind me faster and faster to the mattress on which I lay—down and down it sank, till the dusty odor from the lining of the canopy came stealing into my nostrils.

At that final moment the instinct of self-preservation startled me out of my trance, and I moved at last. There was just room for me to roll myself sidewise off the bed.

As I dropped noiselessly to the floor, the edge of the murderous canopy touched me on the shoulder.

Without stopping to draw my breath, without wiping the cold sweat from my face, I rose instantly on my knees to watch the bed-top. I was literally spellbound by it. If I had heard footsteps behind me, I could not have turned round; if a means of escape had been miraculously provided for me, I could not have moved to take advantage of it. The whole life in me was, at that moment, concentrated in my eyes.

It descended—the whole canopy, with the fringe round it, came down—down—close down; so close that there was not room now to squeeze my finger between the bed-top and the bed. I felt at the sides, and discovered that what had appeared to me from beneath to be the ordinary light canopy of a four-post bed was in reality a thick, broad mattress, the substance of which was concealed by the valance and its fringe. I looked up and saw the four posts rising hideously bare. In the middle of the bed-top was a huge wooden screw that had evidently worked it down through a hole in the ceiling, just as ordinary presses are worked down on the substance selected for compression. The frightful apparatus moved without making the faintest noise. There had been no creaking as it came down; there was now not the faintest sound from the room above. Amidst a dead and awful silence I beheld before me—in the nineteenth century, and in the civilized capital of France—such a machine for secret murder by suffocation as might have existed in the worst days of the Inquisition, in the lonely inns among the Hartz Mountains, in the mysterious tribunals of Westphalia! Still, as I looked on it, I could not move, I could hardly breathe, but I began to recover the power of thinking, and in a moment I discovered the murderous conspiracy framed against me in all its horror.

My cup of coffee had been drugged, and drugged too strongly. I had been saved from being smothered by having taken an overdose of some narcotic. How I had chafed and fretted at the fever fit which had preserved my life by keep-

ing me awake! How recklessly I had confided myself to the
two wretches who had led me into this room, determined,
for the sake of my winnings, to kill me in my sleep by the
surest and most horrible contrivance for secretly accom-
plishing my destruction! How many men, winners like me,
had slept, as I had proposed to sleep, in that bed, and had
never been seen or heard of more! I shuddered at the bare
idea of it.

But ere long all thought was again suspended by the
sight of the murderous canopy moving once more. After it
had remained on the bed—as nearly as I could guess—about
ten minutes, it began to move up again. The villains who
worked it from above evidently believed that their purpose
was now accomplished. Slowly and silently, as it had descended, that horrible bed-top rose toward its former place.
When it reached the upper extremities of the four posts, it
reached the ceiling too. Neither hole nor screw could be
seen; the bed became in appearance an ordinary bed again
—the canopy an ordinary canopy—even to the most suspicious eyes.

Now, for the first time, I was able to move—to rise from
my knees—to dress myself in my upper clothing—and to
consider of how I should escape. If I betrayed by the smallest noise that the attempt to suffocate me had failed, I was
certain to be murdered. Had I made any noise already? I
listened intently, looking toward the door.

No! no footsteps in the passage outside—no sound of a
tread, light or heavy, in the room above—absolute silence
everywhere. Besides locking and bolting my door, I had
moved an old wooden chest against it, which I had found
under the bed. To remove this chest (my blood ran cold
as I thought of what its contents *might* be!) without making
some disturbance was impossible; and, moreover, to think
of escaping through the house, now barred up for the night,
was sheer insanity. Only one chance was left me—the window. I stole to it on tiptoe.

My bedroom was on the first floor, above an entresol,

and looked into the back street. I raised my hand to open the window, knowing that on that action hung, by the merest hair-breadth, my chance of safety. They keep vigilant watch in a House of Murder. If any part of the frame cracked, if the hinge creaked, I was a lost man! It must have occupied me at least five minutes, reckoning by time—five *hours* reckoning by suspense—to open that window. I succeeded in doing it silently—in doing it with all the dexterity of a house-breaker—and then looked down into the street. To leap the distance beneath me would be almost certain destruction! Next, I looked round at the sides of the house. Down the left side ran a thick water-pipe—it passed close by the outer edge of the window. The moment I saw the pipe, I knew I was saved. My breath came and went freely for the first time since I had seen the canopy of the bed moving down upon me!

To some men the means of escape which I had discovered might have seemed difficult and dangerous enough—to *me* the prospect of slipping down the pipe into the street did not suggest even a thought of peril. I had always been accustomed, by the practise of gymnastics, to keep up my schoolboy powers as a daring and expert climber; and knew that my head, hands, and feet would serve me faithfully in any hazards of ascent or descent. I had already got one leg over the window-sill, when I remembered the handkerchief filled with money under my pillow. I could well have afforded to leave it behind me, but I was revengefully determined that the miscreants of the gambling-house should miss their plunder as well as their victim. So I went back to the bed and tied the heavy handkerchief at my back by my cravat.

Just as I had made it tight and fixed it in a comfortable place, I thought I heard a sound of breathing outside the door. The chill feeling of horror ran through me again as I listened. No! dead silence still in the passage—I had only heard the night air blowing softly into the room. The next moment I was on the window-sill—and the next I had a firm grip on the water-pipe with my hands and knees.

I slid down into the street easily and quietly, as I thought I should, and immediately set off at the top of my speed to a branch "Prefecture" of Police, which I knew was situated in the immediate neighborhood. A "Sub-prefect," and several picked men among his subordinates, happened to be up, maturing, I believe, some scheme for discovering the perpetrator of a mysterious murder which all Paris was talking of just then. When I began my story, in a breathless hurry and in very bad French, I could see that the Sub-prefect suspected me of being a drunken Englishman who had robbed somebody; but he soon altered his opinion as I went on, and before I had anything like concluded, he shoved all the papers before him into a drawer, put on his hat, supplied me with another (for I was bareheaded), ordered a file of soldiers, desired his expert followers to get ready all sorts of tools for breaking open doors and ripping up brick flooring, and took my arm, in the most friendly and familiar manner possible, to lead me with him out of the house. I will venture to say that when the Sub-prefect was a little boy, and was taken for the first time to the play, he was not half as much pleased as he was now at the job in prospect for him at the gambling-house!

Away we went through the streets, the Sub-prefect cross-examining and congratulating me in the same breath as we marched at the head of our formidable *posse comitatus*. Sentinels were placed at the back and front of the house the moment we got to it, a tremendous battery of knocks was directed against the door; a light appeared at a window; I was told to conceal myself behind the police—then came more knocks, and a cry of "Open in the name of the law!" At that terrible summons bolts and locks gave way before an invisible hand, and the moment after the Sub-prefect was in the passage, confronting a waiter half dressed and ghastly pale. This was the short dialogue which immediately took place:

"We want to see the Englishman who is sleeping in this house?"

"He went away hours ago."

"He did no such thing. His friend went away; *he* remained. Show us to his bedroom!"

"I swear to you, Monsieur le Sous-prefect, he is not here! he—"

"I swear to you, Monsieur le Garçon, he is. He slept here—he didn't find your bed comfortable—he came to us to complain of it—here he is among my men—and here am I ready to look for a flea or two in his bedstead. Renaudin! (calling to one of the subordinates, and pointing to the waiter), collar that man, and tie his hands behind him. Now, then, gentlemen, let us walk upstairs!"

Every man and woman in the house was secured—the "Old Soldier" the first. Then I identified the bed in which I had slept, and then we went into the room above.

No object that was at all extraordinary appeared in any part of it. The Sub-prefect looked round the place, commanded everybody to be silent, stamped twice on the floor, called for a candle, looked attentively at the spot he had stamped on, and ordered the flooring there to be carefully taken up. This was done in no time. Lights were produced, and we saw a deep raftered cavity between the floor of this room and the ceiling of the room beneath. Through this cavity there ran perpendicularly a sort of case of iron thickly greased; and inside the case appeared the screw, which communicated with the bed-top below. Extra lengths of screw, freshly oiled; levers covered with felt; all the complete upper works of a heavy press—constructed with infernal ingenuity so as to join the fixtures below, and when taken to pieces again to go into the smallest possible compass—were next discovered and pulled out on the floor. After some little difficulty the Sub-prefect succeeded in putting the machinery together, and, leaving his men to work it, descended with me to the bedroom. The smothering canopy was then lowered, but not so noiselessly as I had seen it lowered. When I mentioned this to the Sub-prefect, his answer, simple as it was, had a terrible significance. "My men," said he, "are working down the bed-top for the first time—the men whose money you won were in better practise."

We left the house in the sole possession of two police agents—every one of the inmates being removed to prison on the spot. The Sub-prefect, after taking down my "procès verbal" in his office, returned with me to my hotel to get my passport. "Do you think," I asked, as I gave it to him, "that any men have really been smothered in that bed, as they tried to smother *me?*"

"I have seen dozens of drowned men laid out at the Morgue," answered the Sub-prefect, "in whose pocketbooks were found letters stating that they had committed suicide in the Seine, because they had lost everything at the gaming-table. Do I know how many of those men entered the same gambling-house that *you* entered? won as *you* won? took that bed as *you* took it? slept in it? were smothered in it? and were privately thrown into the river, with a letter of explanation written by the murderers and placed in their pocketbooks? No man can say how many or how few have suffered the fate from which you have escaped. The people of the gambling-house kept their bedstead machinery a secret from us—even from the police! The dead kept the rest of the secret for them. Good-night, or rather good-morning, Monsieur Faulkner! Be at my office again at nine o'clock— in the meantime, au revoir!"

The rest of my story is soon told. I was examined and re-examined; the gambling-house was strictly searched all through from top to bottom; the prisoners were separately interrogated; and two of the less guilty among them made a confession. I discovered that the Old Soldier was the master of the gambling-house—*justice* discovered that he had been drummed out of the army as a vagabond years ago; that he had been guilty of all sorts of villainies since; that he was in possession of stolen property, which the owners identified; and that he, the croupier, another accomplice, and the

woman who had made my cup of coffee, were all in the
secret of the bedstead. There appeared some reason to doubt
whether the inferior persons attached to the house knew
anything of the suffocating machinery; and they received
the benefit of that doubt, by being treated simply as thieves
and vagabonds. As for the Old Soldier and his two head
myrmidons, they went to the galleys; the woman who had
drugged my coffee was imprisoned for I forget how many
years; the regular attendants at the gambling-house were
considered "suspicious," and placed under "surveillance";
and I became, for one whole week (which is a long time),
the head "lion" in Parisian society. My adventure was
dramatized by three illustrious play-makers, but never saw
theatrical daylight; for the censorship forbade the introduction on the stage of a correct copy of the gambling-house
bedstead.

One good result was produced by my adventure, which
any censorship must have approved: it cured me of ever
again trying "Rouge et Noir" as an amusement. The sight
of a green cloth, with packs of cards and heaps of money
on it, will henceforth be forever associated in my mind with
the sight of a bed canopy descending to suffocate me in the
silence and darkness of the night.

THE CAPTURE OF BILL SIKES

By Charles Dickens

It was nearly two hours before daybreak; that time which, in the autumn of the year, may be truly called the dead of night; when the streets are silent and deserted; when even sound appears to slumber, and profligacy and riot have staggered home to dream; it was at this still and silent hour that the Jew sat watching in his old lair, with face so distorted and pale, and eyes so red and bloodshot, that he looked less like a man than like some hideous phantom: moist from the grave, and worried by an evil spirit.

He sat crouching over a cold hearth, wrapped in an old torn coverlet, with his face turned toward a wasting candle that stood upon a table by his side. His right hand was raised to his lips, and as, absorbed in thought, he bit his long black nails, he disclosed among his toothless gums a few such fangs as should have been a dog's or rat's.

Stretched upon a mattress on the floor lay Noah Claypole, fast asleep. Toward him the old man sometimes directed his eyes for an instant, and then brought them back again to the candle; which, with long-burned wick drooping almost double, and hot grease falling down in clots upon the table, plainly showed that his thoughts were busy elsewhere.

Indeed they were. Mortification at the overthrow of his notable scheme; hatred of the girl who had dared to palter with strangers; an utter distrust of the sincerity of her refusal to yield him up; bitter disappointment at the loss of his revenge on Sikes; the fear of detection, and ruin, and death; and a fierce and deadly rage kindled by all; these were the passionate considerations which, following close upon each other with rapid and ceaseless whirl, shot through the brain of Fagin, as every evil thought and blackest purpose lay working at his heart.

He sat without changing his attitude in the least, or appearing to take the smallest heed of time, until his quick ear seemed to be attracted by a footstep in the street.

"At last," muttered the Jew, wiping his dry and fevered mouth. "At last!"

The bell rang gently as he spoke. He crept upstairs to the door, and presently returned accompanied by a man muffled to the chin, who carried a bundle under one arm. Sitting down and throwing back his outer coat, the man displayed the burly frame of Sikes.

"There!" he said, laying the bundle on the table. "Take care of that, and do the most you can with it. It's been trouble enough to get; I thought I should have been here three hours ago."

Fagin laid his hand upon the bundle, and locking it in the cupboard, sat down again without speaking. But he did not take his eyes off the robber for an instant during this action; and now that they sat over against each other, face to face, he looked fixedly at him, with his lips quivering so violently, and his face so altered by the emotions which had mastered him, that the housebreaker involuntarily drew back his chair and surveyed him with a look of real affright.

"Wot now?" cried Sikes. "Wot do you look at a man so for?"

The Jew raised his right hand and shook his trembling forefinger in the air; but his passion was so great that the power of speech was for the moment gone.

"Damme!" said Sikes, feeling in his breast with a look of alarm. "He's gone mad. I must look to myself here."

"No, no," rejoined Fagin, finding his voice. "It's not—you're not the person, Bill. I've no—no fault to find with you."

"Oh, you haven't, haven't you?" said Sikes, looking

sternly at him, and ostentatiously passing a pistol into a more convenient pocket. "That's lucky—for one of us. Which one that is, don't matter."

"I've got that to tell you, Bill," said the Jew, drawing his chair nearer, "will make you worse than me."

"Ay?" returned the robber, with an incredulous air. "Tell away. Look sharp, or Nance will think I'm lost."

"Lost!" cried Fagin. "She has pretty well settled that, in her own mind, already."

Sikes looked with an aspect of great perplexity into the Jew's face, and reading no satisfactory explanation of the riddle there, clinched his coat-collar in his huge hand and shook him soundly.

"Speak, will you!" he said; "or if you don't, it shall be for want of breath. Open your mouth and say wot you've got to say in plain words. Out with it, you thundering old cur—out with it!"

"Suppose that lad that's lying there—" Fagin began.

Sikes turned round to where Noah was sleeping, as if he had not previously observed him. "Well?" he said, resuming his former position.

"Suppose that lad," pursued the Jew, "was to peach—to blow upon us all—first seeking out the right folks for the purpose, and then having a meeting with 'em in the street to paint our likenesses, describe every mark that they might know us by, and the crib where we might be most easily taken. Suppose he was to do all this, and besides to blow upon a plant we've all been in, more or less—of his own fancy; not grabbed, trapped, tried, earwigged by the parson and brought to it on bread and water—but of his own fancy; to please his own taste; stealing out at nights to find those most interested against us, and peaching to them. Do you hear me?" cried the Jew, his eyes flashing with rage. "Suppose he did all this, what then?"

"What then!" replied Sikes, with a tremendous oath. "If he was left alive till I came, I'd grind his skull under the iron heel of my boot into as many grains as there are hairs upon his head."

"What if *I* did it?" cried the Jew, almost in a yell. "*I* that know so much, and could hang so many besides myself!"

"I don't know," replied Sikes, clenching his teeth and turning white at the mere suggestion. "I'd do something in the jail that 'ud get me put in irons; and if I was tried along with you, I'd fall upon you with them in the open court, and beat your brains out afore the people. I should have such strength," muttered the robber, poising his brawny arm, "that I could smash your head as if a loaded wagon had gone over it."

"You would?"

"Would I!" said the housebreaker. "Try me."

"If it was Charley, or the Dodger, or Bet, or—"

"I don't care who," replied Sikes, impatiently. "Whoever it was, I'd serve them the same."

Fagin looked hard at the robber; and, motioning him to be silent, stooped over the bed upon the floor, and shook the sleeper to rouse him. Sikes leaned forward in his chair, looking on with his hands upon his knees, as if wondering much what all this questioning and preparation was to end in.

"Bolter, Bolter! Poor lad!" said Fagin, looking up with an expression of devilish anticipation, and speaking slowly and with marked emphasis. "He's tired—tired with watching for *her* so long—watching for *her,* Bill."

"Wot d'ye mean?" asked Sikes, drawing back.

The Jew made no answer, but bending over the sleeper again, hauled him into a sitting posture. When his assumed name had been repeated several times, Noah rubbed his eyes, and, giving a heavy yawn, looked sleepily about him.

"Tell me that again—once again, just for him to hear," said the Jew, pointing to Sikes as he spoke.

"Tell yer what?" asked the sleepy Noah, shaking himself pettishly.

"That about—NANCY," said the Jew, clutching Sikes by the wrist, as if to prevent his leaving the house before he had heard enough. "You followed her?"

"Yes."

"To London Bridge?"

"Yes."

"Where she met two people?"

"So she did."

"A gentleman and a lady that she had gone to of her own accord before, who asked her to give up all her pals, and Monks first, which she did—and to describe him, which she did—and to tell them what house it was that we meet at, and go to, which she did—and where it could be best watched from, which she did—and what time the people went there, which she did. She did all this. She told it all every word without a threat, without a murmur—she did—did she not?" cried the Jew, half mad with fury.

"All right," replied Noah, scratching his head. "That's just what it was!"

"What did they say about last Sunday?" demanded the Jew.

"About last Sunday!" replied Noah, considering. "Why, I told yer that before."

"Again. Tell it again!" cried Fagin, tightening his grasp on Sikes, and brandishing his other hand aloft, as the foam flew from his lips.

"They asked her," said Noah, who, as he grew more wakeful, seemed to have a dawning perception who Sikes was, "they asked her why she didn't come, last Sunday, as she promised. She said she couldn't."

"Why—why?" interrupted the Jew, triumphantly. "Tell him that."

"Because she was forcibly kept at home by Bill, the man she had told them of before," replied Noah.

"What more of him?" cried the Jew. "What more of the man she had told them of before? Tell him that, tell him that."

"Why, that she couldn't very easily get out-of-doors unless he knew where she was going to," said Noah; "and so the first time she went to see the lady, she—ha! ha! ha! it made me laugh when she said it, that it did—she gave him a drink of laudanum."

"Hell's fire!" cried Sikes, breaking fiercely from the Jew. "Let me go!"

Flinging the old man from him, he rushed from the room, and darted, wildly and furiously, up the stairs.

"Bill, Bill!" cried the Jew, following him hastily. "A word. Only a word."

The word would not have been exchanged, but that the housebreaker was unable to open the door, on which he was expending fruitless oaths and violence when the Jew came panting up.

"Let me out," said Sikes. "Don't speak to me; it's not safe. Let me out, I say."

"Hear me speak a word," rejoined the Jew, laying his hand upon the lock. "You won't be—"

"Well?" replied the other.

"You won't be—too—violent, Bill?" whined the Jew.

The day was breaking, and there was light enough for the men to see each other's faces. They exchanged one brief glance; there was a fire in the eyes of both which could not be mistaken.

"I mean," said Fagin, showing that he felt all disguise was now useless, "not too violent for safety. Be crafty, Bill, and not too bold."

Sikes made no reply; but pulling open the door, of which the Jew had turned the lock, dashed into the silent streets.

Without one pause, or moment's consideration; without once turning his head to the right or left, or raising his eyes to the sky or lowering them to the ground, but looking straight before him with savage resolution: his teeth so tightly compressed that the strained jaw seemed starting through his skin, the robber held on his headlong course, nor muttered a word, nor relaxed a muscle, until he reached his own door. He opened it, softly, with a key; strode lightly up the stairs; and entering his own room, double-locked the door, and lifting the heavy table against it, drew back the curtain of the bed.

The girl was lying, half dressed, upon it. He had roused her from her sleep, for she raised herself with a hurried and startled look.

"Get up!" said the man.

"It is you, Bill!" said the girl, with an expression of pleasure at his return.

"It is," was the reply. "Get up."

There was a candle burning, but the man hastily drew it from the candlestick and hurled it under the grate. Seeing the faint light of early day, without, the girl rose to undraw the curtain.

"Let it be," said Sikes, thrusting his hand before her. "There's light enough for wot I've got to do."

"Bill," said the girl, in a low voice of alarm, "why do you look like that at me?"

The robber sat regarding her, for a few seconds, with dilated nostrils and heaving breast; and then, grasping her by the head and throat, dragged her into the middle of the room, and looking once toward the door, placed his heavy hand upon her mouth.

"Bill, Bill!" gasped the girl, wrestling with the strength of mortal fear—"I—I won't scream or cry—not once—hear me—speak to me—tell me what I have done?"

"You know, you she-devil!" returned the robber, suppressing his breath. "You were watched to-night; every word you said was heard."

"Then spare my life for the love of Heaven, as I spared yours," rejoined the girl, clinging to him. "Bill, dear Bill, you can not have the heart to kill me. Oh! think of all I have given up, only this one night, for you. You shall have time to think, and save yourself this crime; I will not loose my hold, you can not throw me off. Bill, Bill, for dear God's sake, for your own, for mine, stop before you spill my blood! I have been true to you, upon my guilty soul I have!"

The man struggled violently to release his arms; but those of the girl were clasped round his, and tear her as he would, he could not tear them away.

"Bill," cried the girl, striving to lay her head upon his breast, "the gentleman, and that dear lady, told me to-night of a home in some foreign country where I could end my days in solitude and peace. Let me see them again, and beg them, on my knees, to show the same mercy and goodness to you; and let us both leave this dreadful place, and far apart lead better lives, and forget how we have lived, except in prayers, and never see each other more. It is never too late to repent. They told me so—I feel it now—but we must have time—a little, little time!"

The housebreaker freed one arm, and grasped his pistol. The certainty of immediate detection if he fired flashed across his mind even in the midst of his fury, and he beat it twice with all the force he could summon upon the up-turned face that almost touched his own.

She staggered and fell, nearly blinded with the blood that rained down from a deep gash in her forehead; but raising herself, with difficulty, on her knees, drew from her bosom a white handkerchief—Rose Maylie's own—and holding it up, in her folded hands, as high toward Heaven as her feeble strength would allow, breathed one prayer for mercy to her Maker.

It was a ghastly figure to look upon. The murderer, staggering backward to the wall, and shutting out the sight with his hand, seized a heavy club and struck her down.

Of all bad deeds that under cover of the darkness had been committed within wide London's bounds since night hung over it, that was the worst. Of all the horrors that rose with an ill scent upon the morning air, that was the foulest and most cruel.

The sun—the bright sun, that brings back, not light alone, but new life, and hope, and freshness to man—burst upon the crowded city in clear and radiant glory. Through costly colored glass and paper-mended window, through cathedral dome and rotten crevice, it shed its equal ray. It lighted up the room where the murdered woman lay. It did. He tried to shut it out, but it would stream in. If the sight had been a ghastly one in the dull morning, what was it, now, in all that brilliant light!

He had not moved; he had been afraid to stir. There had been a moan and motion of the hand; and with terror added to rage, he had struck and struck again. Once he threw a rug over it; but it was worse to fancy the eyes, and imagine them moving toward him, than to see them glaring upward, as if watching the reflection of the pool of gore that quivered and danced in the sunlight on the ceiling. He had plucked it off again. And there was the body—mere flesh and blood, no more—but such flesh, and so much blood!

He struck a light, kindled a fire, and thrust the club into it. There was hair upon the end, which blazed and shrunk into a light cinder, and, caught by the air, whirled up the chimney. Even that frightened him, sturdy as he was; but he held the weapon till it broke; and then piled it on the coals to burn away and smolder into ashes. He washed himself, and rubbed his clothes; there were spots that would not be removed, but he cut the pieces out, and burned them. How those stains were dispersed about the room! The very feet of the dog were bloody.

All this time he had never once turned his back upon the corpse; no, not for a moment. Such preparations completed, he moved, backward, toward the door, dragging the dog with him, lest he should soil his feet anew and carry out new evidences of the crime into the streets. He shut the door softly, locked it, took the key, and left the house.

He crossed over, and glanced up at the window, to be sure that nothing was visible from the outside. There was the curtain still drawn, which she would have opened to admit the light she never saw again. It lay nearly under there. *He* knew that. God, how the sun poured down upon the very spot!

The glance was instantaneous. It was a relief to have got free of the room. He whistled on the dog, and walked rapidly away.

He went through Islington; strode up the hill at Highgate on which stands the stone in honor of Whittington; turned down to Highgate Hill, unsteady of purpose, and uncertain where to go; struck off to the right again, almost as soon as he began to descend it; and taking the footpath across the fields, skirted Caen Wood, and so came out on Hampstead Heath. Traversing the hollow by the Vale of Health, he mounted the opposite bank, and crossing the road which joins the villages of Hampstead and Highgate, made along the remaining portion of the Heath to the fields at North End, in one of which he laid himself down under a hedge, and slept.

Soon he was up again, and away—not far into the country, but back toward London by the high-road—then back again—then over another part of the same ground as he had already traversed—then wandering up and down in fields, and lying on ditches' brinks to rest, and starting up to make for some other spot, and do the same, and ramble on again.

Where could he go, that was near and not too public, to get some meat and drink? Hendon. That was a good place, not far off, and out of most people's way. Thither he directed his steps—running sometimes, and sometimes, with a strange perversity, loitering at a snail's pace, or stopping altogether and idly breaking the hedges with his stick. But when he got there, all the people he met—the very children at the doors—seemed to view him with suspicion. Back he turned again, without the courage to purchase bit or drop, though he had tasted no food for many hours; and once more he lingered on the Heath, uncertain where to go.

He wandered over miles and miles of ground, and still came back to the old place. Morning and noon had passed, and the day was on the wane, and still he rambled to and

fro, and up and down, and round and round, and still lingered about the same spot.

At last he got away, and shaped his course for Hatfield.

It was nine o'clock at night, when the man, quite tired
out, and the dog, limping and lame from the unaccustomed
exercise, turned down the hill by the church of the quiet
village, and plodding along the little street, crept into a
small public-house, whose scanty light had guided them to
the spot. There was a fire in the tap-room, and some
country laborers were drinking before it. They made room
for the stranger, but he sat down in the furthest corner, and
ate and drank alone, or rather with his dog, to whom he
cast a morsel of food from time to time.

The conversation of the men assembled here turned upon
the neighboring land and farmers; and when those topics
were exhausted, upon the age of some old man who had
been buried on the previous Sunday; the young men present
considering him very old, and the old men present declaring
him to have been quite young—not older, one white-haired
grandfather said, than he was—with ten or fifteen years of
life in him at least—if he had taken care; if he had taken
care.

There was nothing to attract attention, or excite alarm,
in this. The robber, after paying his reckoning, sat silent
and unnoticed in his corner, and had almost dropped asleep,
when he was half awakened by the noisy entrance of a new-
comer.

This was an antic-fellow, half peddler and half mounte-
bank, who traveled about the country on foot, to vend hones,
strops, razors, washballs, harness paste, medicine for dogs
and horses, cheap perfumery, cosmetics, and such-like
wares, which he carried in a case slung to his back. His
entrance was the signal for various homely jokes with the
countrymen, which slackened not until he had made his supper, and opened his box of treasures, when he ingeniously
contrived to unite business with amusement.

"And what be that stoof? Good to eat, Harry?" asked a

grinning countryman, pointing to some composition-cakes in one corner.

"This," said the fellow, producing one—"this is the infallible and invaluable composition for removing all sorts of stain, rust, dirt, mildew, spick, speck, spot, or spatter, from silk, satin, linen, cambric, cloth, crape, stuff, carpet, merino, muslin, bombazeen, or woolen stuff. Wine-stains, fruit-stains, beer-stains, water-stains, paint-stains, pitch-stains, any stains, all come out at one rub with the infallible and invaluable composition. If a lady stains her honor, she has only need to swallow one cake and she's cured at once—for it's poison. If a gentleman wants to prove his, he has only need to bolt one little square, and he has put it beyond question—for it's quite as satisfactory as a pistol-bullet, and a great deal nastier in the flavor, consequently the more credit in taking it. One penny a square. With all these virtues, one penny a square!"

There were two buyers directly, and more of the listeners plainly hesitated. The vender observing this, increased in loquacity.

"It's all bought up as fast as it can be made," said the fellow. "There are fourteen water-mills, six steam-engines, and a galvanic battery, always a-working upon it, and they can't make it fast enough, though the men work so hard that they die off, and the widows is pensioned directly, with twenty pound a year for each of the children, and a premium of fifty for twins. One penny a square! Two halfpence is all the same, and four farthings is received with joy. One penny a square! Wine-stains, fruit-stains, beer-stains, water-stains, paint-stains, pitch-stains, mud-stains, blood-stains. Here is a stain upon the hat of a gentleman in the company that I'll take clean out before he can order me a pint of ale."

"Hah!" cried Sikes, starting up. "Give that back."

"I'll take it clean out, sir," replied the man, winking to the company, "before you can come across the room to get it. Gentlemen, all observe the dark stain upon this gentleman's hat, no wider than a shilling, but thicker than a half-crown. Whether it is a wine-stain, fruit-stain, beer-stain, water-stain, paint-stain, pitch-stain, mud-stain, or blood-stain—"

The man got no further, for Sikes, with a hideous imprecation, overthrew the table, and tearing the hat from him, burst out of the house.

With the same perversity of feeling and irresolution that had fastened upon him, despite himself, all day, the murderer, finding that he was not followed, and that they most probably considered him some drunken sullen fellow, turned back up the town, and getting out of the glare of the lamps of a stage-coach that was standing in the street, was walking past, when he recognized the mail from London, and saw that it was standing at the little post-office. He almost knew what was to come; but he crossed over, and listened.

The guard was standing at the door, waiting for the letter-bag. A man, dressed like a gamekeeper, came up at the moment, and he handed him a basket which lay ready on the pavement.

"That's for your people," said the guard. "Now, look alive in there, will you. Damn that 'ere bag, it warn't ready night afore last; this won't do, you know!"

"Anything new up in town, Ben?" asked the gamekeeper, drawing back to the window-shutters, the better to admire the horses.

"No, nothing that I knows on," replied the man, pulling on his gloves. "Corn's up a little. I heerd talk of a murder, too, down Spitalfields way, but I don't reckon much upon it."

"Oh, that's quite true," said a gentleman inside who was looking out of the window. "And a dreadful murder it was."

"Was it, sir?" rejoined the guard, touching his hat. "Man or woman, pray, sir?"

"A woman," replied the gentleman. "It is supposed—"

"Now, Ben," cried the coachman, impatiently.

"Damn that 'ere bag," cried the guard; "are you gone to sleep in there?"

"Coming!" cried the office-keeper, running out.

"Coming," growled the guard. "Ah, and so's the young 'ooman of property that's going to take a fancy to me, but I don't know when. Here, give hold. All ri—ight!"

The horn sounded a few cheerful notes, and the coach was gone.

Sikes remained standing in the street, apparently unmoved by what he had just heard, and agitated by no stronger feeling than a doubt where to go. At length he went back again, and took the road which leads from Hatfield to St. Albans.

He went on, doggedly; but as he left the town behind him and plunged into the solitude and darkness of the road, he felt a dread and awe creeping upon him which shook him to the core. Every object before him, substance or shadow, still or moving, took the semblance of some fearful thing; but these fears were nothing compared to the sense that haunted him of that morning's ghastly figure following at his heels. He could trace its shadow in the gloom, supply the smallest item of the outline, and note how stiff and solemn it seemed to stalk along. He could hear its garments rustling in the leaves; and every breath of wind came laden with that last low cry. If he stopped, it did the same. If he ran, it followed—not running too: that would have been a relief; but like a corpse endowed with the mere machinery of life, and borne on one slow melancholy wind that never rose or fell.

At times, he turned, with desperate determination, resolved to beat this phantom off, though it should look him dead; but the hair rose on his head, and his blood stood still, for it had turned with him and was behind him then. He had kept it before him that morning, but it was behind him now—always. He leaned his back against a bank, and felt that it stood above him, visibly out against the cold night sky. He threw himself upon the road—on his back upon the road. At his head it stood, silent, erect, and still—a living gravestone, with its epitaph in blood.

Let no man talk of murderers escaping justice, and hint that Providence must sleep. There were twenty score of violent deaths in one long minute of that agony of fear.

There was a shed in a field he passed that offered shelter for the night. Before the door were three tall poplar trees, which made it very dark within; and the wind moaned through them with a dismal wail. He *could not* walk on till daylight came again; and here he stretched himself close to the wall—to undergo new torture.

For now a vision came before him, as constant and more terrible than that from which he had escaped. Those widely staring eyes, so lustreless and so glassy that he had better borne to see them than think upon them, appeared in the midst of the darkness: light in themselves, but giving light to nothing. There were but two, but they were everywhere. If he shut out the sight, there came the room with every well-known object—some, indeed, that he would have forgotten, if he had gone over its contents from memory—each in its accustomed place. The body was in *its* place, and its eyes were as he saw them when he stole away. He got up, and rushed into the field without. The figure was behind him. He re-entered the shed, and shrank down once more. The eyes were there, before he had laid himself along.

And here he remained, in such terror as none but he can know, trembling in every limb, and the cold sweat starting from every pore, when suddenly there arose upon the night wind the noise of distant shouting and the roar of voices mingled in alarm and wonder. Any sound of men in that lonely place, even though it conveyed a real cause of alarm, was something to him. He regained his strength and energy at the prospect of personal danger; and, springing to his feet, rushed into the open air.

The broad sky seemed on fire. Rising into the air with showers of sparks, and rolling one above the other, were sheets of flame, lighting the atmosphere for miles round, and driving clouds of smoke in the direction where he stood. The shouts grew louder as new voices swelled the roar, and he could hear the cry of "Fire!" mingled with the ringing of an alarm-bell, the fall of heavy bodies, and the crackling of flames as they twined round some new obstacle, and shot aloft as though refreshed by food. The noise increased as he looked. There were people there—men and women— light, bustle. It was like new life to him. He darted onward —straight, headlong—dashing through brier and brake, and leaping gate and fence as madly as the dog, who careered with loud and sounding bark before him.

He came upon the spot. There were half-dressed figures tearing to and fro, some endeavoring to drag the frightened horses from the stables, others driving the cattle from the yard and outhouses, and others coming laden from the burning pile, amid a shower of falling sparks and the tumbling down of red-hot beams. The apertures, where doors and windows stood an hour ago, disclosed a mass of raging fire: walls rocked and crumbled into the burning well; the molten lead and iron poured down, white-hot, upon the ground. Women and children shrieked, and men encouraged each other with noisy shouts and cheers. The clanking of the engine-pumps, and the spurting and hissing of the water as it fell upon the blazing wood, added to the tremendous roar. He shouted, too, till he was hoarse; and, flying from memory and himself, plunged into the thickest of the throng.

Hither and thither he dived that night: now working at the pumps, and now hurrying through the smoke and flame, but never ceasing to engage himself wherever noise and men were thickest. Up and down the ladders, upon the roofs of buildings, over floors that quaked and trembled with his weight, under the lee of falling bricks and stones, in every part of that great fire was he; but he bore a charmed life, and had neither scratch nor bruise, nor weariness nor thought, till morning dawned again, and only smoke and blackened ruins remained.

This mad excitement over, there returned, with tenfold

force, the dreadful consciousness of his crime. He looked suspiciously about him, for the men were conversing in groups, and he feared to be the subject of their talk. The dog obeyed the significant beck of his finger, and they drew off, stealthily, together. He passed near an engine where some men were seated, and they called to him to share in their refreshment. He took some bread and meat; and as he drank a draft of beer, heard the firemen, who were from London, talking about the murder. "He has gone to Birmingham, they say," said one; "but they'll have him yet, for the scouts are out, and by to-morrow night there'll be a cry all through the country."

He hurried off, and walked till he almost dropped upon the ground; then lay down in a lane, and had a long but broken and uneasy sleep. He wandered on again, irresolute and undecided, and oppressed with the fear of another solitary night.

Suddenly he took the desperate resolution of going back to London.

"There's somebody to speak to there, at all events," he thought. "A good hiding-place, too. They'll never expect to nab me there, after this country scent. Why can't I lay by for a week or so, and, forcing blunt from Fagin, get abroad to France? Damme, I'll risk it."

He acted upon this impulse without delay, and choosing the least frequented roads, began his journey back, resolved to lie concealed within a short distance of the metropolis, and, entering it at dusk by a circuitous route, to proceed straight to that part of it which he had fixed on for his destination.

The dog, though—if any descriptions of him were out, it would not be forgotten that the dog was missing, and had probably gone with him. This might lead to his apprehension as he passed along the streets. He resolved to drown him, and walked on, looking about for a pond, picking up a heavy stone and tying it to his handkerchief as he went.

The animal looked up into his master's face while these preparations were making; and, whether his instinct apprehended something of their purpose, or the robber's sidelong look at him was sterner than ordinary, skulked a little further in the rear than usual, and cowered as he came more slowly along. When his master halted at the brink of a pool, and looked round to call him, he stopped outright.

"Do you hear me call? Come here!" cried Sikes.

The animal came up from the very force of habit; but as Sikes stooped to attach the handkerchief to his throat, he uttered a low growl and started back.

"Come back!" said the robber, stamping on the ground.

The dog wagged his tail, but moved not. Sikes made a running noose and called him again.

The dog advanced, retreated, paused an instant, turned, and scurried away at his hardest speed.

The man whistled again and again, and sat down and waited in the expectation that he would return. But no dog appeared, and at length he resumed his journey.

Near to that part of the Thames on which the church at Rotherhithe abuts, where the buildings on the banks are dirtiest and the vessels on the river blackest with the dust of colliers and the smoke of close-built, low-roofed houses, there exists, at the present day, the filthiest, the strangest, the most extraordinary of the many localities that are hidden in London, wholly unknown, even by name, to the great mass of its inhabitants.

To reach this place, the visitor has to penetrate through a maze of close, narrow, and muddy streets, thronged by the roughest and poorest of waterside people, and devoted to the traffic they may be supposed to occasion. The cheapest and least delicate provisions are heaped in the shops; the coarsest and commonest articles of wearing apparel dangle at the salesman's door, and stream from the house-parapet and windows. Jostling with unemployed laborers of the lowest class, ballast-heavers, coal-whippers, brazen women, ragged children, and the very raff and refuse of the river, he makes his way with difficulty along, assailed by offensive sights and smells from the narrow alleys which branch off on the right and left, and deafened by the clash of ponderous wagons that bear great piles of merchandise from the stacks of warehouses that rise from every corner. Arriving, at length, in streets remoter and less frequented than those through which he has passed, he walks beneath tottering house-fronts projecting over the pavement, dismantled walls that seem to totter as he passes, chimneys half crushed, half hesitating to fall, windows guarded by rusty iron bars that time and dirt have almost eaten away, and every imaginable sign of desolation and neglect.

In such a neighborhood, beyond Dockhead in the borough of Southwark, stands Jacob's Island, surrounded by a muddy ditch, six or eight feet deep, and fifteen or twenty wide when the tide is in, once called Mill Pond, but known in these days as Folly Ditch. It is a creek or inlet from the Thames, and can always be filled at high water by opening the sluices at the Lead Mills from which it took its old name. At such times a stranger, looking from one of the wooden bridges thrown across it at Mill Lane, will see the inhabitants of the houses on either side lowering from their back doors and windows buckets, pails, domestic utensils of all kinds, in which to haul the water up; and when his eye is turned from these operations to the houses themselves, his utmost astonishment will be excited by the scene before him. Crazy wooden galleries common to the backs of half a dozen houses, with holes from which to look upon the slime beneath; windows, broken and patched, with poles thrust out on which to dry the linen that is never there; rooms so small, so filthy, so confined, that the air would seem too tainted even for the dirt and squalor which they shelter; wooden chambers thrusting themselves out above the mud and threatening to fall into it—as some have done; dirt-besmeared walls and decaying foundations; every repulsive lineament of poverty, every loathsome indication of filth, rot, and garbage; all these ornament the banks of Folly Ditch.

In Jacob's Island, the warehouses are roofless and empty; the walls are crumbling down; the windows are windows no more; the doors are falling into the streets; the chimneys are blackened, but they yield no smoke. Thirty or forty years ago, before losses and chancery suits came upon it, it was a thriving place; but now it is a desolate island indeed. The houses have no owners; they are broken open and entered upon by those who have the courage; and there they live and there they die. They must have powerful motives for a secret residence, or be reduced to a destitute condition indeed, who seek a refuge in Jacob's Island.

In an upper room of one of these houses—a detached house of fair size, ruinous in other respects, but strongly defended at door and window, of which house the back commanded the ditch in manner already described—there were assembled three men, who, regarding each other every now and then with looks expressive of perplexity and expectation, sat for some time in profound and gloomy silence. One of these was Toby Crackit, another Mr. Chitling, and the third a robber of fifty years, whose nose had been almost beaten in in some old scuffle, and whose face bore a frightful scar which might probably be traced to the same occasion. This man was a returned transport, and his name was Kags.

"I wish," said Toby, turning to Mr. Chitling, "that you had picked out some other crib when the two old ones got too warm, and had not come here, my fine feller."

"Why didn't you, blunderhead?" said Kags.

"Well, I thought you'd have been a little more glad to see me than this," replied Mr. Chitling, with a melancholy air.

"Why, look'e, young gentleman," said Toby, "when a man keeps himself so very ex-clusive as I have done, and by that means has a snug house over his head, with nobody prying and smelling about it, it's rather a startling thing to have the honor of a wisit from a young gentleman (however respectable and pleasant a person he may be to play cards with a conweniency) circumstanced as you are."

"Especially when the exclusive young man has got a friend stopping with him that's arrived sooner than was expected from foreign parts, and is too modest to want to be presented to the Judges on his return," added Mr. Kags.

There was a short silence, after which Toby Crackit, seeming to abandon as hopeless any further effort to maintain his usual devil-may-care swagger, turned to Chitling and said:

"When was Fagin took, then?"

"Just at dinner-time—two o'clock this afternoon. Charley and I made our lucky up the wash'us chimney, and Bolter got into the empty water-butt, head downward; but his legs were so precious long that they stuck out at the top, and so they took him too."

"And Bet?"

"Poor Bet! She went to see the body, to speak to who it was," replied Chitling, his countenance falling more and more, "and went off mad, screaming and raving, and beating her head against the boards; so they put a strait weskut on her and took her to the hospital—and there she is."

"Wot's come of young Bates?" demanded Kags.

"He hung about, not to come over here afore dark, but he'll be here soon," replied Chitling. "There's nowhere else to go to now, for the people at the Cripples are all in custody, and the bar of the ken—I went up there and see it with my own eyes—is filled with traps."

"This is a smash," observed Toby, biting his lips. "There's more than one will go with this."

"The sessions are on," said Kags: "if they get the inquest over, and Bolter turns King's evidence, as of course he will, from what he's said already, they can prove Fagin an accessory before the fact, and get the trial on on Friday, and he'll swing in six days from this, by G—!"

"You should have heard the people groan," said Chitling;

"the officers fought like devils, or they'd have torn him away. He was down once, but they made a ring round him, and fought their way along. You should have seen how he looked about him, all muddy and bleeding, and clung to them as if they were his dearest friends. I can see 'em now not able to stand upright with the pressing of the mob, and dragging him along amongst 'em; I can see the people jumping up, one behind another, and snarling with their teeth and making at him like wild beasts; I can see the blood upon his hair and beard, and hear the cries with which the women worked themselves into the centre of the crowd at the street corner, and swore they'd tear his heart out!"

The horror-stricken witness of this scene pressed his hands upon his ears, and with his eyes closed, got up and paced violently to and fro, like one distracted.

While he was thus engaged, and the two men sat by in silence with their eyes fixed upon the floor, a pattering noise was heard upon the stairs, and Sikes's dog bounded into the room. They ran to the window, downstairs, and into the street. The dog had jumped in at an open window; he made no attempt to follow them, nor was his master to be seen.

"What's the meaning of this?" said Toby, when they had returned. "He can't be coming here. I—I—hope not."

"If he was coming here, he'd have come with the dog," said Kags, stooping down to examine the animal, who lay panting on the floor. "Here! Give us some water for him; he has run himself faint."

"He's drunk it all up, every drop," said Chitling, after watching the dog some time in silence. "Covered with mud —lame—half blind—he must have come a long way."

"Where can he have come from!" exclaimed Toby. "He's been to the other kens, of course, and, finding them filled with strangers, come on here where he's been many a time and often. But where can he have come from first, and how comes he here alone without the other!"

"He" (none of them called the murderer by his old name)

—"he can't have made away with himself. What do you think?" said Chitling.

Toby shook his head.

"If he had," said Kags, "the dog 'ud want to lead us away to where he did it. No. I think he's got out of the country and left the dog behind. He must have given him the slip somehow, or he wouldn't be so easy."

This solution, appearing the most probable one, was adopted as the right; and the dog, creeping under a chair, coiled himself up to sleep, without more notice from anybody.

It being now dark, the shutter was closed, and a candle lighted and placed upon the table. The terrible events of the last two days had made a deep impression on all three, increased by the danger and uncertainty of their own position. They drew their chairs closer together, starting at every sound. They spoke little, and that in whispers, and were as silent and awe-stricken as if the remains of the murdered woman lay in the next room.

They had sat thus some time, when suddenly was heard a hurried knocking at the door below.

"Young Bates," said Kags, looking angrily round, to check the fear he felt himself.

The knocking came again. No, it wasn't he. He never knocked like that.

Crackit went to the window, and, shaking all over, drew in his head. There was no need to tell them who it was; his pale face was enough. The dog, too, was on the alert in an instant, and ran whining to the door.

"We must let him in," he said, taking up the candle.

"Isn't there any help for it?" asked the other man, in a hoarse voice.

"None. He *must* come in."

"Don't leave us in the dark," said Kags, taking down a candle from the chimney-piece, and lighting it with such a trembling hand that the knocking was twice repeated before he had finished.

Crackit went down to the door, and returned, followed by a man with the lower part of his face buried in a handkerchief, and another tied over his head under his hat. He drew them slowly off. Blanched face, sunken eyes, hollow cheeks, beard of three days' growth, wasted flesh, short, thick breath; it was the very ghost of Sikes.

He had his hand upon a chair which stood in the middle of the room, but shuddering as he was about to drop into it, and seeming to glance over his shoulder, dragged it back close to the wall—as close as it would go—ground it against it—and sat down.

Not a word had been exchanged. He looked from one to another in silence. If an eye were furtively raised and met his, it was instantly averted. When his hollow voice broke silence, they all three started. They seemed never to have heard its tones before.

"How came that dog here?" he asked.

"Alone. Three hours ago."

"To-night's paper says that Fagin's taken. Is it true, or a lie?"

"True."

They were silent again.

"Damn you all," said Sikes, passing his hand across his forehead. "Have you nothing to say to me?"

There was an uneasy movement among them, but nobody spoke.

"You that keep this house," said Sikes, turning his face to Crackit, "do you mean to sell me, or to let me lie here till this hunt is over?"

"You may stop here, if you think it safe," returned the person addressed, after some hesitation.

Sikes carried his eyes slowly up the wall behind him, rather trying to turn his head than actually doing it, and said: "Is—it—the body—is it buried?"

They shook their heads.

"Why isn't it?" he retorted, with the same glance behind

him. "Wot do they keep such ugly things above the ground for?—Who's that knocking?"

Crackit intimated, by a motion of his hand as he left the room, that there was nothing to fear; and directly came back with Charley Bates behind him. Sikes sat opposite the door, so that the moment the boy entered the room he encountered his figure.

"Toby," said the boy, falling back, as Sikes turned his eyes toward him, "why didn't you tell me this downstairs?"

There had been something so tremendous in the shrinking off of the three that the wretched man was willing to propitiate even this lad. Accordingly, he nodded, and made as though he would shake hands with him.

"Let me go into some other room," said the boy, retreating still further.

"Charley!" said Sikes, stepping forward, "don't you—don't you know me?"

"Don't come nearer me," answered the boy, still retreating and looking, with horror in his eyes, upon the murderer's face. "You monster!"

The man stopped half-way, and they looked at each other, but Sikes's eyes sank gradually to the ground.

"Witness you three," cried the boy, shaking his clenched fist and becoming more and more excited as he spoke. "Witness you three—I'm not afraid of him—if they come here after him, I'll give him up; I will. I tell you out at once. He may kill me for it if he likes, or if he dares, but if I'm here, I'll give him up. I'd give him up if he was to be boiled alive. Murder! Help! If there's the pluck of a man among you three, you'll help me. Murder! Help! Down with him!"

Pouring out these cries, and accompanying them with violent gesticulation, the boy actually threw himself, single-handed, upon the strong man, and in the intensity of his energy, and the suddenness of his surprise, brought him heavily to the ground.

The three spectators seemed quite stupefied. They offered no interference, and the boy and man rolled on the ground together; the former, heedless of the blows that showered upon him, wrenching his hands tighter and tighter in the garments about the murderer's breast, and never ceasing to call for help with all his might.

The contest, however, was too unequal to last long. Sikes had him down, and his knee was on his throat, when Crackit pulled him back with a look of alarm, and pointed to the window. There were lights gleaming below, voices in loud and earnest conversation, the tramp of hurried footsteps—endless they seemed in number—crossing the nearest wooden bridge. One man on horseback seemed to be among the crowd, for there was the noise of hoofs rattling on the uneven pavement. The gleam of lights increased; the footsteps came more thickly and noisily on. Then came a loud knocking at the door, and then a hoarse murmur from such a multitude of angry voices as would have made the boldest quail.

"Help!" shrieked the boy, in a voice that rent the air. "He's here! Break down the door!"

"In the King's name," cried the voices without, and the hoarse cry rose again, but louder.

"Break down the door!" screamed the boy. "I tell you they'll never open it. Run straight to the room where the light is. Break down the door!"

Strokes, thick and heavy, rattled upon the door and lower window-shutters as he ceased to speak, and a loud huzza burst from the crowd, giving the listener for the first time some adequate idea of its immense extent.

"Open the door of some place where I can lock this screeching hell-babe," cried Sikes, fiercely, running to and fro, and dragging the boy now as easily as if he were an empty sack. "That door. Quick!" He flung him in, bolted it, and turned the key. "Is the downstairs door fast?"

"Double-locked and chained," replied Crackit, who, with the other two men, still remained quite helpless and bewildered.

"The panels—are they strong?"

"Lined with sheet-iron."

"And the windows too?"

"Yes, and the windows."

"Damn you!" cried the desperate ruffian, throwing up the sash and menacing the crowd. "Do your worst! I'll cheat you yet!"

Of all the terrific yells that ever fell on mortal ears, none could exceed the cry of the infuriated throng. Some shouted to those who were nearest to set the house on fire; others roared to the officers to shoot him dead. Among them all, none showed such fury as the man on horseback, who, throwing himself out of the saddle, and bursting through the crowd as if he were parting water, cried, beneath the window, in a voice that rose above all others: "Twenty guineas to the man who brings a ladder!"

The nearest voices took up the cry, and hundreds echoed it. Some called for ladders, some for sledge-hammers; some ran with torches to and fro as if to seek them, and still came back and roared again; some spent their breath in impotent curses and execrations; some pressed forward with the ecstasy of madmen, and thus impeded the progress of those below; some among the boldest attempted to climb up by the waterspout and crevices in the wall; and all waved to and fro, in the darkness beneath, like a field of corn moved by an angry wind, and joined from time to time in one loud furious roar.

"The tide," cried the murderer, as he staggered back into the room and shut the faces out—"the tide was in as I came up. Give me a rope, a long rope. They're all in front. I may drop into the Folly Ditch, and clear off that way. Give me a rope, or I shall do three more murders and kill myself."

The panic-stricken men pointed to where such articles were kept; the murderer, hastily selecting the longest and strongest cord, hurried up to the house-top.

All the windows in the rear of the house had been long ago bricked up, except one small trap in the room where the boy was locked, and that was too small even for the passage of his body. But, from this aperture, he had never ceased to call on those without to guard the back; and thus when the murderer emerged at last on the house-top by the door in the roof, a loud shout proclaimed the fact to those in front, who immediately began to pour around, pressing upon each other in one unbroken stream.

He planted a board which he had carried up with him for the purpose so firmly against the door that it must be matter of great difficulty to open it from the inside; and creeping over the tiles, looked over the low parapet.

The water was out, and the ditch a bed of mud.

The crowd had been hushed during these few moments, watching his motions and doubtful of his purpose, but the instant they perceived it and knew it was defeated, they raised a cry of triumphant execration to which all their previous shouting had been whispers. Again and again it rose. Those who were at too great a distance to know its meaning took up the sound: it echoed and re-echoed; it seemed as though the whole city had poured its population out to curse him.

On pressed the people from the front—on, on, on, in a strong struggling current of angry faces, with here and there a glaring torch to light them up, and show them out in all their wrath and passion. The houses on the opposite side of the ditch had been entered by the mob; sashes were thrown up, or torn bodily out; there were tiers and tiers of faces in every window, and cluster upon cluster of people clinging to every house-top. Each little bridge (and there were three in sight) bent beneath the weight of the crowd upon it. Still the current poured on to find some nook or hole from which to vent their shouts, and only for an instant see the wretch.

"They have him now," cried a man on the nearest bridge. "Hurrah!"

The crowd grew light with uncovered heads; and again the shout uprose.

"I will give fifty pounds," cried an old gentleman from

the same quarter, "to the man who takes him alive. I will remain here till he comes to ask me for it."

There was another roar. At this moment the word was passed among the crowd that the door was forced at last, and that he who had first called for the ladder had mounted into the room. The stream abruptly turned, as this intelligence ran from mouth to mouth; and the people at the windows, seeing those upon the bridges pouring back, quitted their stations, and running into the street, joined the concourse that now thronged pell-mell to the spot they had left; each man crushing and striving with his neighbor, and all panting with impatience to get near the door and look upon the criminal as the officers brought him out. The cries and shrieks of those who were pressed almost to suffocation, or trampled down and trodden underfoot in the confusion, were dreadful; the narrow ways were completely blocked up; and at this time, between the rush of some to regain the space in front of the house and the unavailing struggles of others to extricate themselves from the mass, the immediate attention was distracted from the murderer, although the eagerness for his capture was increased.

The man had shrunk down, thoroughly quelled by the ferocity of the crowd and the impossibility of escape; but seeing this sudden change with no less rapidity than it had occurred, he sprang upon his feet, determined to make an effort for his life by dropping into the ditch.

Roused into new strength and energy, and stimulated by the noise within the house, which announced that an entrance had really been effected, he set his foot against the stack of chimneys, fastened one end of the rope tightly and firmly round it, and with the other made a strong running noose by the aid of his hands and teeth almost in a second. He could let himself down by the cord to within a less distance of the ground than his own height, and had his knife ready in his hand to cut it then and drop.

At the very instant when he brought the loop over his head previous to slipping it beneath his arm-pits, and when the old gentleman before mentioned (who had clung so tight to the railing of the bridge as to resist the force of the crowd and retain his position) earnestly warned those about him that the man was about to lower himself down—at that very instant the murderer, looking behind him on the roof, threw his arms above his head, and uttered a yell of terror.

"The eyes again!" he cried, in an unearthly screech.

Staggering as if struck by lightning, he lost his balance and tumbled over the parapet.   The noose was at his neck. It ran up with his weight, tight as a bowstring, and swift as the arrow it speeds.   He fell for five-and-thirty feet.   There was a sudden jerk, a terrific convulsion of the limbs; and there he hung, with the open knife clenched in his stiffening hand.

The old chimney quivered with the shock, but stood it bravely.   The murderer swung lifeless against the wall; and the boy, thrusting aside the dangling body which obscured his view, called to the people to come and take him out, for God's sake.

A dog which had lain concealed till now ran backward and forward on the parapet with a dismal howl, and, collecting himself for a spring, jumped for the dead man's shoulders.   Missing his aim, he fell into the ditch, turning completely over as he went, and, striking his head against a stone, dashed out his brains.

RAPPACCINI'S DAUGHTER

By Nathaniel Hawthorne

A YOUNG man named Giovanni Guasconti came very long ago from the more southern region of Italy to pursue his studies at the University of Padua. Giovanni, who had but a scanty supply of gold ducats in his pocket, took lodgings in a high and gloomy chamber of an old edifice which looked not unworthy to have been the palace of a Paduan noble, and which, in fact, exhibited over its entrance the armorial bearings of a family long since extinct. The young stranger, who was not unstudied in the great poem of his country, recollected that one of the ancestors of this family, and perhaps an occupant of this very mansion, had been pictured by Dante as a partaker of the immortal agonies of his Inferno. These reminiscences and associations, together with the tendency to heartbreak natural to a young man for the first time out of his native sphere, caused Giovanni to sigh heavily as he looked around the desolate and ill-furnished apartment.

"Holy Virgin, signor!" cried old Dame Lisabetta, who, won by the youth's remarkable beauty of person, was kindly endeavoring to give the chamber a habitable air; "what a sigh was that to come out of a young man's heart! Do you find this old mansion gloomy? For the love of Heaven, then, put your head out of the window, and you will see as bright sunshine as you have left in Naples."

Guasconti mechanically did as the old woman advised, but could not quite agree with her that the Lombard sunshine was as cheerful as that of Southern Italy. Such as it was, however, it fell upon a garden beneath the window, and expended its fostering influences on a variety of plants which seemed to have been cultivated with exceeding care.

"Does this garden belong to the house?" asked Giovanni.

"Heaven forbid, signor, unless it were fruitful of better pot-herbs than any that grow there now," answered old Lisabetta. "No; that garden is cultivated by the own hands of Signor Giacomo Rappaccini, the famous doctor who, I warrant him, has been heard of as far as Naples. It is said that he distils these plants into medicines that are as potent as a charm. Oftentimes you may see the Signor Doctor at work, and perchance the signora his daughter, too, gathering the strange flowers that grow in the garden."

The old woman had now done what she could for the aspect of the chamber, and, commending the young man to the protection of the saints, took her departure.

Giovanni still found no better occupation than to look down into the garden beneath his window. From its appearance he judged it to be one of those botanic gardens which were of earlier date in Padua than elsewhere in Italy, or in the world. Or, not improbably, it might once have been the pleasure-place of an opulent family; for there was the ruin of a marble fountain in the centre, sculptured with rare art, but so woefully shattered that it was impossible to trace the original design from the chaos of remaining fragments. The water, however, continued to gush and sparkle into the sunbeams as cheerfully as ever. A little gurgling sound ascended to the young man's window and made him feel as if a fountain were an immortal spirit that sung its song unceasingly, and without heeding the vicissitudes around it, while one century embodied it in marble and another scattered the perishable garniture on the soil. All about the pool into which the water subsided grew various plants that seemed to require a plentiful supply of moisture for the nourishment of gigantic leaves, and in some instances flowers of gorgeous magnificence. There was one shrub in particular, set in a marble vase in the midst of the pool, that bore a profusion of purple blossoms, each of which had the lustre and richness of a gem; and the whole together made a show so resplendent that it seemed enough to illuminate the garden, even had there been no sunshine. Every portion of the soil was peopled with plants and herbs which, if less beautiful, still bore tokens of assiduous care, as if all had their individual virtues, known to the scientific mind that fostered them. Some were placed in urns rich with old carving and others in common garden-pots; some crept serpent-like along the ground, or climbed on high, using whatever means of ascent was offered them. One plant had wreathed itself round a statue of Vertumnus, which was thus quite veiled and shrouded in a drapery of hanging foliage so happily arranged that it might have served a sculptor for a study.

While Giovanni stood at the window he heard a rustling behind a screen of leaves, and became aware that a person was at work in the garden. His figure soon emerged into view, and showed itself to be that of no common laborer, but a tall, emaciated, sallow and sickly-looking man dressed in a scholar's garb of black. He was beyond the middle term of life, with gray hair, and a thin gray beard, and a face singularly marked with intellect and cultivation, but which could never, even in his more youthful days, have expressed much warmth of heart.

Nothing could exceed the intentness with which this scientific gardener examined every shrub which grew in his path; it seemed as if he was looking into their inmost nature, making observations in regard to their creative essence, and discovering why one leaf grew in this shape and another in that, and wherefore such and such flowers differed among themselves in hue and perfume. Nevertheless, in spite of the deep intelligence on his part, there was no approach to intimacy between himself and these vegetable existences. On the contrary, he avoided their actual touch or the direct inhaling of their odors with a caution that impressed Giovanni most disagreeably; for the man's de-

meanor was that of one walking among malignant influences, such as savage beasts or deadly snakes or evil spirits
which, should he allow them one moment of license, would
wreak upon him some terrible fatality. It was strangely
frightful to the young man's imagination to see this air of
insecurity in a person cultivating a garden—that most simple and innocent of human toils, and which had been alike
the joy and labor of the unfallen parents of the race. Was
this garden, then, the Eden of the present world? and this
man with such a perception of harm in what his own hands
caused to grow—was he the Adam?

The distrustful gardener, while plucking away the dead
leaves or pruning the too luxuriant growth of the shrubs,
defended his hands with a pair of thick gloves. Nor were
these his only armor. When, in his walk through the garden, he came to the magnificent plant that hung its purple
gems beside the marble fountain, he placed a kind of mask
over his mouth and nostrils, as if all this beauty did but
conceal a deadlier malice. But, finding his task still too
dangerous, he drew back, removed the mask, and called
loudly, but in the infirm voice of a person affected with inward disease:

"Beatrice! Beatrice!"

"Here am I, my father! What would you?" cried a rich
and youthful voice from the window of the opposite house—
a voice as rich as a tropical sunset, and which made Giovanni, though he knew not why, think of deep hues of purple
or crimson and of perfumes heavily delectable. "Are you in
the garden?"

"Yes, Beatrice," answered the gardener, "and I need your
help."

Soon there emerged from under a sculptured portal the
figure of a young girl arrayed with as much richness of
taste as the most splendid of the flowers, beautiful as the
day, and with a bloom so deep and vivid that one shade more
would have been too much. She looked redundant with life,
health, and energy; all of which attributes were bound down

and compressed, as it were, and girdled tensely in their luxuriance by her virgin zone. Yet Giovanni's fancy must have grown morbid while he looked down into the garden, for the impression which the fair stranger made upon him was as if here were another flower, the human sister of those vegetable ones, as beautiful as they—more beautiful than the richest of them—but still to be touched only with a glove, nor to be approached without a mask. As Beatrice came down the garden path it was observable that she handled and inhaled the odor of several of the plants which her father had most sedulously avoided.

"Here, Beatrice," said the latter; "see how many needful offices require to be done to our chief treasure. Yet, shattered as I am, my life might pay the penalty of approaching it so closely as circumstances demand. Henceforth, I fear, this plant must be consigned to your sole charge."

"And gladly will I undertake it," cried again the rich tones of the young lady as she bent toward the magnificent plant and opened her arms as if to embrace it. "Yes, my sister, my splendor, it shall be Beatrice's task to nurse and serve thee, and thou shalt reward her with thy kisses and perfume-breath, which to her is as the breath of life."

Then, with all the tenderness in her manner that was so strikingly expressed in her words, she busied herself with such attentions as the plant seemed to require; and Giovanni, at his lofty window, rubbed his eyes, and almost doubted whether it were a girl tending her favorite flower or one sister performing the duties of affection to another.

The scene soon terminated. Whether Doctor Rappaccini had finished his labors in the garden or that his watchful eye had caught the stranger's face, he now took his daughter's arm and retired. Night was already closing in; oppressive exhalations seemed to proceed from the plants and steal upward past the open window, and Giovanni, closing the lattice, went to his couch and dreamed of a rich flower and beautiful girl. Flower and maiden were different, and yet the same, and fraught with some strange peril in either shape.

But there is an influence in the light of morning that tends to rectify whatever errors of fancy, or even of judgment, we may have incurred during the sun's decline, or among the shadows of the night, or in the less wholesome glow of moonshine. Giovanni's first movement on starting from sleep was to throw open the window and gaze down into the garden which his dreams had made so fertile of mysteries. He was surprised, and a little ashamed, to find how real and matter-of-fact an affair it proved to be in the first rays of the sun, which gilded the dewdrops that hung upon leaf and blossom, and, while giving a brighter beauty to each rare flower, brought everything within the limits of ordinary experience. The young man rejoiced that in the heart of the barren city he had the privilege of overlooking this spot of lovely and luxuriant vegetation. It would serve, he said to himself, as a symbolic language to keep him in communion with Nature. Neither the sickly and thought-worn Doctor Giacomo Rappaccini, it is true, nor his brilliant daughter, was now visible; so that Giovanni could not determine how much of the singularity which he attributed to both was due to their own qualities, and how much to his wonder-working fancy. But he was inclined to take a most rational view of the whole matter.

In the course of the day he paid his respects to Signor Pietro Baglioni, professor of medicine in the university, a physician of eminent repute to whom Giovanni had brought a letter of introduction. The professor was an elderly personage, apparently of genial nature and habits that might almost be called jovial; he kept the young man to dinner and made himself very agreeable by the freedom and liveliness of his conversation, especially when warmed by a flask or two of Tuscan wine. Giovanni, conceiving that men of science, inhabitants of the same city, must needs be on familiar terms with one another, took an opportunity to mention the name of Doctor Rappaccini. But the professor did not respond with so much cordiality as he had anticipated.

"Ill would it become a teacher of the divine art of medicine," said Professor Pietro Baglioni, in answer to a question of Giovanni, "to withhold due and well-considered praise of a physician so eminently skilled as Rappaccini. But, on the other hand, I should answer it but scantily to my conscience were I to permit a worthy youth like yourself, Signor Giovanni, the son of an ancient friend, to imbibe erroneous ideas respecting a man who might hereafter chance to hold your life and death in his hands. The truth is, our worshipful Doctor Rappaccini has as much science as any member of the faculty—with perhaps one single exception—in Padua or all Italy, but there are certain grave objections to his professional character."

"And what are they?" asked the young man.

"Has my friend Giovanni any disease of body or heart, that he is so inquisitive about physicians?" said the professor, with a smile. "But, as for Rappaccini, it is said of him—and I, who know the man well, can answer for its truth—that he cares infinitely more for science than for mankind. His patients are interesting to him only as subjects for some new experiment. He would sacrifice human life—his own among the rest—or whatever else was dearest to him, for the sake of adding so much as a grain of mustard-seed to the great heap of his accumulated knowledge."

"Methinks he is an awful man indeed," remarked Guasconti, mentally recalling the cold and pursely intellectual aspect of Rappaccini. "And yet, worshipful professor, is it not a noble spirit? Are there many men capable of so spiritual a love of science?"

"God forbid!" answered the professor somewhat testily —"at least, unless they take sounder views of the healing art than those adopted by Rappaccini. It is his theory that all medicinal virtues are comprised within those substances which we term vegetable poisons. These he cultivates with his own hands, and is said even to have produced new varieties of poison more horribly deleterious than Nature, without the assistance of this learned person, would ever have plagued the world with. That the Signor Doctor does less mischief than might be expected with such dangerous substances is undeniable. Now and then, it must be owned, he has effected—or seemed to effect—a marvelous cure. But, to tell you my private mind, Signor Giovanni, he should receive little credit for such instances of success—they being probably the work of chance—but should be held strictly accountable for his failures, which may justly be considered his own work."

The youth might have taken Baglioni's opinions with many grains of allowance had he known that there was a professional warfare of long continuance between him and Doctor Rappaccini, in which the latter was generally thought to have gained the advantage. If the reader be inclined to judge for himself, we refer him to certain black-letter tracts on both sides preserved in the medical department of the University of Padua.

"I know not, most learned professor," returned Giovanni, after musing on what had been said of Rappaccini's exclusive zeal for science—"I know not how dearly this physician may love his art, but surely there is one object more dear to him. He has a daughter."

"Aha!" cried the professor, with a laugh. "So now our friend Giovanni's secret is out! You have heard of this daughter, whom all the young men in Padua are wild about, though not half a dozen have ever had the good hap to see her face. I know little of the Signora Beatrice save that Rappaccini is said to have instructed her deeply in his science, and that, young and beautiful as fame reports her, she is already qualified to fill a professor's chair. Perchance her father destines her for mine. Other absurd rumors there be, not worth talking about or listening to. So now, Signor Giovanni, drink off your glass of Lacryma."

Guasconti returned to his lodgings somewhat heated with the wine he had quaffed, and which caused his brain to swim with strange fantasies in reference to Doctor Rappaccini and the beautiful Beatrice. On his way, happening to pass by a florist's, he bought a fresh bouquet of flowers.

Ascending to his chamber, he seated himself near the window, but within the shadow thrown by the depth of the wall, so that he could look down into the garden with little risk of being discovered. All beneath his eye was a solitude. The strange plants were basking in the sunshine, and now and then nodding gently to one another, as if in acknowledgment of sympathy and kindred. In the midst, by the shattered fountain, grew the magnificent shrub, with its purple gems clustering all over it; they glowed in the air and gleamed back again out of the depths of the pool, which thus seemed to overflow with colored radiance from the rich reflection that was steeped in it. At first, as we have said, the garden was a solitude. Soon, however, as Giovanni had half hoped, half feared, would be the case, a figure appeared beneath the antique sculptured portal and came down between the rows of plants, inhaling their various perfumes as if she were one of those beings of old classic fable that lived upon sweet odors. On again beholding Beatrice the young man was even startled to perceive how much her beauty exceeded his recollection of it—so brilliant, so vivid in its character, that she glowed amid the sunlight, and, as Giovanni whispered to himself, positively illuminated the more shadowy intervals of the garden path. Her face being now more revealed than on the former occasion, he was struck by its expression of simplicity and sweetness—qualities that had not entered into his idea of her character, and which made him ask anew what manner of mortal she might be. Nor did he fail again to observe or imagine an analogy between the beautiful girl and the gorgeous shrub that hung its gemlike flowers over the fountain—a resemblance which Beatrice seemed to have indulged a fantastic humor in heightening both by the arrangement of her dress and the selection of its hues.

Approaching the shrub, she threw open her arms as with

a passionate ardor, and drew its branches into an intimate
embrace—so intimate that her features were hidden in its
leafy bosom and her glistening ringlets all intermingled with
the flowers.

"Give me thy breath, my sister," exclaimed Beatrice, "for
I am faint with common air. And give me this flower of
thine, which I separate with gentlest fingers from the stem,
and place it close beside my heart."

With these words the beautiful daughter of Rappaccini
plucked one of the richest blossoms of the shrub, and was
about to fasten it in her bosom. But now, unless Giovanni's
drafts of wine had bewildered his senses, a singular incident occurred. A small orange-colored reptile of the lizard
or chameleon species chanced to be creeping along the path
just at the feet of Beatrice. It appeared to Giovanni, but
at the distance from which he gazed he could scarcely have
seen anything so minute—it appeared to him, however, that
a drop or two of moisture from the broken stem of the
flower descended upon the lizard's head. For an instant the
reptile contorted itself violently, and then lay motionless in
the sunshine. Beatrice observed this remarkable phenomenon and crossed herself sadly, but without surprise; nor
did she therefore hesitate to arrange the fatal flower in her
bosom. There it blushed, and almost glimmered with the
dazzling effect of a precious stone, adding to her dress and
aspect the one appropriate charm which nothing else in the
world could have supplied. But Giovanni, out of the shadow
of his window, bent forward and shrank back, and murmured and trembled.

"Am I awake? Have I my senses?" said he to himself.
"What is this being? Beautiful shall I call her, or inexpressibly terrible?"

Beatrice now strayed carelessly through the garden, approaching closer beneath Giovanni's window; so that he was
compelled to thrust his head quite out of its concealment in
order to gratify the intense and painful curiosity which she
excited. At this moment there came a beautiful insect over

the garden wall; it had perhaps wandered through the city and found no flowers nor verdure among those antique haunts of men until the heavy perfumes of Doctor Rappaccini's shrubs had lured it from afar. Without alighting on the flowers this winged brightness seemed to be attracted by Beatrice, and lingered in the air and fluttered about her head. Now, here it could not be but that Giovanni Guasconti's eyes deceived him. Be that as it might, he fancied that while Beatrice was gazing at the insect with childish delight it grew faint and fell at her feet. Its bright wings shivered; it was dead—from no cause that he could discern, unless it were the atmosphere of her breath. Again Beatrice crossed herself and sighed heavily as she bent over the dead insect.

An impulsive movement of Giovanni drew her eyes to the window. There she beheld the beautiful head of the young man—rather a Grecian than an Italian head, with fair, regular features and a glistening of gold among his ringlets—gazing down upon her like a being that hovered in midair. Scarcely knowing what he did, Giovanni threw down the bouquet which he had hitherto held in his hand.

"Signora," said he, "there are pure and healthful flowers: wear them for the sake of Giovanni Gausconti."

"Thanks, signor!" replied Beatrice, with her rich voice, that came forth as it were like a gush of music, and with a mirthful expression, half childish and half woman-like. "I accept your gift, and would fain recompense it with this precious purple flower; but if I toss it into the air, it will not reach you. So Signor Guasconti must even content himself with my thanks."

She lifted the bouquet from the ground, and then, as if inwardly ashamed at having stepped aside from her maidenly reserve to respond to a stranger's greeting, passed swiftly homeward through the garden. But, few as the moments were, it seemed to Giovanni, when she was on the point of vanishing beneath the sculptured portal, that his beautiful bouquet was already beginning to wither in her grasp. It was an idle thought: there could be no possibility of distinguishing a faded flower from a fresh one at so great a distance.

For many days after this incident the young man avoided the window that looked into Doctor Rappaccini's garden as if something ugly and monstrous would have blasted his eyesight had he been betrayed into a glance. He felt conscious of having put himself, to a certain extent, within the influence of an unintelligible power by the communication which he had opened with Beatrice. The wisest course would have been, if his heart were in any real danger, to quit his lodgings, and Padua itself, at once; the next wiser, to have accustomed himself as far as possible to the familiar and daylight view of Beatrice, thus bringing her rigidly and systematically within the limits of ordinary experience. Least of all, while avoiding her sight, should Giovanni have remained so near this extraordinary being that the proximity, and possibility even of intercourse, should give a kind of substance and reality to the wild vagaries which his imagination ran riot continually in producing. Guasconti had not a deep heart—or, at all events, its depths were not sounded now—but he had a quick fancy and an ardent southern temperament which rose every instant to a higher fever-pitch. Whether or no Beatrice possessed those terrible attributes— that fatal breath, the affinity with those so beautiful and deadly flowers—which were indicated by what Giovanni had witnessed, she had at least instilled a fierce and subtle poison into his system. It was not love, although her rich beauty was a madness to him, nor horror, even while he fancied her spirit to be imbued with the same baneful essence that seemed to pervade her physical frame, but a wild offspring of both love and horror that had each parent in it and burned like one and shivered like the other. Giovanni knew not what to dread; still less did he know what to hope; yet hope and dread kept a continual warfare in his breast, alternately vanquishing one another and starting up afresh to renew the contest. Blessed are all simple emotions, be they dark or bright! It is the lurid intermixture of the two that produces the illuminating blaze of the infernal regions.

Sometimes he endeavored to assuage the fever of his spirit by a rapid walk through the streets of Padua or beyond its gates; his footsteps kept time with the throbbings of his brain, so that the walk was apt to accelerate itself to a race. One day he found himself arrested; his arm was seized by a portly personage who had turned back on recognizing the young man and expended much breath in overtaking him.

"Signor Giovanni! Stay, my young friend!" cried he. "Have you forgotten me? That might well be the case if I were as much altered as yourself."

It was Baglioni, whom Giovanni had avoided ever since their first meeting, from a doubt that the professor's sagacity would look too deeply into his secrets. Endeavoring to recover himself, he stared forth wildly from his inner world into the outer one, and spoke like a man in a dream:

"Yes; I am Giovanni Guasconti. You are Professor Pietro Baglioni. Now let me pass."

"Not yet—not yet, Signor Giovanni Guasconti," said the professor, smiling, but at the same time scrutinizing the youth with an earnest glance. "What! Did I grow up side by side with your father, and shall his son pass me like a stranger in these old streets of Padua? Stand still, Signor Giovanni, for we must have a word or two before we part."

"Speedily, then, most worshipful professor—speedily!" said Giovanni, with feverish impatience. "Does not Your Worship see that I am in haste?"

Now, while he was speaking, there came a man in black along the street, stooping and moving feebly like a person in inferior health. His face was all overspread with a most sickly and sallow hue, but yet so pervaded with an expression of piercing and active intellect that an observer might have easily overlooked the merely physical attributes, and have seen only this wonderful energy. As he passed, this person exchanged a cold and distant salutation with Baglioni, but fixed his eyes upon Giovanni with an intentness that seemed to bring out whatever was within him worthy of notice. Nevertheless, there was a peculiar quietness in the look, as if taking merely a speculative, not a human, interest in the young man.

"It is Doctor Rappaccini," whispered the professor, when the stranger had passed. "Has he ever seen your face before?"

"Not that I know," answered Giovanni, starting at the name.

"He *has* seen you! he must have seen you!" said Baglioni, hastily. "For some purpose or other, this man of science is making a study of you. I know that look of his: it is the same that coldly illuminates his face as he bends over a bird, a mouse or a butterfly which in pursuance of some experiment he has killed by the perfume of a flower— a look as deep as Nature itself, but without Nature's warmth of love. Signor Giovanni, I will stake my life upon it you are the subject of one of Rappaccini's experiments."

"Will you make a fool of me?" cried Giovanni, passionately. "That, Signor Professor, were an untoward experiment."

"Patience, patience!" replied the imperturbable professor. "I tell thee, my poor Giovanni, that Rappaccini has a scientific interest in thee. Thou hast fallen into fearful hands. And the Signora Beatrice—what part does she act in this mystery?"

But Guasconti, finding Baglioni's pertinacity intolerable, here broke away, and was gone before the professor could again seize his arm. He looked after the young man intently, and shook his head.

"This must not be," said Baglioni to himself. "The youth is the son of my old friend, and shall not come to any harm from which the arcana of medical science can preserve him. Besides, it is too insufferable an impertinence in Rappaccini thus to snatch the lad out of my own hands, as I may say, and make use of him for his infernal experiments. This daughter of his! It shall be looked to. Perchance, most learned Rappaccini, I may foil you where you little dream of it!"

Meanwhile, Giovanni had pursued a circuitous route, and at length found himself at the door of his lodgings. As he crossed the threshold he was met by old Lisabetta, who smirked and smiled and was evidently desirous to attract his attention—vainly, however, as the ebullition of his feelings had momentarily subsided into a cold and dull vacuity. He turned his eyes full upon the withered face that was puckering itself into a smile, but seemed to behold it not. The old dame, therefore, laid her grasp upon his cloak.

"Signor, signor!" whispered she, still with a smile over the whole breadth of her visage, so that it looked not unlike a grotesque carving in wood, darkened by centuries. "Listen, signor! There is a private entrance into the garden."

"What do you say?" exclaimed Giovanni, turning quickly about, as if an inanimate thing should start into feverish life. "A private entrance into Doctor Rappaccini's garden?"

"Hush, hush! Not so loud!" whispered Lisabetta, putting her hand over his mouth. "Yes, into the worshipful doctor's garden, where you may see all his fine shrubbery. Many a young man in Padua would give gold to be admitted among those flowers."

Giovanni put a piece of gold into her hand.

"Show me the way," said he.

A surmise, probably excited by his conversation with Baglioni, crossed his mind that this interposition of old Lisabetta might perchance be connected with the intrigue, whatever were its nature, in which the professor seemed to suppose that Doctor Rappaccini was involving him. But such a suspicion, though it disturbed Giovanni, was inadequate to restrain him. The instant he was aware of the possibility of approaching Beatrice, it seemed an absolute necessity of his existence to do so. It mattered not whether she were angel or demon: he was irrevocably within her sphere, and must obey the law that whirled him onward in ever lessening circles toward a result which he did not attempt to foreshadow. And yet, strange to say, there came across him a sudden doubt whether this intense interest on his part were not delusory, whether it were really of so deep and positive a nature as to justify him in now thrusting himself into an incalculable position, whether it were not merely the fantasy of a young man's brain only slightly or not at all connected with his heart.

He paused, hesitated, turned half about, but again went on. His withered guide led him along several obscure passages, and finally undid a door through which, as it was opened, there came the sight and sound of rustling leaves with the broken sunshine glimmering among them. Giovanni stepped forth, and, forcing himself through the entanglement of a shrub that wreathed its tendrils over the hidden entrance, he stood beneath his own window, in the open area of Doctor Rappaccini's garden.

How often is it the case that when impossibilities have come to pass, and dreams have condensed their misty substance into tangible realities, we find ourselves calm and even coldly self-possessed, amid circumstances which it would have been a delirium of joy or agony to anticipate! Fate delights to thwart us thus. Passion will choose his own time to rush upon the scene, and lingers sluggishly behind when an appropriate adjustment of events would seem to summon his appearance. So was it now with Giovanni. Day after day his pulses had throbbed with feverish blood at the improbable idea of an interview with Beatrice, and of standing with her face to face in this very garden, basking in the Oriental sunshine of her beauty and snatching from her full gaze the mystery which he deemed the riddle of his own existence. But now there was a singular and untimely equanimity within his breast. He threw a glance around the garden to discover if Beatrice or her father were present, and perceiving that he was alone, began a critical observation of the plants.

The aspect of one and all of them dissatisfied him: their gorgeousness seemed fierce, passionate, and even unnatural. There was hardly an individual shrub which a wanderer straying by himself through a forest would not have been startled to find growing wild, as if an unearthly face had glared at him out of the thicket. Several, also, would have shocked a delicate instinct by an appearance of artificialness, indicating that there had been such a commixture, and, as it were, adultery of various vegetable species that the production was no longer of God's making, but the monstrous offspring of man's depraved fancy, glowing with only an evil mockery of beauty. They were probably the result of experiment, which in one or two cases had succeeded in mingling plants individually lovely into a compound possessing the questionable and ominous character that distinguished the whole growth of the garden. In fine, Giovanni recognized but two or three plants in the collection, and those of a kind that he well knew to be poisonous. While busy with these contemplations he heard the rustling of a silken garment, and turning beheld Beatrice emerging from beneath the sculptured portal.

Giovanni had not considered with himself what should be his deportment—whether he should apologize for his intrusion into the garden or assume that he was there with the privity at least, if not by the desire, of Doctor Rappaccini or his daughter. But Beatrice's manner placed him at his ease, though leaving him still in doubt by what agency he had gained admittance. She came lightly along the path, and met him near the broken fountain. There was surprise in her face, but brightened by a simple and kind expression of pleasure.

"You are a connoisseur in flowers, signor," said Beatrice, with a smile, alluding to the bouquet which he had flung her from the window; "it is no marvel, therefore, if the sight of my father's rare collection has tempted you to take a nearer view. If he were here, he could tell you many strange and interesting facts as to the nature and habits of these shrubs, for he has spent a lifetime in such studies, and this garden is his world."

"And yourself, lady?" observed Giovanni. "If fame says true, you likewise are deeply skilled in the virtues indicated by these rich blossoms and these spicy perfumes. Would you deign to be my instructress, I should prove an apter scholar than under Signor Rappaccini himself."

"Are there such idle rumors?" asked Beatrice, with the music of a pleasant laugh. "Do people say that I am skilled in my father's science of plants? What a jest is there! No; though I have grown up among these flowers I know no more of them than their hues and perfume, and sometimes methinks I would fain rid myself of even that small knowledge. There are many flowers here—and those not the least brilliant—that shock and offend me when they meet my eye. But pray, signor, do not believe these stories about my science; believe nothing of me save what you see with your own eyes."

"And must I believe all that I have seen with my own eyes?" asked Giovanni, pointedly, while the recollection of former scenes made him shrink. "No, signora; you demand too little of me. Bid me believe nothing save what comes from your own lips."

It would appear that Beatrice understood him. There came a deep flush to her cheek, but she looked full into Giovanni's eyes and responded to his gaze of uneasy suspicion with a queenlike haughtiness:

"I do so bid you, signor," she replied. "Forget whatever you may have fancied in regard to me; if true to the outward senses, still it may be false in its essence. But the words of Beatrice Rappaccini's lips are true from the heart outward; those you may believe."

A fervor glowed in her whole aspect and beamed upon Giovanni's consciousness like the light of truth itself. But while she spoke there was a fragrance in the atmosphere around her, rich and delightful, though evanescent, yet which the young man, from an indefinable reluctance, scarcely dared to draw into his lungs. It might be the odor of the flowers. Could it be Beatrice's breath which thus embalmed her words with a strange richness, as if by steeping them in her heart. A faintness passed like a shadow over Giovanni, and flitted away; he seemed to gaze through the beautiful girl's eyes into her transparent soul, and felt no more doubt or fear.

The tinge of passion that had colored Beatrice's manner vanished; she became gay, and appeared to derive a pure delight from her communion with the youth, not unlike what the maiden of a lonely island might have felt conversing with a voyager from the civilized world. Evidently her experience of life had been confined within the limits of that garden. She talked now about matters as simple as the daylight or summer clouds, and now asked questions in reference to the city or Giovanni's distant home, his friends, his mother and his sisters—questions indicating such seclusion and such lack of familiarity with modes and forms that Giovanni responded as if to an infant. Her spirit gushed out before him like a fresh rill that was just catching its first glimpse of the sunlight and wondering at the reflections of earth and sky which were flung into its bosom. There came thoughts, too, from a deep source, and fantasies of a gemlike brilliancy, as if diamonds and rubies sparkled upward among the bubbles of the fountain. Ever and anon there gleamed across the young man's mind a sense of wonder that he should be walking side by side with the being who had so wrought upon his imagination, whom he had idealized in such hues of terror, in whom he had positively witnessed such manifestations of dreadful attributes—that he should be conversing with Beatrice like a brother, and should find her so human and so maiden-like. But such reflections were only momentary; the effect of her character was too real not to make itself familiar at once.

In this free intercourse they had strayed through the

garden, and now, after many turns among its avenues, were come to the shattered fountain beside which grew the magnificent shrub with its treasury of glowing blossoms. A fragrance was diffused from it which Giovanni recognized as identical with that which he had attributed to Beatrice's breath, but incomparably more powerful. As her eyes fell upon it, Giovanni beheld her press her hand to her bosom, as if her heart were throbbing suddenly and painfully.

"For the first time in my life," murmured she, addressing the shrub, "I had forgotten thee."

"I remember, signora," said Giovanni, "that you once promised to reward me with one of those living gems for the bouquet which I had the happy boldness to fling to your feet. Permit me now to pluck it as a memorial of this interview."

He made a step toward the shrub with extended hand. But Beatrice darted forward, uttering a shriek that went through his heart like a dagger. She caught his hand and drew it back with the whole force of her slender figure. Giovanni felt her touch thrilling through his fibres.

"Touch it not," exclaimed she, in a voice of agony—"not for thy life! It is fatal."

Then, hiding her face, she fled from him and vanished beneath the sculptured portal. As Giovanni followed her with his eyes he beheld the emaciated figure and pale intelligence of Doctor Rappaccini, who had been watching the scene, he knew not how long, within the shadow of the entrance.

No sooner was Guasconti alone in his chamber than the image of Beatrice came back to his passionate musings invested with all the witchery that had been gathering around it ever since his first glimpse of her, and now likewise imbued with a tender warmth of girlish womanhood. She was human; her nature was endowed with all gentle and feminine qualities; she was worthiest to be worshiped; she was capable, surely, on her part, of the height and heroism of love. Those tokens which he had hitherto considered as proofs of a frightful peculiarity in her physical and moral system were now either forgotten or by the subtle sophistry of passion transmitted into a golden crown of enchantment; rendering Beatrice the more admirable by so much as she was the more unique. Whatever had looked ugly was now beautiful; or, if incapable of such a change, it stole away and hid itself among those shapeless half-ideas which throng the dim region beyond the daylight of our perfect consciousness.

Thus did Giovanni spend the night, nor fell asleep until the dawn had begun to awake the slumbering flowers in Doctor Rappaccini's garden, whither his dreams doubtless led him. Up rose the sun in his due season, and flinging his beams upon the young man's eyelids, awoke him to a sense of pain. When thoroughly aroused, he became sensible of a burning and tingling agony in his hand, in his right hand— the very hand which Beatrice had grasped in her own when he was on the point of plucking one of the gemlike flowers. On the back of that hand there was now a purple print like that of four small fingers, and the likeness of a slender thumb upon his wrist. Oh, how stubbornly does love, or even that cunning semblance of love which flourishes in the imagination, but strikes no depth of root into the heart— how stubbornly does it hold its faith until the moment comes when it is doomed to vanish into the mist! Giovanni wrapped a handkerchief about his hand, and wondered what evil thing had stung him, and soon forgot his pain in a reverie of Beatrice.

After the first interview, a second was in the inevitable course of what we call fate. A third, a fourth, and a meeting with Beatrice in the garden was no longer an incident in Giovanni's daily life, but the whole space in which he might be said to live, for the anticipation and memory of that ecstatic hour made up the remainder. Nor was it otherwise with the daughter of Rappaccini. She watched for the youth's appearance, and flew to his side with confidence as unreserved as if they had been playmates from early infancy

—as if they were such playmates still. If by any unwonted chance he failed to come at the appointed moment, she stood beneath the window and sent up the rich sweetness of her tones to float around him in his chamber and echo and reverberate throughout his heart. "Giovanni, Giovanni! Why tarriest thou? Come down!" and down he hastened into that Eden of poisonous flowers.

But with all this intimate familiarity there was still a reserve in Beatrice's demeanor so rigidly and invariably sustained that the idea of infringing it scarcely occurred to his imagination. By all appreciable signs they loved—they had looked love with eyes that conveyed the holy secret from the depths of one soul into the depths of the other, as if it were too sacred to be whispered by the way; they had even spoken love in those gushes of passion when their spirits darted forth in articulated breath like tongues of long-hidden flame—and yet there had been no seal of lips, no clasp of hands, nor any slightest caress such as love claims and hallows. He had never touched one of the gleaming ringlets of her hair; her garment—so marked was the physical barrier between them—had never been waved against him by a breeze. On the few occasions when Giovanni had seemed tempted to overstep the limit, Beatrice grew so sad, so stern, and, withal, wore such a look of desolate separation shuddering at itself that not a spoken word was requisite to repel him. At such times he was startled at the horrible suspicions that rose monster-like out of the caverns of his heart and stared him in the face. His love grew thin and faint as the morning mist; his doubts alone had substance. But when Beatrice's face brightened again after the momentary shadow, she was transformed at once from the mysterious, questionable being whom he had watched with so much awe and horror; she was now the beautiful and unsophisticated girl whom he felt that his spirit knew with a certainty beyond all other knowledge.

A considerable time had now passed since Giovanni's last meeting with Baglioni. One morning, however, he was disagreeably surprised by a visit from the professor, whom he had scarcely thought of for whole weeks, and would willingly have forgotten still longer. Given up, as he had long been, to a pervading excitement, he could tolerate no companions except upon condition of their perfect sympathy with his present state of feeling; such sympathy was not to be expected from Professor Baglioni.

The visitor chatted carelessly for a few moments about the gossip of the city and the university, and then took up another topic.

"I have been reading an old classic author lately," said he, "and met with a story that strangely interested me. Possibly you may remember it. It is of an Indian prince who sent a beautiful woman as a present to Alexander the Great. She was as lovely as the dawn and gorgeous as the sunset, but what especially distinguished her was a certain rich perfume in her breath richer than a garden of Persian roses. Alexander, as was natural to a youthful conqueror, fell in love at first sight with this magnificent stranger. But a certain sage physician, happening to be present, discovered a terrible secret in regard to her."

"And what was that?" asked Giovanni, turning his eyes downward to avoid those of the professor.

"That this lovely woman," continued Baglioni, with emphasis, "had been nourished with poisons from her birth upward, until her whole nature was so imbued with them that she herself had become the deadliest poison in existence. Poison was her element of life. With that rich perfume of her breath she blasted the very air. Her love would have been poison—her embrace, death. Is not this a marvelous tale?"

"A childish fable," answered Giovanni, nervously starting from his chair. "I marvel how Your Worship finds time to read such nonsense among your graver studies."

"By the by," said the professor, looking uneasily about him, "what singular fragrance is this in your apartment? Is it the perfume of your gloves? It is faint, but delicious, and yet, after all, by no means agreeable. Were I to breathe it long, methinks it would make me ill. It is like the breath of a flower, but I see no flowers in the chamber."

"Nor are there any," replied Giovanni, who had turned pale as the professor spoke; "nor, I think, is there any fragrance except in Your Worship's imagination. Odors, being a sort of element combined of the sensual and the spiritual, are apt to deceive us in this manner. The recollection of a perfume—the bare idea of it—may easily be mistaken for a present reality."

"Ay, but my sober imagination does not often play such tricks," said Baglioni; "and were I to fancy any kind of odor, it would be that of some vile apothecary-drug wherewith my fingers are likely enough to be imbued. Our worshipful friend Rappaccini, as I have heard, tinctures his medicaments with odors richer than those of Araby. Doubtless, likewise, the fair and learned Signora Beatrice would minister to her patients with drafts as sweet as a maiden's breath, but woe to him that sips them!"

Giovanni's face evinced many contending emotions. The tone in which the professor alluded to the pure and lovely daughter of Rappaccini was a torture to his soul, and yet the intimation of a view of her character opposite to his own gave instantaneous distinctness to a thousand dim suspicions which now grinned at him like so many demons. But he strove hard to quell them, and to respond to Baglioni with a true lover's perfect faith.

"Signor Professor," said he, "you were my father's friend; perchance, too, it is your purpose to act a friendly part toward his son. I would fain feel nothing toward you save respect and deference, but I pray you to observe, signor, that there is one subject on which we must not speak. You know not the Signora Beatrice; you can not, therefore, estimate the wrong—the blasphemy, I may even say—that is offered to her character by a light or injurious word."

"Giovanni! my poor Giovanni!" answered the professor, with a calm expression of pity. "I know this wretched girl far better than yourself. You shall hear the truth in respect to the poisoner Rappaccini and his poisonous daughter—yes, poisonous as she is beautiful. Listen, for even should you do violence to my gray hairs it shall not silence me. That old fable of the Indian woman has become a truth by the deep and deadly science of Rappaccini and in the person of the lovely Beatrice."

Giovanni groaned and hid his face.

"Her father," continued Baglioni, "was not restrained by natural affection from offering up his child in this horrible manner as the victim of his insane zeal for science. For—let us do him justice—he is as true a man of science as ever distilled his own heart in an alembic. What, then, will be your fate? Beyond a doubt, you are selected as the material of some new experiment. Perhaps the result is to be death—perhaps a fate more awful still. Rappaccini, with what he calls the interest of science before his eyes, will hesitate at nothing."

"It is a dream!" muttered Giovanni to himself. "Surely it is a dream!"

"But," resumed the professor, "be of good cheer, son of my friend! It is not yet too late for the rescue. Possibly we may even succeed in bringing back this miserable child within the limits of ordinary nature from which her father's madness has estranged her. Behold this little silver vase; it was wrought by the hands of the renowned Benvenuto Cellini, and is well worthy to be a love-gift to the fairest dame in Italy. But its contents are invaluable. One little sip of this antidote would have rendered the most virulent poisons of the Borgias innocuous; doubt not that it will be as efficacious against those of Rappaccini. Bestow the vase and the precious liquid within it on your Beatrice, and hopefully await the result."

Baglioni laid a small exquisitely-wrought silver phial on the table and withdrew, leaving what he had said to produce its effects upon the young man's mind.

"We will thwart Rappaccini yet," thought he, chuckling

to himself, as he descended the stairs. "But let us confess the truth of him: he is a wonderful man—a wonderful man indeed—a vile empiric, however, in his practise, and therefore not to be tolerated by those who respect the good old rules of the medical profession."

Throughout Giovanni's whole acquaintance with Beatrice he had occasionally, as we have said, been haunted by dark surmises as to her character; yet so thoroughly had she made herself felt by him as a simple, natural, most affectionate and guileless creature that the image now held up by Professor Baglioni looked as strange and incredible as if it were not in accordance with his own original conception. True, there were ugly recollections connected with his first glimpses of the beautiful girl: he could not quite forget the bouquet that withered in her grasp, and the insect that perished amid the sunny air by no ostensible agency save the fragrance of her breath. These incidents, however, dissolving in the pure light of her character, had no longer the efficacy of facts, but were acknowledged as mistaken fantasies, by whatever testimony of the senses they might appear to be substantiated. There is something truer and more real than what we can see with the eyes and touch with the finger. On such better evidence had Giovanni founded his confidence in Beatrice, though rather by the necessary force of her high attributes than by any deep and generous faith on his part. But now his spirit was incapable of sustaining itself at the height to which the early enthusiasm of passion had exalted it; he fell down groveling among earthly doubts, and defiled therewith the pure whiteness of Beatrice's image. Not that he gave her up: he did but distrust. He resolved to institute some decisive test that should satisfy him once for all whether there were those dreadful peculiarities in her physical nature which could not be supposed to exist without some corresponding monstrosity of soul. His eyes, gazing down afar, might have deceived him as to the lizard, the insect, and the flowers; but if he could witness at the distance of a few paces the sudden blight of one fresh

and healthful flower in Beatrice's hand, there would be room
for no further question. With this idea he hastened to the
florist's and purchased a bouquet that was still gemmed
with the morning dewdrops.

It was now the customary hour of his daily interview
with Beatrice. Before descending into the garden Giovanni
failed not to look at his figure in the mirror—a vanity to be
expected in a beautiful young man, yet, as displaying itself
at that troubled and feverish moment, the token of a certain shallowness of feeling and insincerity of character. He
did gaze, however, and said to himself that his features had
never before possessed so rich a grace, nor his eyes such
vivacity, nor his cheeks so warm a hue of superabundant
life.

"At least," thought he, "her poison has not yet insinuated
itself into my system. I am no flower, to perish in her
grasp."

With that thought he turned his eyes on the bouquet,
which he had never once laid aside from his hand. A thrill
of indefinable horror shot through his frame on perceiving
that those dewy flowers were already beginning to droop;
they wore the aspect of things that had been fresh and
lovely yesterday. Giovanni grew white as marble and stood
motionless before the mirror, staring at his own reflection
there as at the likeness of something frightful. He remembered Baglioni's remark about the fragrance that seemed
to pervade the chamber: it must have been the poison in his
breath. Then he shuddered—shuddered at himself. Recov-
ering from his stupor, he began to watch with curious eye a
spider that was busily at work hanging its web from the
antique cornice of the apartment, crossing and recrossing
the artful system of interwoven lines, as vigorous and active
a spider as ever dangled from an old ceiling. Giovanni bent
toward the insect and emitted a deep, long breath. The
spider suddenly ceased its toil; the web vibrated with a
tremor originating in the body of the small artisan. Again
Giovanni sent forth a breath, deeper, longer and imbued

with a venomous feeling out of his heart; he knew not whether he were wicked or only desperate. The spider made a convulsive grip with his limbs, and hung dead across the window.

"Accursed! accursed!" muttered Giovanni, addressing himself. "Hast thou grown so poisonous that this deadly insect perishes by thy breath?"

At that moment a rich, sweet voice came floating up from the garden:

"Giovanni, Giovanni! It is past the hour. Why tarriest thou? Come down!"

"Yes," muttered Giovanni, again: "she is the only being whom my breath may not slay. Would that it might!"

He rushed down, and in an instant was standing before the bright and loving eyes of Beatrice. A moment ago his wrath and despair had been so fierce that he could have desired nothing so much as to wither her by a glance, but with her actual presence there came influences which had too real an existence to be at once shaken off—recollections of the delicate and benign power of her feminine nature, which had so often enveloped him in a religious calm; recollections of many a holy and passionate outgush of her heart, when the pure fountain had been unsealed from its depths and made visible in its transparency to his mental eye; recollections which, had Giovanni known how to estimate them, would have assured him that all this ugly mystery was but an earthly illusion, and that, whatever mist of evil might seem to have gathered over her, the real Beatrice was a heavenly angel. Incapable as he was of such high faith, still her presence had not utterly lost its magic. Giovanni's rage was quelled into an aspect of sullen insensibility. Beatrice, with a quick spiritual sense, immediately felt that there was a gulf of blackness between them which neither he nor she could pass. They walked on together, sad and silent, and came thus to the marble fountain, and to its pool of water on the ground, in the midst of which grew the shrub that bore gemlike blossoms. Giovanni was affrighted at the eager enjoyment—the appetite, as it were—with which he found himself inhaling the fragrance of the flowers.

"Beatrice," asked he, abruptly, "whence came this shrub?"

"My father created it," answered she, with simplicity.

"Created it! created it!" repeated Giovanni. "What mean you, Beatrice?"

"He is a man fearfully acquainted with the secrets of nature," replied Beatrice, "and at the hour when I first drew breath this plant sprang from the soil, the offspring of his science, of his intellect, while I was but his earthly child. Approach it not," continued she, observing with terror that Giovanni was drawing nearer to the shrub; "it has qualities that you little dream of. But I, dearest Giovanni—I grew up and blossomed with the plant, and was nourished with its breath. It was my sister, and I loved it with a human affection; for—alas! hast thou not suspected it?—there was an awful doom."

Here Giovanni frowned so darkly upon her that Beatrice paused and trembled. But her faith in his tenderness reassured her and made her blush that she had doubted for an instant.

"There was an awful doom," she continued—"the effect of my father's fatal love of science—which estranged me from all society of my kind. Until Heaven sent thee, dearest Giovanni, oh, how lonely was thy poor Beatrice!"

"Was it a hard doom?" asked Giovanni, fixing his eyes upon her.

"Only of late have I known how hard it was," answered she, tenderly. "Oh, yes; but my heart was torpid, and therefore quiet."

Giovanni's rage broke forth from his sullen gloom like a lightning-flash out of a dark cloud.

"Accursed one!" cried he, with venomous scorn and anger. "And, finding thy solitude wearisome, thou hast severed me likewise from all the warmth of life and enticed me into thy region of unspeakable horror!"

"Giovanni!" exclaimed Beatrice, turning her large bright eyes upon his face. The force of his words had not found its way into her mind; she was merely thunderstruck.

"Yes, poisonous thing!" repeated Giovanni, beside himself with passion. "Thou hast done it! Thou hast blasted me! Thou hast filled my veins with poison! Thou hast made me as hateful, as ugly, as loathsome and deadly a creature as thyself—a world's wonder of hideous monstrosity! Now—if our breath be, happily, as fatal to ourselves as to all others—let us join our lips in one kiss of unutterable hatred, and so die."

"What has befallen me?" murmured Beatrice, with a low moan out of her heart. "Holy Virgin, pity me—a poor heartbroken child!"

"Thou? Dost thou pray?" cried Giovanni, still with the same fiendish scorn. "Thy very prayers as they come from thy lips taint the atmosphere with death. Yes, yes, let us pray! Let us to church and dip our fingers in the holy water at the portal: they that come after us will perish as by a pestilence. Let us sign crosses in the air: it will be scattering curses abroad in the likeness of holy symbols."

"Giovanni," said Beatrice, calmly, for her grief was beyond passion, "why dost thou join thyself with me thus in those terrible words? I, it is true, am the horrible thing thou namest me, but thou—what hast thou to do save with one other shudder at my hideous misery to go forth out of the garden and mingle with thy race, and forget that there ever crawled on earth such a monster as poor Beatrice?"

"Dost thou pretend ignorance?" asked Giovanni, scowling upon her. "Behold! This power have I gained from the pure daughter of Rappaccini!"

There was a swarm of summer insects flitting through the air in search of the food promised by the flower-odors of the fatal garden. They circled round Giovanni's head, and were evidently attracted toward him by the same influence which had drawn them for an instant within the sphere of several of the shrubs. He sent forth a breath among them, and smiled bitterly at Beatrice, as at least a score of the insects fell dead upon the ground.

"I see it! I see it!" shrieked Beatrice. "It is my father's fatal science! No, no, Giovanni, it was not I! Never, never! I dreamed only to love thee and be with thee a little time, and so to let thee pass away, leaving but thine image in mine heart. For, Giovanni—believe it—though my body be nourished with poison, my spirit is God's creature and craves love as its daily food. But my father! he has united us in this fearful sympathy. Yes, spurn me! tread upon me! kill me! Oh, what is death, after such words as thine? But it was not I; not for a world of bliss would I have done it!"

Giovanni's passion had exhausted itself in its outburst from his lips. There now came across him a sense—mournful and not without tenderness—of the intimate and peculiar relationship between Beatrice and himself. They stood, as it were, in an utter solitude which would be made none the less solitary by the densest throng of human life. Ought not, then, the desert of humanity around them to press this insulated pair closer together? If they should be cruel to one another, who was there to be kind to them? Besides, thought Giovanni, might there not still be a hope of his returning within the limits of ordinary nature, and leading Beatrice—the redeemed Beatrice—by the hand? Oh, weak and selfish and unworthy spirit, that could dream of an earthly union and earthly happiness as possible after such deep love had been so bitterly wronged as was Beatrice's love by Giovanni's blighting words! No, no! there could be no such hope. She must pass heavily with that broken heart across the borders; she must bathe her hurts in some font of Paradise and forget her grief in the light of immortality, and there be well.

But Giovanni did not know it.

"Dear Beatrice," said he, approaching her, while she shrank away, as always at his approach, but now with a different impulse—"dearest Beatrice, our fate is not yet so desperate. Behold! There is a medicine, potent, as a wise physician has assured me, and almost divine in its efficacy. It is composed of ingredients the most opposite to those by which thy awful father has brought this calamity upon thee and me. It is distilled of blessed herbs. Shall we not quaff it together, and thus be purified from evil?"

"Give it me," said Beatrice, extending her hand to receive the little silver phial which Giovanni took from his bosom. She added with a peculiar emphasis, "I will drink, but do thou await the result."

She put Baglioni's antidote to her lips, and at the same moment the figure of Rappaccini emerged from the portal and came slowly toward the marble fountain. As he drew near the pale man of science seemed to gaze with a triumphant expression at the beautiful youth and maiden, as might an artist who should spend his life in achieving a picture or a group of statuary, and finally be satisfied with his success. He paused; his bent form grew erect with conscious power; he spread out his hands over them in the attitude of a father imploring a blessing upon his children. But those were the same hands that had thrown poison into the stream of their lives! Giovanni trembled. Beatrice shuddered very nervously, and pressed her hand upon her heart.

"My daughter," said Rappaccini, "thou art no longer lonely in the world. Pluck one of these precious gems from thy sister-shrub, and bid thy bridegroom wear it in his bosom. It will not harm him now. My science and the sympathy between thee and him have so wrought within his system that he now stands apart from common men, as thou dost, daughter of my pride and triumph, from ordinary women. Pass on, then, through the world, most dear to one another and dreadful to all besides."

"My father," said Beatrice, feebly—and still, as she spoke, she kept her hand upon her heart—"wherefore didst thou inflict this miserable doom upon thy child?"

"Miserable!" exclaimed Rappaccini. "What mean you, foolish girl? Dost thou deem it misery to be endowed with marvelous gifts against which no power nor strength could avail an enemy, misery to be able to quell the mightiest with a breath, misery to be as terrible as thou art beautiful? Wouldst thou, then, have preferred the condition of a weak woman, exposed to all evil and capable of none?"

"I would fain have been loved, not feared," murmured Beatrice, sinking down upon the ground. "But now it matters not. I am going, father, where the evil which thou hast striven to mingle with my being will pass away like a dream —like the fragrance of these poisonous flowers which will no longer taint my breath among the flowers of Eden. Farewell, Giovanni! Thy words of hatred are like lead within my heart, but they too will fall away as I ascend. Oh, was there not from the first more poison in thy nature than in mine?"

To Beatrice—so radically had her earthly part been wrought upon by Rappaccini's skill—as poison had been life, so the powerful antidote was death. And thus the poor victim of man's ingenuity and of thwarted nature, and of the fatality that attends all such efforts of perverted wisdom, perished there at the feet of her father and Giovanni.

Just at that moment Professor Pietro Baglioni looked forth from the window and called loudly, in a tone of triumph mixed with horror, to the thunder-stricken man of science:

"Rappaccini, Rappaccini! And is *this* the upshot of your experiment?"

ZODOMIRSKY'S DUEL

By Alexandre Dumas

CHAPTER I

At the time of this story our regiment was stationed in the dirty little village of Valins, on the frontier of Austria.

It was the fourth of May in the year 182—, and I, with several other officers, had been breakfasting with the Aide-de-Camp in honor of his birthday, and discussing the various topics of the garrison.

"Can you tell us without being indiscreet," asked Sub-Lieutenant Stamm of Andrew Michaelovitch, the Aide-de-Camp, "what the Colonel was so eager to say to you this morning?"

"A new officer," he replied, "is to fill the vacancy of captain."

"His name?" demanded two or three voices.

"Lieutenant Zodomirsky, who is betrothed to the beautiful Mariana Ravensky."

"And when does he arrive?" asked Major Belayef.

"He *has* arrived. I have been presented to him at the Colonel's house. He is very anxious to make your acquaintance, gentlemen, and I have therefore invited him to dine with us. But that reminds me, Captain, you must know him," he continued, turning to me; "you were both in the same regiment at St. Petersburg."

"It is true," I replied. "We studied there together. He was then a brave, handsome youth, adored by his comrades,

328

in every one's good graces, but of a fiery and irritable temper."

"Mademoiselle Ravensky informed me that he was a skilful duelist," said Stamm. "Well, he will do very well here; a duel is a family affair with us. You are welcome, Monsieur Zodomirsky. However quick your temper, you must be careful of it before me, or I shall take upon myself to cool it."

And Stamm pronounced these words with a visible sneer.

"How is it that he leaves the Guards? Is he ruined?" asked Cornet Naletoff.

"I have been informed," replied Stamm, "that he has just inherited from an old aunt about twenty thousand rubles. No, poor devil! he is consumptive."

"Come, gentlemen," said the Aide-de-Camp, rising, "let us pass to the saloon and have a game of cards. Koloff will serve dinner while we play."

We had been seated some time, and Stamm, who was far from rich, was in the act of losing sixty rubles, when Koloff announced:

"Captain Zodomirsky."

"Here you are, at last!" cried Michaelovitch, jumping from his chair. "You are welcome."

Then, turning to us, he continued: "These are your new comrades, Captain Zodomirsky; all good fellows and brave soldiers."

"Gentlemen," said Zodomirsky, "I am proud and happy to have joined your regiment. To do so has been my greatest desire for some time, and if I am welcome, as you courteously say, I shall be the happiest man in the world."

"Ah! good day, Captain," he continued, turning to me and holding out his hand. "We meet again. You have not forgotten an old friend, I hope?"

As he smilingly uttered these words, Stamm, to whom his back was turned, darted at him a glance full of bitter hatred. Stamm was not liked in the regiment; his cold and taciturn nature had formed no friendship with any of us. I could not understand his apparent hostility toward Zodomirsky, whom I believed he had never seen before.

Some one offered Zodomirsky a cigar. He accepted it, lit at the cigar of an officer near him, and began to talk gaily to his new comrades.

"Do you stay here long?" asked Major Belayef.

"Yes, monsieur," replied Zodomirsky. "I wish to stay with you as long as possible," and as he pronounced these words he saluted us all round with a smile. He continued: "I have taken a house near that of my old friend Ravensky whom I knew at St. Petersburg. I have my horses there, an excellent cook, a passable library, a little garden, and a target; and there I shall be quiet as a hermit, and happy as a king. It is the life that suits me."

"Ha! you practise shooting!" said Stamm, in such a strange voice, accompanied by a smile so sardonic, that Zodomirsky regarded him in astonishment.

"It is my custom every morning to fire twelve balls," he replied.

"You are very fond of that amusement, then?" demanded Stamm, in a voice without any trace of emotion; adding, "I do not understand the use of shooting, unless it is to hunt with."

Zodomirsky's pale face was flushed with a sudden flame. He turned to Stamm, and replied in a quiet but firm voice: "I think, monsieur, that you are wrong in calling it lost time to learn to shoot with a pistol; in our garrison life an imprudent word often leads to a meeting between comrades, in which case he who is known for a good shot inspires respect among those indiscreet persons who amuse themselves in asking useless questions."

"Oh! that is not a reason, Captain. In duels, as in everything else, something should be left to chance. I maintain my first opinion, and say that an honorable man ought not to take too many precautions."

"And why?" asked Zodomirsky.

"I will explain to you," replied Stamm. "Do you play at cards, Captain?"

"Why do you ask that question?"

"I will try to render my explanation clear, so that all will understand it. Every one knows that there are certain players who have an enviable knack, while shuffling the pack, of adroitly making themselves master of the winning card. Now, I see no difference, myself, between the man who robs his neighbor of his money and the one who robs him of his life." Then he added, in a way to take nothing from the insolence of his observation, "I do not say this to you, in particular, Captain; I speak in general terms."

"It is too much as it is, monsieur!" cried Zodomirsky, "I beg Captain Alexis Stephanovitch to terminate this affair with you." Then, turning to me, he said: "You will not refuse me this request?"

"So be it, Captain," replied Stamm quickly. "You have told me yourself you practise shooting every day, while I practise only on the day I fight. We will equalize the chances. I will settle details with Monsieur Stephanovitch."

Then he rose and turned to our host.

"*Au revoir,* Michaelovitch," he said. "I will dine at the Colonel's." And with these words he left the room.

The most profound silence had been kept during this altercation; but, as soon as Stamm disappeared, Captain Pravdine, an old officer, addressed himself to us all.

"We can not let them fight, gentlemen," he said.

Zodomirsky touched him gently on his arm.

"Captain," he said, "I am a newcomer among you; none of you know me. I have yet, as it were, to win my spurs; it is impossible for me to let this quarrel pass without fighting. I do not know what I have done to annoy this gentleman, but it is evident that he has some spite against me."

"The truth of the matter is that Stamm is jealous of you, Zodomirsky," said Cornet Naletoff. "It is well known that he is in love with Mademoiselle Ravensky."

"That, indeed, explains all," he replied. "However, gen-

tlemen, I thank you for your kind sympathy in this affair
from the bottom of my heart."

"And now to dinner, gentlemen!" cried Michaelovitch.
"Place yourselves as you choose. The soup, Koloff; the
soup!"

Everybody was very animated. Stamm seemed forgotten;
only Zodomirsky appeared a little sad. Zodomirsky's health
was drunk; he seemed touched with this significant attention, and thanked the officers with a broken voice.

"Stephanovitch," said Zodomirsky to me, when dinner
was over, and all had risen, "since M. Stamm knows you
are my second and has accepted you as such, see him, and
arrange everything with him; accept all his conditions; then
meet Captain Pravdine and me at my rooms. The first who
arrives will wait for the other. We are now going to Monsieur Ravensky's house."

"You will let us know the hour of combat?" said several
voices.

"Certainly, gentlemen. Come and bid a last farewell to
one of us."

We all parted at the Ravensky's door, each officer shaking hands with Zodomirsky as with an old friend.

CHAPTER II

STAMM was waiting for me when I arrived at his house.
His conditions were these: Two sabres were to be planted at
a distance of one pace apart; each opponent to extend his
arm at full length and fire at the word "*three*." One pistol
alone was to be loaded.

I endeavored in vain to obtain another mode of combat.

"It is not a victim I offer to M. Zodomirsky," said Stamm,
"but an adversary. He will fight as I propose, or I will not
fight at all; but in that case I shall prove that M. Zodomirsky is brave only when sure of his own safety."

Zodomirsky's orders were imperative. I accepted.

When I entered Zodomirsky's rooms, they were vacant; he had not arrived. I looked round with curiosity. They were furnished in a rich but simple manner, and with evident taste. I drew a chair near the balcony and looked out over the plain. A storm was brewing; some drops of rain fell already, and thunder moaned.

At this instant the door opened, and Zodomirsky and Pravdine entered. I advanced to meet them.

"We are late, Captain," said Zodomirsky, "but it was unavoidable."

"And what says Stamm?" he continued.

I gave him his adversary's conditions. When I had ended, a sad smile passed over his face; he drew his hand across his forehead and his eyes glittered with feverish lustre.

"I had foreseen this," he murmured. "You have accepted, I presume?"

"Did you not give me the order yourself?"

"Absolutely," he replied.

Zodomirsky threw himself in a chair by the table, in which position he faced the door. Pravdine placed himself near the window, and I near the fire. A presentiment weighed down our spirits. A mournful silence reigned.

Suddenly the door opened and a woman muffled in a mantle which streamed with water, and with the hood drawn over her face, pushed past the servant, and stood before us. She threw back the hood, and we recognized Mariana Ravensky!

Pravdine and I stood motionless with astonishment. Zodomirsky sprang toward her.

"Great heavens! what has happened, and why are you here?"

"Why am I here, George?" she cried. "Is it *you* who ask me, when this night is perhaps the last of your life? Why am I here? To say farewell to you. It is only two hours since I saw you, and not one word passed between us of to-morrow. Was that well, George?"

"But I am not alone here," said Zodomirsky in a low

voice. "Think, Mariana. Your reputation—your fair fame—"

"Are you not all in all to me, George? And in such a time as this, what matters anything else?"

She threw her arm about his neck and pressed her head against his breast.

Pravdine and I made some steps to quit the room.

"Stay, gentlemen," she said lifting her head. "Since you have seen me here, I have nothing more to hide from you, and perhaps you may be able to help me in what I am about to say." Then, suddenly flinging herself at his feet:

"I implore you, I command you, George," she cried, "not to fight this duel with Monsieur Stamm. You will not end two lives by such a useless act! Your life belongs to me; it is no longer yours. George, do you hear? You will not do this."

"Mariana! Mariana! in the name of Heaven do not torture me thus! Can I refuse to fight? I should be dishonored —lost! If I could do so cowardly an act, shame would kill me more surely than Stamm's pistol."

"Captain," she said to Pravdine, "you are esteemed in the regiment as a man of honor; you can, then, judge about affairs of honor. Have pity on me, Captain, and tell him he can refuse such a duel as this. Make him understand that it is not a duel, but an assassination; speak, speak, Captain, and if he will not listen to me, he will to you."

Pravdine was moved. His lips trembled and his eyes were dimmed with tears. He rose, and, approaching Mariana, respectfully kissed her hand, and said with a trembling voice:

"To spare you any sorrow, Mademoiselle, I would lay down my life; but to counsel M. Zodomirsky to be unworthy of his uniform by refusing this duel is impossible. Each adversary, your betrothed as well as Stamm, has a right to propose his conditions. But whatever be the conditions, the Captain is in circumstances which render this duel absolutely necessary. He is known as a skilful duelist; to refuse

Stamm's conditions were to indicate that he counts upon his skill."

"Enough, Mariana, enough," cried George. "Unhappy girl! you do not know what you demand. Do you wish me, then, to fall so low that you yourself would be ashamed of me? I ask you, are you capable of loving a dishonored man?"

Mariana had let herself fall upon a chair. She rose, pale as a corpse, and began to put her mantle on.

"You are right, George, it is not I who would love you no more, but you who would hate me. We must resign ourselves to our fate. Give me your hand, George; perhaps we shall never see each other again. To-morrow! to-morrow! my love."

She threw herself upon his breast, without tears, without sobs, but with a profound despair.

She wished to depart alone, but Zodomirsky insisted on leading her home.

Midnight was striking when he returned.

"You had better both retire," said Zodomirsky as he entered. "I have several letters to write before sleeping. At five we must be at the rendezvous."

I felt so wearied that I did not want telling twice. Pravdine passed into the saloon, I into Zodomirsky's bedroom, and the master of the house into his study.

The cool air of the morning woke me. I cast my eyes upon the window, where the dawn commenced to appear. I heard Pravdine also stirring. I passed into the saloon, where Zodomirsky immediately joined us. His face was pale but serene.

"Are the horses ready?" he inquired.

I made a sign in the affirmative.

"Then, let us start," he said.

We mounted into the carriage and drove off.

CHAPTER III

"Ah," said Pravdine all at once, "there is Michaelovitch's carriage. Yes, yes, it is he with one of ours, and there is Naletoff, on his Circassian horse. Good! the others are coming behind. It is well we started so soon."

The carriage had to pass the house of the Ravenskys. I could not refrain from looking up; the poor girl was at her window, motionless as a statue. She did not even nod to us.

"Quicker! quicker!" cried Zodomirsky to the coachman. It was the only sign by which I knew that he had seen Mariana.

Soon we distanced the other carriages, and arrived upon the place of combat—a plain where two great pyramids rose, passing in this district by the name of the "Tomb of the Two Brothers." The first rays of the sun darting through the trees began to dissipate the mists of night.

Michaelovitch arrived immediately after us, and in a few minutes we formed a group of nearly twenty persons. Then we heard the crunch of other steps upon the gravel. They were those of our opponents. Stamm walked first, holding in his hand a box of pistols. He bowed to Zodomirsky and the officers.

"Who gives the word to fire, gentlemen?" he asked.

The two adversaries and the seconds turned toward the officers, who regarded them with perplexity.

No one offered. No one wished to pronounce that terrible "three," which would sign the fate of a comrade.

"Major," said Zodomirsky to Belayef, "will you render me this service?"

Thus asked, the Major could not refuse, and he made a sign that he accepted.

"Be good enough to indicate our places, gentlemen," continued Zodomirsky, giving me his sabre and taking off his coat; "then load, if you please."

"That is useless," said Stamm. "I have brought the pistols; one of the two is loaded, the other has only a gun-cap."

"Do you know which is which?" said Pravdine.

"What does it matter?" replied Stamm, "Monsieur Zodomirsky will choose."

"It is well," said Zodomirsky.

Belayef drew his sabre and thrust it in the ground midway between the two pyramids. Then he took another sabre and planted it before the first. One pace alone separated the two blades. Each adversary was to stand behind a sabre, extending his arm at full length. In this way each had the muzzle of his opponent's pistol at six inches from his heart. While Belayef made these preparations Stamm unbuckled his sabre and divested himself of his coat. His seconds opened his box of pistols, and Zodomirsky, approaching, took without hesitation the nearest to him. Then he placed himself behind one of the sabres.

Stamm regarded him closely; not a muscle of Zodomirsky's face moved, and there was not about him the least appearance of bravado, but of the calmness of courage.

"He is brave," murmured Stamm.

And taking the pistol left by Zodomirsky he took up his position behind the other sabre, in front of his adversary.

They were both pale, but while the eyes of Zodomirsky burned with implacable resolution, those of Stamm were uneasy and shifting. I felt my heart beat loudly.

Belayef advanced. All eyes were fixed on him.

"Are you ready, gentlemen?" he asked.

"We are waiting, Major," replied Zodomirsky and Stamm together, and each lifted his pistol before the breast of the other.

A death-like silence reigned. Only the birds sang in the bushes near the place of combat. In the midst of this silence the Major's voice resounding made every one tremble.

"One."

"Two."

"*Three.*"

Then we heard the sound of the hammer falling on the cap of Zodomirsky's pistol. There was a flash, but no sound followed it.

Stamm had not fired, and continued to hold the mouth of his pistol against the breast of his adversary.

"Fire!" said Zodomirsky, in a voice perfectly calm.

"It is not for you to command, Monsieur," said Stamm; "it is I who must decide whether to fire or not, and that depends on how you answer what I am about to say."

"Speak, then; but in the name of Heaven speak quickly."

"Never fear, I will not abuse your patience."

We were all ears.

"I have not come to kill you, Monsieur," continued Stamm. "I have come with the carelessness of a man to whom life holds nothing, while it has kept none of the promises it has made to him. You, Monsieur, are rich, you are beloved, you have a promising future before you: life must be dear to you. But fate has decided against you: it is you who must die and not I. Well, Monsieur Zodomirsky, give me your word not to be so prompt in the future to fight duels, and I will not fire."

"I have not been prompt to call you out, Monsieur," replied Zodomirsky in the same calm voice; "you have wounded me by an outrageous comparison, and I have been compelled to challenge you. Fire, then; I have nothing to say to you."

"My conditions can not wound your honor," insisted Stamm. "Be our judge, Major," he added, turning to Belayef. "I will abide by your opinion; perhaps M. Zodomirsky will follow my example."

"M. Zodomirsky has conducted himself as bravely as possible; if he is not killed, it is not his fault." Then, turning to the officers round, he said:

"Can M. Zodomirsky accept the imposed condition?"

"He can! he can!" they cried, "and without staining his honor in the slightest."

Zodomirsky stood motionless.

"The Captain consents," said old Pravdine, advancing. "Yes, in the future he will be less prompt."

"It is you who speak, Captain, and not M. Zodomirsky," said Stamm.

"Will you affirm my words, Monsieur Zodomirsky?" asked Pravdine, almost supplicating in his eagerness.

"I consent," said Zodomirsky, in a voice scarcely intelligible.

"Hurrah! hurrah!" cried all the officers, enchanted with this termination. Two or three threw up their caps.

"I am more charmed than any one," said Stamm, "that all has ended as I desired. Now, Captain, I have shown you that before a resolute man the art of shooting is nothing in a duel, and that if the chances are equal a good shot is on the same level as a bad one. I did not wish in any case to kill you. Only I had a great desire to see how you would look death in the face. You are a man of courage; accept my compliments. The pistols were not loaded." Stamm, as he said these words, fired off his pistol. There was no report!

Zodormirsky uttered a cry which resembled the roar of a wounded lion.

"By my father's soul!" he cried, "this is a new offense, and more insulting than the first. Ah! it is ended, you say? No. Monsieur, it must recommence, and this time the pistols shall be loaded, if I have to load them myself."

"No, Captain," replied Stamm, tranquilly, "I have given you your life, I will not take it back. Insult me if you wish, I will not fight with you."

"Then it is with me you will fight, Monsieur Stamm," cried Pravdine, pulling off his coat. "You have acted like a scoundrel; you have deceived Zodomirsky and his seconds, and, in five minutes if your dead body is not lying at my feet, there is no such thing as justice."

Stamm was visibly confused. He had not bargained for this.

"And if the Captain does not kill you, I will!" said Naletoff.

"Or I!" "Or I!" cried with one voice all the officers.

"The devil! I can not fight with you all," replied Stamm. "Choose one among you, and I will fight with him, though it will not be a duel, but an assassination."

"Reassure yourself, Monsieur," replied Major Belayef; "we will do nothing that the most scrupulous honor can complain of. All our officers are insulted, for under their uniform you have conducted yourself like a rascal. You can not fight with all; it is even probable you will fight with none. Hold yourself in readiness, then. You are to be judged. Gentlemen, will you approach?"

We surrounded the Major, and the fiat went forth without discussion. Every one was of the same opinion.

Then the Major, who had played the rôle of president, approached Stamm, and said to him:

"Monsieur, you are lost to all the laws of honor. Your crime was premeditated in cold blood. You have made M. Zodomirsky pass through all the sensations of a man condemned to death, while you were perfectly at ease, you who knew that the pistols were not loaded. Finally, you have refused to fight with the man whom you have doubly insulted."

"Load the pistols! load them!" cried Stamm, exasperated. "I will fight with any one!"

But the Major shook his head with a smile of contempt.

"No, Monsieur Lieutenant," he said, "you will fight no more with your comrades. You have stained your uniform. We can no longer serve with you. The officers have charged me to say that, not wishing to make your deficiencies known to the Government, they ask you to give in your resignation on the cause of bad health. The surgeon will sign all necessary certificates. To-day is the 3d of May: you have from now to the 3d of June to quit the regiment."

"I will quit it, certainly; not because it is your desire, but mine," said Stamm, picking up his sabre and putting on ¦ is coat.

Then he leaped upon his horse, and galloped off toward the village, casting a last malediction to us all.

We all pressed round Zodomirsky. He was sad; more than sad, gloomy.

"Why did you force me to consent to this scoundrel's conditions, gentlemen?" he said. "Without you, I should never have accepted them."

"My comrades and I," said the Major, "will take all the responsibility. You have acted nobly, and I must tell you in the name of us all, M. Zodomirsky, that you are a man of honor." Then, turning to the officers: "Let us go, gentlemen; we must inform the Colonel of what has passed."

"We mounted into the carriages. As we did so we saw Stamm in the distance galloping up the mountainside from the village upon his horse. Zodomirsky's eyes followed him.

"I know not what presentiment torments me," he said, "but I wish his pistol had been loaded, and that he had fired."

He uttered a deep sigh, then shook his head, as if with that he could disperse his gloomy thoughts.

"Home," he called to the driver.

We took the same route that we had come by, and consequently again passed Mariana Ravensky's window. Each of us looked up, but Mariana was no longer there.

"Captain," said Zodomirsky, "will you do me a service?"

"Whatever you wish," I replied.

"I count upon you to tell my poor Mariana the result of this miserable affair."

"I will do so. And when?"

"Now. The sooner the better. Stop!" cried Zodomirsky to the coachman. He stopped, and I descended, and the carriage drove on.

*　　*　　*　　*　　*　　*　　*

Zodomirsky had hardly entered when he saw me appear in the doorway of the saloon. Without doubt my face was pale, and wore a look of consternation, for Zodomirsky sprang toward me, crying:

"Great heavens, Captain! What has happened?"

I drew him from the saloon.

"My poor friend, haste, if you wish to see Mariana alive. She was at her window; she saw Stamm gallop past. Stamm being alive, it followed that you were dead. She uttered a cry, and fell. From that moment she has never opened her eyes."

"Oh, my presentiments!" cried Zodomirsky, "my presentiments!" and he rushed hatless and without his sabre, into the street.

On the staircase of Mlle. Ravensky's house he met the doctor, who was coming down.

"Doctor," he cried, stopping him, "she is better, is she not?"

"Yes," he answered, "better, because she suffers no more."

"Dead!" murmured Zodomirsky, growing white, and supporting himself against the wall. "Dead!"

"I always told her, poor girl! that, having a weak heart, she must avoid all emotion—"

But Zodomirsky had ceased to listen. He sprang up the steps, crossed the hall and the saloon, calling like a madman:

"Mariana! Mariana!"

At the door of the sleeping chamber stood Mariana's old nurse, who tried to bar his progress. He pushed by her, and entered the room.

Mariana was lying motionless and pale upon her bed. Her face was calm as if she slept. Zodomirsky threw himself upon his knees by the bedside, and seized her hand. It was cold, and in it was clenched a curl of black hair.

"My hair!" cried Zodomirsky, bursting into sobs. "Yes, yours," said the old nurse, "your hair that she cut off herself on quitting you at St. Petersburg. I have often told her it would bring misfortune to one of you."

If any one desires to learn what became of Zodomirsky, let him inquire for Brother Vassili, at the Monastery of Troitza.

The holy brothers will show the visitor his tomb. They know neither his real name nor the causes which, at twenty-six, had made him take the robe of a monk. Only they say, vaguely, that it was after a great sorrow, caused by the death of a woman whom he loved.

WHO WAS SHE?

By Bayard Taylor

Come, now, there may as well be an end of this! Every time I meet your eyes squarely, I detect the question just slipping out of them. If you had spoken it, or even boldly looked it; if you had shown in your motions the least sign of a fussy or fidgety concern on my account; if this were not the evening of my birthday, and you the only friend who remembered it; if confession were not good for the soul, though harder than sin to some people, of whom I am one— well, if all reasons were not at this instant converged into a focus, and burning me rather violently, in that region where the seat of emotion is supposed to lie, I should keep my trouble to myself.

Yes, I have fifty times had it on my mind to tell you the whole story. But who can be certain that his best friend will not smile—or, what is worse, cherish a kind of charitable pity ever afterward—when the external forms of a very serious kind of passion seem trivial, fantastic, foolish? And the worst of all is that the heroic part which I imagined I was playing proves to have been almost the reverse. The only comfort which I can find in my humiliation is that I am capable of feeling it. There isn't a bit of a paradox in this, as you will see; but I only mention it, now, to prepare you for, maybe, a little morbid sensitiveness of my moral nerves.

The documents are all in this portfolio under my elbow. I had just read them again completely through when you were announced. You may examine them as you like afterward: for the present, fill your glass, take another Cabaña, and keep silent until my "ghastly tale" has reached its most lamentable conclusion.

The beginning of it was at Wampsocket Springs, three years ago last summer. I suppose most unmarried men who have reached, or passed, the age of thirty—and I was then thirty-three—experience a milder return of their adolescent warmth, a kind of fainter second spring, since the first has not fulfilled its promise. Of course, I wasn't clearly conscious of this at the time: who is? But I had had my youthful passion and my tragic disappointment, as you know: I had looked far enough into what Thackeray used to call the cryptic mysteries to save me from the Scylla of dissipation, and yet preserved enough of natural nature to keep me out of the Pharisaic Charybdis. My devotion to my legal studies had already brought me a mild distinction; the paternal legacy was a good nest-egg for the incubation of wealth—in short, I was a fair, respectable "party," desirable to the humbler mammas, and not to be despised by the haughty exclusives.

The fashionable hotel at the Springs holds three hundred, and it was packed. I had meant to lounge there for a fortnight and then finish my holidays at Long Branch; but eighty, at least, out of the three hundred were young and moved lightly in muslin. With my years and experience I felt so safe that to walk, talk, or dance with them became simply a luxury, such as I had never—at least so freely—possessed before. My name and standing, known to some families, were agreeably exaggerated to the others, and I enjoyed that supreme satisfaction which a man always feels when he discovers, or imagines, that he is popular in society. There is a kind of premonitory apology implied in my saying this, I am aware. You must remember that I am culprit, and culprit's counsel, at the same time.

You have never been at Wampsocket? Well, the hills sweep around in a crescent, on the northern side, and four or five radiating glens, descending from them, unite just above the village. The central one, leading to a waterfall (called "Minne-hehe" by the irreverent young people, because there is so little of it), is the fashionable drive and promenade; but the second ravine on the left, steep, crooked, and cumbered with bowlders which have tumbled from somewhere and lodged in the most extraordinary groupings, became my favorite walk of a morning. There was a foot-path in it, well-trodden at first, but gradually fading out as it became more like a ladder than a path, and I soon discovered that no other city feet than mine were likely to scale a certain rough slope which seemed the end of the ravine. With the aid of the tough laurel-stems I climbed to the top, passed through a cleft as narrow as a doorway, and presently found myself in a little upper dell, as wild and sweet and strange as one of the pictures that haunts us on the brink of sleep.

There was a pond—no, rather a bowl—of water in the centre; hardly twenty yards across, yet the sky in it was so pure and far down that the circle of rocks and summer foliage inclosing it seemed like a little planetary ring, floating off alone through space. I can't explain the charm of the spot, nor the selfishness which instantly suggested that I should keep the discovery to myself. Ten years earlier I should have looked around for some fair spirit to be my "minister," but now—

One forenoon—I think it was the third or fourth time I had visited the place—I was startled to find the dent of a heel in the earth, half-way up the slope. There had been rain during the night and the earth was still moist and soft. It was the mark of a woman's boot, only to be distinguished from that of a walking-stick by its semicircular form. A little higher, I found the outline of a foot, not so small as to awake an ecstasy, but with a suggestion of lightness, elasticity, and grace. If hands were thrust through holes in a board-fence, and nothing of the attached bodies seen, I can easily imagine that some would attract and others repel us: with footprints the impression is weaker, of course, but we can not escape it. I am not sure whether I wanted to find the unknown wearer of the boot within my precious personal solitude: I was afraid I should see her, while passing through the rocky crevice, and yet was disappointed when I found no one.

But on the flat, warm rock overhanging the tarn—my special throne—lay some withering wild-flowers and a book! I looked up and down, right and left: there was not the slightest sign of another human life than mine. Then I lay down for a quarter of an hour, and listened: there were only the noises of bird and squirrel, as before. At last, I took up the book, the flat breadth of which suggested only sketches. There were, indeed, some tolerable studies of rocks and trees on the first pages; a few not very striking caricatures, which seemed to have been commenced as portraits, but recalled no faces I knew; then a number of fragmentary notes, written in pencil. I found no name, from first to last; only, under the sketches, a monogram so complicated and laborious that the initials could hardly be discovered unless one already knew them.

The writing was a woman's, but it had surely taken its character from certain features of her own: it was clear, firm, individual. It had nothing of that air of general debility which usually marks the manuscript of young ladies, yet its firmness was far removed from the stiff, conventional slope which all Englishwomen seem to acquire in youth and retain through life. I don't see how any man in my situation could have helped reading a few lines—if only for the sake of restoring lost property. But I was drawn on, and on, and finished by reading all: thence, since no further harm could be done, I reread, pondering over certain passages until they stayed with me. Here they are, as I set them down, that evening, on the back of a legal blank:

"It makes a great deal of difference whether we wear social forms as bracelets or handcuffs."

"Can we not still be wholly our independent selves, even

while doing, in the main, as others do? I know two who are so; but they are married."

"The men who admire these bold, dashing young girls treat them like weaker copies of themselves. And yet they boast of what they call 'experience'!"

"I wonder if any one felt the exquisite beauty of the noon as I did to-day? A faint appreciation of sunsets and storms is taught us in youth, and kept alive by novels and flirtations; but the broad, imperial splendor of this summer noon! —and myself standing alone in it—yes, utterly alone!"

"The men I seek *must* exist: where are they? How make an acquaintance, when one obsequiously bows himself away, as I advance? The fault is surely not all on my side."

There was much more, intimate enough to inspire me with a keen interest in the writer, yet not sufficiently so to make my perusal a painful indiscretion. I yielded to the impulse of the moment, took out my pencil, and wrote a dozen lines on one of the blank pages. They ran something in this wise:

"IGNOTUS IGNOTÆ!—You have bestowed without intending it, and I have taken without your knowledge. Do not regret the accident which has enriched another. This concealed idyl of the hills was mine, as I supposed, but I acknowledge your equal right to it. Shall we share the possession, or will you banish me?"

There was a frank advance, tempered by a proper caution, I fancied, in the words I wrote. It was evident that she was unmarried, but outside of that certainty there lay a vast range of possibilities, some of them alarming enough. However, if any nearer acquaintance should arise out of the incident, the next step must be taken by her. Was I one of the men she sought? I almost imagined so—certainly hoped so.

I laid the book on the rock, as I had found it, bestowed another keen scrutiny on the lonely landscape, and then descended the ravine. That evening, I went early to the ladies' parlor, chatted more than usual with the various damsels whom I knew, and watched with a new interest those whom I knew not. My mind, involuntarily, had already created a picture of the unknown. She might be twenty-five, I thought; a reflective habit of mind would hardly be developed before that age. Tall and stately, of course; distinctly proud in her bearing, and somewhat reserved in her manners. Why she should have large dark eyes, with long dark lashes, I could not tell; but so I seemed to see her. Quite forgetting that I was (or had meant to be) *Ignotus*, I found myself staring rather significantly at one or the other of the young ladies, in whom I discovered some slight general resemblance to the imaginary character. My fancies, I must confess, played strange pranks with me. They had been kept in a coop so many years that now, when I suddenly turned them loose, their rickety attempts at flight quite bewildered me.

No! there was no use in expecting a sudden discovery. I went to the glen betimes, next morning: the book was gone and so were the faded flowers, but some of the latter were scattered over the top of another rock, a few yards from mine. Ha! this means that I am not to withdraw, I said to myself: she makes room for me! But how to surprise her? —for by this time I was fully resolved to make her acquaintance, even though she might turn out to be forty, scraggy, and sandy-haired.

I knew no other way so likely as that of visiting the glen at all times of the day. I even went so far as to write a line of greeting, with a regret that our visits had not yet coincided, and laid it under a stone on the top of *her* rock. The note disappeared, but there was no answer in its place. Then I suddenly remembered her fondness for the noon hours, at which time she was "utterly alone." The hotel *table d'hôte* was at one o'clock: her family, doubtless, dined later, in their own rooms. Why, this gave me, at least, her place in society! The question of age, to be sure, remained unsettled; but all else was safe.

The next day I took a late and large breakfast, and sacri-

ficed my dinner. Before noon the guests had all straggled
back to the hotel from glen and grove and lane, so bright
and hot was the sunshine. Indeed, I could hardly have supported the reverberation of heat from the sides of the ravine, but for a fixed belief that I should be successful. While
crossing the narrow meadow upon which it opened, I caught
a glimpse of something white among the thickets higher up.
A moment later it had vanished, and I quickened my pace,
feeling the beginning of an absurd nervous excitement in
my limbs. At the next turn, there it was again! but only for
another moment. I paused, exulting, and wiped my drenched
forehead. "She can not escape me!" I murmured between
the deep draughts of cooler air I inhaled in the shadow of a
rock.

A few hundred steps more brought me to the foot of the
steep ascent, where I had counted on overtaking her. I was
too late for that, but the dry, baked soil had surely been
crumbled and dislodged, here and there, by a rapid foot. I
followed, in reckless haste, snatching at the laurel branches
right and left, and paying little heed to my footing. About
one-third of the way up I slipped, fell, caught a bush which
snapped at the root, slid, whirled over, and before I fairly
knew what had happened, I was lying doubled up at the
bottom of the slope.

I rose, made two steps forward, and then sat down with
a groan of pain; my left ankle was badly sprained, in addition to various minor scratches and bruises. There was a
revulsion of feeling, of course—instant, complete, and
hideous. I fairly hated the Unknown. "Fool that I was!"
I exclaimed, in the theatrical manner, dashing the palm of
my hand softly against my brow: "lured to this by the fair
traitress! But, no!—not fair: she shows the artfulness of
faded, desperate spinsterhood; she is all compact of enamel,
'liquid bloom of youth' and hair dye!"

There was a fierce comfort in this thought, but it couldn't
help me out of the scrape. I dared not sit still, lest a sun-
stroke should be added, and there was no resource but to hop

or crawl down the rugged path, in the hope of finding a forked sapling from which I could extemporize a crutch. With endless pain and trouble I reached a thicket, and was feebly working on a branch with my pen-knife, when the sound of a heavy footstep surprised me.

A brown harvest-hand, in straw hat and shirt-sleeves, presently appeared. He grinned when he saw me, and the thick snub of his nose would have seemed like a sneer at any other time.

"Are you the gentleman that got hurt?" he asked. "Is it pretty tolerable bad?"

"Who said I was hurt?" I cried, in astonishment.

"One of your town-women from the hotel—I reckon she was. I was binding oats, in the field over the ridge; but I haven't lost no time in comin' here."

While I was stupidly staring at this announcement, he whipped out a big clasp-knife, and in a few minutes fashioned me a practicable crutch. Then, taking me by the other arm, he set me in motion toward the village.

Grateful as I was for the man's help, he aggravated me by his ignorance. When I asked if he knew the lady, he answered: "It's more'n likely *you* know her better." But where did she come from? Down from the hill, he guessed, but it might ha' been up the road. How did she look? was she old or young? what was the color of her eyes? of her hair? There, now, I was too much for him. When a woman kept one o' them speckled veils over her face, turned her head away, and held her parasol between, how were you to know her from Adam? I declare to you, I couldn't arrive at one positive particular. Even when he affirmed that she was tall, he added, the next instant: "Now I come to think on it, she stepped mighty quick; so I guess she must ha' been short."

By the time we reached the hotel, I was in a state of fever; opiates and lotions had their will of me for the rest of the day. I was glad to escape the worry of questions, and the conventional sympathy expressed in inflections of the voice which are meant to soothe, and only exasperate. The next morning, as I lay upon my sofa, restful, patient, and properly cheerful, the waiter entered with a bouquet of wild flowers.

"Who sent them?" I asked.

"I found them outside your door, sir. Maybe there's a card; yes, here's a bit o' paper."

I opened the twisted slip he handed me, and read: "From your dell—and mine." I took the flowers; among them were two or three rare and beautiful varieties which I had only found in that one spot. Fool, again! I noiselessly kissed, while pretending to smell them, had them placed on a stand within reach, and fell into a state of quiet and agreeable contemplation.

Tell me, yourself, whether any male human being is ever too old for sentiment, provided that it strikes him at the right time and in the right way! What did that bunch of wild flowers betoken? Knowledge, first; then, sympathy; and finally, encouragement, at least. Of course she had seen my accident, from above; of course she had sent the harvest laborer to aid me home. It was quite natural she should imagine some special, romantic interest in the lonely dell, on my part, and the gift took additional value from her conjecture.

Four days afterward, there was a hop in the large dining-room of the hotel. Early in the morning, a fresh bouquet had been left at my door. I was tired of my enforced idleness, eager to discover the fair unknown (she was again fair, to my fancy!), and I determined to go down, believing that a cane and a crimson velvet slipper on the left foot would provoke a glance of sympathy from certain eyes, and thus enable me to detect them.

The fact was, the sympathy was much too general and effusive. Everybody, it seemed, came to me with kindly greetings; seats were vacated at my approach, even fat Mrs. Huxter insisting on my taking her warm place, at the head of the room. But Bob Leroy—you know him—as gallant a gentleman as ever lived, put me down at the right point, and kept me there. He only meant to divert me, yet gave me the only place where I could quietly inspect all the younger ladies, as dance or supper brought them near.

One of the dances was an old-fashioned cotillon, and one of the figures, the "coquette," brought every one, in turn, before me. I received a pleasant word or two from those whom I knew, and a long, kind, silent glance from Miss May Danvers. Where had been my eyes? She was tall, stately, twenty-five, had large dark eyes, and long dark lashes! Again the changes of the dance brought her near me; I threw (or strove to throw) unutterable meanings into my eyes, and cast them upon hers. She seemed startled, looked suddenly away, looked back to me, and—blushed. I knew her for what is called "a nice girl"—that is, tolerably frank, gently feminine, and not dangerously intelligent. Was it possible that I overlooked so much character and intellect?

As the cotillon closed, she was again in my neighborhood, and her partner led her in my direction. I was rising painfully from my chair, when Bob Leroy pushed me down again, whisked another seat from somewhere, planted it at my side, and there she was!

She knew who was her neighbor, I plainly saw; but instead of turning toward me, she began to fan herself in a nervous way and to fidget with the buttons of her gloves. I grew impatient.

"Miss Danvers!" I said, at last.

"Oh!" was all her answer, as she looked at me for a moment.

"Where are your thoughts?" I asked.

Then she turned, with wide, astonished eyes, coloring softly up to the roots of her hair. My heart gave a sudden leap.

"How can you tell, if I can not?" she asked.

"May I guess?"

She made a slight inclination of the head, saying nothing. I was then quite sure.

"The second ravine to the left of the main drive?"

This time she actually started; her color became deeper, and a leaf of the ivory fan snapped between her fingers.

"Let there be no more a secret!" I exclaimed. "Your flowers have brought me your messages; I knew I should find you—"

Full of certainty, I was speaking in a low, impassioned voice. She cut me short by rising from her seat; I felt that she was both angry and alarmed. Fisher, of Philadelphia, jostling right and left in his haste, made his way toward her. She fairly snatched his arm, clung to it with a warmth I had never seen expressed in a ballroom, and began to whisper in his ear. It was not five minutes before he came to me, alone, with a very stern face, bent down, and said:

"If you have discovered our secret, you will keep silent. You are certainly a gentleman."

I bowed, coldly and savagely. There was a draught from the open window; my ankle became suddenly weary and painful, and I went to bed. Can you believe that I didn't guess, immediately, what it all meant? In a vague way, I fancied that I had been premature in my attempt to drop our mutual incognito, and that Fisher, a rival lover, was jealous of me. This was rather flattering than otherwise; but when I limped down to the ladies' parlor, the next day, no Miss Danvers was to be seen. I did not venture to ask for her; it might seem importunate, and a woman of so much hidden capacity was evidently not to be wooed in the ordinary way.

So another night passed by; and then, with the morning, came a letter which made me feel, at the same instant, like a fool and a hero. It had been dropped in the Wampsocket post-office, was legibly addressed to me and delivered with some other letters which had arrived by the night mail. Here it is; listen!

"NOTO IGNOTA!—Haste is not a gift of the gods, and you have been impatient, with the usual result. I was almost prepared for this, and

thus am not wholly disappointed. In a day or two more you will discover your mistake, which, so far as I can learn, has done no particular
harm. If you wish to find *me*, there is only one way to seek me;
should I tell you what it is, I should run the risk of losing you—that
is, I should preclude the manifestation of a certain quality which I
hope to find in the man who may—or, rather, must—be my friend.
This sounds enigmatical, yet you have read enough of my nature, as
written in those random notes in my sketch-book, to guess, at least,
how much I require. Only this let me add: mere guessing is useless.

"Being unknown, I can write freely. If you find me, I shall be justi-
fied; if not, I shall hardly need to blush, even to myself, over a futile
experiment.

"It is possible for me to learn enough of your life, henceforth, to
direct my relation toward you. This may be the end; if so, I shall
know it soon. I shall also know whether you continue to seek me.
Trusting in your honor as a man, I must ask you to trust in mine,
as a woman."

I *did* discover my mistake, as the Unknown promised.
There had been a secret betrothal between Fisher and Miss
Danvers, and, singularly enough, the momentous question
and answer had been given in the very ravine leading to my
upper dell! The two meant to keep the matter to themselves; but therein, it seems, I thwarted them; there was a
little opposition on the part of their respective families, but
all was amicably settled before I left Wampsocket.

The letter made a very deep impression upon me. What
was the one way to find her? What could it be but the
triumph that follows ambitious toil—the manifestation of
all my best qualities as a man? Be she old or young, plain
or beautiful, I reflected, hers is surely a nature worth knowing, and its candid intelligence conceals no hazards for me.
I have sought her rashly, blundered, betrayed that I set her
lower, in my thoughts, than her actual self: let me now
adopt the opposite course, seek her openly no longer, go back
to my tasks, and, following my own aims vigorously and
cheerfully, restore that respect which she seemed to be on
the point of losing. For, consciously or not, she had communicated to me a doubt, implied in the very expression of
her own strength and pride. She had meant to address me

as an equal, yet, despite herself, took a stand a little above that which she accorded to me.

I came back to New York earlier than usual, worked steadily at my profession and with increasing success, and began to accept opportunities (which I had previously declined) of making myself personally known to the great, impressible, fickle, tyrannical public. One or two of my speeches in the hall of the Cooper Institute, on various occasions—as you may perhaps remember—gave me a good headway with the party, and were the chief cause of my nomination for the State office which I still hold. (There, on the table, lies a resignation, written to-day, but not yet signed. We'll talk of it afterward.) Several months passed by, and no further letter reached me. I gave up much of my time to society, moved familiarly in more than one province of the kingdom here, and vastly extended my acquaintance, especially among the women; but not one of them betrayed the mysterious something or other—really I can't explain precisely what it was!—which I was looking for. In fact, the more I endeavored quietly to study the sex, the more confused I became.

At last, I was subjected to the usual onslaught from the strong-minded. A small but formidable committee entered my office one morning and demanded a categorical declaration of my principles. What my views on the subject were, I knew very well; they were clear and decided; and yet, I hesitated to declare them! It wasn't a temptation of Saint Anthony—that is, turned the other way—and the belligerent attitude of the dames did not alarm me in the least; but *she!* What was *her* position? How could I best please her? It flashed upon my mind, while Mrs. —— was making her formal speech, that I had taken no step for months without a vague, secret reference to *her.* So I strove to be courteous, friendly, and agreeably noncommittal; begged for further documents, and promised to reply by letter in a few days.

I was hardly surprised to find the well-known hand on the envelope of a letter shortly afterward. I held it for a

minute in my palm, with an absurd hope that I might sym-
pathetically feel its character before breaking the seal. Then
I read it with a great sense of relief.

"I have never assumed to guide a man, except toward the full
exercise of his powers. It is not opinion in action, but opinion in a
state of idleness or indifference, which repels me. I am deeply glad
that you have gained so much since you left the country. If, in shaping
your course, you have thought of me, I will frankly say that, *to that
extent,* you have drawn nearer. Am I mistaken in conjecturing that
you wish to know my relation to the movement concerning which you
were recently interrogated? In this, as in other instances which may
come, I must beg you to consider me only as a spectator. The more
my own views may seem likely to sway your action, the less I shall
be inclined to declare them. If you find this cold or unwomanly, remember that it is not easy!"

Yes! I felt that I had certainly drawn much nearer to her.
And from this time on, her imaginary face and form became
other than they were. She was twenty-eight—three years
older; a very little above the middle height, but not tall;
serene, rather than stately, in her movements; with a calm,
almost grave face, relieved by the sweetness of the full, firm
lips; and finally eyes of pure, limpid gray, such as we fancy
belonged to the Venus of Milo. I found her thus much more
attractive than with the dark eyes and lashes—but she did
not make her appearance in the circles which I frequented.

Another year slipped away. As an official personage, my
importance increased, but I was careful not to exaggerate
it to myself. Many have wondered (perhaps you among
the rest) at my success, seeing that I possess no remarkable
abilities. If I have any secret, it is simply this—doing faithfully, with all my might, whatever I undertake. Nine-tenths
of our politicians become inflated and careless, after the first
few years, and are easily forgotten when they once lose
place.

I am a little surprised now that I had so much patience
with the Unknown. I was too important, at least, to be
played with; too mature to be subjected to a longer test; too

earnest, as I had proved, to be doubted, or thrown aside without a further explanation.

Growing tired, at last, of silent waiting, I bethought me of advertising. A carefully written "Personal," in which *Ignotus* informed *Ignota* of the necessity of his communicating with her, appeared simultaneously in the "Tribune," "Herald," "World," and "Times." I renewed the advertisement as the time expired without an answer, and I think it was about the end of the third week before one came, through the post, as before.

Ah, yes! I had forgotten. See! my advertisement is pasted on the note, as a heading or motto for the manuscript lines. I don't know why the printed slip should give me a particular feeling of humiliation as I look at it, but such is the fact. What she wrote is all I need read to you:

"I could not, at first, be certain that this was meant for me. If I were to explain to you why I have not written for so long a time, I might give you one of the few clews which I insist on keeping in my own hands. In your public capacity, you have been (so far as a woman may judge) upright, independent, wholly manly: in your relations with other men I learn nothing of you that is not honorable: toward women you are kind, chivalrous, no doubt, overflowing with the *usual* social refinements, but— Here, again, I run hard upon the absolute necessity of silence. The way to me, if you care to traverse it, is so simple, so very simple! Yet, after what I have written, I can not even wave my hand in the direction of it, without certain self-contempt. When I feel free to tell you, we shall draw apart and remain unknown forever.

"You desire to write? I do not prohibit it. I have heretofore made no arrangement for hearing from you, in turn, because I could not discover that any advantage would accrue from it. But it seems only fair, I confess, and you dare not think me capricious. So, three days hence, at six o'clock in the evening, a trusty messenger of mine will call at your door. If you have anything to give her for me, the act of giving it must be the sign of a compact on your part that you will allow her to leave immediately, unquestioned and unfollowed."

You look puzzled, I see: you don't catch the real drift of her words? Well, that's a melancholy encouragement. Neither did I, at the time: it was plain that I had disappointed her in some way, and my intercourse with or manner toward women had something to do with it. In vain I ran over as much of my later social life as I could recall. There had been no special attention, nothing to mislead a susceptible heart; on the other side, certainly no rudeness, no want of "chivalrous" (she used the word!) respect and attention. What, in the name of all the gods, was the matter?

In spite of all my efforts to grow clearer, I was obliged to write my letter in a rather muddled state of mind. I had *so* much to say! sixteen folio pages, I was sure, would only suffice for an introduction to the case; yet, when the creamy vellum lay before me and the moist pen drew my fingers toward it, I sat stock dumb for half an hour. I wrote, finally, in a half-desperate mood, without regard to coherency or logic. Here's a rough draft of a part of the letter, and a single passage from it will be enough:

"I can conceive of no simpler way to you than the knowledge of your name and address. I have drawn airy images of you, but they do not become incarnate, and I am not sure that I should recognize you in the brief moment of passing. Your nature is not of those which are instantly legible. As an abstract power, it has wrought in my life and it continually moves my heart with desires which are unsatisfactory because so vague and ignorant. Let me offer you, personally, my gratitude, my earnest friendship, you would laugh if I were *now* to offer more."

Stay! here is another fragment, more reckless in tone:

"I want to find the woman whom I can love—who can love me. But this is a masquerade where the features are hidden, the voice disguised, even the hands grotesquely gloved. Come! I will venture more than I ever thought was possible to me. You shall know my deepest nature as I myself seem to know it. Then, give me the commonest chance of learning yours, through an intercourse which shall leave both free, should we not feel the closing of the inevitable bond!"

After I had written that, the pages filled rapidly. When the appointed hour arrived, a bulky epistle, in a strong linen envelope, sealed with five wax seals, was waiting on my table. Precisely at six there was an announcement: the door opened, and a little outside, in the shadow, I saw an old woman, in a thread-bare dress of rusty black.

"Come in!" I said.

"The letter!" answered a husky voice. She stretched out a bony hand, without moving a step.

"It is for a lady—very important business," said I, taking up the letter; "are you sure that there is no mistake?"

She drew her hand under the shawl, turned without a word, and moved toward the hall door.

"Stop!" I cried: "I beg a thousand pardons! Take it— take it! You are the right messenger!"

She clutched it, and was instantly gone.

Several days passed, and I gradually became so nervous and uneasy that I was on the point of inserting another "Personal" in the daily papers, when the answer arrived. It was brief and mysterious; you shall hear the whole of it:

"I thank you. Your letter is a sacred confidence which I pray you never to regret. Your nature is sound and good. You ask no more than is reasonable, and I have no real right to refuse. In the one respect which I have hinted, *I* may have been unskilful or too narrowly cautious: I must have the certainty of this. Therefore, as a generous favor, give me six months more! At the end of that time I will write to you again. Have patience with these brief lines: another word might be a word too much."

You notice the change in her tone? The letter gave me the strongest impression of a new, warm, almost anxious interest on her part. My fancies, as first at Wampsocket, began to play all sorts of singular pranks: sometimes she was rich and of an old family, sometimes moderately poor and obscure, but always the same calm, reposeful face and clear gray eyes. I ceased looking for her in society, quite sure that I should not find her, and nursed a wild expectation of suddenly meeting her, face to face, in the most unlikely places and under startling circumstances. However, the end of it all was patience—patience for six months.

There's not much more to tell; but this last letter is hard for me to read. It came punctually, to a day. I knew it would, and at the last I began to dread the time, as if a heavy note were falling due, and I had no funds to meet it. My head was in a whirl when I broke the seal. The fact in it stared at me blankly, at once, but it was a long time before the words and sentences became intelligible.

"The stipulated time has come, and our hidden romance is at an end. Had I taken this resolution a year ago, it would have saved me many vain hopes, and you, perhaps, a little uncertainty. Forgive me, first, if you can, and then hear the explanation:

"You wished for a personal interview: *you have had, not one, but many.* We have met, in society, talked face to face, discussed the weather, the opera, toilettes, Queechy, Aurora Floyd, Long Branch and Newport, and exchanged a weary amount of fashionable gossip; and you never guessed that I was governed by any deeper interest! I have purposely uttered ridiculous platitudes, and you were as smilingly courteous as if you enjoyed them: I have let fall remarks whose hollowness and selfishness could not have escaped you, and have waited in vain for a word of sharp, honest, manly reproof. Your manner to me was unexceptionable, as it was to all other women: but there lies the source of my disappointment, of—yes—of my sorrow!

"You appreciate, I can not doubt, the qualities in woman which men value in one another—culture, independence of thought, a high and earnest apprehension of life; but you know not how to seek them. It is not true that a mature and unperverted woman is flattered by receiving only the general obsequiousness which most men give to the whole sex. In the man who contradicts and strives with her, she discovers a truer interest, a nobler respect. The empty-headed, spindle-shanked youths who dance admirably, understand something of billiards, much less of horses, and still less of navigation, soon grow inexpressibly wearisome to us; but the men who adopt their social courtesy, never seeking to arouse, uplift, instruct us, are a bitter disappointment.

"What would have been the end, had you really found me? Certainly a sincere, satisfying friendship. No mysterious magnetic force has drawn you to me or held you near me, nor has my experiment inspired me with an interest which can not be given up without a personal pang. I am grieved, for the sake of all men and all women. Yet, understand me! I mean no slightest reproach. I esteem and honor you for what you are. Farewell!"

There! Nothing could be kinder in tone, nothing more humiliating in substance. I was sore and offended for a few days; but I soon began to see, and ever more and more clearly, that she was wholly right. I was sure, also, that any further attempt to correspond with her would be vain. It all comes of taking society just as we find it, and supposing that conventional courtesy is the only safe ground on which men and women can meet.

The fact is—there's no use in hiding it from myself (and I see, by your face, that the letter cuts into your own conscience)—she is a free, courageous, independent character, and—I am not.

But who *was* she?

MADEMOISELLE OLYMPE ZABRISKI

By Thomas Bailey Aldrich

CHAPTER I

We are accustomed to speak with a certain light irony of the tendency which women have to gossip, as if the sin itself, if it is a sin, were of the gentler sex, and could by no chance be a masculine peccadillo. So far as my observation goes, men are as much given to small talk as women, and it is undeniable that we have produced the highest type of gossiper extant. Where will you find, in or out of literature, such another droll, delightful, chatty busybody as Samuel Pepys, Esq., Secretary to the Admiralty in the reigns of those fortunate gentlemen Charles II and James II of England? He is the king of tattlers, as Shakespeare is the king of poets.

If it came to a matter of pure gossip, I would back Our Club against the Sorosis or any women's club in existence. Whenever you see in your drawing-room four or five young fellows lounging in easy chairs, cigar in hand, and now and then bringing their heads together over the small round Japanese table which is always the pivot of these social circles, you may be sure that they are discussing Tom's engagement, or Dick's extravagance, or Harry's hopeless passion for the younger Miss Fleurdelys. It is here old Tippleton gets execrated for that everlasting *bon mot* of his which was quite a success at dinner-parties forty years ago; it is here the belle of the season passes under the scalpels of merciless young surgeons; it is here B's financial condition

363

is handled in a way that would make B's hair stand on end; it is here, in short, that everything is canvassed—everything that happens in our set, I mean—much that never happens, and a great deal that could not possibly happen. It was at Our Club that I learned the particulars of the Van Twiller affair.

It was great entertainment to Our Club, the Van Twiller affair, though it was rather a joyless thing, I fancy, for Van Twiller. To understand the case fully, it should be understood that Ralph Van Twiller is one of the proudest and most sensitive men living. He is a lineal descendant of Wouter Van Twiller, the famous old Dutch governor of New York—Nieuw Amsterdam, as it was then; his ancestors have always been burgomasters or admirals or generals, and his mother is the Mrs. Vanrensselaer Vanzandt Van Twiller whose magnificent place will be pointed out to you on the right bank of the Hudson as you pass up the historic river toward Idlewild. Ralph is about twenty-five years old. Birth made him a gentleman, and the rise of real estate—some of it in the family since the old governor's time —made him a millionaire. It was a kindly fairy that stepped in and made him a good fellow also. Fortune, I take it, was in her most jocund mood when she heaped her gifts in this fashion on Van Twiller, who was, and will be again, when this cloud blows over, the flower of Our Club.

About a year ago there came a whisper—if the word "whisper" is not too harsh a term to apply to what seemed a mere breath floating gently through the atmosphere of the billiard-room—imparting the intelligence that Van Twiller was in some kind of trouble. Just as everybody suddenly takes to wearing square-toed boots, or to drawing his neck-scarf through a ring, so it became all at once the fashion, without any preconcerted agreement, for everybody to speak of Van Twiller as a man in some way under a cloud. But what the cloud was, and how he got under it, and why he did not get away from it, were points that lifted themselves into the realm of pure conjecture. There was no man in the club with strong enough wing to his imagination to soar to the supposition that Van Twiller was embarrassed in money matters. Was he in love? That appeared nearly as improbable; for if he had been in love all the world—that is, perhaps a hundred first families—would have known all about it instantly.

"He has the symptoms," said Delaney, laughing. "I remember once when Jack Fleming—"

"Ned!" cried Fleming, "I protest against any allusion to that business."

This was one night when Van Twiller had wandered into the club, turned over the magazines absently in the reading-room, and wandered out again without speaking ten words. The most careless eye would have remarked the great change that had come over Van Twiller. Now and then he would play a game of billiards with De Peyster or Haseltine, or stop to chat a moment in the vestibule with old Duane; but he was an altered man. When at the club, he was usually to be found in the small smoking-room upstairs, seated on a fauteuil fast asleep, with the last number of "The Nation" in his hand. Once, if you went to two or three places of an evening, you were certain to meet Van Twiller at them all. You seldom met him in society now.

By and by came whisper number two—a whisper more emphatic than number one, but still untraceable to any tangible mouthpiece. This time the whisper said that Van Twiller *was* in love. But with whom? The list of possible Mrs. Van Twillers was carefully examined by experienced hands, and a check placed against a fine old Knickerbocker name here and there, but nothing satisfactory arrived at. Then that same still small voice of rumor, but now with an easily detected staccato sharpness to it, said that Van Twiller was in love—with an actress! Van Twiller, whom it had taken all these years and all this waste of raw material in the way of ancestors to bring to perfection—Ralph Van Twiller, the net result and flower of his race, the descendant of Wouter, the son of Mrs. Vanrensselaer Vanzandt Van Twiller—in love with an actress! That was too ridiculous to be believed—and so everybody believed it.

Six or seven members of the club abruptly discovered in themselves an unsuspected latent passion for the histrionic art. In squads of two or three they stormed successively all the theatres in town—Booth's, Wallack's, Daly's Fifth Avenue (not burned down then), and the Grand Opera House. Even the shabby homes of the drama over in the Bowery, where the Germanic Thespis has not taken out his naturalization papers, underwent rigid exploration. But no clew was found to Van Twiller's mysterious attachment. The *opéra bouffe,* which promised the widest field for investigation, produced absolutely nothing, not even a crop of suspicions. One night, after several weeks of this, Delaney and I fancied that we caught sight of Van Twiller in the private box of an uptown theatre, where some thrilling trapeze performance was going on, which we did not care to sit through; but we concluded afterward that it was only somebody who looked like him. Delaney, by the way, was unusually active in this search. I dare say he never quite forgave Van Twiller for calling him Muslin Delaney. Ned is fond of ladies' society, and that's a fact.

The Cimmerian darkness which surrounded Van Twiller's inamorata left us free to indulge in the wildest conjectures. Whether she was black-tressed Melpomene, with bowl and dagger, or Thalia, with the fair hair and the laughing face, was only to be guessed at. It was popularly conceded, however, that Van Twiller was on the point of forming a dreadful *mésalliance.*

Up to this period he had visited the club regularly. Suddenly he ceased to appear. He was not to be seen on Fifth Avenue, or in the Central Park, or at the houses he generally frequented. His chambers—and mighty comfortable chambers they were—on Thirty-fourth Street were deserted. He had dropped out of the world, shot like a bright particular star from his orbit in the heaven of the best society.

The following conversation took place one night in the smoking-room:

"Where's Van Twiller?"

"Who's seen Van Twiller?"

"What has become of Van Twiller?"

Delaney picked up the "Evening Post," and read—with a solemnity that betrayed young Firkins into exclaiming, "By Joye, now!—"

"Married, on the 10th instant, by the Rev. Friar Laurence, at the residence of the bride's uncle, Montague Capulet, Esq., Miss Adrienne Le Couvreur to Mr. Ralph Van Twiller, both of this city. No cards."

"Free List suspended," murmured De Peyster.

"It strikes me," said Frank Livingstone, who had been ruffling the leaves of a magazine at the other end of the table, "that you fellows are in a great fever about Van Twiller."

"So we are."

"Well, he has simply gone out of town."

"Where?"

"Up to the old homestead on the Hudson."

"It's an odd time of year for a fellow to go into the country."

"He has gone to visit his mother," said Livingstone.

"In February?"

"I didn't know, Delaney, that there was any statute in force prohibiting a man from visiting his mother in February if he wants to."

Delaney made some light remark about the pleasure of communing with Nature with a cold in her head, and the topic was dropped.

Livingstone was hand in glove with Van Twiller, and if any man shared his confidence it was Livingstone. He was aware of the gossip and speculation that had been rife in the club, but he either was not at liberty or did not think it worth while to relieve our curiosity. In the course of a week or two it was reported that Van Twiller was going to Europe; and go he did. A dozen of us went down to the "Scythia" to see him off. It was refreshing to have something as positive as the fact that Van Twiller had sailed.

CHAPTER II

SHORTLY after Van Twiller's departure the whole thing came out. Whether Livingstone found the secret too heavy a burden, or whether it transpired through some indiscretion on the part of Mrs. Vanrensselaer Vanzandt Van Twiller, I can not say; but one evening the entire story was in the possession of the club.

Van Twiller had actually been very deeply interested— not in an actress, for the legitimate drama was not her humble walk in life, but—in Mademoiselle Olympe Zabriski, whose really perilous feats on the trapeze had astonished New York the year before, though they had failed to attract Delaney and me the night we wandered into the up-town theatre on the trail of Van Twiller's mystery.

That a man like Van Twiller should be fascinated even for an instant by a common circus-girl seems incredible; but it is always the incredible thing that happens. Besides, Mademoiselle Olympe was not a common circus-girl; she was a most daring and startling gymnaste, with a beauty and a grace of movement that gave to her audacious performance almost an air of prudery. Watching her wondrous dexterity and pliant strength, both exercised without apparent effort, it seemed the most natural proceeding in the world that she should do those unpardonable things. She had a way of melting from one graceful posture into another like the dissolving figures thrown from a stereopticon. She was a lithe, radiant shape out of the Grecian mythology, now poised up there above the gaslights, and now gleaming through the air like a slender gilt arrow.

I am describing Mademoiselle Olympe as she appeared to Van Twiller on the first occasion when he strolled into the theatre where she was performing. To me she was a girl of eighteen or twenty years of age (maybe she was much older, for pearl powder and distance keep these people perpetually young), slightly but exquisitely built, with sinews of silver wire; rather pretty, perhaps, after a manner, but showing plainly the effects of the exhaustive draughts she was making on her physical vitality. Now, Van Twiller was an enthusiast on the subject of calisthenics. "If I had a daughter," Van Twiller used to say, "I wouldn't send her to a boarding school, or a nunnery; I'd send her to a gymnasium for the first five years. Our American women have no physique. They are lilies, pallid, pretty—and perishable. You marry an American woman, and what do you marry? A headache. Look at English girls. They are at least roses, and last the season through."

Walking home from the theatre that first night, it flitted through Van Twiller's mind that if he could give this girl's set of nerves and muscles to any one of the two hundred high-bred women he knew, he would marry her on the spot and worship her forever.

The following evening he went to see Mademoiselle Olympe again. "Olympe Zabriski," he soliloquized as he sauntered through the lobby—"what a queer name! Olympe is French and Zabriski is Polish. It is her *nom de guerre,* of course; her real name is probably Sarah Jones. What kind of creature can she be in private life, I wonder? I wonder if she wears that costume all the time, and if she springs to her meals from a horizontal bar. Of course she rocks the baby to sleep on the trapeze." And Van Twiller went on making comical domestic tableaux of Mademoiselle Zabriski, like the clever, satirical dog he was, until the curtain rose.

This was on a Friday. There was a matinée the next day, and he attended that, though he had secured a seat for the usual evening entertainment. Then it became a habit of Van Twiller's to drop into the theatre for half an hour or so every night, to assist at the interlude, in which she appeared. He cared only for her part of the programme, and timed his visits accordingly. It was a surprise to himself when he reflected, one morning, that he had not missed a single performance of Mademoiselle Olympe for nearly two weeks.

"This will never do," said Van Twiller. "Olympe"—he called her Olympe, as if she were an old acquaintance, and so she might have been considered by that time—"is a wonderful creature; but this will never do. Van, my boy, you must reform this altogether."

But half-past nine that night saw him in his accustomed orchestra chair, and so on for another week. A habit leads a man so gently in the beginning that he does not perceive he is led—with what silken threads and down what pleasant avenues it leads him! By and by the soft silk threads become iron chains, and the pleasant avenues Avernus!

Quite a new element had lately entered into Van Twiller's enjoyment of Mademoiselle Olympe's ingenious feats—a vaguely born apprehension that she might slip from that swinging bar; that one of the thin cords supporting it might snap, and let her go headlong from the dizzy height. Now and then, for a terrible instant, he would imagine her lying a glittering, palpitating heap at the foot-lights, with no color in her lips! Sometimes it seemed as if the girl were tempting this kind of fate. It was a hard, bitter life, and nothing but poverty and sordid misery at home could have driven her to it. What if she should end it all some night, by just unclasping that little hand? It looked so small and white from where Van Twiller sat!

This frightful idea fascinated while it chilled him, and helped to make it nearly impossible for him to keep away from the theatre. In the beginning his attendance had not interfered with his social duties or pleasures; but now he came to find it distasteful after dinner to do anything but read, or walk the streets aimlessly, until it was time to go to the play. When that was over, he was in no mood to go anywhere but to his rooms. So he dropped away by insensible degrees from his habitual haunts, was missed, and began to be talked about at the club. Catching some intimation of this, he ventured no more in the orchestra stalls, but shrouded himself behind the draperies of the private box in which Delaney and I thought we saw him on one occasion.

Now, I find it very perplexing to explain what Van Twiller was wholly unable to explain to himself. He was not in love with Mademoiselle Olympe. He had no wish to speak to her, or to hear her speak. Nothing could have been easier, and nothing further from his desire, than to know her personally. A Van Twiller personally acquainted with a strolling female acrobat! Good heavens! That was something possible only with the discovery of perpetual motion. Taken from her theatrical setting, from her lofty perch, so to say, on the trapeze-bar, Olympe Zabriski would have shocked every aristocratic fibre in Van Twiller's body. He was simply fascinated by her marvelous grace and *élan,* and the magnetic recklessness of the girl. It was very young in him and very weak, and no member of the Sorosis, or all the Sorosisters together, could have been more severe on Van Twiller than he was on himself. To be weak, and to know it, is something of a punishment for a proud man. Van Twiller took his punishment, and went to the theatre, regularly.

"When her engagement comes to an end," he meditated, "that will finish the business."

Mademoiselle Olympe's engagement finally did come to an end and she departed. But her engagement had been highly beneficial to the treasury-chest of the up-town theatre, and before Van Twiller could get over missing her she had returned from a short Western tour, and her immediate reappearance was underlined on the play-bills.

On the dead wall opposite the windows of Van Twiller's sleeping-room there appeared, as if by necromancy, an aggressive poster with MADEMOISELLE OLYMPE ZABRISKI on it in letters at least a foot high. This thing stared him in the face when he woke up one morning. It gave him a sensation as if she had called on him overnight and left her card.

From time to time through the day he regarded that poster with a sardonic eye. He had pitilessly resolved not to repeat the folly of the previous month. To say that this moral victory cost him nothing would be to deprive it of merit. It cost him many internal struggles. It is a fine thing to see a man seizing his temptation by the throat, and wrestling with it, and trampling it underfoot like St. Anthony. This was the spectacle Van Twiller was exhibiting to the angels.

The evening Mademoiselle Olympe was to make her reappearance, Van Twiller, having dined at the club, and feeling more like himself than he had felt for weeks, returned to his chamber, and, putting on dressing-gown and slippers, piled up the greater portion of his library about him, and fell to reading assiduously. There is nothing like a quiet evening at home with some slight intellectual occupation, after one's feathers have been stroked the wrong way.

When the lively French clock on the mantelpiece—a base of malachite surmounted by a flying bronze Mercury with its arms spread gracefully in the air, and not remotely suggestive of Mademoiselle Olympe in the act of executing her grand flight from the trapeze—when the clock, I repeat, struck nine, Van Twiller paid no attention to it. That was certainly a triumph. I am anxious to render Van Twiller all the justice I can, at this point of the narrative, inasmuch as when the half hour sounded musically, like a crystal ball dropping into a silver bowl, he rose from the chair automatically, thrust his feet into his walking-shoes, threw his overcoat across his arm, and strode out of the room.

To be weak and to scorn your weakness, and not to be able to conquer it, is, as has been said, a hard thing; and I suspect it was not with unalloyed satisfaction that Van Twiller found himself taking his seat in the back part of the private box night after night during the second engagement of Mademoiselle Olympe. It was so easy not to stay away!

In this second edition of Van Twiller's fatuity, his case was even worse than before. He not only thought of Olympe quite a number of times between breakfast and dinner, he not only attended the interlude regularly, but he began, in spite of himself, to occupy his leisure hours at night by dreaming of her. This was too much of a good thing, and Van Twiller regarded it so. Besides, the dream was always the same—a harrowing dream, a dream singularly adapted to shattering the nerves of a man like Van Twiller. He would imagine himself seated at the theatre (with all the members of Our Club in the parquette), watching Mademoiselle Olympe as usual, when suddenly that young lady would launch herself desperately from the trapeze, and come flying through the air like a fire-brand hurled at his private box. Then the unfortunate man would wake up with cold drops standing on his forehead.

There is one redeeming feature in this infatuation of Van Twiller's which the sober moralist will love to look upon— the serene unconsciousness of the person who caused it. She went through her *rôle* with admirable aplomb, drew her salary, it may be assumed, punctually, and appears from first to last to have been ignorant that there was a miserable slave wearing her chains nightly in the left-hand proscenium box.

That Van Twiller, haunting the theatre with the persistency of an ex-actor, conducted himself so discreetly as not to draw the fire of Mademoiselle Olympe's blue eyes shows that Van Twiller, however deeply under a spell, was not in love. I say this, though I think if Van Twiller had not been Van Twiller, if he had been a man of no family and no position and no money, if New York had been Paris and Thirty-fourth Street a street in the Latin Quarter— but it is useless to speculate on what might have happened. What did happen is sufficient.

It happened, then, in the second week of Queen Olympe's second unconscious reign, that an appalling Whisper floated up the Hudson, effected a landing at a point between Spuyten Duyvil Creek and Cold Spring, and sought out a stately mansion of Dutch architecture standing on the bank of the river. The Whisper straightway informed the lady dwelling in this mansion that all was not well with the last of the Van Twillers; that he was gradually estranging himself from his peers, and wasting his nights in a play-house watching a misguided young woman turning unmaidenly somersaults on a piece of wood attached to two ropes.

Mrs. Vanrensselaer Vanzandt Van Twiller came down to town by the next train to look into this little matter.

She found the flower of the family taking an early breakfast at 11 A. M., in his cosy apartments on Thirty-fourth Street. With the least possible circumlocution she confronted him with what rumor had reported of his pursuits, and was pleased, but not too much pleased, when he gave her an exact account of his relations with Mademoiselle Zabriski, neither concealing nor qualifying anything. As a confession, it was unique, and might have been a great deal less entertaining. Two or three times in the course of the narrative, the matron had some difficulty in preserving the gravity of her countenance. After meditating a few minutes, she tapped Van Twiller softly on the arm with the tip of her parasol, and invited him to return with her the next day up the Hudson and make a brief visit at the home of his ancestors. He accepted the invitation with outward alacrity and inward disgust.

When this was settled, and the worthy lady had withdrawn, Van Twiller went directly to the establishment of Messrs. Ball, Black, and Company, and selected, with unerring taste, the finest diamond bracelet procurable. For his mother? Dear me, no! She had the family jewels.

I would not like to state the enormous sum Van Twiller paid for this bracelet. It was such a clasp of diamonds as would have hastened the pulsation of a patrician wrist. It was such a bracelet as Prince Camaralzaman might have sent to the Princess Badoura, and the Princess Badoura—might have been very glad to get,

In the fragrant Levant morocco case, where these happy jewels lived when they were at home, Van Twiller thoughtfully placed his card, on the back of which he had written a line begging Mademoiselle Olympe Zabriski to accept the accompanying trifle from one who had witnessed her graceful performances with interest and pleasure. This was not done inconsiderately. "Of course, I must inclose my card, as I would to any lady," Van Twiller had said to himself. "A Van Twiller can neither write an anonymous letter nor make an anonymous present." Blood entails its duties as well as its privileges.

The casket despatched to its destination, Van Twiller felt easier in his mind. He was under obligations to the girl for many an agreeable hour that might otherwise have passed heavily. He had paid the debt, and he had paid it *en prince,* as became a Van Twiller. He spent the rest of the day in looking at some pictures at Goupil's, and at the club, and in making a few purchases for his trip up the Hudson. A conspicuousness that this trip up the Hudson was a disorderly retreat came over him unpleasantly at intervals.

When he returned to his rooms late at night, he found a note lying on the writing-table. He started as his eyes caught the words "——— Theatre" stamped in carmine letters on one corner of the envelope. Van Twiller broke the seal with trembling fingers.

Now, this note some time afterward fell into the hands of Livingstone, who showed it to Stuyvesant, who showed it to Delaney, who showed it to me, and I copied it as a literary curiosity. The note ran as follows:

MR. VAN TWILLER DEAR SIR—i am verry greatfull to you for that Bracelett. it come just in the nic of time for me. The Mademoiselle Zabriski dodg is about Plaid out. my beard is getting to much for me. i shall have to grow a mustash and take to some other line of business, i dont no what now, but will let you no. You wont feel bad if i sell that Bracelett. i have seen Abrahams Moss and he says he will do the square thing. Pleas accep my thanks for youre Beautifull and Unexpected present.

Youre respectfull servent,
CHARLES MONTMORENCI WALTERS.

The next day Van Twiller neither expressed nor felt any unwillingness to spend a few weeks with his mother at the old homestead.

And then he went abroad.

A GOOD-FOR-NOTHING

By Hjalmar Hjorth Boyesen

CHAPTER I

RALPH GRIM was born a gentleman. He had the misfortune of coming into the world some ten years later than might reasonably have been expected. Colonel Grim and his lady had celebrated twelve anniversaries of their wedding-day, and had given up all hopes of ever having a son and heir, when this late comer startled them by his unexpected appearance. The only previous addition to the family had been a daughter, and she was then ten summers old.

Ralph was a very feeble child, and could only with great difficulty be persuaded to retain his hold of the slender thread which bound him to existence. He was rubbed with whiskey, and wrapped in cotton, and given mare's milk to drink, and God knows what not, and the Colonel swore a round oath of paternal delight when at last the infant stopped gasping in that distressing way and began to breathe like other human beings. The mother, who, in spite of her anxiety for the child's life, had found time to plot for him a career of future magnificence, now suddenly set him apart for literature, because that was the easiest road to fame, and disposed of him in marriage to one of the most distinguished families of the land. She cautiously suggested this to her husband when he came to take his seat at her bedside; but to her utter astonishment she found that he had been indulging a similar train of thought, and had already

377

destined the infant prodigy for the army. She, however, could not give up her predilection for literature, and the Colonel, who could not bear to be contradicted in his own house, as he used to say, was getting every minute louder and more flushed, when, happily, the doctor's arrival interrupted the dispute.

As Ralph grew up from infancy to childhood, he began to give decided promise of future distinction. He was fond of sitting down in a corner and sucking his thumb, which his mother interpreted as the sign of that brooding disposition peculiar to poets and men of lofty genius. At the age of five, he had become sole master in the house. He slapped his sister Hilda in the face, or pulled her hair, when she hesitated to obey him, tyrannized over his nurse, and sternly refused to go to bed in spite of his mother's entreaties. On such occasions, the Colonel would hide his face behind his newspaper, and chuckle with delight; it was evident that nature had intended his son for a great military commander. As soon as Ralph himself was old enough to have any thoughts about his future destiny, he made up his mind that he would like to be a pirate. A few months later, having contracted an immoderate taste for candy, he contented himself with the comparatively humble position of a baker; but when he had read "Robinson Crusoe" he manifested a strong desire to go to sea in the hope of getting wrecked on some desolate island. The parents spent long evenings gravely discussing these indications of uncommon genius, and each interpreted them in his or her own way.

"He is not like any other child I ever knew," said the mother.

"To be sure," responded the father, earnestly. "He is a most extraordinary child. I was a very remarkable child too, even if I do say it myself; but, as far as I remember, I never aspired to being wrecked on an uninhabited island."

The Colonel probably spoke the truth; but he forgot to take into account that he had never read "Robinson Crusoe."

Of Ralph's school-days there is but little to report, for,

to tell the truth, he did not fancy going to school, as the discipline annoyed him. The day after his having entered the gymnasium, which was to prepare him for the Military Academy, the principal saw him waiting at the gate after his class had been dismissed. He approached him, and asked why he did not go home with the rest.

"I am waiting for the servant to carry my books," was the boy's answer.

"Give me your books," said the teacher.

Ralph reluctantly obeyed. That day the Colonel was not a little surprised to see his son marching up the street, and every now and then glancing behind him with a look of discomfort at the principal, who was following quietly in his train, carrying a parcel of school-books. Colonel Grim and his wife, divining the teacher's intention, agreed that it was a great outrage, but they did not mention the matter to Ralph. Henceforth, however, the boy refused to be accompanied by his servant. A week later he was impudent to the teacher of gymnastics, who whipped him in return. The Colonel's rage knew no bounds; he rode in great haste to the gymnasium, reviled the teacher for presuming to chastise *his* son, and committed the boy to the care of a private tutor.

At the age of sixteen, Ralph went to the capital with the intention of entering the Military Academy. He was a tall, handsome youth, slender of stature, and carried himself as erect as a candle. He had a light, clear complexion of almost feminine delicacy; blond, curly hair, which he always kept carefully brushed; a low forehead, and a straight, finely modeled nose. There was an expression of extreme sensitiveness about the nostrils, and a look of indolence in the dark-blue eyes. But the *ensemble* of his features was pleasing, his dress irreproachable, and his manners bore no trace of the awkward self-consciousness peculiar to his age. Immediately on his arrival in the capital he hired a suite of rooms in the aristocratic part of the city, and furnished them rather expensively, but in excellent taste. From a bosom friend, whom he met by accident in the restaurant's pavilion in the park, he learned that a pair of antlers, a stuffed eagle, or falcon, and a couple of swords, were indispensable to a well-appointed apartment. He accordingly bought these articles at a curiosity shop. During the first weeks of his residence in the city he made some feeble efforts to perfect himself in mathematics, in which he suspected he was somewhat deficient. But when the same officious friend laughed at him, and called him "green," he determined to trust to fortune, and henceforth devoted himself the more assiduously to the French ballet, where he had already made some interesting acquaintances.

The time for the examination came; the French ballet did not prove a good preparation; Ralph failed. It quite shook him for the time, and he felt humiliated. He had not the courage to tell his father; so he lingered on from day to day, sat vacantly gazing out of his window, and tried vainly to interest himself in the busy bustle down on the street. It provoked him that everybody else should be so light hearted, when he was, or at least fancied himself, in trouble. The parlor grew intolerable; he sought refuge in his bedroom. There he sat one evening (it was the third day after the examination), and stared out upon the gray stone walls which on all sides inclosed the narrow courtyard. The round stupid face of the moon stood tranquilly dozing like a great Limburger cheese suspended under the sky.

Ralph, at least, could think of a no more fitting simile. But the bright-eyed young girl in the window hard by sent a longing look up to the same moon, and thought of her distant home on the fjords, where the glaciers stood like hoary giants, and caught the yellow moonbeams on their glittering shields of snow. She had been reading "Ivanhoe" all the afternoon, until the twilight had overtaken her quite unaware, and now she suddenly remembered that she had forgotten to write her German exercise. She lifted her face and saw a pair of sad, vacant eyes gazing at her from the next window in the angle of the court. She was a little startled at first, but in the next moment she thought of her German exercise and took heart.

"Do you know German?" she said; then immediately repented that she had said it.

"I do," was the answer.

She took up her apron and began to twist it with an air of embarrassment.

"I didn't mean anything," she whispered, at last. "I only wanted to know."

"You are very kind."

That answer roused her; he was evidently making sport of her.

"Well, then, if you do, you may write my exercise for me. I have marked the place in the book."

And she flung her book over to the window, and he caught it on the edge of the sill, just as it was falling.

"You are a very strange girl," he remarked, turning over the leaves of the book, although it was too dark to read. "How old are you?"

"I shall be fourteen six weeks before Christmas," answered she, frankly.

"Then I excuse you."

"No, indeed," cried she, vehemently. "You needn't excuse me at all. If you don't want to write my exercise, you may send the book back again. I am very sorry I spoke to you, and I shall never do it again."

"But you will not get the book back again without the exercise," replied he, quietly. "Good-night."

The girl stood long looking after him, hoping that he would return. Then, with a great burst of repentance, she hid her face in her lap, and began to cry.

"Oh, dear, I didn't mean to be rude," she sobbed. "But it was Ivanhoe and Rebecca who upset me."

The next morning she was up before daylight, and waited for two long hours in great suspense before the curtain of his window was raised. He greeted her politely; threw a hasty glance around the court to see if he was observed, and then tossed her book dexterously over into her hands.

"I have pinned the written exercise to the flyleaf," he said. "You will probably have time to copy it before breakfast."

"I am ever so much obliged to you," she managed to stammer.

He looked so tall and handsome, and grown-up, and her remorse stuck in her throat, and threatened to choke her. She had taken him for a boy as he sat there in his window the evening before.

"By the way, what is your name?" he asked, carelessly, as he turned to go.

"Bertha."

"Well, my dear Bertha, I am happy to have made your acquaintance."

And he again made her a polite bow, and entered his parlor.

"How provokingly familiar he is," thought she; "but no one can deny that he is handsome."

The bright roguish face of the young girl haunted Ralph during the whole next week. He had been in love at least ten times before, of course; but, like most boys, with young ladies far older than himself. He found himself frequently glancing over to her window in the hope of catching another glimpse of her face; but the curtain was always drawn down, and Bertha remained invisible. During the second week, however, she relented, and they had many a pleasant chat together. He now volunteered to write all her exercises, and she made no objections. He learned that she was the daughter of a well-to-do peasant in the sea-districts of Norway (and it gave him quite a shock to hear it), and that she was going to school in the city, and boarded with an old lady who kept a *pension* in the house adjoining the one in which he lived.

One day in the autumn Ralph was surprised by the sudden arrival of his father, and the fact of his failure in the examination could no longer be kept a secret. The old Colonel flared up at once when Ralph made his confession; the large veins upon his forehead swelled; he grew coppery-red in his face, and stormed up and down the floor, until his son became seriously alarmed; but, to his great relief, he was soon made aware that his father's wrath was not turned against him personally, but against the officials of the Military Academy who had rejected him. The Colonel took it as insult to his own good name and irreproachable standing as an officer; he promptly refused any other explanation, and vainly racked his brain to remember if any youthful folly of his could possibly have made him enemies among the teachers of the Academy. He at last felt satisfied that it was envy of his own greatness and rapid advancement which had induced the rascals to take vengeance on his son. Ralph reluctantly followed his father back to the country town where the latter was stationed, and the fair-haired Bertha vanished from his horizon. His mother's wish now prevailed, and he began, in his own easy way, to prepare himself for the University. He had little taste for Cicero, and still less for Virgil, but with the use of a "pony" he soon gained sufficient knowledge of these authors to be able to talk in a sort of patronizing way about them, to the great delight of his fond parents. He took quite a fancy, however, to the ode in Horace ending with the lines:

> Dulce ridentem,
> Dulce loquentem,
> Lalagen amabo.

And in his thought he substituted for Lalage the fair-haired Bertha, quite regardless of the requirements of the metre.

To make a long story short, three years later Ralph returned to the capital, and after having worn out several tutors, actually succeeded in entering the University.

The first year of college life is a happy time to every young man, and Ralph enjoyed its processions, its parliamentary gatherings, and its leisure, as well as the rest. He was certainly not the man to be sentimental over the loss of a young girl whom, moreover, he had only known for a few weeks. Nevertheless, he thought of her at odd times, but not enough to disturb his pleasure. The standing of his family, his own handsome appearance, and his immaculate linen opened to him the best houses of the city, and he became a great favorite in society. At lectures he was seldom seen, but more frequently in the theatres, where he used to come in during the middle of the first act, take his station in front of the orchestra box, and eye, through his lorgnette, by turns, the actresses and the ladies of the parquet.

CHAPTER II

Two months passed, and then came the great annual ball which the students give at the opening of the second semester. Ralph was a man of importance that evening; first, because he belonged to a great family; secondly, because he was the handsomest man of his year. He wore a large golden star on his breast (for his fellow-students had made him a Knight of the Golden Boar) and a badge of colored ribbons in his buttonhole.

The ball was a brilliant affair, and everybody was in excellent spirits, especially the ladies. Ralph danced incessantly, twirled his soft mustache, and uttered amiable platitudes. It was toward midnight, just as the company was moving out to supper, that he caught the glance of a pair of dark-blue eyes, which suddenly drove the blood to his cheeks and hastened the beating of his heart. But when he looked once more the dark-blue eyes were gone, and his unruly heart went on hammering against his side. He laid his hand on his breast and glanced furtively at his fair neighbor, but she looked happy and unconcerned, for the flavor of the ice cream was delicious. It seemed an endless meal, but, when it was done, Ralph rose, led his partner back to the ballroom, and hastily excused himself. His glance wandered round the wide hall, seeking the well-remembered eyes once more, and, at length, finding them in a remote corner, half hid behind a moving wall of promenaders. In another moment he was at Bertha's side.

"You must have been purposely hiding yourself, Miss Bertha," said he, when the usual greetings were exchanged. "I have not caught a glimpse of you all this evening, until a few moments ago."

"But I have seen you all the while," answered the girl, frankly. "I knew you at once as I entered the hall."

"If I had but known that you were here," resumed Ralph, as it were invisibly expanding with an agreeable sense of dignity, "I assure you, you would have been the very first one I should have sought."

She raised her large grave eyes to his, as if questioning his sincerity; but she made no answer.

"Good gracious!" thought Ralph. "She takes things terribly in earnest."

"You look so serious, Miss Bertha," said he, after a moment's pause. "I remember you as a bright-eyed, flaxen-haired little girl, who threw her German exercise-book to me across the yard, and whose merry laughter still rings pleasantly in my memory. I confess I don't find it quite easy to identify this grave young lady with my merry friend of three years ago."

"In other words, you are disappointed at not finding me the same as I used to be."

"No, not exactly; but—"

Ralph paused and looked puzzled. There was something in the earnestness of her manner which made a facetious compliment seem grossly inappropriate, and in the moment no other escape suggested itself.

"But what?" demanded Bertha, mercilessly.

"Have you ever lost an old friend?" asked he, abruptly.

"Yes; how so?"

"Then," answered he, while his features lighted up with a happy inspiration—"then you will appreciate my situation.

I fondly cherished my old picture of you in my memory. Now I have lost it, and I can not help regretting the loss. I do not mean, however, to imply that this new acquaintance —this second edition of yourself, so to speak—will prove less interesting."

She again sent him a grave, questioning look, and began to gaze intently upon the stone in her bracelet.

"I suppose you will laugh at me," began she, while a sudden blush flitted over her countenance. "But this is my first ball, and I feel as if I had rushed into a whirlpool, from which I have, since the first rash plunge was made, been vainly trying to escape. I feel so dreadfully forlorn. I hardly know anybody here except my cousin, who invited me, and I hardly think I know him either."

"Well, since you are irredeemably committed," replied Ralph, as the music, after some prefatory flourishes, broke into the delicious rhythm of a Strauss waltz, "then it is no use struggling against fate. Come, let us make the plunge together. Misery loves company."

He offered her his arm, and she rose, somewhat hesitatingly, and followed.

"I am afraid," she whispered, as they fell into line with the procession that was moving down the long hall, "that you have asked me to dance merely because I said I felt forlorn. If that is the case, I should prefer to be led back to my seat."

"What a base imputation!" cried Ralph.

There was something so charmingly *naïve* in this self-depreciation—something so altogether novel in his experience, and, he could not help adding, just a little bit countrified. His spirits rose; he began to relish keenly his position as an experienced man of the world, and, in the agreeable glow of patronage and conscious superiority, chatted with hearty *abandon* with his little rustic beauty.

"If your dancing is as perfect as your German exercises were," said she, laughing, as they swung out upon the floor, "then I promise myself a good deal of pleasure from our meeting."

"Never fear," answered he, quickly reversing his step, and whirling with many a capricious turn away among the thronging couples.

When Ralph drove home in his carriage toward morning he briefly summed up his impressions of Bertha in the following adjectives: intelligent, delightfully unsophisticated, a little bit verdant, but devilish pretty.

Some weeks later Colonel Grim received an appointment at the fortress of Aggershuus, and immediately took up his residence in the capital. He saw that his son cut a fine figure in the highest circles of society, and expressed his gratification in the most emphatic terms. If he had known, however, that Ralph was in the habit of visiting, with alarming regularity, at the house of a plebeian merchant in a somewhat obscure street, he would, no doubt, have been more chary of his praise. But the Colonel suspected nothing, and it was well for the peace of the family that he did not. It may have been cowardice in Ralph that he never mentioned Bertha's name to his family or to his aristocratic acquaintances; for, to be candid, he himself felt ashamed of the power she exerted over him, and by turns pitied and ridiculed himself for pursuing so inglorious a conquest. Nevertheless it wounded his egotism that she never showed any surprise at seeing him, that she received him with a certain frank unceremoniousness, which, however, was very becoming to her; that she invariably went on with her work heedless of his presence, and in everything treated him as if she had been his equal. She persisted in talking with him in a half sisterly fashion about his studies and his future career, warned him with great solicitude against some of his reprobate friends, of whose merry adventures he had told her; and if he ventured to compliment her on her beauty or her accomplishments, she would look up gravely from her sewing, or answer him in a way which seemed to banish the idea of love-making into the land of the impossible. He was constantly tormented by the suspicion that she secretly disapproved of him, and that from a mere moral interest in his welfare she was conscientiously laboring to make him a better man. Day after day he parted from her feeling humiliated, faint-hearted, and secretly indignant both at himself and her, and day after day he returned only to renew the same experience. At last it became too intolerable, he could endure it no longer. Let it make or break, certainty, at all risks, was at least preferable to this sickening suspense. That he loved her, he could no longer doubt; let his parents foam and fret as much as they pleased; for once he was going to stand on his own legs. And in the end, he thought, they would have to yield, for they had no son but him.

Bertha was going to return to her home on the sea-coast in a week. Ralph stood in the little low-ceiled parlor, as she imagined, to bid her good-by. They had been speaking of her father, her brothers, and the farm, and she had expressed the wish that if he ever should come to that part of the country he might pay them a visit. Her words had kindled a vague hope in his breast, but in their very frankness and friendly regard there was something which slew the hope they had begotten. He held her hand in his, and her large confiding eyes shone with an emotion which was beautiful, but was yet not love.

"If you were but a peasant born like myself," said she, in a voice which sounded almost tender, "then I should like to talk to you as I would to my own brother; but—"

"No, not brother, Bertha," cried he, with sudden vehemence; "I love you better than I ever loved any earthly being, and if you knew how firmly this love has clutched at the roots of my heart, you would perhaps—you would at least not look so reproachfully at me."

She dropped his hand, and stood for a moment silent.

"I am sorry that it should have come to this, Mr. Grim," said she, visibly struggling for calmness. "And I am perhaps more to blame than you."

"Blame," muttered he, "why are you to blame?"

"Because I do not love you; although I sometimes feared that this might come. But then again I persuaded myself that it could not be so."

He took a step toward the door, laid his hand on the knob, and gazed down before him.

"Bertha," began he, slowly, raising his head, "you have always disapproved of me, you have despised me in your heart, but you thought you would be doing a good work if you succeeded in making a man of me."

"You use strong language," answered she, hesitatingly; "but there is truth in what you say."

Again there was a long pause, in which the ticking of the old parlor clock grew louder and louder.

"Then," he broke out at last, "tell me before we part if I can do nothing to gain—I will not say your love—but only your regard? What would you do if you were in my place?"

"My advice you will hardly heed, and I do not even know that it would be well if you did. But if I were a man in your position, I should break with my whole past, start out into the world where nobody knew me, and where I should be dependent only upon my own strength, and there I would conquer a place for myself, if it were only for the satisfaction of knowing that I was really a man. Here cushions are sewed under your arms, a hundred invisible threads bind you to a life of idleness and vanity, everybody is ready to carry you on his hands, the road is smoothed for you, every stone carefully moved out of your path, and you will probably go to your grave without having ever harbored one earnest thought, without having done one manly deed."

Ralph stood transfixed, gazing at her with open mouth; he felt a kind of stupid fright, as if some one had suddenly seized him by the shoulders and shaken him violently. He tried vainly to remove his eyes from Bertha. She held him as by a powerful spell. He saw that her face was lighted with an altogether new beauty; he noticed the deep glow upon her cheek, the brilliancy of her eye, the slight quiver of her lip. But he saw all this as one sees things in a half-trance, without attempting to account for them; the door between his soul and his senses was closed.

"I know that I have been bold in speaking to you in this way," she said at last, seating herself in a chair at the window. "But it was yourself who asked me. And I have felt all the time that I should have to tell you this before we parted."

"And," answered he, making a strong effort to appear calm, "if I follow your advice, will you allow me to see you once more before you go?"

"I shall remain here another week, and shall, during that time, always be ready to receive you."

"Thank you. Good-by."

"Good-by."

Ralph carefully avoided all the fashionable thorough-fares; he felt degraded before himself, and he had an idea that every man could read his humiliation in his counte-nance. Now he walked on quickly, striking the sidewalk with his heels; now, again, he fell into an uneasy, reckless saunter, according as the changing moods inspired defiance of his sentence, or a qualified surrender. And, as he walked on, the bitterness grew within him, and he piteously reviled himself for having allowed himself to be made a fool of by "that little country goose," when he was well aware that there were hundreds of women of the best families of the land who would feel honored at receiving his attentions. But this sort of reasoning he knew to be both weak and con-temptible, and his better self soon rose in loud rebellion.

"After all," he muttered, "in the main thing she was right. I am a miserable good-for-nothing, a hothouse plant, a poor stick, and if I were a woman myself, I don't think I should waste my affections on a man of that calibre."

Then he unconsciously fell to analyzing Bertha's charac-ter, wondering vaguely that a person who moved so timidly in social life, appearing so diffident, from an ever-present fear of blundering against the established forms of etiquette, could judge so quickly, and with such a merciless certainty, whenever a moral question, a question of right and wrong, was at issue. And, pursuing the same train of thought, he contrasted her with himself, who moved in the highest spheres of society as in his native element, heedless of moral scruples, and conscious of no loftier motive for his actions than the immediate pleasures of the moment.

As Ralph turned the corner of a street, he heard himself hailed from the other sidewalk by a chorus of merry voices.

"Ah, my dear Baroness," cried a young man, springing across the street and grasping Ralph's hand (all his student friends called him the Baroness), "in the name of this illustrious company, allow me to salute you. But why the deuce —what is the matter with you? If you have the *Katzenjammer*,* soda-water is the thing. Come along—it's my treat!"

The students instantly thronged around Ralph, who stood distractedly swinging his cane and smiling idiotically.

"I am not quite well," said he; "leave me alone."

"No, to be sure, you don't look well," cried a jolly youth, against whom Bertha had frequently warned him; "but a glass of sherry will soon restore you. It would be highly immoral to leave you in this condition without taking care of you."

Ralph again vainly tried to remonstrate; but the end was, that he reluctantly followed.

He had always been a conspicuous figure in the student world; but that night he astonished his friends by his eloquence, his reckless humor, and his capacity for drinking. He made a speech for "Woman," which bristled with wit, cynicism, and sarcastic epigrams. One young man, named Vinter, who was engaged, undertook to protest

Katzenjammer is the sensation a man has the morning after a carousal.

against his sweeping condemnation, and declared that Ralph, who was a universal favorite among the ladies, ought to be the last to revile them.

"If," he went on, "the Baroness should propose to six well-known ladies here in this city whom I could mention, I would wager six Johannisbergers, and an equal amount of champagne, that every one of them would accept him."

The others loudly applauded this proposal, and Ralph accepted the wager. The letters were written on the spot, and immediately despatched. Toward morning, the merry carousal broke up, and Ralph was conducted in triumph to his home.

CHAPTER III

Two days later, Ralph again knocked on Bertha's door, He looked paler than usual, almost haggard; his immaculate linen was a little crumpled, and he carried no cane; his lips were tightly compressed, and his face wore an air of desperate resolution.

"It is done," he said, as he seated himself opposite her. "I am going."

"Going!" cried she, startled at his unusual appearance. "How, where?"

"To America. I sail to-night. I have followed your advice, you see. I have cut off the last bridge behind me."

"But, Ralph," she exclaimed, in a voice of alarm. "Something dreadful must have happened. Tell me quick; I must know it."

"No; nothing dreadful," muttered he, smiling bitterly. "I have made a little scandal, that is all. My father told me to-day to go to the devil, if I chose, and my mother gave me five hundred dollars to help me along on the way. If you wish to know, here is the explanation."

And he pulled from his pocket six perfumed and carefully folded notes, and threw them into her lap.

"Do you wish me to read them?" she asked, with growing surprise.

"Certainly. Why not?"

She hastily opened one note after the other, and read.

"But, Ralph," she cried, springing up from her seat, while her eyes flamed with indignation, "what does this mean? What have you done?"

"I didn't think it needed any explanation," replied he, with feigned indifference. "I proposed to them all, and, you see, they all accepted me. I received all these letters to-day. I only wished to know whether the whole world regarded me as such a worthless scamp as you told me I was."

She did not answer, but sat mutely staring at him, fiercely crumpling a rose-colored note in her hand. He began to feel uncomfortable under her gaze, and threw himself about uneasily in his chair.

"Well," said he, at length, rising, "I suppose there is nothing more. Good-by."

"One moment, Mr. Grim," demanded she, sternly. "Since I have already said so much, and you have obligingly revealed to me a new side of your character, I claim the right to correct the opinion I expressed of you at our last meeting."

"I am all attention."

"I did think, Mr. Grim," began she, breathing hard, and steadying herself against the table at which she stood, "that you were a very selfish man—an embodiment of selfishness, absolute and supreme, but I did not believe that you were wicked."

"And what convinced you that I was selfish, if I may ask?"

"What convinced me?" repeated she, in a tone of inexpressible contempt. "When did you ever act from any generous regard for others? What good did you ever do to anybody?"

"You might ask, with equal justice, what good I ever did to myself."

"In a certain sense, yes; because to gratify a mere momentary wish is hardly doing one's self good."

"Then I have, at all events, followed the Biblical precept, and treated my neighbor very much as I treat myself."

"I did think," continued Bertha, without heeding the remark, "that you were at bottom kind-hearted, but too hopelessly well-bred ever to commit an act of any decided complexion, either good or bad. Now I see that I have misjudged you, and that you are capable of outraging the most sacred feelings of a woman's heart in mere wantonness, or for the sake of satisfying a base curiosity, which never could have entered the mind of an upright and generous man."

The hard, benumbed look in Ralph's face thawed in the warmth of her presence, and her words, though stern, touched a secret spring in his heart. He made two or three vain attempts to speak, then suddenly broke down, and cried:

"Bertha, Bertha, even if you scorn me, have patience with me, and listen."

And he told her, in rapid, broken sentences, how his love for her had grown from day to day, until he could no longer master it; and how, in an unguarded moment, when his pride rose in fierce conflict against his love, he had done this reckless deed of which he was now heartily ashamed. The fervor of his words touched her, for she felt that they were sincere. Large mute tears trembled in her eyelashes as she sat gazing tenderly at him, and in the depth of her soul the wish awoke that she might have been able to return this great and strong love of his; for she felt that in this love lay the germ of a new, of a stronger and better man. She noticed, with a half-regretful pleasure, his handsome figure, his delicately shaped hands, and the noble cast of his features; an overwhelming pity for him rose within her, and she began to reproach herself for having spoken so harshly, and, as she now thought, so unjustly. Perhaps he read in her eyes the unspoken wish. He seized her hand,

and his words fell with a warm and alluring cadence upon her ear.

"I shall not see you for a long time to come, Bertha," said he, "but if at the end of five or six years your hand is still free, and I return another man—a man to whom you could safely intrust your happiness—would you then listen to what I may have to say to you? For I promise, by all that we both hold sacred—"

"No, no," interrupted she, hastily. "Promise nothing. It would be unjust to yourself, and perhaps also to me; for a sacred promise is a terrible thing, Ralph. Let us both remain free; and, if you return and still love me, then come, and I shall receive you and listen to you. And even if you have outgrown your love, which is, indeed, more probable, come still to visit me wherever I may be, and we shall meet as friends and rejoice in the meeting."

"You know best," he murmured. "Let it be as you have said."

He arose, took her face between his hands, gazed long and tenderly into her eyes, pressed a kiss upon her forehead, and hastened away.

That night Ralph boarded the steamer for Hull, and three weeks later landed in New York.

CHAPTER IV

THE first three months of Ralph's sojourn in America were spent in vain attempts to obtain a situation. Day after day he walked down Broadway, calling at various places of business, and night after night he returned to his cheerless room with a faint heart and declining spirits. It was, after all, a more serious thing than he had imagined, to cut the cable which binds one to the land of one's birth. There a hundred subtile influences, the existence of which no one suspects until the moment they are withdrawn, unite to keep one in the straight path of rectitude, or at least of external respectability; and Ralph's life had been all in society; the opinion of his fellow-men had been the one force to which he implicitly deferred, and the conscience by which he had been wont to test his actions had been nothing but the aggregate judgment of his friends. To such a man the isolation and the utter irresponsibility of a life among strangers was tenfold more dangerous; and Ralph found, to his horror, that his character contained innumerable latent possibilities which the easy-going life in his home probably never would have revealed to him. It often cut him to the quick, when, on entering an office in his daily search for employment, he was met by hostile or suspicious glances, or when, as it occasionally happened, the door was slammed in his face, as if he were a vagabond or an impostor. Then the wolf was often roused within him, and he felt a momentary wild desire to become what the people here evidently believed him to be. Many a night he sauntered irresolutely about the gambling places in obscure streets, and the glare of light, the rude shouts and clamors in the same moment repelled and attracted him. If he went to the devil, who would care? His father had himself pointed out the way to him; and nobody could blame him if he followed the advice. But then again a memory emerged from that chamber of his soul which still he held sacred; and Bertha's deep-blue eyes gazed upon him with their earnest look of tender warning and regret.

When the summer was half gone, Ralph had gained many a hard victory over himself, and learned many a useful lesson; and at length he swallowed his pride, divested himself of his fine clothes, and accepted a position as assistant gardener at a villa on the Hudson. And as he stood perspiring with a spade in his hand, and a cheap broad-brimmed straw hat on his head, he often took a grim pleasure in picturing to himself how his aristocratic friends at home would receive him if he should introduce himself to them in this new costume.

"After all, it was only my position they cared for," he

reflected, bitterly; "without my father's name what would I be to them?"

Then, again, there was a certain satisfaction in knowing that, for his present situation, humble as it was, he was indebted to nobody but himself; and the thought that Bertha's eyes, if they could have seen him now, would have dwelt upon him with pleasure and approbation, went far to console him for his aching back, his sunburned face, and his swollen and blistered hands.

One day, as Ralph was raking the gravel-walks in the garden, his employer's daughter, a young lady of seventeen, came out and spoke to him. His culture and refinement of manner struck her with wonder, and she asked him to tell her his history; but then he suddenly grew very grave, and she forbore pressing him. From that time she attached a kind of romantic interest to him, and finally induced her father to obtain him a situation that would be more to his taste. And, before winter came, Ralph saw the dawn of a new future glimmering before him. He had wrestled bravely with fate, and had once more gained a victory. He began the career in which success and distinction awaited him as proofreader on a newspaper in the city. He had fortunately been familiar with the English language before he left home, and by the strength of his will he conquered all difficulties. At the end of two years he became attached to the editorial staff; new ambitious hopes, hitherto foreign to his mind, awoke within him; and with joyous tumult of heart he saw life opening its wide vistas before him, and he labored on manfully to repair the losses of the past, and to prepare himself for greater usefulness in times to come. He felt in himself a stronger and fuller manhood, as if the great arteries of the vast universal world-life pulsed in his own being. The drowsy, indolent existence at home appeared like a dull remote dream from which he had awaked, and he blessed the destiny which, by its very sternness, had mercifully saved him; he blessed her, too, who, from the very want of love for him, had, perhaps, made him worthier of love.

The years flew rapidly. Society had flung its doors open to him, and what was more, he had found some warm friends, in whose houses he could come and go at pleasure. He enjoyed keenly the privilege of daily association with high-minded and refined women; their eager activity of intellect stimulated him, their exquisite ethereal grace and their delicately chiseled beauty satisfied his æsthetic cravings, and the responsive vivacity of their nature prepared him ever new surprises. He felt a strange fascination in the presence of these women, and the conviction grew upon him that their type of womanhood was superior to any he had hitherto known. And by way of refuting his own argument, he would draw from his pocketbook the photograph of Bertha, which had a secret compartment there all to itself, and, gazing tenderly at it, would eagerly defend her against the disparaging reflections which the involuntary comparison had provoked. And still, how could he help seeing that her features, though well molded, lacked animation; that her eye, with its deep, trustful glance, was not brilliant, and that the calm earnestness of her face, when compared with the bright, intellectual beauty of his present friends, appeared pale and simple, like a violet in a bouquet of vividly colored roses? It gave him a quick pang, when, at times, he was forced to admit this; nevertheless, it was the truth.

After six years of residence in America, Ralph had gained a very high reputation as a journalist of rare culture and ability, and in 1867 he was sent to the World's Exhibition in Paris, as correspondent of the paper on which he had during all these years been employed. What wonder, then, that he started for Europe a few weeks before his presence was needed in the imperial city, and that he steered his course directly toward the fjord valley where Bertha had her home? It was she who had bidden him Godspeed when he fled from the land of his birth, and she, too, should receive his first greeting on his return.

CHAPTER V

THE sun had fortified itself behind a citadel of flaming clouds, and the upper forest region shone with a strange ethereal glow, while the lower plains were wrapped in shadow; but the shadow itself had a strong suffusion of color. The mountain peaks rose cold and blue in the distance.

Ralph, having inquired his way of the boatman who had landed him at the pier, walked rapidly along the beach, with a small valise in his hand, and a light summer overcoat flung over his shoulder. Many half-thoughts grazed his mind, and ere the first had taken shape, the second and the third came and chased it away. And still they all in some fashion had reference to Bertha; for in a misty, abstract way, she filled his whole mind; but for some indefinable reason, he was afraid to give free rein to the sentiment which lurked in the remoter corners of his soul.

Onward he hastened, while his heart throbbed with the quickening tempo of mingled expectation and fear. Now and then one of those chill gusts of air, which seem to be careering about aimlessly in the atmosphere during early summer, would strike into his face, and recall him to a keener self-consciousness.

Ralph concluded, from his increasing agitation, that he must be very near Bertha's home. He stopped and looked around him. He saw a large maple at the roadside, some thirty steps from where he was standing, and the girl who was sitting under it, resting her head in her hand and gazing out over the sea, he recognized in an instant to be Bertha. He sprang up on the road, not crossing, however, her line of vision, and approached her noiselessly from behind.

"Bertha," he whispered.

She gave a little joyous cry, sprang up, and made a gesture as if to throw herself in his arms; then suddenly checked herself, blushed crimson, and moved a step backward.

"You came so suddenly," she murmured.

"But, Bertha," cried he (and the full bass of his voice rang through her very soul), "have I gone into exile and waited these many years for so cold a welcome?"

"You have changed so much, Ralph," she answered, with that old grave smile which he knew so well, and stretched out both her hands toward him. "And I have thought of you so much since you went away, and blamed myself because I had judged you so harshly, and wondered that you could listen to me so patiently, and never bear me any malice for what I said."

"If you had said a word less," declared Ralph, seating himself at her side on the greensward, "or if you had varnished it over with politeness, then you would probably have failed to produce any effect and I should not have been burdened with that heavy debt of gratitude which I now owe you. I was a pretty thick-skinned animal in those days, Bertha. You said the right word at the right moment; you gave me a bold and a good piece of advice, which my own ingenuity would never have suggested to me. I will not thank you, because, in so grave a case as this, spoken thanks sound like a mere mockery. Whatever I am, Bertha, and whatever I may hope to be, I owe it all to that hour."

She listened with rapture to the manly assurance of his voice; her eyes dwelt with unspeakable joy upon his strong, bronzed features, his full thick blond beard, and the vigorous proportions of his frame. Many and many a time during his absence had she wondered how he would look if he ever came back, and with that minute conscientiousness which, as it were, pervaded her whole character, she had held herself responsible before God for his fate, prayed for him, and trembled lest evil powers should gain the ascendency over his soul.

On their way to the house they talked together of many things, but in a guarded, cautious fashion, and without the cheerful abandonment of former years. They both, as it were, groped their way carefully in each other's minds, and each vaguely felt that there was something in the other's thought which it was not well to touch unbidden. Bertha saw that all her fears for him had been groundless, and his very appearance lifted the whole weight of responsibility from her breast; and still, did she rejoice at her deliverance from her burden? Ah, no; in this moment she knew that that which she had foolishly cherished as the best and noblest part of herself had been but a selfish need of her own heart. She feared that she had only taken that interest in him which one feels in a thing of one's own making, and now, when she saw that he had risen quite above her; that he was free and strong, and could have no more need of her, she had, instead of generous pleasure at his success, but a painful sense of emptiness, as if something very dear had been taken from her.

Ralph, too, was loth to analyze the impression his old love made upon him. His feelings were of so complex a nature, he was anxious to keep his more magnanimous impulses active, and he strove hard to convince himself that she was still the same to him as she had been before they had ever parted. But, alas! though the heart be warm and generous, the eye is a merciless critic. And the man who had moved on the wide arena of the world, whose mind had housed the large thoughts of this century, and expanded with its invigorating breath—was he to blame because he had unconsciously outgrown his old provincial self, and could no more judge by its standards?

Bertha's father was a peasant, but he had, by his lumber trade, acquired what in Norway was called a very handsome fortune. He received his guest with dignified reserve, and Ralph thought he detected in his eyes a lurking look of distrust. "I know your errand," that look seemed to say, "but you had better give it up at once. It will be of no use for you to try."

And after supper, as Ralph and Bertha sat talking confidingly with each other at the window, he sent his daughter a quick, sharp glance, and then, without ceremony, commanded her to go to bed. Ralph's heart gave a great thump within him; not because he feared the old man, but because his words, as well as his glances, revealed to him the sad history of these long, patient years. He doubted no longer that the love which he had once so ardently desired was his at last; and he made a silent vow that, come what might, he would remain faithful.

As he came down to breakfast the next morning, he found Bertha sitting at the window, engaged in hemming what appeared to be a rough kitchen towel. She bent eagerly over her work, and only a vivid flush upon her cheek told him that she had noticed his coming. He took a chair, seated himself opposite her, and bade her "good-morning." She raised her head, and showed him a sweet, troubled countenance, which the early sunlight illumined with a high spiritual beauty. It reminded him forcibly of those pale, sweet-faced saints of Fra Angelico, with whom the frail flesh seems ever on the point of yielding to the ardent aspirations of the spirit. And still even in this moment he could not prevent his eyes from observing that one side of her forefinger was rough from sewing, and that the whiteness of her arm, which the loose sleeves displayed, contrasted strongly with the browned and sunburned complexion of her hands.

After breakfast they again walked together on the beach, and Ralph, having once formed his resolution, now talked freely of the New World—of his sphere of activity there; of his friends and of his plans for the future; and she listened to him with a mild, perplexed look in her eyes, as if trying vainly to follow the flight of his thoughts. And he wondered, with secret dismay, whether she was still the same strong, brave-hearted girl whom he had once accounted almost bold; whether the life in this narrow valley, amid a hundred petty and depressing cares, had not cramped her spiritual growth, and narrowed the sphere of her thought. Or was she still the same, and was it only he who had changed? At last he gave utterance to his wonder, and she answered him in those grave, earnest tones which seemed in themselves to be half a refutation of his doubts.

"It was easy for me to give you daring advice then, Ralph," she said. "Like most school-girls, I thought that life was a great and glorious thing, and that happiness was a fruit which hung within reach of every hand. Now I have lived for six years trying single-handed to relieve the want and suffering of the needy people with whom I come in contact, and their squalor and wretchedness have sickened me, and, what is still worse, I feel that all I can do is as a drop in the ocean, and, after all, amounts to nothing. I know I am no longer the same reckless girl who, with the very best intention, sent you wandering through the wide world; and I thank God that it proved to be for your good, although the whole now appears quite incredible to me. My thoughts have moved so long within the narrow circle of these mountains that they have lost their youthful elasticity, and can no more rise above them."

Ralph detected, in the midst of her despondency, a spark of her former fire, and grew eloquent in his endeavors to persuade her that she was unjust to herself, and that there was but a wider sphere of life needed to develop all the latent powers of her rich nature.

At the dinner-table, her father again sat eying his guest with the same cold look of distrust and suspicion. And when the meal was at an end, he rose abruptly and called his daughter into another room. Presently Ralph heard his angry voice resounding through the house, interrupted now and then by a woman's sobs, and a subdued, passionate pleading. When Bertha again entered the room, her eyes were very red, and he saw that she had been weeping. She threw a shawl over her shoulders, beckoned to him with her hand, and he arose and followed her. She led the way silently until they reached a thick copse of birch and alder near the strand. She dropped down upon a bench between two trees, and he took his seat at her side.

"Ralph," began she, with a visible effort, "I hardly know

what to say to you; but there is something which I must tell you—my father wishes you to leave us at once."

"And *you,* Bertha?"

"Well—yes—I wish it too."

She saw the painful shock which her words gave him, and she strove hard to speak. Her lips trembled, her eyes became suffused with tears, which grew and grew, but never fell; she could not utter a word.

"Well, Bertha," answered he, with a little quiver in his voice, "if you, too, wish me to go, I shall not tarry. Good-by."

He rose quickly, and, with averted face, held out his hand to her; but as she made no motion to grasp the hand, he began distractedly to button his coat, and moved slowly away.

"Ralph."

He turned sharply, and, before he knew it, she lay sobbing upon his breast.

"Ralph," she murmured, while the tears almost choked her words, "I could not have you leave me thus. It is hard enough—it is hard enough—"

"What is hard, beloved?"

She raised her head abruptly, and turned upon him a gaze full of hope and doubt, and sweet perplexity.

"Ah, no, you do not love me," she whispered, sadly.

"Why should I come to seek you, after these many years, dearest, if I did not wish to make you my wife before God and men? Why should I—"

"Ah, yes, I know," she interrupted him with a fresh fit of weeping, "you are too good and honest to wish to throw me away, now when you have seen how my soul has hungered for the sight of you these many years, how even now I cling to you with a despairing clutch. But you can not disguise yourself, Ralph, and I saw from the first moment that you loved me no more."

"Do not be such an unreasonable child," he remonstrated, feebly. "I do not love you with the wild, irrational passion of former years; but I have the tenderest regard for you, and my heart warms at the sight of your sweet face, and I shall do all in my power to make you as happy as any man can make you who—"

"Who does not love me," she finished.

A sudden shudder seemed to shake her whole frame, and she drew herself more tightly up to him.

"Ah, no," she continued, after a while, sinking back upon her seat. "It is a hopeless thing to compel a reluctant heart. I will accept no sacrifice from you. You owe me nothing, for you have acted toward me honestly and uprightly, and I shall be a stronger or—at least—a better woman for what you gave me—and—for what you could not give me, even though you would."

"But, Bertha," exclaimed he, looking mournfully at her, "it is not true when you say that I owe you nothing. Six years ago, when first I wooed you, you could not return my love, and you sent me out into the world, and even refused to accept any pledge or promise for the future."

"And you returned," she responded, "a man such as my hope had pictured you; but, while I had almost been standing still, you had outgrown me, and outgrown your old self, and, with your old self, outgrown its love for me, for your love was not of your new self, but of the old. Alas! it is a sad tale, but it is true."

She spoke gravely now, and with a steadier voice, but her eyes hung upon his face with an eager look of expectation, as if yearning to detect there some gleam of hope, some contradiction of the dismal truth. He read that look aright and it pierced him like a sharp sword. He made a brave effort to respond to its appeal, but his features seemed hard as stone, and he could only cry out against his destiny, and bewail his misfortune and hers.

Toward evening, Ralph was sitting in an open boat, listening to the measured oar-strokes of the boatmen who were rowing him out to the nearest stopping-place of the steamer. The mountains lifted their great placid heads up among the sun-bathed clouds, and the fjord opened its cool depths as if to make room for their vast reflections. Ralph felt as if he were floating in the midst of the blue infinite space, and, with the strength which this feeling inspired, he tried to face boldly the thought from which he had but a moment ago shrunk as from something hopelessly sad and perplexing.

And in that hour he looked fearlessly into the gulf which separates the New World from the Old. He had hoped to bridge it; but, alas! it can not be bridged.